the m...
Irish Independe...

'An Irish Janet Evanovich meets *Sex And ...* ...y,
high-street style. A lusty romp of a book'
Mirror on *Hot Property*

'Tip top romantic escapism'
Pauline McLynn on *Hot Property*

'As easy to get into as a warm bath, and
tremendously good fun as well.'
Daily Mail on *Hot Property*

'A witty read combining drug crime, property and,
of course, true love'
Heat on *Hot Property*

'A lot of fun . . . it will thoroughly engage and
entertain you'
Irish World on *Gazumped!*

'Great fun'
Irish Independent on *Gazumped!*

Also by Sarah O'Brien

Hot Property
Gazumped!
Love Happens

SARAH O'BRIEN

A Girl Thing

HODDER
HEADLINE
IRELAND

A CIP catalogue record for this title is
available from the British Library

ISBN 0 340 83780 2
Ireland ISBN (Including Northern Ireland) 0 340 83776 4

Typeset in Plantin Light by
Palimpsest Book Production Limited, Polmont, Stirlingshire

Printed and bound by Clays Ltd, St Ives plc

Hodder Headline's policy is to use papers that are natural,
renewable and recyclable products and made from wood grown
in sustainable forests. The logging and manufacturing
processes are expected to conform to the
environmental regulations of the country of origin.

Hodder & Stoughton and Hodder Headline Ireland
Divisions of Hodder Headline
338 Euston Road
London NW1 3BH

NOTE ON THE AUTHOR

Sarah O'Brien has a dual personality – she is both Helena Close and Patricia Rainsford, two best friends since childhood. They have collaborated on everything from teenage romance to weddings, babies and career paths. It was only a matter of time before they began writing together.

Helena has worked in public relations and journalism and Patricia teaches part-time. Both live in Limerick, Ireland, with an assortment of children, husbands, cats and dogs. *A Girl Thing* is their fourth book.

ACKNOWLEDGEMENTS

We'd like to thank – as always – our families and friends, our publisher Ciara Considine and our agent Faith O'Grady. Also all at Hodder Headline Ireland and Hodder UK – especially Ciara Doorley and Alex Bonham and Nick, the nice man who copy-edited our manuscript.

A message to the brave and faithful – you'll never walk alone

This book is dedicated to Stevie G, Xabi Alonso, Robbie Fowler Mark Two, Rafa Benitez, Anthony Foley, John 'The Bull' Hayes (the legend), Gael Garcia Bernal, Paul Abbott, the women who gave us 'girl lessons' (badly needed and not all that successful) and of course – the mighty men of Munster.

I

'But I love you,' my stalker said as two policemen steered him towards the door.

'I love you, too,' said one of the policemen – a huge man in his late forties with sparse hair and a gut that was straining against the buttons of his uniform jacket. He turned his head to wink at me. The other cop laughed.

My stalker sniffed angrily and looked at me over his shoulder as he was marched across the large open reception area of Fab City Radio. Sophie was standing in the open doorway of my office, hands on her hips, supervising the proceedings. Suddenly exhausted, I flopped onto the chair behind my desk.

Over the station loudspeaker system, John Howard, the lunchtime news presenter, was doing a telephone interview with a school principal who was complaining about her leaking roof.

Just as the cortège reached the doors Shane appeared. In other circumstances I'd have been amused by the look of sheer amazement on his face. He didn't say a word, just nodded good day to the policemen and watched the trio disappear through the wood-and-glass swing doors. Dee-Dee Ronan,

Fab City Radio's receptionist and switchboard operator, ran over to him. 'They arrested Jamie's admirer,' she said.

Shane looked at Dee-Dee and she preened under his gaze, flicking her waist-length blonde hair like a horse's mane. He looked inquiringly at me where I was still sitting behind the desk and then walked towards me. I noticed that the door of my office was warped. Shane closed it as best he could. It was suddenly very warm and very quiet in my glorified cubbyhole of an office.

'That's the guy who's been stealing the underwear off Jamie's clothes line,' Sophie said to Shane as she ran to look out the window. 'Oh my God! Look! They really do put their hand on your head when they put you into a squad car.'

Shane looked puzzled.

'I told you about the underwear,' I said.

He shrugged.

'Do you remember?' I asked.

'Vaguely,' he said.

'Look at him – bloody weirdo,' Sophie said to the window pane.

Shane examined me as if he was trying to gauge how I was feeling. I tried for a big carefree smile but my face felt frozen.

'I think it's discrimination – nobody ever takes any of *my* underwear,' he said, smiling at me.

'He actually didn't take Jamie's either, as it happens,' Sophie said, laughing and joining us at my desk. 'He thought he did but none of those lacy knickers and bras actually belong to Jamie – she wears old women's underwear.'

I scowled at her.

'But he *thought* they were yours?' Shane said, directing his question at me as he perched on my desk.

I nodded.

'How do you know?'

Sophie picked up a pair of red lacy boxer shorts from the floor. 'He brought them with him.'

'Shit,' Shane said. 'I recognise those knickers – they belong to Heather.'

'I might have guessed,' Sophie said as she held the item up by its label. 'Only Heather would own Yves St Laurent *knickers*.'

Shane ignored her. 'Is that the guy who has been ringing you?' he said to me.

I took a deep breath and nodded. 'He's probably from that stupid singles' bar you made me go to,' I said, turning back to glare at Sophie.

She put her hands in the air. 'Get lost – it's nothing to do with me.'

'Just that you drag me to every dive in town, trawling for men.'

Sophie tutted and straightened her short skirt. 'You go of your own free will.'

'No, I don't – you break my spirit and force me to go.'

Sophie folded her arms and gave her tinkly girlish laugh. How could this single-minded, hard-headed horse-dealer of a businesswoman have come packaged like a sweet-faced Madonna?

'Who did a whole programme about the singles scene?' she asked me, with a disarming tilt of her head.

I wasn't at all disarmed and just shrugged in reply.

'You may not have wanted to go in the first place but you certainly got mileage out of it,' Sophie continued.

'Yes, and a stalker,' I said and tried to look cross. But she was right – it wasn't her, it was me. Lots of people go to bars and don't end up having a huge scene with a stalker as a consequence. Mind you, they also don't end up with a humdinger of a radio documentary of which they were inordinately proud. Swings and roundabouts.

'Why don't you two stop bitching and just tell me what happened while I was out?' Shane said.

Sophie gave a melodramatic sweep of her hands. 'OK. It was a sunny Tuesday lunchtime. I was in my office on the phone. Jamie had just finished her show and was in here.' She sat beside him on the desktop.

They made a very handsome pair – Shane and Sophie – he was as dark as she was blonde. As tall as she was short. As vague as she was focused. The list was endless. Considering their oppositeness it was amazing that they were such good friends.

'Anyway, I could hear all this commotion going on—'

'He called twelve times while I was on air,' I interrupted as the events of that morning began to make some kind of sense. '*Twelve times!* Dee-Dee recognised his voice and only put him through once. Then he arrived in person.'

'With flowers,' Sophie said, leaning back to sniff one of the red roses, which arched elegantly to one side of its basket.

I rolled my eyes.

'And *Heather*'s underwear,' she continued.

'He barged his way into my office,' I said, suddenly beginning to shake as I remembered the shock of the door flying open and this small man with the thick glasses and enormous flower basket appearing out of nowhere. I laughed nervously. 'Barged in – just like that. Plonked the flowers on the desk. Started pulling underwear from his pocket. Told me that he loved me and knew we were fated to be together.'

I stopped to take a breath and Sophie and Shane kept their stares fixed to my face. I took another breath.

'He closed the door and put the filing cabinet up against it . . . I asked him to leave. He said he couldn't because we had to be together . . .'

Sophie came and sat on the windowsill behind my chair and leaned forward to put her arm around my shoulders.

'He's just an idiot,' she said to Shane. 'The Guards said it. Harmless. But it wasn't nice for Jamie.'

'Why did you have to call the police?' Shane said. 'What did he do?'

'Nothing really, but he wouldn't leave,' I said.

'Dee-Dee and I pushed open the door and tried to get him out but he wouldn't go,' Sophie continued. 'Just sat on that chair there, staring at Jamie. I know he looks like the bloke on the Mr Muscle ads but he's a determined little bugger.'

'So who called the police?' Shane said.

'I did,' Sophie replied. 'I was really only bluffing but he called my bluff and they came which was just as well as we—'

A sharp knock on the door was followed by the sudden appearance of Dee-Dee's broad, pretty face.

'Someone to see you, Sophie,' she trilled, looking at Shane as she spoke. Dee-Dee couldn't help herself – if Shane was in a room he was always the focus of her attention. I smiled at her – at least some things were still normal.

Sophie didn't move. 'Stall them.'

Dee-Dee widened her eyeliner-festooned blue eyes and rolled them wildly. Then she disappeared. In her place stood a tall dark-haired familiar-looking man who smiled at all of us.

I stared at him, wondering who the hell he was. In spite of my recent trauma I couldn't help noticing the casual elegance of his clothes. Sand-coloured linen pants and open-necked white linen shirt. Why couldn't someone like *this* stalk me? Oh no, I had to get Mr Muscle. Mind you, this man didn't look like he'd ever need to go to singles' bars to get cosy with members of the opposite sex.

'Steve!' Sophie exclaimed, jumping up. The man called Steve held both of his hands out towards her. She grabbed them in hers and they kissed the air. Jesus, she was one secretive cow – keeping this gorgeous man to herself. Wait until I got her alone.

'Did you forget I was arriving?' he asked her in a teasing voice.

As soon as he spoke and I could add the soft, sexy voice to the chiselled good looks I recognised him. Steve Lowe – ex-RTE TV and radio presenter. Our big-deal new star acquisition at Fab City Radio. Sophie had talked about almost nothing else for at least three months as she and the directors went about attracting him to Limerick and then negotiating the details with his agent. I tuned back in to the conversation in the office.

'. . . And so the police had to come and arrest him,' Sophie was saying in a high-pitched laughing voice. 'Anyway – where are my manners – let me introduce you. Steve Lowe, this is Shane Ali – our chief sound engineer.'

Steve shook Shane's hand vigorously.

'And this is Jamie Ryan – presenter of our award-winning morning magazine show.'

Steve Lowe looked at me. A broad smile lit up his tanned face. 'I've heard it – first class,' he said, moving towards me. 'No wonder you're the object of such great devotion.'

I stood up. Steve took my hand in his across my desk and as our skin made contact I swear to God I felt a bolt of electricity shoot up my arm. I pulled away from him in shock and sat back down. My office chair swivelled from the impact of the sudden sitting. Steve continued to look at me. Beads of perspiration were beginning to form on my forehead and my heart beat a tattoo in my chest. Christ! I needed a holiday.

'Are you all right?' he asked, his dark eyes searching my face.

I nodded. My mouth had suddenly gone as dry as the Sahara so I couldn't speak.

'Are you sure?' he persisted, his face serious now. 'I know we've been laughing but stalkers can be pretty damn scary – all jokes aside.'

I shook my head. 'I'm fine . . . really,' I managed to squeak.

Steve nodded. 'Good.' He looked at me for a few more long seconds and then he moved his gaze back to Sophie. I felt suddenly cold, as though the sun had moved behind a cloud.

'So, Sophie,' he said in that chocolate-brown voice of his, 'tell me this – do I have an office?'

'Indeed you do!' she said. 'Come along with me and we'll introduce you to everybody and get you set up.'

Steve smiled and waved elegantly at Shane and me. We waved back like contestants on *Who Wants To Be A Millionaire?* and then they were gone.

'So – that's the great Steve Lowe,' Shane said.

'So it seems,' I said.

'What do you think of him?'

I looked at Shane in surprise. 'What do you mean?'

'It's not a hard question, Jamie – what do you think of the big-shot?'

'He seems . . .' I paused as adjectives like fabulous, sexy, magnificent, warm, dynamic flooded into my head '. . . seems really nice, doesn't he?'

Shane shrugged. 'A bit smarmy.'

'Just because *you* have no social graces, Shane Ali.'

'My aunts all think I'm a great boy – very polite and good-looking.'

I laughed.

'You OK?' he asked.

I looked quizzically at him.

'Not traumatised by the stalker?' he said.

'A bit.'

Shane smiled. 'Look, I'm sure Sophie's right – he's just a harmless idiot.'

'I hope you're right,' I said.

'Shane, Kieran needs you in the sound booth – there's something wrong with one of the microphones,' Dee-Dee's voice announced. I looked up. As usual she was at my door but for once she was looking at me instead of at Shane.

'I'd better earn my keep,' he said, standing up. He smiled and waved and sidled past Dee-Dee in the doorway. She was still looking at me instead of at Shane, which was slightly worrying.

'What do you think of the new boy?' she hissed as soon as Shane was out of earshot.

I nodded and smiled and once again superlatives flooded my head. But I didn't say a word.

'Oh . . . my . . . God!' Dee-Dee said, closing her eyes and mock-swooning. 'You wouldn't kick him out of bed for eating toast, would you?'

She opened her eyes and looked eagerly at me. I shook my head.

'He's not married, you know – I read about him in *OK*. He's divorced – Jesus, who'd divorce *him*?'

She paused and I thought for one second that maybe she was looking for me to contribute to the conversation. But I needn't have worried – Dee-Dee was in water-cooler mode and was firmly intent on delivering information.

'And he's thirty-nine – not that he looks it. Mary says his teeth are capped but I think they're just *naturally* perfect, don't you?'

I shrugged.

She looked over her shoulder. 'I think I'll go see if the boss and the new boy would like some coffee.'

I nodded and shrugged this time. Dee-Dee spun on a spiky stiletto heel and the blonde hair-curtain shimmered.

'Oh yes,' she said, spinning back quickly. 'Your sister-in-law rang – she didn't want to talk to you, just said to remind you to pick the kids up and that they had a half-day and were finished at one – OK?'

Dee-Dee tottered away. I jumped up from my seat and looked at my watch. Shit! Half-twelve! Shit! Shit! Shit!

2

I arrived at the school with five minutes to spare. The gods were definitely on my side since not only was there very little traffic en route but I also managed to get a big fat empty parking space right outside the school. A quick root in the glove compartment revealed three books of used-up parking discs. I knew that I wouldn't have enough time to get to a shop and back before the kids were let out. I switched on my hazard lights in the hope that the flashing might make my car invisible to passing traffic wardens.

The schoolyard was full of assorted parents and minders, all waiting for the doors to open and the excited hordes to emerge. I was relieved that I was on time. I hated being late for Mark and Fiona but it wasn't just about that. I also wanted their mother – Marielouise – to be able to relax and feel that she wasn't so alone. It's tough being a single parent and I loved my niece and nephew so it was no hardship for me to help out from time to time. I felt the familiar pang in my chest as I thought of my brother Conor. I really missed him so I couldn't even imagine how badly his wife and children felt without him.

Before I could slip into maudlin reverie the front

door of the school opened and the older children came pouring out in a flurry of high-pitched screams and laughs and chatter. I was making my way inside to find the Senior Infants classroom when Mark appeared with his sister in tow.

'Jamie!' my six-year-old niece squealed as she broke free of her brother's hand and launched herself at me. I picked her up and swung her in the air, squeezing her tightly and kissing the top of her head. Mark sauntered towards us, a look of total disdain on his face.

'You're not supposed to run away from me, Fiona,' he said as I placed his sister back on the terrazzo floor.

Fiona shrugged and shook her head, making her long ash-blonde ponytail swing and the pencils in her metal pencil-case rattle inside her bag. 'But it's Jamie,' she insisted with the cutest lisp I ever heard. Mark looked at me and I winked.

'Hey, Mark, how are you?' I said, bending down to give him a hug. He had a look around to see if any of his friends were in view and then he hugged me back quickly.

'She's only six,' I whispered into his ear as we hugged. 'Not as grown-up as you.'

We exchanged knowing glances. Then, taking each of them by the hand, I made my way out of the school building, across the playground and out to my very conveniently parked car. Fiona talked me into buying ice cream so we dumped the school bags in the car and went across the road to a small shop. As I watched my nephew and niece in animated conversation about the relative merits of different ice creams I noticed for the umpteenth time how like his father Mark looked.

Though Conor was five years older than me, I could clearly remember how he'd looked as a child. The same stubbly blond hair as Mark. The same sallow skin. The same big grey eyes. The same serious expression on his face. Mind you, Conor didn't have as much reason to be serious as his son did. He hadn't had to deal with having his father disappear when he was only just seven.

It was a year and a half now since my brother had boarded a plane to Shannon at Heathrow and had somehow evaporated en route. When it happened I was positive that there was some reasonable explanation. Mistaken identity, for example. Maybe he never got on board that plane? Maybe he'd stayed over to do some business at the London branch of his company and forgotten to tell anybody?

But Bill Hehir, Conor's partner in Bilcon IT Solutions, said that wasn't the case. He was able to tell us that yes, Conor had been in London, sorting out a problem in their office. And Bill was also able to confirm that Conor had left to return home as scheduled. One of the London employees of Bilcon had actually driven Conor to Heathrow.

And Bill would know, because he wasn't just Conor's business partner – he was also his best friend. They'd set up Bilcon in Plassey Technological Park twelve years earlier when they'd still been raw graduates from UL. So as far as anybody could tell it seemed that Conor had just dropped off the face of the Earth without any explanation. Well, except for that first week when Bill came to me with some mixed-up story about how he felt that Conor hadn't been himself for a while – he'd been preoccupied and distracted and making stupid mistakes at work.

Conor had asked Bill to meet him for a drink the night before he left for London. Bill had had to cancel at the last minute and said that Conor seemed unusually upset even though they arranged to meet when he got home. As Bill spoke my stomach knotted and the word he wasn't saying was flashing like a neon light in my head. Eventually I couldn't bear it any longer and just had to say it out loud.

'Are you saying Conor committed suicide?'

Bill shrugged. 'It's a possibility – that's all I'm saying.'

I shook my head. 'I just know that Conor would never kill himself.'

'You can never be certain of what is going on in someone else's life.'

'Well, I'm certain of *that*,' I said.

'I hope you're right.'

I hoped I was right, too.

In those first days and weeks – and even months – I went through other possible explanations both in my head and with the police but they all proved fruitless. And Bill never spoke about the possibility of suicide again. Eventually we had no choice but to accept that Conor was gone and that was about all of it. Conor stopped being the centre of anybody's priorities – except ours – and became merely a photograph on the Garda missing-persons website.

But when somebody is missing there's always this tiny voice rooted deep in the back of your head, whispering that maybe he'll turn up. Maybe one fine day – and for no particular reason – he'll walk back into his life just as suddenly and unexpectedly as he'd disappeared out of it. He'll tell us that he had an accident, hit his head, lost his memory. He'll tell us that he was kidnapped and held hostage. Taken by aliens. He'll tell us something – anything – and then we'll all live happily ever after.

My father's face will fill out again and my mother will lose that haunted look in the back of her eyes. Marielouise and the kids will be ecstatic to be together again as a family. But maybe most of all, poor old Mark will be able to get on with being an eight-year-old without the burden of having to make up to his mother and sister for the lost father in their lives.

Mark and Fiona eventually made their ice cream choices and I drove them home to where their housekeeper, Eileen, was waiting at the door. She usually picked them up from school when Marielouise was working but her car was in the garage.

I hugged Mark who gave me a proper hug back this time. Then I tickled Fiona, who I noticed had managed to embed chocolate ice cream in her hair behind her ear. She kissed me and got out of the car after making me promise that I'd come and see them soon. I waved goodbye and drove back to the office, my eyes smarting with the seemingly endless tears brought about by Conor's disappearance. But I didn't cry. I wouldn't. I'd already spent too much time crying and it had done no good – now I had to try and move on.

In an effort to distract myself I thought about Steve Lowe. What had *that* been about? Maybe it was one of those freak electrical things? Perhaps I'd also developed an ability to bend spoons or something like that. When I arrived at the Fab City office Sarah Quinlan's afternoon show was blaring charts music all over the station. I went straight to my office, still a little raw from my delve into the Conor sadness. Dee-Dee, Raina and Helen – the three Fab City secretaries all waved at me and I waved back. There was no sign of Shane or Sophie.

I closed the banjaxed door as much as it would close. I'd have to call Ger Farrell, the station janitor, and see if he could fix it. Sitting at my desk, desperately trying to think of something to do that would take my mind off my troubles, I pulled a folder marked *Programme Ideas* from a drawer and began to flick through it.

But I couldn't concentrate and as the thumping strains of 'Carwash' pumped out of the speakers mounted on my office wall the tears finally came. One after another they plopped onto the papers that I'd spread out on the desk. I was so preoccupied that I never even knew there was anybody in the room with me until I heard a low cough. I started and looked up from my tear-spattered work to see Steve Lowe standing on the other side of my desk.

'Sorry,' he said when he saw my face.

I shook my head, sniffed and wiped away tears with the palm of my hand. 'No, no, you're fine – can I do something for you? How are you getting on? Settling in?'

I shuffled the papers back into a heap and stuffed them into their folder.

'Look – I'll go – you've had a bad day and now here I am as well adding to your problems, barging in here . . .'

'No, I'm fine – it's not that – that's nothing . . .' The pent-up tears began to escape again and Steve pulled a chair over close to my desk.

'Listen,' he said. 'Sometimes it's good to talk – Jesus, I couldn't tell you the number of things in my life I've bottled up and where did it get me? Nowhere – or at least nowhere good.'

I nodded and relaxed a little and just let the tears flow.

'So?' he said after a few seconds of my silent crying.

I raised my eyebrows in reply, still unable to speak.

'How about talking to a sympathetic stranger?'

I searched in my handbag for a tissue and noisily blew my nose. Then I looked at Steve and almost against my will the words began to come tumbling out. Steve nodded and shook his head and mmm'd and ah-ha'd as I told him about Conor and all that had happened. We sat there for ages as I spilled out all the upset and by the end of it two things had happened.

The first thing – as predicted by Steve – was that I felt better than I'd felt in an awful long time. Light and refreshed and relieved. He hugged me before he left and reassured me that it'd been an honour and a pleasure to listen to me.

I sat in my empty office, surrounded now by the strains of 'Sylvia's Mother', and thought about what had transpired and that was when I realised the other thing that had happened. Steve hadn't predicted it. I'd never have guessed such a thing was possible and I knew that if I told Shane he'd laugh his arse off.

I'd fallen madly in love with Steve Lowe.

3

Next morning my alarm went off at seven – an hour earlier than usual. I turned it off and surveyed my dim bedroom.

'Steve Lowe,' I said to the ceiling. The name rolled off my tongue like honey or my favourite wine. Such a lovely name. Noble. Strong. Sexy.

I shook my head and jumped out of bed. I showered quickly and for the first time in ages wondered what I'd wear for work. This was going to be a huge problem. I didn't want the whole station to know that I fancied Steve Lowe but on the other hand my range of clothes was so scant and predictable that even the tiniest change would be noticed. I opened my pine wardrobe and looked at the contents. Jeans – lots of them. Jumpers, T-shirts. One black dress for funerals. A skirt that I'd bought for a meeting four years ago. One pair of black trousers that Sophie had bought me last Christmas but that I'd never worn. I took it off the hanger and found a new white fitted T-shirt. I dressed and looked at my image in the full-length pine-framed mirror.

'Olive Oyl,' I said to my reflection. And that's exactly who I looked like – Popeye's girlfriend. The trousers seemed to make me look taller and thinner than ever – if that was possible. The figure-hugging T-shirt looked like it was desperately seeking some bust to cling on to and my damp cropped hair stood on end. For the millionth time I envied Sophie her vast knowledge of all things girlie.

From the time I was thirteen it became obvious that I didn't fit into Girl Land. At first I tried. I read the magazines, experimented with make-up and talked endlessly about boys. I was serving my time and believed I was doing well – so well, in fact, that I was actually looking forward to my first public appearance – the Lismore Community Centre under-age disco.

My training schedule for the big night was worthy of any athlete. Under the tutelage of my best-friend-at-the-time, Lizzie Buckley, I was raring to go. I bought new clothes, had my hair cut in a most unflattering Princess Diana rip-off and spent hours and hours with Lizzie experimenting with different shades of eyeshadow and lipstick.

D-Day finally arrived and as Lizzie and I walked into the crowded, noisy hall I felt like Madonna: sexy, hip and cool. The music started and we were off. Darren Healy, my current heart-throb, arrived with his crew and my cup overflowed with happiness. Lizzie convinced me that Darren was looking at me all the time and that she just *knew* he fancied me. Unfortunately Freddie Black, the school anorak, was a lot more forthcoming than Darren and asked me to dance almost immediately.

Lizzie and the girls were skitting laughing as he

propelled me around the hall. I was literally head and shoulders taller than him – if I'd had a bosom his face would have been buried in it.

'Hungry Eyes' seemed to go on for at least an hour as we danced and as if that wasn't bad enough I also had to dance with Freddie through 'Careless Whisper' and 'Borderline'. By the end of the set Freddie had welded himself to me and I knew that he was hoping for a long-term relationship – or at least a one-night stand. Avoiding his gaze, I made my excuses as Madonna finished singing. I headed to the loo, wondering how I was going to manage to duck Freddie for the rest of the night.

The bathroom emptied as I was going through the doors – 'Ride on Time' blaring out behind me and a throng of teenage girls screaming '*I love that song*' stampeding past me. I fixed my make-up, admired myself in the spotty mirror over the sink and then nipped into a cubicle for a pee. Mid-pee the outside door opened and I heard the distinctive squealing of Lizzie and my friends. I was just on the point of calling out to them when Lizzie's voice rose above the babble.

'Did you see Freddie the Geek dancing with Big Bird?' she said.

I froze.

The others roared with laughter.

'No, don't laugh, they're the perfect couple – I think he suits her much better than Darren Healy. I mean, he's so small and she's so tall – the two biggest freaks in the school. Imagine the children they'd have.'

Tears sprang to my eyes and I tugged at the hem

of my skirt in a vain attempt to cover more of my
long skinny legs. My heart thumped so loudly that I
could hear it in my ears and all I wanted to do was
escape. I closed the toilet without flushing, sat on top
of it with my knees pulled up to my chin so that I
wouldn't be discovered and waited an eternity until
they left. Silent tears streamed down my face as I
heard Lizzie's words over and over in my head. *Big
Bird. Freak. Big Bird. Freak.*

And when they did eventually leave I just made a
run for it. Out of the toilets, through the teenager-
filled corridor and into the night. I didn't stop running
until I got home. And that was it for me with Girl
Land.

I never spoke to Lizzie again and though I did
manage to go out with Darren Healy for a while he
was a big disappointment. I made a few decisions that
night. I was good at sport, I was good at school and I
was obviously no good at this girl lark. Much as I hated
to admit it, I thought that Lizzie was probably right –
I *was* a bit of a freak. And that was fine with me: they
could keep it all – the make-up and the preening and
the bitching – I didn't want any of it.

In retrospect I could see that that was how I survived
my adolescence. But now I was an adult woman and
beginning to realise that I'd thrown the baby out with
the bathwater.

However, I couldn't completely escape Girl Land
since it was part of my daily life. Ironically, my
mother's career was a world filled with the beautifi-
cation of every part of the female body. She owned

Poise, a beauty salon that provided every treatment and pampering known to woman, and sometimes man too. I blamed David Beckham for the latter. He started the male manicure and depilation trends and now even Limerick men were queuing up to be waxed and cleansed and moisturised.

Needless to say, I avoided Poise like the plague. I shaved my legs once a month with a Gillette razor and they looked fine to me. But now I wished that I had some miracle foundation that would hide my pasty skin. And some eyeshadow and lipstick wouldn't go astray, either. I rooted in my so-called make-up drawer and under a pile of half-used tubes and bottles found a small cosmetics bag that Mam had given me years ago before she lost hope in me.

I opened it and spread the tubs and palettes out in front of me. It couldn't be that difficult, could it? I flipped open a tube of foundation and lathered it on my face. It didn't look bad at all. Then I chose some brown eyeshadow and a bright pink lipstick. And some black mascara. The mascara was the hardest to apply, because I kept poking myself in the eye with the wand. Finally I swept some blusher across my cheeks the way my mother used to do.

I went downstairs and into the kitchen. Shane was frying eggs at the cooker. He wore a white terry dressing gown that was way too small for him.

'Morning, Shane. Did you grow overnight or did the dressing gown shrink?' I said as I filled the kettle.

'Is your dad coming over for the game tonight?' he said, without turning around.

'Does a bear shit in the woods?' I said, popping slices of bread into the toaster.

Shane flipped his eggs onto a plate, sat down at the kitchen table, and looked at me, his mouth hanging open.

'What?' I asked, frowning.

He shook his head.

'Haven't you ever seen a bit of make-up before?' I said, deciding that attack was the best form of defence.

'Not on you.' He cut up his eggs but kept looking at me.

Heather came in then, dressed to the nines and tying up her blonde hair. 'I've a shoot in one hour, Shaney – how do I look?' She did a little twirl in front of him, bent, kissed him on the lips and smiled sweetly at me.

'Jamie, you look . . . different,' she said, coming closer for a better look.

I ignored her and buttered my toast.

'Make-up,' said Shane.

'I can see that,' Heather said, stifling a laugh as she helped herself to some of Shane's toast.

'Did Shane give you back your knickers?' I said, smiling at her. I knew this reference to my stalker friend would shut her up.

Much as we loved Shane, Sophie and I just couldn't get on with his fiancée, Heather Moore (or Header More as we liked to call her). She was a model and very beautiful and that was about the size of it. There really wasn't much going on upstairs and what there was was pretty bitchy stuff. She reminded me of a cat. Elegant, sleek and gorgeous on the out-side but completely selfish inside, claws always sharp and ready for action.

I stood up and, bringing my toast with me, I went upstairs to the bathroom and examined my face. In the harsh morning light I could see Heather's point. I scrubbed my face clean with a sponge and soap. Maybe I'd swallow my pride and ask Sophie for some make-up lessons. I checked my watch and then, as I ran downstairs, I mentally went through my tasks for the day.

'See you later,' I shouted at nobody in particular as I picked up my briefcase and denim jacket and rushed out the door.

I arrived at the station at eight on the dot and waved at Dee-Dee as I made my way through the open-plan office to my desk. I could see Johnny G – the radio presenter currently on air – in the soundproof studio. He winked at me as he caught my eye. The door of my office was gone, I presumed to be fixed. I sat at my desk, switched on my computer and checked my e-mail. This was something I had done religiously every morning since Conor's disappearance. He had been a great man for e-mails and we used to constantly chat online throughout our work day.

I concentrated on my workload for the day and tried to clear my mind of everything except the prepar-ation for my show. I loved radio. I loved everything about it. That five minutes before going on air. The buzz and excitement, the anticipation. The hours in a microcosmic world that I controlled. Our station owner – John Marshall – was now branching into the world of television but it held no appeal for me.

I worked at my computer and tried not to look up every time the front door opened. I'd have to stop all this silly swooning around Steve Lowe. I was a grown woman – all six foot of me – and had never acted like a love-struck fool in my life. Why did Steve have that effect on me? I worked furiously on my notes, refusing to look away from the screen.

I heard Steve before I saw him. He was leaning over Dee-Dee's desk, smiling intently at her. Sophie was standing behind him and caught my look and threw her gaze beseechingly to Heaven. But I barely noticed. I was way too busy trying to control the queasy feeling in my stomach and the strange palpitations in my heart. Christ, this was worse than having the flu. I wondered if there was some kind of drug I could take to stop it. Maybe I was coming down with something after all – something terminal, judging by the way my body was reacting.

Steve walked away from reception and came straight towards me. My head felt like it was going to float away from my body and I was sure that the whole station could hear my heart thumping. I prepared what I thought was a winning smile and looked directly at him as he approached.

He looked straight at me, nodded hello and walked to his office. My face went scarlet and I bent down, pretending to root for something in a drawer as Sophie approached.

'Jamie, there's a new salsa class starting up and—What's wrong with your face?' she asked.

'The heating is on the blink again. Salsa? I don't think so, not after yesterday.'

Sophie laughed and took off her fitted suit jacket. She looked stunning in a simple pinstripe work suit. Her blonde hair was fixed in an intricate chignon that looked as though it must have taken a couple of weeks to do. As I examined her face I thought first that she had no make-up on but then realised that it was there, all right, but barely perceptible. So that was the way you avoided the panto look – less is more.

'What has our stalker friend got to do with salsa classes? His name is Pierce Thomson, by the way.'

'How do you know that?'

'I was talking to a sergeant in Henry Street this morning.'

'So what's the story with him?' I asked.

'They're not charging him but they cautioned him. They said he was harmless.'

'How consoling. They probably said the same thing once about the Boston Strangler. I'm still not going to the salsa class, Sophie, darling. I can't dance – you know that.'

She smiled at me. 'So that's why we should take lessons. I went out on my date last night . . .'

'How did it go with the rugby player?'

Sophie rolled her eyes. 'Cauliflower ears and cauliflower brain. Listen to me – anyway, I met Rico in the restaurant . . .'

'Rico? Didn't you have a date with Tony Moran, the prop for Shannon?'

'Will you let me finish? Rico was the waiter. He does that part-time. His real job is teaching the salsa classes.'

'I see where this is leading. So we're swapping the singles bars for the salsa. Great. Now I'll get the Latin American stalkers.'

Sophie cocked her head to one side. 'You could do a great piece for your show. Great music . . .'

I threw a balled-up Post-It at her. 'Quit while you're ahead, girl.'

Sophie laughed and ducked the small missile. 'Did you hear Johnny G's dedication to you this morning?'

I shook my head.

'He played "Misty".'

'"Misty"?'

'Come on, Jamie – the song from the movie *Play Misty For Me*.'

I shook my head.

'Where Clint Eastwood is a dj being stalked by a murdering female fan. Do you watch *anything* besides football matches?'

'Bastard! I'll get him back!'

Sophie laughed as she walked away.

We had a staff meeting at nine o'clock. Despite my lectures to myself, I could feel anticipatory butterflies beginning to flutter in my stomach as the clock ticked away the minutes to the meeting. Shane had come in by then and was being accosted as usual by every young female – and one or two males as well

– in the building. The minute Shane Ali appeared every computer in the place went on the blink. Strange, strange world.

I looked across at him now as he knelt on the floor, checking out Raina Burke's hard drive. I knew that technically he was gorgeous. It's in the gene mix – Pakistani father, Hyde Road mother. Once the Irish spread their wings the looks definitely improved. But Shane was such a good friend he was nearly one of the girls, or else I was one of the boys. We lived together in perfect harmony, happily watching Sky Sports while various respective boyfriends and girlfriends flitted through our lives. I never found Shane attractive. God, it would be like fancying my brother.

I shook my head as Conor's face floated in front of me for the umpteenth time that morning. Why was he in my head so much today? The date wasn't significant, was it? I checked the calendar. 20 April. Nope. It didn't ring any bells except that he'd been gone exactly eighteen months, one week and three days. When do you stop counting? And if you stop counting does that mean you care less?

My mobile bleated and I shook myself out of my sombre thoughts. I looked at the screen. Mam. I took a deep breath and answered.

'Hi, Mam.'

'Jamie. Glad I caught you before you went on air. Listen, I have a client here, Miss Limerick actually, and, well, we're a bit behind because we both decided she needed a full wax and anyway she's the first guest on your show today and—'

'Mam, I've a meeting now so could you—'

'I'm telling you as quickly as possible, dear. I said to your father this morning, I said, you see our Jamie? No patience. Just like you. No patience at all . . .'

'Mam?' I tried to keep my voice level but it was hard.

'So, I told Linda – Miss Limerick – a lovely girl – beautiful manner – that I'd ring you and tell you she'll be a little late.'

'How late? Five minutes? Ten?' I was getting furious by now.

My mother chuckled. 'It's a full wax, Jamie, love. An hour at least.'

I inhaled and spoke quietly. 'Tell Miss Limerick that if she's not here at the designated time I won't allow her on my show. It's a programme, not a drop-in centre. I don't mind a bit if she's hairy or not as long as she's here on time. Goodbye, Mother.'

I hung up and dashed into Sophie's office, which also served as a boardroom, flustered and late for the meeting. I knew I was right about the Miss Limerick thing but I also knew that by the end of the day I'd feel guilty and ashamed about the conversation I'd just had with Mam. She had that effect on me. Always.

4

I looked into Steve Lowe's eyes and realised for the first time that they were blue, not brown, and that there were tiny gold flecks near the pupils. His hair flopped over his forehead in a rakish Hugh Grant sort of way and when he smiled deep lines appeared at each side of his mouth. He smiled now, but not at me. He smiled at Sophie. She, on the other hand, smiled at nobody. Instead she conducted the meeting with her usual businesslike efficiency and intelligence. Our Sophie might be blonde but add the 'dumb' at your peril. Johnny G passed me a piece of paper as Steve began to speak about how RTE had raised their ratings and how we could do the same.

I read Johnny's note.

Stalker playlist
Misty
Every breath you take
The Look of Love
Follow me
You'll never walk alone (or again)

Jamie, please add to this at your discretion . . .
Love Johnny xxxx

I narrowed my eyes and, glaring at Johnny, I began to write:

Murderer's playlist
Bang Bang
I shot the sheriff (and Johnny)
Licence to kill
Murder on the Dancefloor

I pushed my note over towards him and heard his stifled laugh as he read it.

Steve and Sophie were in the middle of a discussion on ratings and population demographics. I was kind of baffled by this talk – I mean, if the show is good enough then people will tune in. Sophie was probably the most ambitious person I knew and 'good enough' wouldn't do if 'the best' was still available. Steve talked now about his plans for his drive-time show. He had the most wonderful radio voice and I was looking forward already to listening to him on my way home from work every day.

'What do you think, Jamie?' Sophie smiled sweetly at me, rolling her pen between her fingers. Everybody seemed to be looking at me, expecting gems of wisdom. I rooted in my subconscious for a wisp of the last few sentences of conversation.

'Hard news or magazine style – which do you think works best?' she asked.

'There are already a number of national stations doubling up on the hard-news approach. Why don't we mix hard news with magazine?' I answered.

Steve reached out and put his hand on my bare arm. 'That's it, Jamie. That's exactly what I want to do.' He turned and addressed Sophie but forgot to take his hand away. Which was a very bad idea as my skin seemed to be on fire and his hand would begin to sizzle very soon. The butterflies in my stomach woke up and rioted and my head did the floaty drunken thing again.

'Excuse me, I need to go out for a . . . bathroom . . .' I mumbled. I stood up and tried not to run out of the room. I dashed into the nearby toilet. God, I was definitely coming down with something. This had never happened to me before – not even when I was ten and fell in love with the Liverpool football team and in particular with John Barnes.

I checked my face in the mirror. Jesus, I was as pale as a ghost. And – shit – I had a stripe of foundation that had escaped my earlier scrubbing running down the side of my face. I rubbed at it now with some wet tissue and, taking a deep breath, I went back into the meeting. Steve smiled at me as I sat down and I smiled back and promptly turned bright red. I could see Johnny giving me strange looks so I picked up my notebook and read imaginary notes like they were the most interesting thing in the world.

'So, Jamie, we were just talking about the press party on Saturday night. I'm hoping everybody from the station will be there,' said Sophie, gathering up her own notes.

I'd forgotten about the party to announce details of Fab City TV. In my PS days (pre-Steve) this would not have posed a problem. I had it down to a fine art – after a quick shower throw on any clean and ironed items of clothing nearest at hand. Maybe lipstick, seeing as it was a party. Go to party, nod and smile and watch clock so that am home in time for *Match of the Day*. Now it was a whole different ball game. Literally.

As the meeting broke up and I went back to my office to prepare for my three-hour stint on air all I could think about was my wardrobe, which was more minuscule than capsule. There was nothing for it – I'd have to go clothes shopping and I'd have to drag Sophie with me. I needed serious girl lessons and she was the woman for the job.

Before I knew it the recently depilated Miss Limerick arrived and began babbling on about Sienna Miller and some skirt she'd worn that was obviously going to change people's lives. I tuned out, trying to staunch the feeling of desperation as she wittered on and on. How the hell was I going to get a decent inter- view out of her on air? Luckily, Johnny wasn't only good for puns, he was also our station Casanova and he rescued me from the skirt conversation by taking Miss Limerick for coffee. I escaped into the studio and, clearing all the debris from my mind, began psyching myself up for my show.

★

By quarter to eight that night I had everything in place for a perfect evening. My favourite wine was chilling in the fridge. Dad and Shane were already set up in their usual football-viewing chairs. All we needed now was for Liverpool to beat United. I opened my wine and poured a glass, sipping it in the kitchen as I microwaved popcorn. I could never manage to drink beer, much to Shane's disgust. He claimed that wine-drinking football fans were cissies and I had to constantly remind him that I was actually a female. Familiarity breeds invisibility.

I brought the warm popcorn into the living room and took my usual seat next to Dad. He was deep in conversation with Shane about the team selection. I looked at him affectionately as he chatted. He'd aged ten years since Conor's disappearance. Poor Dad. He never talked about it. And when the subject came up at all his face closed down and became unreadable. Once, about a year ago, I'd caught him crying in the middle of a Liverpool match. We'd been on our own that night: Shane had had an anniversary date with Heather that he couldn't get out of. Liverpool scored and I roared and glanced at Dad and tears were streaming down his face and I knew by the look of him that the goal hadn't even registered. I looked back at the screen but reached out and held his hand. He squeezed mine in return and that was it.

He turned to me now and grabbed some popcorn. 'We'll do it, Jamie. We'll beat them tonight, I can feel it in my water.'

'Don't jinx us, Dad.'

'I've got ten euro on United to win,' said Shane,
without taking his eyes from the screen. Just as the
match started I heard a key in the lock. I glared at
Shane and I knew he could see me but he chose
to ignore me. Heather burst into the room in a
blur of shopping bags, high spirits and expensive
perfume.

'Hi. We finished the shoot early so here I am,' she
said.

We all nodded but kept our gazes on the TV.

'Shaney, did you hear me?' she asked and went over
to him, blocking the TV screen as she passed. Our
heads leaned to the left. She kissed him and then passed
by the TV again. Our heads leaned to the right. She
went out to the kitchen and came back in with a glass
of wine and we all did the head-cocking thing again.
She sat on the arm of Shane's chair, playing with his
hair and kissing his face. Then she started whispering
into his ear. I was finding it increasingly difficult not
to laugh. Dad looked at me and winked and a tiny
bubble of laughter escaped from me.

'Who's in red?' asked Heather.

Nobody answered. She was Shane's fiancée so he
should have done the honours.

We didn't win. It was a scoreless draw and
Heather's presence grew more frustrating than the
lack of goals. She was the type of person who thought
silence was wrong. If there was silence then somebody just had to break it immediately. My mother
was exactly the same.

Sometimes I wondered what Shane saw in her. She

was beautiful in a Caprice sort of way, even I could see that. But they were engaged and I wondered how Shane would cope with the constant chatter after they were married. During the match she talked and talked until her voice became like a pneumatic drill on a distant building site. We all managed to tune her out, even Shane.

Luckily, they headed off to bed early and I made tea for Dad before he went home. We sat on the sofa, which faced the huge picture window that overlooked the Shannon. The view was easily the best one in the city and was worth the exorbitant rent.

Shane and I had lived here for almost five years. Originally, Sophie had lived with us. Then she and Paul – her ex-fiancé – had bought a house together in the suburbs prior to their shock break-up three months ago. I was surprised when Brad and Jen split but Sophie and Paul bowled me over completely.

Dad looked tired as he sipped his tea.

'You OK, Dad?' I asked.

'Disappointed, love, that's all,' he said, his face sad. It took me a second to realise that he was talking about the match.

'I know. Same here.' I smiled at him.

'How's work? Your mother started telling me some long story about you and Miss Limerick but I lost the thread of it halfway through.'

I grinned at him. Boy, did I know how that could happen. 'We're opening a TV station – did I tell you that?'

'You did. And I read about it in the *Leader* last

weekend. Won't that be great for you? Mam is telling everyone you'll be on the telly.'

'No, I won't. I like what I'm doing. Cameras make me jittery.'

'You're the prettiest girl I know, love. You're like a model. You'll be great on the telly.'

'And you're one biased dad,' I said, laughing.

'Bill called in to see me today.'

I smiled tightly. For all that Bill and Conor had been best friends since they were seventeen and I eleven, Bill and I had an edgy relationship. And worse than that – a chequered history. But I didn't say anything negative about him to my father. I never would. My parents loved him and in fairness he also loved them and was very good to them – especially since Conor's disappearance.

'Is that right?' I said.

He rubbed his hands together as if they were cold. 'Poor Bill. He misses him so much.'

I finished my tea. 'We all miss him.'

Dad said nothing.

'Anyway, who are we playing next?' I asked and forced myself to smile.

'Chelsea. And we'll beat them for definite.'

'Dad, shut up, you jinx.'

5

Getting Sophie to agree to girl lessons was much harder than I thought it would be. It was Friday afternoon and I'd just finished a hectic show. It included a weightlifting nun and a Nigerian asylum-seeker who was fluent in Irish. It was a terrific show, and I loved it when that happened, when all the pieces fell together like a jigsaw. I had coffee with Sophie in her office, which was a regular Friday-afternoon ritual with us.

'You've got to help me with the Girl Thing,' I said as I sipped my bought-in cappuccino.

Sophie eyed me above the rim of her reading glasses. 'No.'

'Bitch. Why not? You spent years trying to drag me into shops and beauty salons so why the big change?'

She shook her blonde head and took off her glasses. 'Jamie, Jamie, Jamie. That's exactly the reason why I won't. Look at all the time you wasted.'

I laughed. 'You better help me. Salsa classes?' I knew I had her now.

'OK. There are conditions, though.'

'Anything, Soph, as long as you help me.'

Sophie sipped her coffee, an evil smile playing on her lips.

'One – no cribbing, moaning or groaning. What I say goes.'

I nodded eagerly.

'Two – a couple of hours in Poise – I'll keep the peace between you and your mother, I promise.'

'Do we have to?'

Sophie nodded. 'Three – I pick the clothes, shoes, everything. No jeans and jumpers, no T-shirts, no old women's knickers.'

I rolled my eyes. 'Agreed, you bully.'

'I'll pick you up first thing in the morning.'

'So, who's going to the bash anyway?' I asked casually.

Sophie narrowed her eyes and gave me the evil little smile again. I tried to look unreadable.

'Why do you suddenly want to do all this girl stuff?' she asked.

'Can't I even buy some new clothes?'

'Of course, but usually you have to be dragged kicking and screaming to the shops and then when you get there you buy the same stuff all the time.'

I smiled at my friend. 'Stop hassling me – who's going to the do?'

'Everybody, including that rat-fink ex-fiancé of mine.'

'Why did you invite him?'

'No choice. Paul is the solicitor handling the legal side of things for the new TV station. Anyway, guess who else is coming?'

'Brad Pitt?'

'Nearly as good-looking. The dead sexy Rico.'

'Salsa Rico?'

Sophie nodded, her eyes dancing. 'And he's bringing his brother. I hope he's a bit taller than Rico.'

'I'm not interested, Soph.'

She gave me a quizzical look. 'You should be, because he's your partner for the salsa lessons.'

I sighed. 'Great.'

Sophie stared at me for a few long seconds and my heart began to speed up as I became convinced that she could read my mind. It wasn't that I minded telling her what I felt – she was my best friend in the world, after all, and I'd trust her with my life. But until I knew how I actually felt I wasn't able to talk about it.

'Are you really all right?' she asked.

I nodded, damning the blush that was slowly creeping up my throat into my face.

'Of course I am.'

She continued to stare. 'Sure?'

I laughed. 'Really, Soph, I'm a big girl, all six feet of me.'

She smiled at me. 'We'll have a great day tomorrow. Wait and see – you might end up enjoying it.'

But Sophie was so wrong about that. The day started very well – she and I had breakfast in Brown Thomas followed by a leisurely stroll around the shop. Sophie did all the hard work and I traipsed after her like a lost dog.

I had all the usual problems with clothes that have

plagued me since I was a tall gangly teenager. Nothing fitted. All the trousers and dresses were too short. The jacket sleeves looked like they'd shrunk. Even Sophie, the best shopper in the world, was becoming disheartened. Then one of the shop assistants produced a dress that actually fitted. And it wasn't bad as dresses go. Black, plain and not too short. I came out of the tiny cubicle and stood in front of Sophie and the shop assistant.

'Well?' I asked, pulling the silky material down over my arse.

'That dress was made for you,' said Sophie and the assistant nodded her head vigorously in agreement.

'Do you swear that I don't look like Big Bird?' I asked plaintively.

'I promise you,' Sophie answered.

'You have a great figure – did you ever think of modelling?' the shop assistant asked.

Sophie laughed. 'The thing you don't realise is that while she certainly has the looks she has a very bad attitude. We'll take the dress.'

I stole a glance at the price tag and looked in alarm at Sophie.

'We'll take it,' she insisted. 'Now, shoes, a bag and a nice jacket.'

'Will we rob the bank now or later?' I said as I went back into the cubicle.

By lunchtime we'd purchased all the accessories. Well, Sophie had and I'd watched and handed over my credit card when asked. Working on radio, where you're heard and not seen, makes you lazy about your appearance – especially if you're already anti-Girl Land. But it'd been a long time since I'd met anyone like Steve.

We had lunch in a small pub across the road from my mother's beauty salon. As we sat eating our chicken wraps, surrounded by our bags, I remembered that Sophie's ex would be at the party.

'How do you feel about Paul being there tonight?' I asked, sipping my coffee.

Sophie's face darkened at the mention of her ex-fiancé's name. I could see the hurt in her eyes.

She shrugged and picked at some lettuce on her plate. 'I'm well over him now, Jamie. I don't care if he comes or not.'

'He'll never bring her, will he?'

Sophie looked at me. 'I couldn't care less. He can bring whoever he likes.'

'Her' was a solicitor colleague of Paul's who'd been having an affair with him for the past two years. The length of his and Sophie's engagement, to be precise. Three months ago, Sophie had discovered that instead of being in Killarney at some Law Society function Paul and Rachel were loved-up in Paris. Apparently Rachel's husband had discovered the little trip and duly informed Sophie on the telephone. All that, and the ink wasn't even dry on their new twenty-five-year mortgage.

'You had a lucky escape, Soph,' I said, and meant it. She could have married the cheating coward.

'Whatever doesn't kill you makes you strong. My

mother used to tell me that. Anyway, Jamie, what about you? Any man on the horizon?'

I blushed to the roots of my hair.

She looked at me inquiringly. 'Oh my God! You haven't been wrangling with Billy Boy again, have you?'

I glared at my friend. 'You must be joking.'

She eyed me over the rim of her water glass. 'Sure?'

'Yes. Positive. Now shut up.'

Sophie smiled. 'Come on, let's get your arse across the road and we'll see what we can do with you,' she said and went to pay the bill.

My mother's salon was busier than Colbert Station at Christmas. God, she was really packing them in, I thought as Sophie and I stood in the crowded reception area. I hadn't realised that the beauty business was so lucrative – or so full of beautiful women. The waiting hordes looked fabulous already – why on earth were they here at all? Baffling.

'Jamie! Sophie!' called my mother, as she came towards us in a blur of perfectly groomed efficiency.

She smiled at us and I noticed again how good she looked for her age. She was fifty-five years old, but looked younger. Her shoulder-length brown hair framed a heart-shaped face. Her features were neat and even and everything about her, from her beautifully shaped eyebrows to her tastefully painted nails, was perfectly maintained. As Shane said of her – she was one classy bird. And in her presence I felt like a bird too. Unfortunately and as usual it was Big Bird.

I couldn't understand how a neat, well-proportioned woman could have given birth to such a gangly string of a football-loving daughter. When I was younger I used to think that I'd been switched at birth but one look at my father's angular frame and brown eyes and I knew whose genes I'd inherited. Conor, on the other hand, was like a cross between both parents – neat even features in a tall frame. And let's face it, tall is grand if you're a boy. Tall is five foot ten inches – tops – if you're a girl. Another inch and the jokes start.

I noticed for the first time that Fab City radio was piped through both floors of the salon. Mam brought us to where a young girl with a high, tight ponytail – a hairstyle that Johnny G called 'the poor woman's facelift' – ordered me onto a table and began massaging my face. I almost fell asleep, it felt so good. I could hear my mother and Sophie chatting on and on about lip gloss and highlights and skin peels. This wasn't so bad after all. I mean, I didn't actually have to do anything – I'd be quite willing to do this once or twice a year if it helped me to look like Sophie and Heather, I thought.

When I was finally massaged enough the girl applied some cold goo that smelled like salad. Then I was ordered to a basin where a waiting stylist felt my hair and discussed its texture with Sophie and Mam.

'Very dry – we'll have to give it a deep root,' said the young stylist.

I watched Mam and Sophie in the mirror nod sagely at each other over my head.

'And a once-off colour – cranberry – that would be lovely because she's so dark.'

Everybody nodded again.

'Are you happy with that so?' the hairdresser asked. I was just about to answer when I realised that Sophie had answered for me.

While the stylist went to work I looked at my face in the mirror. I was covered in a thick lime-green face mask and now my hair was being coated in a pinky-purple gunk. I laughed out loud, picked up *Hello!* magazine and settled down for a long read as some space-age hairdryer thing was lowered over my head.

'Jamie?' a familiar voice said after a few minutes.

I jumped and banged my head on the rim of the drying gadget.

'Ouch,' I said. Pushing the yoke away, I looked up at Bill Hehir.

I blushed but it didn't matter because my face was currently lime green anyway.

'Jamie?' he said again, a small smile playing on his lips.

'Bill,' I said and turned back to the mirror.

He was standing behind me and spoke to my image.

'Looking well, Jamie. A little seasick, maybe?' He smiled and patted me on the shoulder like you would a small child. I found Bill Hehir infuriating at the best of times – and this was not the best of times.

'I was looking for your mother but I found you instead.'

'Lucky you. What do you want?'

He smiled that maddening smile again. 'What are you offering?'

'Green mud.' I held his gaze in the mirror, trying to muster some dignity. He stared back at me, his face already showing signs of a five o'clock shadow. I'd known this man since I was a child and he still made me feel as awkward and uncomfortable now as he had way back then. Mr Bill Perfect Man Hehir. Mr No Emotion. Mr Never-Casual Business Genius. Mr Love 'em and Leave 'em Hehir.

'Bill, how are you? I got your message,' sang my mother as she kissed Bill. 'This place is in turmoil today. There's that TV party tonight and some fashion show in Adare . . .' Mam smiled at Bill and fanned her face with her hand.

'You look terrific, Anna. All the hard work suits you,' said Bill.

'I don't know what I'd do without my work,' Mam said.

Bill reached out and put a hand lightly on my mother's shoulder.

She'd always liked Bill. He had become a surrogate son and played the role to perfection. I always felt that with Bill – everything was a role – an act that you had to perform correctly. Still, I was glad that somebody else was around to share the burden of my parents' sorrow, whatever his motives.

Mam and Bill chatted away and I zoned in and out of the conversation surrounding me. Sophie, the bitch, was nowhere to be seen. The stylist came back to check my hair and moved me to a basin to rinse out the colour. I could hear snatches of chat, something about my dad and tickets for a football match.

I was led away then, back to the face-pack area. Mam and Bill smiled at me as I passed.

'See you tonight, Jamie. I can't wait to see how all the – um – colouring turns out,' he said. I smiled falsely at him, cracking my face mask in the process. His eyes danced with amusement and I wanted to kick him. Hard, and preferably in the balls.

'Who's he?' asked Poor Man's Facelift as she chiselled the hardened mud from my face.

'A friend of my mother's,' I said.

'Cute in an old-fashioned way. He looks like those matinée idols that my Granny loves. You know, those guys with too-neat hair and man faces?'

I laughed. 'Man faces?'

'Yeah. I mean some of the lookers nowadays have kinda . . . well, girl faces. He's got a man face.'

'He's a bit of a shit.'

The girl stopped cleansing for a second and looked at me, a ball of green-tinged cotton wool in her hand. 'A very sexy shit.'

I laughed. 'That's a matter of opinion.'

'I love your show,' she said as she cleaned off the last of the gunk.

'Thanks. I never get tired of hearing that,' I said just as Sophie came back, holding her freshly painted nails out in front of her like one of the walking dead.

6

I got home at six and couldn't stop fiddling with my hair as I slipped into my new gear. I thought I looked presentable – but then again, what would I know? Sophie had insisted that I buy a Wonderbra and chicken fillets. I stood in front of the mirror in my bedroom, admiring this ingenious invention that gave you a bust for clothes to hang on to. I finished my dressing, looked at myself and decided that even if *I* was a total idiot at this stuff Sophie was a genius and she loved me so she'd never let me go out looking crap. I took a deep breath and decided that I was just going to have to believe Sophie. Anyway, part of me was actually beginning to believe that I didn't look too bad. My hair was a sculpted halo of shiny black with a deep cranberry colour running through it. The dress was tight black silk that fitted like a glove. Mind you, I'd been a bit disappointed when Sophie had informed me on the way home that twice a year in the salon was not often enough. Twice a *week* would be more like it. I didn't think that was going to be happening any time soon.

I heard Shane and Heather coming in and I went downstairs to try out my new look on them.

'Jamie, Jamie, meet Titbit,' said Heather as I came into the kitchen.

She unfolded a blanket and I looked into the face of a half-grown boxer pup. He looked me up and down with malignant eyes.

'Is he yours?' I said, debating whether to rub him or not. I put out my hand and he growled.

'Jesus,' I said.

'Rescue dog,' said Shane.

'He has some abandonment issues, but we'll fix you up, honey-bunny sweetie-pie,' said Heather.

'He'll be staying here, because Heather travels so much,' said Shane, refusing to meet my gaze.

'He's seeing the dog psychologist on Monday, aren't you, babycakes?' she said as she kissed the pup.

I wondered if the psychologist might take a look at Heather too but I didn't say it out loud. Instead, I looked at Shane and he knew I was thinking it. That'd do for now.

'Jamie, you look different,' he said and stood back to have a better look. 'You look hot. You're a total babe.'

'Flattery will get you everywhere,' I said and waited for Heather's reaction to the new me. There wasn't any. She gave me a cursory once-over, smiled pityingly and went off into the living room with Titbit.

'You'll knock 'em dead tonight. I'm dying to see their faces. God, the hair, that dress . . .'

'Enough, Shane. The dog can stay,' I said, laughing.

'No. I'm bowled over, man. And you love football – the perfect girlfriend!'

'Yeah, right. That's why I get the stalkers.'

I decided to walk to the Clarion, the hotel where the launch party was being held. It was literally a ten-minute walk – I could see its tall structure from my living-room window – and, anyway, it was a really mild April evening. I felt great as I walked along by the river, the best I'd felt in a very long time and I smiled in anticipation of the night ahead.

As I walked I realised that doing all the girl stuff that I'd done today actually does give you confidence – like putting on a mask or a fancy-dress costume. Preparing a face to meet the faces that we meet, I thought as bits of schooldays T. S. Eliot floated into my head. Jesus, I was beginning to wax lyrical.

And then the heavens opened. No black clouds. No drizzle first. No warning. No umbrella. I began to run against the sheets of driving rain, desperately looking for some shelter. I thought about taking off my short jacket to cover my hair but realised that the hair by then was an also-ran. I finally found shelter in a shop doorway, just as the rain eased off. Bloody typical. Stupid bloody country. Sunny spring evening one minute, followed the next by a monsoon.

I arrived at the Clarion looking like the proverbial drowned rat. I decided that my best bet was to run to the loo and stick my head under the hand-drier. I know it wasn't salon chic but it'd have to do. I walked through the lobby without raising my gaze from the floor and just as I was about to turn into the ladies' toilet I heard my name.

'Jamie? Jamie, what in the name of God happened? I left you alone for a couple of hours and . . . and this?'

I looked down into Sophie's face and smiled wanly at her. 'The rain. I walked and, well, it flogged.' I shrugged and shook my legs. Water was dripping down the inside of my thighs.

'Did you ever hear of umbrellas? Nobody goes out without an umbrella after having their hair done,' said Sophie.

'How was I supposed to know that?'

Sophie raised her eyebrows.

I sighed. 'Another Girl Thing, I presume.'

'Jesus, look at the state of you,' said Sophie just as a knot of people passed. They stopped to have a look at me and suddenly I was the main attraction in the lobby as more people came towards us.

'Bit of a colour-run problem, Jamie?' said Johnny G from the back of the crowd. I glared at him and noticed that Bill Hehir was standing next to him, grinning from ear to ear. Bastard. I stuck my tongue out at them and marched into the loo. And then I saw myself. Cranberry colour ran down my neck and shoulders like fake blood in a vampire movie. Mascara rimmed my eyes and my dress was so wet that it looked like it was welded onto me. Tears brimmed in my eyes and I wiped them away with the back of my hand. I should never have bothered with this girl bullshit. No matter how hard I tried I seemed to be destined to fuck up at this lark. I should have worn the jeans and not gone within an ass's roar of the beauty salon. Poise, my arse. They should have called it Hell.

Tears came again and then Sophie was standing next to me, spreading her make-up out on the marble worktop like a surgeon laying out his scalpels.

'Stop crying, you eejit, you'll make it worse,' she said as she grabbed my face and began to repair the damage.

'They should have told me the hair colour would run,' I said after a few minutes of Sophie cleansing and re-applying.

She stopped and looked at me. Then both of us burst out laughing.

When we arrived back the party was in full swing. I didn't look too bad – Sophie had done a great job. My problem now was the dress. It seemed to be getting tighter and tighter. I stretched it down over my body and smiled at all the familiar faces as I surveyed the room for a sighting of Steve. I could see Bill Hehir in the far corner, standing alone and sipping a glass of wine. He raised his glass to me when he caught my eye. I gave him a cursory nod and turned away to continue my search.

I ended up out on the wooden deck, where all the smokers had gathered. Steve was in the middle of a crowd of admirers – I could hear his lovely distinctive voice as he recounted some anecdote about his days at RTE. He saw me and came towards me, the crowd dividing like the Red Sea for him.

'Jamie, you look gorgeous,' he said and kissed my cheek. Then he put his hand on my shoulder and, turning back to the crowd, continued his tale. I stood next to him, enjoying the weight of his hand and the smell of expensive aftershave. I eyed him as he talked and if he'd said that minute let's go into the loo for a bonk I'd have jumped at the chance. He had the shiniest hair I'd ever seen and a way of smiling at you that made you feel like the most special person in the room.

Sophie arrived then and grabbed me to introduce me to Rico and his brother.

Steve stopped his storytelling and air-kissed Sophie and the Spanish boys. Then he put his hand on Sophie's shoulder and continued to talk to his captive audience.

She kind of shrugged his arm off and took a cigarette from Rico. They both lit up, giggling as Rico struck a match and held it out to her.

Rico's brother stood beside him, looking up at me.

'You don't smoke,' I said to Sophie. She giggled again and I realised that she was pissed.

'I do now. This is Raphael,' she said as the diminutive Spaniard stretched himself to kiss me on the cheek. It landed on my neck.

'And this,' she said, turning her body towards Rico and moulding herself to him while running her hand through his hair, 'is the lovely Rico.'

Rico smiled at me and kissed my cheek. I must say he was very handsome, in a dark Mediterranean sort of way, and he had a great body. It must be all the salsa dancing, I thought as I whipped a glass of wine from a passing waiter's tray. I scanned the deck for Steve but I knew instinctively that he was gone. It felt like a change in the atmosphere.

'Let's go inside,' I said and we went back into the party.

Johnny G was doing hip dj stuff on a turntable in the corner – God, couldn't he ever take a night off? People were beginning to dance and Steve was on the floor with Dee-Dee. I stood watching them as I zoned in and out of conversation with Sophie and the Spaniards. Dee-Dee's sheet of poker-straight hair shimmered as Steve led her expertly around the floor. Steve saw me and waved. I waved back, willing him to come over. Instead he carried on dancing, with Raina Burke now, followed by Sarah Quinlan from the *Afternoon Show* and then Helen O'Connor from the evening slot.

'He'll be running out of radio presenters soon. He'll have to move on to the TV recruits next,' said Sophie, laughing.

I laughed too. 'It's just his way – he likes mixing with people,' I said as I took another glass of wine from a very good-looking waiter.

'Unlike Mr Moody Blues,' said Sophie, nodding over at Bill Hehir. 'What is his problem? It's a party, for God's sake, not a bloody wake.'

I shrugged and downed the glass of wine in one go. 'Look at him in his Armani suit. Jesus, his idea of casual is loosening his tie.'

'Does he ever smile?' Sophie asked, slugging back a green-coloured drink.

'Once. When he was eight,' I said. 'But it was a complete accident.'

Sophie guffawed and then grabbed me by the hand. 'Duck, quick, he's coming over.'

'Who, Bill?' I said but swivelled around with her to face the French doors leading to the deck. I could see Rico and his brother outside having another fag.

'Worse. Paddy Shine – and he's making a beeline for you. If he captures you I'm running, Jamie, I swear I am.'

Paddy Shine did the late-night slot at Fab City. He called his show *Shine On* but we held daily competitions to rename it – none of them flattering. Paddy was an old-school union-mad presenter who didn't realise what the word 'libellous' meant. He'd had us in court more times than Judge Judy and Sophie threatened to fire him on a regular basis. But firing Paddy would be like trying to fire SIPTU. My biggest problem with Paddy was that he absolutely loved me – ever since he'd discovered my affection for football.

'Jamie, at last someone normal. How are you, girl?' he said, putting his arm around my waist. He was a small middle-aged man with a bald head and a pot belly. And the biggest honker of a nose I'd ever seen.

'Hi, Paddy, how's it going?' I said, desperately looking for a means of escape. Sophie, true to her word, had disappeared.

'Will you look at himself out on the floor like Fred Astaire,' he said, nodding over at Steve. 'These big noises from RTE are all the same. I'd swear there's a factory up in Montrose producing these fellas.'

'He's a good presenter,' I said as I scanned the room for Sophie. I spotted Shane and Heather looking like the golden couple and talking to Bill. And

Bill was smiling. Jesus, he was really getting into party mode. Paddy's voice droned on and I nodded and smiled and didn't pay the least bit of attention to what he was saying. It was one of my best attributes – being able to zone in and out of conversations and still keep the gist. A real gift, I thought and continued my scanning. I took another glass of wine from a passing waiter. I'd need plenty of fortification to put up with Paddy.

It was Shane who rescued me eventually. I was on my fourth glass of wine and was beginning to yawn. Paddy had just gone through the Premiership team by team and was halfway through the first division when Shane arrived with Heather and Bill in tow. I smiled gratefully at Shane as he began to discuss the mighty fall of Leeds United with Paddy.

'Jamie,' said Bill, half smiling at me. I hated that.

'Bill,' I said. 'Enjoying yourself?'

He shrugged. 'Not really. Same old same old, isn't it?'

Heather stood between Paddy and Shane, a look of complete and utter boredom on her face.

'Don't be such a party-pooper,' I said.

He shrugged slightly. 'So that's what you call a person who tells it like it is?'

I smiled. 'Gotta go, gotta mingle – have a little fun, even. Remember that word – fun – or has it been banned from your vocabulary?' I said and walked away, delighted with my parting shot. Every blow I could land on Bill Hehir felt like justice.

My dress seemed to be really tight now or else I

was just pissed and bloated from alcohol. I headed for the loo and had the pleasure of passing Paul – Sophie's ex – on the way. He was with some legal-eagle friends of his.

'Well, scumbag, how's it going? Still hoodwinking away down at the Courthouse?' I said and, boy, was *that* a conversation stopper. Paul and his friends looked at me like I'd fallen from Mars.

'I'd better let you go. I know you want to get back to lying and cheating. Good evening – ahem – gentlemen,' I said and walked away.

I looked at myself in the mirror of the bathroom and decided that I looked grand but drunk. I also decided it was time I went home – otherwise I'd make a complete fool of myself. I pulled at my too-tight dress and realised that it had shrunk after the wetting. Jesus, was that another girl rule? Buy a really expensive dress that you can only wear weather permitting? I yanked the dress down as far as it would go and went back towards the party to say my goodbyes. I'd just make the second half of *Match of the Day*, I thought – and then I walked straight into Steve.

'Oh,' I said, as I pulled back from him, 'it's you.'

He reached out a hand and stroked my cheek. 'OK?'

I nodded like a robot, mesmerised by his eyes. He smiled at me and lines appeared at each side of his mouth and I was taken away with how cute and boyish it made him look. He leaned towards me and kissed me very gently on the mouth, like he was kissing something precious that would melt at any moment. Then he pulled away and walked towards the main exit. I leaned against the wall, barely registering the party noises in the room beyond. My legs felt like jelly and my heart pounded. I took a deep breath and went into the mêlée in search of Sophie. She was standing near the open French doors with Rico and Bill.

'I'm off,' I said as I approached.

'Jamie, it's only ten-thirty. Please stay – we're just starting here,' said Sophie, twining her arm around Rico's waist.

'I'm leaving too,' Bill said. 'Want a lift?'

'No, I'm fine, I'll walk,' I said and left. Bill followed.

'Sure about the lift?' he said again as we walked through the lobby to the exit.

'Positive,' I said. I wanted to be alone with my delicious kiss. I wanted to savour and relive it. I could do that on the short walk home.

'OK. But Jamie, you don't have any dress covering your bum, so I'd walk with my back to the wall if I were you,' he said. And, chucking me on the chin, he walked off in the direction of the car park.

I stood and watched and suddenly the image of Bill's retreating back threw me into a flashback of another night when I had watched him walk away. That time, though, I had been lying in bed. To hell with Bill Hehir! I was damned if I was going to waste my time thinking about him.

I put a hand behind my back and felt for my dress. It wasn't there. The thing had shrunk right up to knickers-level at the back, maintaining its length at the front as if to fool me. I took off my jacket and, wrapping it around my waist, I began the short walk home. I didn't care about the dress or Bill or football at that moment. All I knew was that at the start of the evening I had liked Steve. Found him attractive. Wouldn't kick him out of bed for eating toast, as Dee-Dee had said. Now it was a whole different ball game. After the kiss I was sure. I wanted him now, come hell or high water. And, by God, I intended to land him.

7

The sun was very warm for April and I closed my eyes, savouring the feel of it on my vitamin D-starved skin. It was Sunday afternoon, one of those rare days where everything seemed right with the world, even the weather. 'Pet days' my dad called them and I smiled to myself as I remembered this phrase from childhood. I was in the People's Park with Mark and Fiona. They'd run straight off to the playground as soon as we'd arrived, leaving me dozing on a nearby bench.

I could hear their voices now as they played energetically on the slide and I opened my eyes to check on them. They waved over at me and I waved back. I closed my eyes again, exhausted from the happenings of the previous night. These happenings – unfortunately – had had nothing to do with Steve Lowe and everything to do with Titbit. Titbit's psychiatric problems really came into their own at night and he'd whined and barked and growled the hours away while I'd tried to sleep with a pillow over my head. Heather had assured me this morning that once Titbit had seen his shrink he'd be absolutely fine. Why didn't I believe her? I made a mental note to do a programme on dogs' owners and the lengths they'd go to for their pets.

'Jamie, you be Liverpool and I'll be United,' said Mark as he bounded up in front of me, his new Nike football under his arm.

'Where's your sister?' I asked as I got up from my cosy nest and tried to summon the energy for a game of soccer with a highly charged eight-year-old.

'On the swings. Come on, Jamie, you promised,' he said and pulled me by the hand to the grassy area that ran next to the playground.

'OK, OK, I'm coming. I'll just tell Fiona what we're doing, she might want to play,' I said.

Mark looked at me derisively. 'She's a girl, Jamie. Only you and boys like soccer.' He bounced the ball near his feet, then headed it away towards the green.

I went over to Fiona. She sat on a swing next to a pretty black girl with beaded hair and brown saucer eyes.

'Zara has four new Bratz, can she come to McDonald's with us?' Fiona asked in her cute lispy voice. Her blonde plaits had come undone and she had a stripe of mud on her cheek. Fiona could never stay clean and tidy and she reminded me so much of myself at that age. Mam was forever fixing me and telling me that she couldn't understand how I un-ravelled after five minutes. I always thought this made me sound like a piece of knitting. But looking at Fiona now I completely understood what she meant. I bent and kissed her clean cheek.

'We're going to play ball just over there. Do you and your new friend want to come?'

The girls looked at me, then at each other and then they both shook their heads without saying a word. These little misses would never need Girl Lessons.

'OK, we'll be just there,' I said, pointing to where Mark was playing.

I ran at my nephew then and tackled him as he tried to sweep the ball through my legs. We both crashed to the ground in a heap and fell on top of each other, laughing.

I got up and rubbed my hands together.

'Mark Ryan, let the war begin,' I said and he knew exactly what I meant. Serious football. First person to make it to ten goals was the champion. We made makeshift goals from our coats and jumpers and the competition started in earnest.

Mark was beating me 7–6 when I took an over-enthusiastic shot at his goal. The ball sailed over his head and into a nearby oak tree.

'That's a point in Gaelic football,' I said and my nephew shook his head pityingly at me.

'I'll have to climb the tree,' he said.

I shook my head. 'No way. Your track record is too bad. It's not long since you broke your arm.'

Mark scowled. 'That was ages ago. It's fine now.'

'It *wasn't* ages ago and your First Communion is next Saturday – your mother will kill me if you fall out of the tree. Move over, I'll get it.'

Mark stood back and I climbed the tree with great

aplomb. I was only sorry that none of my friends were around to admire me. At the top, just as I stretched out my hand to tip the ball onto the grass, I heard a sudden cry from the direction of the playground, followed by Mark's frightened voice.

'Jamie, Jamie, quick, Fiona's upside down,' he shouted. I shielded my eyes with my hand against the glare from the sun and searched out Fiona. Then I saw her – however she'd managed it, she'd caught her leg in the rope of the swing and was dangling upside down. And roaring like an ass.

'I'm coming, I'm coming, Fiona,' I shouted, and began to climb down the tree, worried that if I didn't get there fast enough she'd fall and get hurt.

I was halfway down when I saw him. The Man. He seemed to come out of nowhere and made a beeline for the now-hysterical Fiona. He had a full beard and dark sunglasses and a red baseball cap turned back to front. I was just about to scream at him when something stopped me. I watched him then as I clung onto a thick oak branch. I watched him as he gently untangled the crying child and put her on the ground. I watched as he knelt down in front of her. I watched like you'd watch a match replay in slow motion, knowing in your heart that you'd seen this scene before.

And then I came alive and, sliding down the last few feet of tree, I ran towards my niece and The Man, shouting gibberish as I did so. He stood up quickly and looked at me through his dark glasses before running off towards the park exit.

I knelt down in front of Fiona. She had a small scratch on her forehead.

'Are you OK, baby?' I said as I hugged her to me.

Mark had followed me over and stood in front of me, watching the proceedings.

'Why are you crying, Jamie?' he asked.

I wiped my eyes with my sleeve. I hadn't realised that I'd been crying. I pulled away from Fiona and held her little face in my hands.

'Listen, sweetie, what did he say to you? What did the man say?' I said, giving her what I hoped was a reassuring smile.

She smiled back at me. 'Nothing. Just lifted me down. Can we have ice cream in McDonald's too?'

'Of course, honey. Didn't he say anything to you?'

Fiona pushed a wisp of blonde hair that had escaped from her plait off her face and sniffed. 'Nope. Can we go now?'

'Jamie, my ball?' said Mark.

I sighed and took each child by the hand. 'OK, I'll get the ball. But you two must stand right under the tree where I can see you.'

We continued our afternoon with McDonald's and ice cream and a peek at the grumpy Titbit and my head was buzzing with the encounter in the park. I knew that I couldn't even think of the ramifications of it until I had the children safely deposited with their mother. I'd rented a DVD that morning for them as a final treat before they went home at seven and as they watched it I went to the kitchen to make coffee. Shane was there, cooking pasta and wearing his i-pod. I considered telling him what I'd seen – or thought I'd seen – but the discovery was too new and raw to say it out loud yet. I wanted the kids to be gone and safe before I spoke the words and made it a reality.

So when the DVD was over they said their good-byes to Shane and Titbit and sang some *You're A Star* song in the car on the way home. I smiled and made all the right aunt noises while inside me my emotions ran riot. Finally I pulled into the drive of my brother's house, a big modern luxury home on the Ennis Road. Marielouise was waiting at the door as my car pulled up. I kissed the children, waved and smiled at Marielouise and reversed down the paved drive.

As soon as I was around the corner I pulled up and lay my head on the steering wheel. Tears were starting to come again and I wiped them away with my hand. Then, suddenly, I knew what to do. I rooted for my phone in my big untidy handbag, I flipped it open and dialled, sniffing back tears as I waited for a response.

'Hi, it's me.'

'What's wrong?'

'I saw him.'

'Who?'

'I saw him today in the park. I saw Conor.'

8

'You don't believe me.'

'I believe that you *think* you saw him.'

I shook my head and looked directly into Bill's eyes. 'You're humouring me, that's all.'

We were sitting in Bill's pristine living room. All cream carpets and blond wood, and fitted with every gadget known to man. The lights were voice-activated, the curtains closed and opened electronically. The stereo was state of the art. The TV was a plasma job, the newest version. We were sitting on a deep leather sofa, a small table in front of us with a cafetière of untouched coffee on it. Bill began to pour coffee into delicate cream-coloured mugs.

'Don't patronise me. I know it was Conor.'

Bill continued to pour coffee.

'Well?' I said.

He put a single teaspoonful of sugar into a mug, added a tiny drop of milk, stirred twice and handed the drink to me.

'Did you have something to eat, Jamie? There are steaks in the fridge, or if you like I could order in – that new Thai place is really good . . .'

'Answer me.' I looked at him over the rim of my mug. He shrugged and put his hands in the air.

'OK, OK. I don't know, Jamie. I simply don't know. I want to believe you but sometimes the mind plays tricks – there could have been something about that man that reminded you of Conor . . .'

I shook my head vigorously, the violent movement making me spill coffee onto my jeans. 'It was him, Bill. I just know it in my heart – it was Conor and he saw Fiona in trouble. I know it was him.'

Tears came again and I tried to swallow them back. Bill took a linen napkin from the table and handed it to me. I wiped my eyes and looked at him.

'What shall I do? Should I go to the police?'

He reached out and put a hand lightly over mine. 'Jamie, you'll only drag it all back up again. For yourself, for your parents, for those kids. We're all just coming to terms with it now a year and a half later . . .'

'So you don't believe me. That's fine.' I looked directly at him. 'I shouldn't have expected anything else.'

'I'm trying to be reasonable here. Logical.'

'And I'm being unreasonable and illogical? Thanks for the vote of confidence. But do you know something? I saw him today – think about the consequences of that instead of whether I dreamt it or not.'

'I didn't say you dreamt it, Jamie. Sometimes when you're stressed the mind—'

'Spare me that bullshit – in fact, I shouldn't have come here at all, shouldn't have told you. Typical of you: patronise me, trivialise what I saw today – Mr Fucking Know-It-All.'

Bill looked at me solemnly, running a hand through his neatly cropped hair. 'I don't want you to go off on wild-goose chases, that's all.'

I laughed harshly. 'Since when did you care about my well-being? I'm not you, Bill. I can't just forget about people that I love.'

'Stop, Jamie – stop before you say something you'll regret.'

I glared at him. 'Or maybe *do* something I'll regret?' It was out before I could help myself but the anger and confusion in his face made me pleased.

It hadn't always been like that between us. Until three years earlier he'd just been my brother's pal – part of the furniture. And then Munster played Wasps in Dublin.

I browbeat Sophie into coming to the match. Promised we'd shop as well. And then on the Friday night she met that bastard Paul in a pub full of Munster fans. Sophie was madly in love and in spite of her protestations I wasn't going to be the gooseberry. Which was fine with me. Then next afternoon I happened to bump into Bill at Lansdowne Road. Munster beat the crap out of Wasps and maybe it was all the hugging we did every time they scored but somehow we ended up having drinks and then dinner and then a bit of a rolling maul of our own in Bill's hotel room. I was starting to think that this falling-in-love thing was catching – but Sophie wasn't the only person to hook up with a bollocks that weekend.

On Sunday night I missed the train. For all Sophie's frantic textings to me from the station I couldn't do a goddamn thing about the traffic jam on the Quays and part of me was glad. I went back to Bill's hotel – I knew he'd be there because he was working in Dublin all week.

I knocked gently on the hotel room door but there was no answer. I could hear the shower so I tried the handle. The door opened and I let myself in, laughing at how surprised he'd be to see me. But the joke was on me. In the big double bed we'd shared only hours earlier lay a sleeping woman. Naked.

I turned and ran like the clappers. Found a B&B near the station, cried myself to sleep and then resolved to put Bill out of my head. Sure, he tried to ring me in the weeks that followed but I managed to avoid his calls. And eventually he stopped. The next time I had to talk to him was when we realised that Conor was missing. Bill loved Conor and no matter what else I thought of him I couldn't deny that. Nobody worked harder than him when we were searching in those early months. I didn't know who else to turn to after seeing The Man in the park. But now I was sorry.

'You're missing the point, Jamie,' Bill was saying as I tuned back in to the conversation.

'Oh, am I? I see my brother, I want to find him, and I'm missing the point?' I laughed mirthlessly again and shook my head incredulously at him.

'Maybe *he* doesn't want to be found.'

'What?'

'If it was him today then he doesn't want to show himself – not even to his own children.'

I stared hard at Bill. I had no answer for that. I

stood up. 'I need to use the loo,' I said and marched off without waiting for an answer. I went through the stainless-steel kitchen that looked like an operating theatre and made my way to the loo in the utility area at the rear. I splashed water on my face and examined it in the mirror for crying damage.

A picture of The Man in the park flashed through my mind and I shook my head as if to dissolve the image. Then I washed my hands and wiped them on a luxury white hand towel and made my way back through the kitchen. I noticed a small black and white photograph in a silver frame on the granite island in the centre of the room. I picked up the photo and looked at it. Bill looked back at me, a rare smile on his face. A real smile because you could see it in his eyes too. He had an arm around the most beautiful woman I'd ever seen. Hauntingly lovely face with exquisite bone structure. A face you couldn't take your gaze away from. Maybe she was the woman in his bed in Dublin? Best of luck to her, dealing with that arrogant fucker, I thought as I went back into the living room.

Bill was standing near the French windows and turned around when I came back in. I picked up my handbag from the sofa.

'I'm off – see you,' I said and went out into the terracotta-tiled hallway.

'Wait, Jamie, I—' He ran after me and almost bumped into me at the front door.

'What?' I said as I opened the latch on the door. I could hear birds singing outside.

'Nothing. I'm sorry.' Bill shrugged and held my gaze.

'For what?'

'Conor. I'm sorry about Conor. I want to believe it was him too.'

I could smell his million-dollar aftershave and I could see his stubble. He was not a good ad for the Gillette Mach 3 Turbo.

I walked out the door and down the gravelled drive to my car.

'Hey, Jamie?' he called from the doorway.

I looked up

'It takes two to tango,' Bill said, leaning on the door frame.

I got into my car and after banging the door shut I pulled away without looking back at him.

Next morning, as I prepared to go on air, I filled Sophie in. I was behind schedule so I gave her a bare sketch of the park episode and a brief synopsis of my Bill encounter. Then I left her there, eyes round and a thousand questions on her lips, and went into my sound booth where the world was always right.

My guests included a rapper from the Parish and a man who had stopped twelve people from drowning themselves. What kind of karma was that? To be in the right place at the right time twelve times in a row? I was pleased with my show and when it was over and I handed my womb of a studio to John Howard, our main newsman. I was delighted when Steve gave me the thumbs-up from the doorway of his office. I beamed at him.

'Jamie, these came for you – aren't they gorgeous?' said Dee-Dee as I passed reception.

An enormous hand-tied bouquet of lilies stood in a bag of water on the desk.

'For me?' I said.

Johnny G whistled as he passed. 'Somebody has the hots for Jamie,' he said, winking at Dee-Dee.

'Was there a card?' I asked, searching the flowers. I found the card in the midst of the fragrant blooms. *Beautiful.* That was all it said. I read it again. One single word. Part of me hoped that Steve had sent these to me. But there was something cold and eerie in that single word that screamed *stalker*.

'They're really pretty, Jamie. Who sent them? Did you meet someone new over the weekend?'

I smiled at her. 'Yeah. I met Titbit but he didn't send them because he's busy with his shrink this morning. Who delivered them?'

'Some pimply guy from Interflora. Small, glasses . . . oh Jesus.' Realisation dawned on Dee-Dee's face.

Sophie arrived then and looked at the flowers and then at me and Dee-Dee.

'Stalker?' she asked.

Both of us nodded in unison.

'Oops.'

I walked to my office and Sophie followed.

'What happened?'

'With the stalker? I've no idea but you've reassured me that he's perfectly harmless – that as stalkers go he's up there with the crème de la crème of stalkers . . . he's actually the saint of stalkers . . .'

'Shut up, Jamie. He's as harmless as a pet mouse. No, what happened with *Bill*?'

I rolled my eyes. 'I told you what happened. He thought I was hallucinating, I called him a few choice names and then I left.'

She narrowed her eyes. 'And nobody removed any items of clothing during this encounter?'

'Bitch,' I said. 'So how was your weekend?'

Sophie laughed. 'The old let's-change-the-subject trick.'

I looked at my friend. 'I'm sure it was him, Soph. It was Conor.'

'How sure? On a scale of one to ten, how sure?'

'You don't believe me either.'

'Are you absolutely positive it was him?'

I looked down at my hands. 'When it was happening – yes – absolutely positive. I was just about to shout out his name but then I knew I couldn't because of the kids. But now . . .'

'Now what?'

'After Bill last night and, well, you know yourself. The doubt creeps in.'

'Did you say anything to your parents? Marielouise?'

I shook my head.

'Good,' said Sophie. 'It's better not to just yet, especially with the Communion next Saturday.'

I nodded agreement. Mark was due to make his First Communion on Saturday and my mother had insisted on throwing a party for him. She said it was bad enough that his dad was gone and that he deserved a big fuss.

'You're still coming to it, aren't you, Sophie?' I said, dreading the thought of it already. I'd have to get dressed up – that was always a problem. Secondly, it was Cup Final Day – Liverpool against United – and though I knew there would be a fair smattering of my relatives sneaking into the living room to watch it I also knew that my mother would be very unhappy about that, particularly with me. And the third thing was that Bill would be there and Steve wouldn't. Unless I could think of a pretext for inviting Steve to my nephew's First Communion. That sounded like a non-starter already.

'You can wear your new dress,' said Sophie as if reading my mind.

I shook my head. 'It wouldn't fit Fiona now. It shrunk on Saturday night.'

Sophie started laughing. 'I don't believe it! How do you manage it at all?'

I shrugged. 'I started my girl apprenticeship too late, Soph. Think of all the girl lessons I don't know about – umbrellas, raincoats . . .'

'We'll go shopping again – I need some retail therapy. Anyway, I had a brilliant weekend,' she said slyly. And then Shane was at the door looking for her and she was gone with a wave of her hand before I could get any more information.

As I left the building in the afternoon I met Steve Lowe coming back with takeaway coffee.

'Jamie! Great show this morning. Well done,' he said, sipping his drink through its safety lid. He looked at me intently and for a mad moment I wanted to tell him about seeing Conor.

'I'm doing my first show this evening. Please listen in. It'd really help if I thought you were listening.' He smiled at me and the cute magic lines appeared at each side of his mouth and I felt like I was the only other person on the planet.

'Wouldn't miss it for the world,' I said, looking at his mouth and remembering the delicious understatement of a kiss.

Steve smiled again and my heart started to thump. 'How about going for a drink – say, Wednesday evening. Would you be around?'

Would I be around? Of course I'd be around. In the back of my head I knew that Wednesday evening was important in the world of soccer but maybe we could go to a pub where the game was on the bar's TV. Better still, maybe Steve liked football.

'Definitely.' I hoped I didn't sound too eager.

'Eightish in that lovely cocktail bar – what's it called? Kokomo, that's it.'

'Perfect,' I said.

'Perfect,' he said and neither of us moved.

'Right so,' Steve said eventually. 'It's a date. Take care, Jamie.' He walked in through the station doors and I took off home. I felt like skipping but managed to restrain myself. I heard his voice over and over in my head: *it's a date – it's a date*. I smiled at everyone as I walked along the busy five o'clock pavement. I turned off by the river and the crowds disappeared. I was almost home when I heard footsteps behind me. I turned around quickly but the street was deserted

– the only sounds were muffled city noises and the rush of the swollen river.

Weird, I thought as I tried to shake off the feeling that someone had been following me. My mind was starting to play tricks on me but one thing I knew was absolute gospel – Steve Lowe had asked me out on a date and at that moment that was the most important thing in my life.

9

When is a date not a date? When everybody in the
radio station – including Ger Farrell the janitor –
turns up. I walked into Kokomo on Wednesday
evening at five past eight in a whole new set of clob-
ber that Sophie had picked out the day before and
walked straight into Dee-Dee, resplendent in a
barely-there satin tunic thing over tight-fitting jeans.
She was perched on a stool at the bar next to Steve
and half the station workforce. I was mortified but
I knew I couldn't just walk back out. I'd have to play
it cool.

'Jamie, Jamie, I'm delighted you could make it. Isn't
this great?' he said as he stood up and manoeuvred
me over to his stool. 'Here, sit down next to Dee-Dee
and I'll go get another chair.'

I sat down next to her and we smiled at each other.
I couldn't think of one thing to talk about with her
that didn't concern work. 'Nice top,' I said eventually
as Steve and Johnny G laughed at some joke that
Steve had told.

'Thanks. Topshop,' she said.

'Oh right. Crowded here, isn't it?'

She nodded and looked over at Steve and I knew

then that she'd made the same mistake as me –
she'd thought she was going on a date.

'That skirt is gorgeous – is it yours?' asked Dee-
Dee, reaching out and touching the lovely cotton
material.

'I paid for it, Sophie picked it out,' I said as Steve
came towards us, grinning from ear to ear.

'I'm the luckiest man in the world,' he said looking me up and down. He might as well have plugged
me in. Electric shocks ran through my body. When
he was around I was like an unearthed electrical
appliance.

'Not one, but two gorgeous women in my company,'
he said. 'Would you like a cocktail, Jamie? There's a
menu . . .'

'Actually, I'm just passing, Steve, said I'd drop in
on the way to . . . to my sister-in-law's – you know,
babysitting – good old Auntie Jamie,' I lied and
laughed heartily. Dee-Dee arched an eyebrow. Steve
looked crestfallen.

'That's such a pity, Jamie. We're hoping to make
these Wednesday nights a regular thing with the
staff,' he said, touching my arm with his hand. Very
dangerous territory.

'We used to do it when I was in RTE, and it really
paid off – that's where we had all our good ideas,' he
said. 'Stay for one, just one.'

At that moment Raina Burke, another station secretary, and a bunch of her friends – all equipped with
skimpy satin tops and screechy voices – burst into the
bar and made a beeline for us. Correction: for Steve.

He turned to greet them and I got up and gave a general wave as I left.

'Hey, Jamie, *Match of the Day*?' called Johnny G as I neared the door. But I ignored him.

I drove home feeling hollow and empty. I couldn't compete with all those real girls who didn't have to have Girl Lessons to buy clothes. Sophie could do it with her eyes closed. Heather had been doing it since she was in the womb. All those girls in that bar knew the rules and regulations. I didn't even know the game.

I listened to Paddy Shine's voice on the radio drone on and on about a pack of wandering horses living on Westside Green and then he played the Eagles' 'Take it Easy' – a track from a total of three albums that Paddy played over and over on every show. They were *Best of the Eagles*, *Best of Barry White* and *Best of Kylie*. Paddy had a big thing for Kylie. For some reason, Paddy's show cheered me up now – something about its predictability and uncoolness. I pulled into my drive, turned off the ignition and Paddy's voice and smiled as I opened the front door.

The night wasn't a complete dead loss, I thought as I went to the fridge and poured myself a glass of wine. I didn't stick around competing with all those girls. I kind of played hard to get, really. Separated myself from the masses. Maybe I was better at the girl thing than I thought?

I plonked myself down in front of the TV and flicked on the match, glad to have the house to myself for once. The match was a bore so I put on a DVD – *Collateral*

– that Shane had rented. I knew straight away that he and not Heather had chosen it and I settled down to watch it with my wine beside me.

I must have dozed off because in my dream I heard a baby crying and when I woke I could still hear it. It seemed to be coming from upstairs. I stood up, stiff from my doze, and crept out to the hallway and up the stairs. The crying was coming from my bedroom. The bloody dog, I thought as I opened the door. The room looked like a small typhoon had passed through it followed by a couple of tornados. The stainless-steel curtain rail lay in a tangle of voile on the floor. My lovely red slippers were in shreds near the bed. A cardboard storage box lay in tatters on the mat. I walked further into the room and bent down and picked up a tiny piece of what had once been my birth certificate.

'You're dead,' I said, scanning the room for Titbit. He was sitting under the dressing table, observing me with his malevolent black eyes.

'You little bastard,' I said, taking a step towards him. He growled at me and showed his teeth, as if daring me to come closer.

I slid down to the floor and examined the damage. I realised with horror that the contents of the chewed-up box were my most valuable and treasured possessions. Besides my birth certificate, he's eaten my passport, my degree, my one and only corsage from my debs, my baby shoes and a whole pile of photos. I picked up a half-chewed picture of Conor and me on my First Communion day. I wore the obligatory white dress. The dog had eaten both our legs off but my eyes filled up when I saw Conor's eager boyish face, smiling at the camera, one arm protectively around me. I picked up another picture of Conor, Bill and me at some family party. They were young men in their early twenties, on the brink of setting up their innovative company, and I was an awkward lanky teenager in a Kurt Cobain T-shirt. The dog, symbolically, had bitten off Conor's face, so Bill was the only identifiable one standing there with me, frozen in time. Even back then he wore a shirt and tie, the tie slightly loosened, his face serious. I was looking up at him with a big grin on my face.

Tears dripped onto the half-eaten photo and I wiped my eyes with the sleeve of my lovely new top. But they wouldn't stop coming so I gave in and began to bawl in earnest. Titbit had come out from his hidey-hole and stood in front of me, his head tilted to one side as if he was on the point of asking me a question. I glared at him through my tears. He came over and put his head on my lap and joined in the bawling.

The morning of Mark's Communion dawned bright and sunny and I was glad. It was, after all, a big day for him and sunshine always helped. I bounded out of bed and into the shower, feeling a strange sense of excitement. As I lathered myself in shower gel I tried to work out the source of my excitement. It was Cup Final Day but that wasn't it, I thought as I massaged coconut conditioner – highly recommended by Sophie

– into my hair. My mother was throwing a party but I knew that *definitely* wasn't it: Mam's parties usually filled me with dread. And then I knew what it was. As I rinsed my hair I realised that somewhere in my heart I thought Conor might show up for his son's first Holy Communion. It wasn't unreasonable to assume that he'd be there for Mark's big day. That was the source of the butterflies in my stomach.

I dried myself and dressed in the pale blue linen trouser suit that Sophie had insisted was 'made' for me. I examined myself in the mirror. It did look good, I admitted as I slipped into the delicate sandals that apparently matched the outfit. I wondered if I'd be able to survive the whole day in the new get-up and considered throwing my jeans and runners into a bag. Then I remembered that Sophie would be there and that it wouldn't be worth the grief. She'd cite Girl Rule number forty-five – or something like that: *Thou shalt remain dressed to the nines all day, no matter how painful.*

I laughed to myself at my own joke and made my way downstairs. I was greeted by Titbit who, to put it mildly, was deteriorating seriously in the mental health department. Every time he saw somebody he sprang up and down in the air and then ran around in circles, howling to beat the band. I glared at him now as he ran around the kitchen. I still hadn't forgiven him or his owners for the destruction in my bedroom. Oh, they'd tried to make it up to me – bought me fluffy slippers, fixed my curtains, bought me chocolates, even – but I was determined to milk it for all it was worth. Shane arrived into the kitchen, i-pod on his head already, hair tousled from sleep.

He smiled at me and I could hear the tinny sound of music as he went to the fridge, opened it and stared into it. This was a Shane ritual that baffled me. He'd done exactly the same thing last night before going to bed: did he really think that the contents of the fridge had changed miraculously during the night?

I lifted an earplug from his ear. 'Do you wear your i-pod when you're having sex?' I asked.

Shane flipped the earphones down around his neck. 'No, I wear a condom,' he said, with a grin. 'You look fab – what's up?'

'Mark's First Communion.'

'On Cup Final Day? Those priests have no consideration,' he said as he slapped bread into the toaster and then began to eat peanut butter from a jar with a dessert spoon.

'My peanut butter – don't come the hound,' I said, grabbing the jar.

He smiled at me and winked. That charm might work on other women but it cut no ice with me.

'Where are you watching the match?' I asked, pouring coffee into a clean mug.

'I'm going to watch it here, in the comfort of my own home. Do you think Heather would be insulted if I asked her to do my shopping while the match is on?'

I grinned at him. The doorbell rang and he went to answer it, humming as he did so. I drank my coffee and looked out the window at the lovely spring day.

I felt good and wondered if there was any way I could manoeuvre my day so that I 'accidentally' bumped into Steve. It seemed an awful waste that I'd be all dressed up and the one person I wanted to notice me wouldn't get the chance.

'For you, Jamie,' said Shane, his face obscured by the biggest basket of flowers I'd ever seen.

'Jesus,' I said.

'Nope,' he said. 'Interflora.' He plonked the flowers down on the kitchen table.

I searched in the foliage. 'No card?' I said.

Shane shrugged. 'The delivery woman said they were for you.'

'Woman?'

Shane nodded. 'Small, early thirties, nice t . . . teeth . . .'

I threw a crust at him.

'Who sent them? Was it your stalker?'

'He's not *my* stalker – I don't want him.'

He laughed. 'You know what I mean.'

'He usually lets me know. There's a note, a card, something.'

Shane smiled at me. 'So they're not the stalker's, are they? Because if they are and, well . . . if they're heading for the wheelie bin then I'll take them.'

'Cheapskate.'

'Cup Final Day – she'll do the shopping if she gets these.'

Just then my mobile phone rang, signalling a text message. I read it while Shane buried his head in the fridge again.

I love you. You are the sun in my sky.

A chill ran down my spine. I checked the number but I knew already that I wouldn't recognise it. I was right. I handed the phone to Shane and he read the message.

'Stalker?' he said, looking at me.

I nodded.

Shane could read the unease in my face. 'Look, I think you should call the Guards yourself.'

'They won't do anything – they keep saying that he's harmless.'

'Even so – at least you might feel better if you're doing something about it.'

I nodded. Shane was right. The powerlessness was the worst thing.

'I'll do it right now.'

'Good girl,' he said as he left the kitchen.

I went in search of the phone book and looked up the number for Henry Street Garda Station.

'Hello – could I speak to somebody about stalkers, please?'

10

We arrived at my parents' house at noon. My mother had nominated Sophie and me to be the reception hosts so we left the church as soon as the Communion Mass was over.

I told Sophie about the stalker flowers as we placed champagne flutes on silver trays. My mother did nothing by halves. The caterers were already sorting out the buffet in a specially erected marquee in the large sunny garden.

'Shane's right,' said Sophie, one hand on a slim hip. She wore a simple white dress that managed to be demure and sexy, both at the same time. 'I don't think he's any harm, but it makes sense to keep the cops informed, just to be on the safe side.'

I nodded.

'Did you see Bill in the church?' she asked, looking at me slyly.

'No. Why?'

She shrugged. 'No reason. Anyway, wasn't Mark a total cutie?'

I smiled at the memory of Mark marching up the aisle, his innocent face shining with happiness. I'd scanned the church, looking for The Man in The

Park, but hadn't seen anyone who remotely resembled him.

'They're arriving, Jamie. Let's pop some champagne.'

We opened the bottles and poured the frothy liquid into glasses.

'Your mother said this was just a small family gathering – I'd hate to see her idea of a large one,' said Sophie as we picked up trays and began to serve the throngs of people that were sailing through the front door.

I figured that if I put in a good two hours of daughterly hostessing then my mother wouldn't miss me when the footie started. It seemed like a good plan so I smiled and small talked my way around the garden, enjoying the warm day. Mark was in his element and at one stage he looked around surreptitiously before showing me his pockets. They were full to the brim with notes of all denominations.

'Hitting the 500, Jamie,' he said, with a wink. God, he really was his father's son where money was concerned.

I laughed. 'Any plans for it? Can you give me a deposit for a house?'

He shook his head. 'Sorry, I need it all.'

I looked at my nephew. 'For what, Mark? What are you planning to spend it on?'

Mark's face closed the way my dad's does if he doesn't want to talk to you. 'Nothing. What time's the football on?' he said, taking a chicken sandwich from a nearby trestle table.

There was something about Mark that was making me uneasy but it wasn't the time or place to quiz him. I made a mental note to pursue this conversation at a future date. 'Coverage starts at two o'clock.'

He ran off then and joined a clatter of his cousins on the old slide that had once been mine and Conor's. I saw Marielouise standing by herself near the French doors and walked over to join her.

'Hi,' I said and smiled at my sister-in-law. She looked tired and drawn. She wore a cream linen suit and her blonde hair was tied up loosely.

'You look wonderful, Jamie. I said so to my sister when I saw you at the church. Your suit is lovely and you've done something with your hair.'

I laughed. 'Sophie helped. You know what I'm like where clothes are concerned. Strictly a comfort dresser.'

'Conor is exactly the same.' She looked at me after saying his name. 'I don't know whether to say "is" or "was".'

I nodded and patted her on the arm. 'Today is hard.'

Marielouise nodded back and looked over to where Mark and the other children were running riot around my father.

'Your mam was right, though. It's the best thing for Mark.'

I nodded again.

'I miss him more now. How can that be?'

'It's harder when there's no closure,' I said.

She shook her head. 'Where there's no closure

there's also hope. He might still be out there somewhere, alive, afraid to come home.'

'I think that, too.'

'Listen to me, on Mark's special day. I promised
myself this morning there'd be no morbid talk.'
Marielouise smiled brightly but not with her eyes.

'Oh, look, Bill's just arrived. And is that Rachel
Hynes with him? I never knew those two were an
item again. You never said a thing, Jamie.'

I looked across the garden to where my mother was
greeting Bill and a petite brunette. It was Rachel, all
right, all polished and packaged and gift-wrapped. How
would you like your up-and-coming solicitor? She'd
been Bill's on-off relationship since his hormones had
kicked in twenty years ago. She was shit-hot at her job
and apparently was destined for great things. I'd had
her on my show a couple of times and afterwards I'd felt
like ringing up Bertie Ahern and Tony Blair and telling
them both to resign – that we'd found a replacement
– two for the price of one. She could have run both
countries at a profit, solved the peace-process problems
and searched for weapons of mass destruction in her
spare time. Sophie said that if she was a mother she'd
eat her young.

I knew that I had to do the right thing, so with
Marielouise by my side we walked over towards them.

'I haven't seen you for ages, Jamie,' said Rachel, her
narrow brown eyes examining me from top to toe.

I felt like I was being accused of some crime.
'That's right,' I said, smiling at her.

I could feel Bill's gaze on me. I wanted to slap him.

How can you find someone so infuriating? All he had to do was breathe near me and I wanted to thump the head off him. I wondered if Rachel had seen the picture of the beautiful woman in his kitchen. I considered asking her but it was too bitchy, too Heather – and anyway, what did I care who Bill Hehir slept with? Or how many, for that matter?

Mark came hurtling up the path then, and threw himself into Bill's outstretched arms.

'Marky, my main man, how's it going?' said Bill, hugging the boy to him.

He was Mark's godfather and took the role as seriously as he did everything else in his life. I'd joked with Conor when Mark was born that Bill would be looking to go to Godfather School before assuming the role. Rachel and my mother had detached themselves from us by now and were chatting away like the hammers of hell. Bill knelt down in front of Mark, took a gold envelope from his inside pocket and held it out to the boy.

'Open it,' he said, tousling Mark's hair.

Mark opened the envelope carefully. Inside was a gold sheet of paper. He read it, his eyes growing round with delight. Then he dropped the letter and did a mad dance.

'Yes! Yes! Yes!' he screamed, punching the air.

Then he looked at Bill. 'Really?' he asked, his face suddenly serious.

Bill nodded slowly and Mark threw himself at him. I picked up the letter, curious to know what was causing so much delight. I read it with Marielouise peering over my shoulder. It was a VIP trip to Liverpool next November – corporate box and a meet-and-greet with all the players. Bill had given Mark every boy's dream.

'That's lovely,' I said and my gaze locked with Bill's. He nodded at me, didn't even crack a smile.

'A trip for two, Mark. You'll be taking your beloved aunt,' I said.

Mark glanced at Bill who shook his head.

'Boys' weekend, Jamie – sorry about that,' he said and high-fived Mark.

'Traitor,' I said to my nephew, but he was gone like a bullet to tell everyone.

Rachel rejoined us, linking arms with Bill in the process and looking up at him in a kind of simpering girly way. Jesus, even she could do the Girl Thing – what was wrong with me?

'She's one of mine,' my mother whispered proudly to Marielouise, nodding her head towards Rachel. My mother had this habit of claiming ownership of her better-known clientele. Sophie had disappeared and I went in search of her. I found her in the marquee, chatting up one of the caterers – a boy child, by the look of him.

'See you in a while, Tyrone,' she called as he hastily retreated once he saw me coming. Did I look that scary?

'Tyrone? A name like that puts him in his teens,' I said.

Sophie laughed. 'Wrong. He's twenty-four and very cute.'

'What about Rico?'

She looked at me, puzzled. 'What about him?'

'I thought you and him were . . .'

Sophie laughed and downed her drink in one go. 'That's so pre-fiancé, Jamie.'

I laughed. 'So anything goes now?'

My friend looked at me, her face suddenly serious. 'Absolutely. My days of looking for Mr Right are well over – these days it's more Mr Right Now.'

She put down her empty glass and grabbed up another one as she winked at me. 'How's Bill?'

'Being the perfect godfather. He brought Rachel Hynes.'

Surprise registered on Sophie's half-pissed face. 'Is he tacking with her again? No way.'

'I think they're a perfect match. Both so up their own arses they can't see anything else – perfect,' I said, picking up a chicken drumstick.

Sophie shook her head so vigorously that her drink spilled.

'Answer this. Why is it that when you and he are in the same room together there's such a current of energy between ye that we could run Ardnacrusha power station on it?'

She laughed then and I gave her a dig in the arm. 'You're pissed, Sophie Quinn and it's only two o'clock in the day. And Bill and I don't like each other so *that*'s the current between us, good old-fashioned honest dislike. Now it's time for football.'

'I'm going to find Tyrone – you're no fun,' Sophie said and waltzed out of the marquee. I glanced around the garden. Mam was holding court with a group of women who looked like they resided permanently in her salon. Other guests were chatting away. Rachel was mingling like it was going out of fashion.

I ducked inside the house and headed for the den. There was standing room only. All my male relatives including my dad were glued to the TV.

Bill sat on the couch next to Dad, with Mark beside him. Nobody took their stares from the screen as I searched for somewhere to sit. Finally I ended up sitting practically at Bill's feet and for what seemed like the millionth time this season I watched my beloved Liverpool being beaten. Ninety-two minutes of agony and torture. I vowed to give it all up in favour of something less stressful – like golf. Mark looked sad as the final whistle blew. My dad switched off the TV despite the protests from some of my pro-United relatives. There was no way we were watching them parade the FA Cup around the place. I unfolded my legs and stood up, stiff from my time on the floor.

'Who's on for a game of soccer?' said Bill, standing up and dragging the despondent Mark with him. The boy cheered up instantly at the mention of football.

'Me, me, me,' he said. 'And Jamie. You'll play, won't you, Jamie?'

I nodded and followed them out of the room and into the sunny garden. Fiona flew past me with a gang of shrieking girls in pursuit. Her hairband was askew on her head and her gorgeous pink dress was showing signs of wear and tear.

We set up our playing pitch at the bottom of the garden, using the goalposts that Bill had bought Mark last Christmas. Bill had rounded up another few players, including Paddy Shine, who was an old friend of my dad's, and – of course – my dad himself. We divided into two teams and I examined my bedraggled team-mates. We'd never be the dream team. The game started out as fun and in fairness the children were great, sporting and fair. The adults were the problem. You'd swear we were playing in the FA Cup, the game got so serious.

I took the legs from under Bill in what I considered to be a fair tackle. He responded by doing the same thing to me, smiling as he did so. I reacted like any normal person would: I punched him, meaning to get his shoulder or back but getting him slap in the left eye instead. He held a hand up to his eye and players gathered around him. Paddy, who was the ref, looked at me and shook his head.

I shrugged. 'Fair tackle,' I said, resorting to lying.

'Yeah, if it was a boxing match,' said Bill, taking his hand away from his eye. It looked swollen.

'You'll have a nice shiner there in a couple of hours,' said Paddy.

'Cool,' said Mark. 'A black eye.'

'So, whose throw is it?' I said, bending to pick up the ball.

'It's not yours anyway, Jamie – you're off,' Paddy said.

Paddy's prophecy came true. By the time we were leaving, Bill's eye was almost closed tight, the colour already a vibrant shade of purple. Rachel had put ice on it but it didn't look as though it had helped at all. My mother kept glaring at me, like I'd *meant* to give him a shiner. Or else I'd committed some other sin in her eyes – I didn't bother finding out. I could never please the woman no matter what I did and I'd given up trying since I was about six.

Sophie had disappeared, presumably with Tyrone, so after saying my goodbyes I left the party. As I sat in my car I felt strangely satisfied with myself. I drove home while listening to Fab City radio – a retro about Bob Dylan – and decided that there was nothing like throwing a good hard punch to make you feel better about life.

11

My satisfaction at giving Bill a shiner lasted all the next day. But eventually even that wore off and I was back to The Man in The Park who was haunting me more and more with each passing day. On Monday morning I went into work early and tried to get it all out of my head. I was supposed to be interviewing Tommy Sloane, a local gardener who was entering the Chelsea Flower Show, and I thought that I should know something about my subject.

My relationship with flowers is pretty basic – I like them. They smell nice, they look nice, it can be very romantic if it isn't a stalker who gives you some and that's about it. I knew it wasn't the whole truth, but in my experience flowers came from garage fore-courts – where you buy a bunch out of guilt when visiting your mother. In an effort to remedy my ignor-ance, I Googled the Chelsea Flower Show. Just as I was trying to work up some enthusiasm for the Royal Horticultural Society, Steve appeared in my doorless doorway.

'Knock, knock,' he said with a grin.

My heart flipped in my chest and my lower intes-tines melted.

'Hi!' I said, brightly, wishing I'd tried some of that concealer on the black awake-all-night rings around my eyes. 'You're in early.'

Steve nodded. 'I came in to meet Tommy – bit of moral support.'

'Oh, right,' I said. Steve was the one who'd suggested to Sophie that the radio station get behind Tommy Sloane's Road to Chelsea. It cost a fortune to enter a garden in the Chelsea Flower Show and Tommy was busy fund-raising at the moment. He was fast becoming a local celebrity – all over the local papers and even a spot on the RTE *Nationwide* programme. So it was a good idea for Fab City to be associated with Limerick's answer to Diarmuid Gavin. I hadn't realised that Steve knew Tommy Sloane personally.

'What time is he due in?' Steve asked, sauntering the three steps from the doorway to my desk. He pulled over a plastic bucket chair and sat down opposite me. My God, how could that be so sexy?

'He can't come in until we're on air – has to wait and take delivery of something or other. Dee-Dee said she'd babysit him and I'm here boning up on Chelsea – as you can see.'

I turned my monitor towards him and he smiled. 'I'll look after him when he arrives.'

'That'd be great, Steve – if you're not busy . . . I didn't realise you knew him personally.'

Steve nodded for a full second and then, with a quick glance towards the open doorway, he leaned towards me. My face went red from a sudden rush of desire.

'I'm his sponsor,' he said, his blue eyes dark and serious – and seriously gorgeous.

'Really?' I said in a suddenly breathy voice. 'That's great. I thought Sophie was trying to get the directors to sponsor him as well – did you hear anything about that?'

Steve's eyes clouded with confusion and he sat back in his chair, obviously tied up in thought inside himself. I was just about to interrupt and suggest that he should lean back towards me when to my delight he did.

'I'm not his flower-show sponsor,' he said, his eyes now dancing with amusement. 'The divorce pretty well cleaned me out – well, that and the drink and drugs, if I'm to be honest.'

He paused and I smiled, not caring at all about what he was saying just as long as he was looking at and speaking to me.

'I'm his AA sponsor,' he said.

'Oh,' I said, covering my face with my hands as his words penetrated the veil of lust and longing that had enveloped me. 'Oh my God, Steve, I'm so stupid!'

He touched the back of my hands with both of his. I swallowed hard and peeped at him through my fingers.

'It was a natural mistake,' he said.

'I'm so sorry,' I said.

'Don't be. And don't worry about Tommy while you're on air – I'll do the needful, I promise.'

I raised my head and looked properly at Steve. He held both of my hands in his for a few seconds and then stood up. 'I have a bit of work to do for my show this afternoon.'

I nodded, frantically scrabbling inside my head for a way to keep him with me. And then I did an awful thing. All I can say in my own defence is that both my ability to think and my conscience were momentarily warped by desire and by my belief that I was in love. It also had a reasonably positive outcome so there's that – but all that is just a way for me to try and find excuses for the inexcusable.

'I wonder if I could talk to you for just a minute, Steve?' I heard myself say. 'I have a bit of a problem about my . . . you know . . . situation . . . with my missing brother.'

He looked at me, his face attentive and serious. 'Has something happened?'

I sighed. 'Well, yes and no – I was wondering if I could just talk to you about it . . . maybe get a bit of clarity on the whole situation?'

Steve gave his broad and beautiful smile and pulled the bucket chair close to the desk. 'I told you already – any time you want to talk about it, just holler.'

I dropped my gaze and stared at the pens flung untidily around my desk, momentarily ashamed. But then again, a voice inside me reasoned, you *do* need to talk to somebody and if something good can come from Conor's disappearance then so much the better. I liked that voice the best so I raised my gaze and locked it with Steve's concerned look.

'If it's not taking too much of your time?' I said.

He reached out and took my hand in his. 'Tell me all about it.'

So I did. I told him about Fiona and Mark and The Man in The Park. When I finished Steve didn't say anything for a few seconds. Just held my hand in his and looked serious. I could have happily stayed sitting there like that for the rest of my life. Just being near to Steve was calming for me. He absent-mindedly stroked the back of my hand with his tapered fingers and I closed my eyes.

'What would you like to do?' he said, disturbing my reverie.

I opened my eyes and shrugged as I struggled to keep the subject of my missing brother in focus.

'Seriously,' Steve continued. 'If you had a magic wand and you could do something about this – about Conor – what would you do? Don't think about it too much, Jamie – just answer. Give me the first answer that comes into your head.'

'Look for him,' I said immediately.

Steve nodded. 'OK – how would you do that?'

I shrugged, a familiar feeling of impotence and low-grade rage flooding me. This was my characteristic response to Conor's disappearance: it made me feel simultaneously helpless and angry with him. I preferred it when I was just feeling all gooey and lovesick about Steve.

'Well?' he said.

'I don't know. I mean – where would I start? What would I do?'

Steve raised his eyebrows. 'Ever thought of hiring somebody to have a look for you?'

'You mean like a private investigator?'

Steve nodded.

'But are there even any in Limerick?' I said.

'Bound to be – I know there are loads in Dublin. How do you think Susan got so much dirt on me?'

'Jesus – a PI. Like the movies?'

Steve nodded, placed my hand gently back on the desk and stood up. 'It's a thought, anyway.'

Then he was gone, with a cheerful wave, and as I was all out of personal tragedies with which to engage him, all I could do was wave back. Anyway, I was also very taken with what he'd said. The idea that there might be a way of finding Conor seemed to reignite something inside me.

It was a mad idea. I hadn't a clue how much it would cost – or even if there were any private investigators in Limerick. But then, I did have my savings in the building society that I had been slowly amassing over the past five years in the hope that some day a miracle would transpire and I'd be able to afford to buy a house. It'd be stupid to spend all my hard-earned savings on a whim like this, I knew it would, but then again – if it helped find Conor . . .

I turned to the pile of books on my windowsill and found the *Golden Pages*. A few seconds flicking found me an entry entitled *Detective Agencies* and I read through the list of twenty or more companies. It was completely amazing to me to think that these had been here all the time and I'd never even known it.

One advertisement in particular took my eye. It was a small boxed ad with no fancy artwork, just the name of the detective – Dermot Kilbane – and his qualifications for the job: twelve years as a Garda sergeant and ten years as a detective Garda. I jotted down Dermot Kilbane's phone number and website address and closed the *Golden Pages*.

This was really mad. I couldn't go off half-cocked hiring some cowboy who'd just part me from my money. I mean, if the police in Ireland and England hadn't been able to uncover any trace of Conor how did I think some washed-up ex-Guard would do any better?

I swivelled in my chair, thoughts and ideas and possibilities swirling around in my head. What harm was there in looking? I stopped swivelling and sat staring at the piece of paper with the phone numbers and website. Without thinking any more about it I turned to my computer and tapped in the website address. A head-and-shoulders picture of a middle-aged man under the words *Dermot Kilbane Investigations* appeared on my screen.

I read slowly every single word on the site – ex-policeman, member of the International Association of Private Detectives (IAPD for short). Mr Kilbane was available to advise you on security for your business premises or home. He was happy to undertake insurance-fraud investigation. And he was also willing to conduct discreet and sensitive 'personal' investigations.

There was nothing else of interest on Dermot

Kilbane's site. Pictures of surveillance equipment. Testimonials from satisfied clients identified only by monikers like R.D., West Clare and M.O'S, Limerick City. It all looked very professional and above board. But did I really think it was a good idea to go down such a strange and uncharted road?

I looked at my watch and saw that it was almost ten. Johnny G was bidding his listeners goodbye and introducing the ten o'clock news headlines. I gathered up a few pages about the Chelsea Flower Show I'd printed out, deciding that I'd just have to wing this one, and headed towards the studio. Johnny winked at me and wagged a finger in mock reproach as I ran past him and took my seat at the microphone.

After that it was all fine. A mother of seven from Croom rang in to tell me about the distance-learning PhD she'd just finished. I played music and read from the newspapers and before I knew it the twelve o'clock news headlines were being read.

During the news break Dee-Dee crept in to tell me that Tommy Sloane had arrived and was having coffee with Steve. I asked her to send him in to me in fifteen minutes and she agreed. As she left she was muttering something salacious about Steve and I felt a tiny twinge of jealousy.

Dee-Dee was a very pretty girl. A bit of an airhead but efficient and likeable for all that. It was all very well for Dee-Dee to fancy Shane – Shane was my friend and I had no real interest in his love life. Mind you, I'd probably have preferred Dee-Dee to Header if I'd been allowed to choose. All I knew was that she'd better not be shaking that arse or her Lady Godiva hair in Steve's direction if she knew what was good for her.

I didn't have too much time to dwell on the issue as I was soon back on the air, listening to Ron Sexsmith singing his little heart out and welcoming Tommy Sloane into the studio. I helped him to put on his headphones and did my best to make him feel at ease. I remembered clearly how intimidating and strange a broadcasting studio can be the first time you encounter one.

Tommy was a tall, skinny man who emanated energy like a nuclear power plant. He looked to be in his late thirties and had the general appearance of a handsome carnival man: a row of small hoop earrings in his right ear, longish curly grey-spattered black hair, a bright patterned Hawaiian shirt and faded blue jeans.

As he came in he tripped over a two-foot-tall metal sculpture of a radio transmitter that had been presented to me by the station's directors. It was one ugly piece of work but I had no choice: I had to keep it on display and pretend that I liked it. The only positive thing I could say about it was that the cleaning staff found it great as a doorstop when they were vacuuming out the studio.

I apologised to Tommy and helped him to his chair. He didn't seem to mind. I knew by the way he was looking at everything with interest that he'd never been in a radio studio before. I was a little concerned that he'd be overwhelmed by the experience. I needn't have worried.

As soon as I asked him the first question about his garden he lit up and chatted animatedly. Once Ron stopped singing and we were back on air I repeated the question and then just sat back as Tommy described his Chelsea Flower Show garden.

The garden was called 'Fairy Fort' and it was a floral tribute to the tradition that the original forts or raths were the dwelling places of the fairies. He spoke about his garden with passion and obvious expertise. I didn't interrupt him, just tried to ask questions that would keep him talking. He described the planting of bluebell and cowslip drifts. The positioning of white-thorn bushes and blackthorn bushes. By and large, the details went over my head. Nevertheless, I was very pleased as I knew his great love for his garden would be easily transmitted over the airwaves. All of which would make for both a good show for me and lots of sponsorship for Tommy and his Fairy Fort.

I was right. Before Tommy was off the air the compliments about the programme and offers of money and help flooded in. Companies, schools, individuals – everybody was excited by the description of the garden and wanted to be part of it. Tommy's piece ran over time and brought me up almost to the end of my show. I did the usual Mystery Voice rundown and played one final piece of music – Barber's Adagio for Strings – and then it was one o'clock and time for Fab City News's hour-long lunchtime programme.

When I emerged from my sound cocoon, I discovered that Tommy had left with Steve as soon as he'd finished his piece with me. I wandered back to my office, my head vaguely planning the programmes for the next week. Wasn't there a young local band who'd won some college competition? I thought I remembered Shane talking about them. They might make an interesting show. Where was Shane? He might know how to contact them.

I went back to my office and sat at the desk for a few minutes, ideas for programmes flitting in and out of my head, but I found that I couldn't concentrate. Now that I was back in the real world I was also back in the place where I wasn't in complete control – not even of myself.

I knew that there was only one thing I could do about it. Lifting my phone, I dialled the code for an outside line and then punched in the number. My heart squeezed in my chest when the phone was answered. I wasn't able to speak for a few seconds. But afraid as I was, I knew that I was committed to a course of action and that I wouldn't be able to relax until I saw it through.

'Hello?' the voice said again. 'Dermot Kilbane Investigations – how can I help you?'

12

I parked outside Dermot Kilbane's semi-detached house and for the umpteenth time reconsidered my decision to be there. What the hell was I thinking of? This was real life, not the movies – but then again, in real life weird things like your thirty-five-year-old brother disappearing in broad daylight weren't supposed to happen, were they? In light of that, a consultation with a private investigator was nothing.

I picked up my shoulder bag. It contained a manila file stuffed with newspaper clippings and various bits and pieces relating to Conor's disappearance. Could I really hand it over to this stranger? It felt like all I had of Conor – especially since that mongrel had eaten my photographs of him. I slung the bag over my shoulder and walked up the short drive to the front door.

This house was almost identical to my Auntie Molly's place with its neatly cut grass, cream scalloped blinds and highly polished mahogany door. There were two terracotta pots filled with plants flanking the entrance. Surely a private detective's office had to give some hint of the intrigue its owner was immersed in? I pulled out my piece of paper covered in scrawled directions – 53

Pine Hill. Maybe there were two estates called Pine Hill?

Tentatively I rang the doorbell. The door opened almost immediately and a whippet-thin middle-aged woman in a nurse's uniform looked enquiringly at me.

'Oh,' I said, 'I'm sorry – I must have the wrong house.'

'No problem,' she said, smiling as she began to close the door.

'Sorry – before you go – you don't know where Dermot Kilbane lives, by any chance, do you?'

She stopped and looked at me and then turned her head. 'Dermot!' she shouted. 'Somebody for you.'

Beckoning me to step into the hallway, the woman closed the door and then shot off up the stairs, taking the steps two at a time. Immediately a very heavy man with a thatch of grey hair appeared from the kitchen.

'Jamie Ryan?'

I nodded.

He smiled and extended a hand. 'Dermot Kilbane. Nice to meet you. Come into my office.'

He turned and led me through a small, tidy kitchen into a room that had obviously been a garage until recently. The unplastered walls were painted white and the concrete floor was covered in dark red industrial carpet. All along one wall there was a series of obviously new, and mostly empty, shelves. In the furthest corner of the room stood a desk, two office chairs upholstered in red tweedy fabric and a tall metal filing cabinet. This whole corner of the office was topped off by a huge impressionistic painting of something that looked vaguely like a castle. The painting was so big that it covered at least five feet of wall. He caught me looking at it.

'It's King John's castle,' he said.

I nodded. 'Lovely.'

'My daughter Niamh painted it when she was only fifteen.'

'It's very good,' I said.

He looked fondly at the painting and nodded his head. 'She's at art college now.' He turned back and motioned me to sit down. I did so, watching in morbid fascination as he lowered his bulky form onto a chair. The chair was a reasonably substantial office chair – we had loads of them at Fab City – but even so it didn't look as if it was going to survive its encounter with the detective. Dermot Kilbane was not just a little on the chubby side, he was actually fat. He was a tall man, as you'd expect of an ex-policeman – six-two or more and broad to go with it. In his day he had probably been a fine figure of a man, as my mother might say. However, add four or five stones of excess weight to that already large frame and you were talking seriously big.

He leaned back in his chair and it groaned audibly. 'So? Where shall we start?'

I shrugged and shifted my bag around on my lap.

'Maybe if I tell you a bit about myself first?' he said.

I nodded and smiled. That sounded like a good way to buy time.

'Well, I presume you saw my ad in the phone book?'

I nodded again.

'Did you have a look at my website?'

'Yes.'

'Do you mind me asking what you thought of it?'

I shrugged. 'Very nice.'

'No, really: my sons Dessie and Frank designed it and we're not sure it works – they're still at college – but I think it's pretty good. They told me to get feedback from customers – so? What do you think?'

'It looks fine . . . honestly.'

'Good, good.' He leaned forward and put his elbows on the pale wood desk. 'OK now – I was going to tell you a bit about myself – let's see. OK – I've been a Guard for most of my life – loved it, to be truthful. Unfortunately, though, I had to take early retirement – a bit of trouble with the lungs and the ticker . . .'

'Oh, I'm sorry to hear that,' I said because he paused.

Dermot looked at me thoughtfully for a few seconds and then shook his head. 'It's fine – under control – just think clients might like to know why I left the Force. That's me, really – I've only set up this business in the past year. You know yourself, three kids at college, you have to do something.'

He paused again and looked at me. This time I didn't say anything.

'So? How can I help you, Jamie?'

I looked at him. His face was smooth and round and though I guessed he was in his fifties he didn't seem to have any wrinkles. Underneath his thick grey hair a pair of piercingly blue eyes assessed me as I assessed him. He smiled.

I took a deep breath. 'My brother is missing. His name is Conor Ryan, he's thirty-five years old now – thirty-four when he went missing – and he disappeared without trace just over eighteen months ago.'

I spent almost two hours in Dermot Kilbane's garage-office telling him everything that I knew about Conor's disappearance. Kilbane took reams and reams of notes as I spoke and when I finished he asked me at least a couple of hundred questions. Along the way he made us tea and produced a delicious home-baked apple tart that he said he'd baked himself. By the time we were finished I had not only clarified matters for myself but was also beginning to feel quite confident.

'Do you mind if I ask you a question?' I said as we were having a final cup of tea and slice of apple tart.

He shook his head.

'Do you think The Man in The Park was Conor?'

Dermot didn't answer for a few seconds – he just sat mashing a piece of apple with his fork.

'Could be,' he said eventually.

My heart leapt and it must have shown on my face because he said, 'Might *not* be him as well – there are a lot of men that age and the mind is a mysterious thing: it can play tricks on us.'

'But why would he help Fiona if it wasn't Conor?' I said.

'Most people are kind – I know it's hard to believe when it looks like the world is full of evil bastards but very few people would walk on by and leave a small child tangled upside down in a swing.'

Tears pricked my eyes. 'So I might be imagining it?'

'You could be,' Dermot said softly. 'But do you know something, we really need to find out what happened to Conor.'

I nodded. 'Do you think *you* can find out?'

'I can certainly try. Leave it with me for a week or so and I'll see what I can do: how about that? If I review everything and I think that there's no hope I'll tell you – if not, sure we could keep going for a little while and see what happens.'

'How much do you charge?' I asked, my heart unexpectedly expanding inside me with new hope.

'It varies – obviously I charge any expenses but I do my best to keep the cost down. Listening to you here I'm thinking I should pay London a visit and see what I can turn up. Other than that, I suppose I just need to have a look at all the information I can find on the case.'

'How will you do that?' I said as I hugged my bag close to my chest. I could feel the corners of my Conor folder protruding.

Dermot smiled. 'I still have contacts – it won't be any problem.'

I pulled out the folder and handed it across the desk to Dermot. Without a word he examined the contents. Then he looked up at me, his bright eyes narrowed with concentration. 'Did you put this together?'

I nodded. 'When Conor went missing I cut out the pieces from the paper, kept reports, that kind of thing – stupid, I know, but it made me feel like I was doing something. I even wrote things down on bits of paper: things people said at the time – Bill, the Guards – daft, really.'

'It's not a bit daft – you'd be surprised what helps. Anyway, I'll look after this, I promise and . . .' He stood up and reached out a hand. I took my cue from him and did the same. We shook hands.

'I won't call you unless I have something to report but you feel free to call me any time.'

Dermot handed me a business card and I put it into a pocket in my now very light handbag as we walked in silence back through the Kilbanes' kitchen to the front door. Maybe this morbidly obese retired police-man wouldn't be able to find out anything about Conor. Or maybe he'd find out that the worst we'd feared was true – Conor was dead and we'd never see him again. Still, whether it was my sighting of The Man in The Park or my contracting of Dermot Kilbane's services I felt quite positive for the first time in ages. Whatever the outcome, I had a feeling that we were getting close to the answer.

13

I didn't tell Bill about Dermot Kilbane – I was too sensitive about the whole subject to be able to ward off his scathing opinions. I decided that I wasn't going to tell anybody and for a while that seemed like a good idea. But then the whole thing began to build up inside my head until my hiring of a private detective was becoming an issue in itself. So, a few days later, I told Shane all about Kilbane. We were in our kitchen and I was cooking myself an omelette while he heated some ready-made lasagne in the microwave.

'So?' I said just as the microwave pinged. 'What do you think?'

Shane slid the gelatinous mound out of its plastic container onto a plate before he answered. 'He sounds OK,' he said, getting himself a fork and sitting at the table. Titbit whined at the back door and I looked in despair at Shane.

'Why can't Heather take him to live with her?' I said, adding olives to the salad I had made earlier.

'Poor old dog,' Shane said, getting up to let him in. The dog leapt around the kitchen as if he was on an invisible trampoline. Shane put some lasagne off his own plate in the stainless-steel doggy bowl and Titbit yelped his thanks.

'Want some salad?' I asked as I joined Shane at the table.

He shook his head and grinned. 'No, thanks. I'm fine with this.'

'I honestly don't know how you're not dead, Shane Ali – you never eat vegetables and all I ever see you have for dinner is that pre-packaged shite.'

Shane smiled. He and I had long since agreed to disagree on the subject of food, which was why we made separate meals even when we were both at home together at mealtimes. His mother was a good-quality meat and two veg Irish cook, all of his Pakistani aunts and even his father Ramin were terrific cooks but somehow the cooking gene had skipped Shane.

'I eat fruit,' he said.

'Well, mark my words, when you and Heather get married there'll be none of that stodgy crap for dinner. I'd say her body hasn't seen a carb since she was eleven.'

Shane just grinned again and continued to wolf down his plate of lasagne. Titbit had finished eating and had come over to lie at Shane's feet. He glanced up at me with those malevolent eyes and I looked away.

'So?' Shane said after a few minutes of both of us occupying ourselves with food. 'When will this PI guy get back to you with a report?'

'Don't know – he said for me to ring him if I feel

like it but I suppose I should give him a couple of weeks anyway before I start to hassle him.'

Shane nodded.

'One other thing,' I said as I finished my dinner. He looked at me.

'Please don't tell anybody about this guy – I haven't even told Sophie.'

He stood up and stacked the dirty dishes into a neat pile. 'What guy?' he said just as the doorbell rang. I winked at him and ran out to answer it. Sophie and Heather were standing side by side in the narrow porch and the atmosphere in that confined space was positively charged. They both stepped into the hallway as soon as the door opened.

'Jamie,' they said in tandem. I raised a hand in greeting and pointed towards the kitchen. 'Shane's in there.'

Both of the women set off in the direction of my finger. Heather in the lead with an eye-rolling Sophie behind her.

'Heather's just been telling me all about her new *big* contract for Real Woman cosmetics,' Sophie said, sticking out her tongue at Heather's back.

'The face of Real Woman,' Heather called.

'Lovely,' I said, thinking that there were few women I knew who were less real than Heather. But then – what did I know about Girl Land? I was a rank amateur. Heather rushed to Shane as soon as she got into the kitchen.

'Sweetie,' she said, kissing him provocatively on the lips. Shane put his arms around her and Sophie muttered something about them getting a room and I just ignored them all and made tea.

'Don't you two think my Shane is pretty enough to be a model?' Heather asked.

Sophie and I stood together in front of him and pretended to survey him.

'Not bad,' Sophie said, her arms folded.

'Hmm,' I agreed. 'A bit on the scrawny side – could do with a couple of visits to the gym.'

'Watch your mouth,' Shane said, throwing a dish-cloth. We ducked and it landed on the table.

Heather wound her arms around Shane and looked at Sophie and I. 'Seriously, though – Real Woman are launching a new range of grooming products for men . . .'

'Called Real Man, by any chance?' Sophie interjected.

Heather looked amazed. 'Yes, it is – how did you know that?'

Sophie just shrugged and elbowed me.

'Anyway,' Heather continued. 'I want Shane to try out for the face of Real Man – think of it, Shaney: me and you, Real Woman and Real Man? Come on, please. For me? You two persuade him.'

I threw my hands up in the air and turned back to the table where I poured four mugs of tea. Sophie sat down opposite me. Shane kissed his fiancée. 'I'm happy as a sound tech, love – really.'

Heather pouted and hung her head while Sophie made puking gestures to me behind an upraised hand. Titbit woke up and broke the tension by jumping all over Shane.

'Ohhhhh, baby,' Heather crooned, as she tried to catch him long enough to stroke him. 'Dr Yelverton says you're doing great – I missed you – how have you been?'

'Neurotic,' I muttered into my tea.

Heather ignored me. 'I'm going to pop upstairs and have a bath,' she said to Shane, innuendo dripping from every syllable. 'I've had a long hard day – the shoot was gruelling but Dave says it'll be worth it.'

Sophie and I sipped our tea.

'I think I'll come with you and scrub your back,' Shane said, putting both of his hands on her waist as she led him from the room.

'Thank God,' Sophie said as soon as we could hear that the giggling had moved to the upstairs of the house. 'I mean, listen to that, Jamie – what the hell is that giggling all about? Are they having sex or playing tickling?'

I shrugged and grinned. 'Why are you all dressed up?' I said, taking in Sophie's appearance. She was wearing a halter-necked short black dress and was beautifully made-up. She finished her tea and sat back in her chair, reviewing her new manicure. 'I have a date with Rico.'

'Is Tyrone back at school?'

Sophie scowled and pinched me in the arm.

'Ow,' I said. 'Where are ye going? The Copacabana?'

'You're a regular comedian, Jamie – Pat Shortt wouldn't get a look in.'

'Thanks,' I said. 'This must be your third or fourth date with the lovely Rico – are you two becoming an item?'

'Don't be ridiculous – it's serial lust. I'm onto a great thing here. I've never had better sex – don't get me wrong, Paul was good in a by-the-book solicitor kind of way – but Rico on the other hand . . .' She groaned and bent forward.

'Too much information,' I said.

'You should try it some time,' she said.

'Rico?'

'Well, if you like him I'm sure he'd oblige – but not necessarily him, just the whole idea of casual relationships.'

'I'm tired of that carry-on,' I said. 'I want something else in my life now, Sophie. I want a relationship that isn't just a series of dates – I want it to be going somewhere.'

'To each his own,' Sophie said, standing up. 'Anyway, the reason I'm here is to tell you that the directors have decided to put major cash behind Tommy Sloane's garden.'

'Brilliant! I mean, I think he might be bonkers, Soph, but he's a bit of a genius by all accounts.'

'Exactly,' she said, 'and seemingly there's a lot of money riding on him to win Chelsea.'

'That's good.'

She nodded. 'But even better is that the directors have decided that the best way to capitalise on our investment is for us to go with him when he goes to Chelsea next week to start work on his garden. We'll do daily updates and really build up the tension before the results are announced.'

'Good idea – kind of like a pre-match build-up.'

Sophie shrugged. 'Whatever. Did you know that Tommy has a load of local fans who are all planning to travel to the Flower Show to support him?'

'No, but that figures.'

'Anyway, I've arranged with a small London station to let us use one of their studios so that we can actually broadcast from there.'

'You're a genius, Sophie.'

'Thanks, I know.'

'So who are you sending to cover it – Steve?'

She nodded. 'He's the obvious choice and as well as being high-profile he's Tommy Sloane's pal – did you know that?'

'Yes, he told me.'

'Anyway, the directors want us to make a documentary – kind of *Limerick Does Chelsea* – as well as do the daily broadcasts.'

I nodded. 'Another good idea.'

'Glad you think that – because that's why we're sending you as well.'

14

Sophie took off for her date with Rico almost immediately after she'd dropped the bomb. I staggered into the sitting room and turned on the TV to drown the noises from Shane's room. Plonking myself onto the sofa, I half watched highlights of an Italian football match. Steve and I were going to London together? It was like a dream come true – or maybe a nightmare. If I couldn't manage to wangle my way into his affections with that much continuous contact then I'd have to accept that he wasn't ever going to reciprocate my feelings.

Next morning when I arrived at work there was a fragrant bunch of roses and lilies standing in a glass vase on my desk. I stuck my head out of my still-empty doorway.

'Dee-Dee?' I called. She looked up at me from her computer. 'Stalker flowers?'

Dee-Dee nodded. 'The card is in the bin. Do you want it?'

'No, thanks. Anybody want flowers?' I shouted.

Raina Burke slammed a drawer on a filing cabinet. 'My aunt is in hospital,' she said. 'She had her gall bladder out.'

'Be my guest,' I said, fetching the bouquet and bringing it to her desk.

She thanked me and told me that the janitor had sworn he'd ordered a new door.

'I'll believe it when I see it,' I said, heading back to my desk. But whether or not I had an office door was really the least of my worries. Much higher on my agenda was exactly what I was going to do if I had to present my programme from London. And Sophie wanted me to collect material for a documentary as well. Shit – where was I going to get the head-space to do that when my real interest while I was there would be in seducing Steve Lowe?

Just at that moment Sophie arrived in my office.

'Day after tomorrow – 7.15 flight – here's the print-out. Be there or be square.'

She dropped a sheaf of papers on the desk and turned to leave.

'Soph?'

'Yes?'

'Where will I be staying while I'm in London?'

'A place called The Hampshire. It looks nice on the Internet – Raina found it for you. It's a guest house and it's quite close to both the Royal Hospital where the flower show is on and also LFM – the station you'll be working out of.'

'And Steve?'

'What about Steve?'

I coughed. 'Will he be staying in the same place? Are there any techies coming with us, by the way? I forgot to ask you that.'

Sophie came back over and sat on my desk. She folded her arms and looked at me. 'The LFM people will do most of that and Ian Doyle is coming from here – Shane's choice. He says that Ian will be very good at helping you collect interviews for the documentary.'

She paused and looked at me. I sat completely still.

'Ian has a brother who lives in London so he's staying with him,' she continued. 'You and Steve will be staying in the Hampshire – is that all right with you?'

I felt a slow blush creep up my neck towards my face. I lowered my head and pretended to be looking for something in the top drawer of my desk.

'What's going on, Jamie?'

I rummaged through the paper clips and rubber bands, muttering about biros.

'Jamie?'

I looked up and shrugged. 'Nothing.'

'Do I look as stupid as Heather?'

I bit my lip.

'Have you got a thing for Steve?'

I looked helplessly at her. I wanted to deny it but when Sophie had you under her microscope there was no real escape.

I shrugged again. 'A bit.'

'A bit of a thing?'

'I suppose.'

Sophie rolled her eyes and sighed deeply. 'Steve Lowe is carrying more baggage than a freight train – definitely more baggage than that Ryanair flight you'll be getting to London.'

'I think he's great,' I said, suddenly feeling protective.

'He *is* great – he's just a bit fucked up. You know he's an alcoholic?'

'So what? He's dealt with that and learned from it. I think it's made him more of a man, not less.'

Sophie sighed again. 'Why do you think he and RTE parted company?'

'No idea – and, to be honest, Sophie, I don't think it's any of our business.'

'Well, it is if you're thinking of letting him into your knickers.'

'Don't be so crude – it's not like that.'

Sophie snorted. 'Sorry – I didn't realise you were so sensitive. Tell me what it is like, so.'

I sat there for a few seconds, looking at her. She just didn't understand. Sophie had been hurt and now believed that all men were bastards but that just wasn't the case. Well, if I could accept her insane behaviour running around with Rico and every young fella in town the least she could do was respect my feelings for Steve.

'He's been very nice to me,' I said, hesitating for a moment. 'Kind. A few things have happened . . . you know, I've been upset about Conor and all that stuff and he's been there for me. Listened. Gave me good advice. I know he's handsome and sexy but it isn't just that, Sophie . . . I really like him.'

She didn't answer for a few seconds. 'So that's what all the sudden interest in girl things is about,' she said eventually.

I shrugged.

'You need to be careful.'

'I will be,' I said. 'Anyway, maybe he doesn't feel the same way about me.'

'I'll have to have him beaten up if that's the case,' Sophie said, standing up and straightening her short suit-skirt. 'I'm telling you now, though, I'm not booking you two into a double room in London, no matter how much you beg me.'

I laughed as she winked and left my office.

15

The Ryanair flight from Shannon to Stansted was filled to capacity, so Ian, Steve and I each ended up sitting with strangers. I wasn't sorry. I hate travelling. From the time I was the tiniest child my memories of travel are all about throwing up. As a result, while I love being in different places I dread the journey there.

I always carry a variety of travel-sickness remedies in my handbag. But as most of the medication makes me feel like shite I was hoping to survive the short flight to London without having to resort to much more than a fistful of ginger tablets and some chewing gum. As if it isn't bad enough to be afflicted with travel-sickness I'm also a victim of long-leg syndrome. Which means that economy flights are excruciatingly uncomfortable. In short, between the puking and the complaining, none of it helped with the image I wanted to present to Steve.

Still, even as I wriggled and sighed and chewed like a mad thing and totally pissed off the man sitting next to me I was excited by the prospect of the days ahead. The whole documentary idea had begun to spark my imagination. Having done some preliminary groundwork I was beginning to think that I was going to get seriously good mileage out of the Tommy Sloane fans. I was particularly looking forward to meeting the women that the more serious gardening fans had dubbed the Tommy Sloane Groupies.

But of course the main cause of my excitement was the idea of spending all that time alone with Steve. I had never been the calculating type before and I was a bit worried about the emergence of this in my personality. I told myself that it was just common sense to know what you want and to try and get it. Even if 'it' was another human being.

In the interests of my Steve campaign I had packed all my new clothes and make-up. As a result I'd had to pay exorbitant excess-baggage charges but I was hoping it would be worthwhile. I knew I hadn't imagined that kiss at the TV launch – there had definitely been more to it than a mere gesture of friendship. Nobody kisses you on the lips like that if they just want to be your pal. I couldn't believe that the huge sexual charge I felt every time I was near Steve was all one-sided – but then again, that's probably what Pierce the Stalker thought about me.

It was too confusing, I'd just have to see what happened. I closed my eyes, refusing offers from the stewards of opportunities to purchase scratch cards and Cup-a-Soup. God be with the good old days of the complimentary cup of tea and cellophane-wrapped biscuits.

I hadn't been in London for a couple of years and as soon as I stopped thinking about Steve my thoughts were occupied with Conor. At least we were flying into

Stansted, not Heathrow – that'd be a bit less evocative. But I still couldn't help picturing yet again the face of The Man in The Park. Bill and even Dermot had made me doubt what I'd seen. That morning I'd been so certain that the man in the baseball cap was Conor, and now . . .

I saw what they were all saying – understood that my mind could be playing tricks. But was it really possible to imagine that feeling of recognition in your gut that comes from more than just hair and eyes and general appearance? I didn't know. I was tempted to call Dermot but it'd only been four days so he'd probably not discovered anything of great importance yet. I'd wait until Steve and I got back from London. Steve and I – it had a lovely ring to it.

We arrived at Stansted ten minutes early and after collecting our bags we opted to share a taxi into London. Steve sat in the passenger seat and charmed the London cabbie while Ian and I shared the back. I knew I was never going to survive chugging through London traffic without throwing up all over the love of my life so I popped two travel sickness tablets as soon as the nausea began. Then I tried to distract myself by talking to Ian.

Ian Doyle was twenty-three or twenty-four and Shane said he was probably one of the best sound engineers he'd ever worked with. He also figured Ian was unlikely to stay a sound engineer for too long because his real passion was his band, The Hooplas. I'd had the band on my show a few times and they were really very good. Ian was their lead singer and he was particularly fine. In ordinary life Ian was a quiet enough guy but on stage he had a riveting presence. All helped along by the fact that he was like a very handsome high-cheek-boned cross between Jarvis Cocker, Damon Albarn and the singer in Franz Ferdinand.

'So, Ian,' I said as the taxi chugged slowly through the traffic and I felt the nausea and drugs begin their battle inside me. 'How are The Hooplas?'

'Good. Getting gigs. I'm going to drop in some demos while I'm in London,' he said, tapping his jacket pocket.

'Good idea. I must have you guys back on the programme soon.'

Ian nodded seriously. 'Any time – just give me the word.'

'OK, I will,' I said. We both nodded – and that was it. Ian and I had exhausted our conversation. We had very little in common. I was much too nauseated and preoccupied to try to be acrobatically sociable and I knew that it'd never even enter Ian's head to try and think of things to talk to me about. It was fine, though. For the rest of the journey we settled into a companionable silence. I looked out the cab window at the crowded city streets. It never ceased to amaze me how fast everything – except the cars – moved in London.

We dropped Ian at his brother's flat, arranging to meet up at ten the next morning, and then we continued our slow journey to the guest house. I dozed in the back of the cab while Steve and the driver were deep in animated conversation about the Middle East.

Eventually we were decanted outside The Hampshire and we did the business of checking in. I tried not to look too delighted when we discovered that we'd been allocated adjoining rooms.

I examined my room, which was small but clean and comfortable, and then unpacked my case, for once taking the time to hang up all my clothes. When I was finished I undressed to my underwear, lay down on my bed and fell fast asleep. When I awoke to the sound of a light tapping sound on my bedroom door the room was pitch dark. Struggling to remember where I was, I staggered over to the door and opened it. Steve was standing in the small hallway. I rubbed my face and ran a hand through my hair, though I knew it was a waste of time. There wasn't a doubt in my mind that my face was creased with sleep and my hair was standing up like bristles on a scrubbing brush.

'Jeez – Jamie – sorry!' Steve said, his stare darting away from me and then back and then away from me again. My stomach sank. I must really look a sight if he couldn't bear to look at me.

'You were asleep – I didn't realise.'

'That's OK,' I said, my hand fumbling on the wall to switch on the lights in my room. 'It's dark – what time is it?'

'Nearly nine. I knocked earlier but there was no answer so I figured you were out. Just thought you might like to get a bite to eat – but look, don't worry about it . . .'

'I'm starving, actually,' I said, walking back into the room. 'Hang on a minute and I'll be with you.' And that was when I realised – I was having this whole conversation with the man of my dreams while I was not only looking like a scrubbing brush that an elephant had just sat on but was also in my underwear. And it wasn't even the sexy new underwear that I'd packed so carefully. I was wearing a black cotton crop-top – dubbed The Uniboob by Sophie – and a pair of faded black knickers. I looked down at my feet and saw that I was also still wearing my socks. Jesus. It couldn't get much worse.

I felt the blood rush to my face as humiliation followed realisation. This wasn't fair. Travel sick. Ugly. And now half naked in a scary way. I was never going to be able to seduce this man. I grabbed my discarded clothes off the floor and, stuttering something about him hanging on for a minute, locked myself into the tiny bathroom.

I dressed before I could confirm how awful I looked. Then I splashed cold water on my face and tried to improve my appearance with a smear of make-up and some mascara. I wasn't sure it was working but at least I'd stayed away from clown school. My hair was another day of the week. It was radiating out from my head exactly as I'd feared and I didn't have time to have a shower or even to just wash it. The best I could do was to stick my head under the shower for a few seconds and then try to brush my hair flat. The result wasn't great but it was a small bit of an improvement – if you didn't mind looking like a six-foot choirboy wearing make-up.

I took a series of deep breaths and stepped back

into the bedroom. Steve was sitting on the end of my bed reading an *Irish Times* that he'd retrieved from my tote bag. He looked so at home there on my bed that it made me feel even worse about what had just happened. Luckily, though, hunger overrode humiliation and gave me back some equilibrium.

'Have you any idea where we might find a restaurant?' I said, shivering as a drop of water from my wet hair sneaked down my neck.

Steve looked up at me and smiled as he folded the newspaper. 'I had a walk around earlier and there's a very nice-looking Italian restaurant just a couple of doors away – how about that?'

'Sounds good to me.'

I led the way down the narrow stairs and out onto the street. It was a lovely May evening in London. The small square where we were staying was facing a neat and well-tended green area. Graceful iron lamp-posts lit the still-bustling street as we made our way the short distance to the restaurant. A handsome Italian waiter who told us that his name was Salvatore greeted us as soon as Steve pushed open the door of the restaurant. He ushered us to a table, providing us with menus and recommendations and drinks. Steve, as usual, chatted amicably with the waiter. I smiled at him but was still too embarrassed by what had happened to be able to relax properly.

The restaurant was quite tiny, with maybe ten white-clothed round tables on which were the de rigueur candles. Each table seemed to be occupied by a couple. As we ordered our food I looked around and tried to imagine their lives. They all looked so together and happy – well, nearly all: there was certainly at least one couple who looked like they were wearing the determinedly cheerful faces of those about to break up.

We ordered bruschetta and tagliatelle and heaps of salad. Luckily I remembered that I was dining with an alcoholic and ordered Perrier instead of wine. Steve followed suit and didn't say anything until the waiter was out of earshot.

'There's no need to have water just because of me,' he said, twirling an empty glass between his fingers.

'Oh, no,' I said, feeling myself blush. 'Oh, not at all. I just thought . . . well, what with the travel-sickness tablets and all that I was afraid to chance any alcohol.'

'It's OK, really – I'm Steve Lowe and I'm an alcoholic.' He smiled at me.

I shrugged and bit my lip.

Steve continued to smile at me and I smiled back. Faint dark stubble was appearing along his chin and I really longed to reach out and touch it. But instead I ran a hand through my own hair. The waiter returned with our bruschetta and Perrier and indignantly whipped away the wine glasses.

'I'm glad people know,' Steve said as we started to eat. 'I'm not ashamed of it, really I'm not.'

'Of course not.'

Steve cut through his bruschetta. 'Well, I have plenty to be ashamed of – I did some really shitty things when I was drinking but that's what it is. Now I have to move on. Especially for my girls. Did I ever tell you about them?'

I shook my head, my mouth full of crispy bread and tomatoes. Steve rooted in his inside pocket and produced a wallet-sized photograph of two very pretty little blonde girls.

'Aoife and Aisling,' he said, displaying the picture.

I swallowed and took the photo. 'They are really beautiful.'

His eyes filled with tears and he nodded. 'That was taken a few years ago – they're almost grown-up now.'

'What age are they?'

'Aoife is fourteen, Aisling is twelve – they're terrific kids. I'd love you to meet them.'

I poured oil on my salad. 'I'd love to meet them.'

Steve's fork was poised in mid-air over his plate and he looked deep into my eyes. 'It's funny the way things work out, isn't it? When Aoife was born I was the happiest man in the world – RTE was really happening for me, Susan and I had bought a fabulous old house on the seafront in Bray and then . . .'

His voice trailed off and his eyes, though still looking at me, were unfocused. 'That's when the drinking really started,' he said, suddenly returning his attention to me. 'I mean, I drank a good bit before that but from then on I really hit the bottle if I'm to be honest.'

He paused. I felt bad for him – his life had been destroyed and he was a truly wonderful and brave person to have overcome his addiction so totally. I wasn't all that confident about my responses and I so wanted to say and do the right thing.

But Steve didn't seem to need me to say anything. 'I kept it a secret at first,' he continued. 'You know, just one of the lads, likes a good time, that sort of thing. Susan must have known but she didn't say anything – probably too busy with Aoife and then when Aisling came along she really had her hands full. She should have realised that there was something going on when I managed to miss Aisling's birth because I was delayed at a work do.'

'Poor Susan,' I said.

Steve looked at me for a few seconds. 'I suppose it must have been difficult for her, all right.'

We finished our bruschetta in silence. When we were done the waiter cleared away our starters and brought our main course. Steve refilled our glasses with sparkling water.

'So what happened?' I said, looking at him over my tall crystal water glass.

He didn't answer immediately, just sipped from his own glass and looked at me. 'Do you mind me talking about this stuff?'

I shook my head. 'Not at all – I find it fascinating. And look . . . I feel a bit dumb saying it but the truth is that I have a lot of admiration for people who face up to their problems. It can't be easy.'

Steve smiled. 'It isn't – but it's worth it. I mean, I hardly knew my little girls. They grew up without me, really – I was never there – always out at some function or other. Even when I was home I wasn't really present – always either drunk or hung-over.'

He stopped and curled a strand of tagliatelle between a fork and spoon, then surreptitiously wiped a tear from his eye. I pretended not to notice and got to work on my own pasta. I was really starving so it tasted like the nicest food I'd ever had.

'Eventually I fucked up on every front,' Steve said after a few seconds. 'For a long while I kept the radio show going. I was careful not to drink before I went on air. God knows how many breath mints I must have consumed.'

He stopped and smiled warmly. I returned the smile and felt the mild light-headedness I had come to associate with being around Steve.

'It can't have been easy,' I said. Then, realising I had already said that, I tried again. 'I mean, you were top of your game, weren't you? And then you lost it all.'

He nodded. 'That's true. It's funny – I was really hoping for a permanent move into TV. I don't tell many people this but I have a real ambition to do television – always have had.'

'That's interesting,' I said.

'Yeah, and believe it or not, four years ago I had my own show. Nothing big, you know, but still – *my own show*. It ran for only four weeks – you might remember it? *Lowe's Lowdown*. An afternoon chat show intended to appeal to the intelligent stay-home-Mom demographic.'

I nodded and shrugged at the same time. I'd never even heard of it. But then, I wasn't part of that demographic, was I? Nor was I about to admit my ignorance to Steve.

'And how come that didn't work out?' I asked.

Steve grimaced, seeming not to notice my vagueness. 'I got pissed one lunchtime and then went on air and tried to snog the Rose of Tralee and put my hand up her skirt.'

In spite of myself I laughed. He looked at me and then smiled as well.

'How did she take it?' I said.

'Not well. She hit me with a bottle of Ballygowan.'

'Poor Steve,' I said.

He grinned. 'I was anaesthetised, I didn't feel a thing. Not until the next morning when I was fired.'

'What?'

Steve nodded. 'The production company were afraid that the Rose was going to sue them for sexual harassment. So they got rid of me.'

'So did you go back to radio?'

'For a little while. But I just seemed to really go off the rails from then on and I lost my radio job as well. By then I was not only drinking but doing a bit of coke. Susan had me followed for a while – I told you that. She wasted her money, really: the dogs on the street at that time knew I was drinking and doing drugs and starting to whore around.'

'What happened?'

He shrugged. 'The usual rock-bottom story. Susan chucked me out on my ear and I tried to convince her to take me back so I booked myself into a treatment centre.'

'That was a good idea.'

'Well, it was a cynical move at first. I had no intention of giving up – just thought Susan might believe me if it looked like I was trying.'

'But you *did* stop.'

'The treatment worked accidentally,' Steve said, with a grin. 'It's not supposed to work like that but in my case it did. Here I am – clean and sober for three years now.'

We finished our dinner in silence but the air between us seemed to have taken on a new energy as a result of Steve opening his heart to me. The waiter came to clear the table and we ordered coffee and ice cream. When we were alone again Steve looked shyly at me.

'You probably think I'm a big loser – but I'm glad I told you. It's important to me . . .'

I grabbed his hand. 'I think you might be the bravest person I've ever met.'

He wound his fingers around mine and we sat like that for a few seconds and then sheepishly pulled apart to eat our desserts and drink our coffee. We didn't really speak much while we finished off our meal. My heart was pounding in my chest, though. There was a quality to the way Steve was looking at me that was answering all my questions about that wildly electric energy I'd felt since we'd first met. He insisted on paying the bill and we were silent on the short walk back to the guest house. As we climbed the stairs together I felt as if he was touching me even though we were two or three feet apart.

Once we reached our landing we stood in the small hallway, just looking at each other for a few seconds. I broke the silence first.

'Thanks for dinner,' I said.

Steve just continued to look at me. I felt my heart

pound in my throat and he was just lifting his hand as though to reach out and touch me when his mobile phone rang. He looked cross and I wanted to tell him to ignore it: it was only a stupid phone, after all, and if it was important the caller could ring back. But he shook himself as if he was waking up, pulled the phone from his jacket pocket and looked at the screen.

'Aoife,' he said to me.

'Oh,' I said.

He answered the phone. 'Hi, sweetie.'

I waved at him and let myself into my room, feeling ready to implode with sexual frustration. It just wasn't fair. I wanted him so badly and for the first time since I'd met him I'd been sure that my feelings were reciprocated. As much as I could tell anything in the world I could see that he wanted me too. And then his daughter had to ring like that.

I felt like such a bitch for resenting the poor little girl. He was her dad, after all, and she was entitled to speak to him. I threw myself face down on the bed and tried to calm down. I should have had a bottle of wine in that bloody restaurant – it might have dampened my ardour. Shit, shit, shit.

I closed my eyes and thought of cold showers just as I felt a hand lightly brush my hair. Startled, I sat up.

'The door was open,' Steve said from where he was kneeling on the floor at the end of my bed. 'You mustn't have pushed it . . .'

And that was as far as he got before I pulled his face close and kissed him. Within seconds he was lying on top of me on the big hotel double bed and I wasn't thinking about anything, just allowing myself to feel the pleasurable ache of his weight all along the length of my body and the sensation on my skin as his hands moved under my T-shirt and I felt his lips on my neck.

We pulled at each other's clothes until we were both naked and rolling around as one entity on the bed. Skin and hair and lips and limbs and tongues together – now slow and easy in our touch – now frenzied and wild. We laughed as we accidentally rolled off the bed onto the floor and there just continued what we'd been doing until we both were moaning with pleasure and half screaming with ecstasy. And then we climbed up onto the crumpled bed and rolled ourselves into each other and the bedclothes and fell asleep.

16

When I awoke next morning Steve was looking at me. The sight of his face in front of mine was almost enough for me. I had never felt like this about anyone before. Just to be able to look into his tired but beautiful face and see his dark eyes looking at me in the dusky room filled me with an aching sort of happiness. He smiled slowly and leaned over and kissed me gently. I pulled him close and we kissed and slipped into a slow, languorous lovemaking that seemed to have a quality to it that I'd also never experienced before. It was almost a sadness, or at least some level of emotion so exquisitely tender that I wasn't sure how to identify it.

Afterwards we showered and dressed and hurried to the dining room. Over our full English breakfast we discussed our work schedule. We were due to meet Tommy Sloane at the Royal Hospital at ten and had arranged to hook up with Ian there. After that we were off to LFM so that we could set up at the studio for our broadcasts while we were in London.

We finished talking about work and continued our breakfast in silence. As I polished off my sausages and eggs and buttered myself a small mound of toast

I was conscious that Steve never seemed to take his gaze from my face.

'I need to say something to you,' he said after some time.

I looked at him, my mouth full of toast and my heart beating in sudden fear. Now that I finally had what I wanted I was terrified that I might lose it. It made me feel very vulnerable to be suddenly in so deep – but then again, it also made me feel very alive and I figured that that might be the pay-off.

'Last night was probably one of the most incredibly special nights of my life,' Steve said.

I sipped from my cup of scalding coffee.

'There was a time in my life when I just blundered around from drink to drink and woman to woman, not really connecting with anybody, just grabbing hold of anything that moved.'

He stopped and refilled his coffee cup. I sat back in my chair.

'I feel that there's something very special between us,' he said. 'I could be wrong – it might be just me – but since we first met I've felt a sort of connection.'

He looked at me questioningly and I shook my head. 'You're not wrong,' I said, my heart soaring.

Steve smiled, leaned forward and brushed a fingertip across my lips. 'Which is why I wanted to say this to you.'

He stopped then, as if I should understand what it was he was trying to say. But all I could hear was him saying those few seconds ago that he felt the same as me.

I shrugged. 'Say what, Steve? I'm not sure that I understand you.'

He took a deep breath. 'The problem is that I really like you, Jamie – there's no other way of saying that, is there?'

I smiled and shrugged. So far, so good – I wasn't really seeing a problem with any of this.

'And because I like you, I feel I owe it to you to be straight – I told you last night about the shit that went down in my past.'

I leaned forward, took his right hand in mine and began to stroke the back of it. Steve groaned softly.

'You see, this is the problem,' he said, not pulling away.

I raised my eyebrows and smiled.

He smiled back. 'I'm like a newborn calf as far as my life goes: all shaky legs and drool. I've just managed to start putting things back together – I have the job at Fab City, I'm trying to develop a proper relationship with my kids – and I don't know that I have anything to offer a woman like you.'

I picked up his hand and slowly kissed each finger-tip. Steve tightened his grip on my hand and leaned forward until we were holding both each other's hands and our faces were almost touching across the small table.

'I'm a bloody alcoholic with a hundred problems. I'm broke, divorced – I have two kids. I'm older than you by a good ten years and a lot more fucked up.'

'So?'

'Like I said, I don't know that I can offer you

anything – or, at least, any of the things that you deserve. I can't even think about having a serious relationship until I have everything else sorted out.'

'So?' I said again.

'So what I'm saying is that I really like you and I don't want last night to be a one-night stand. But I also don't want to pretend that I can offer you a proper relationship – at least, not in the immediate future. If you want to walk away now that's fine, Jamie, really.'

Steve lowered his head. 'We can draw a line under what happened and just carry on being friends.'

I looked at the top of his head and the way his hair curved around itself at its crown. Inside myself I was calmer than I'd been in ages.

'What time did you say we'd meet Tommy?' I asked.

'Ten.'

'That gives us a good hour before we have to leave.'

I stood up and pulled him to his feet. 'Come on,' I said, hurrying out of the tiny dining room and up the narrow stairs to my bedroom. Once inside we stood and looked at each other for a few seconds.

'Are you sure about this?' Steve said.

'You're kidding, right?' I said, moving towards him and laughing as I unbuttoned my blouse. 'I've never been so sure of anything in my life.'

The sun was shining and I felt as if I was going to burst with happiness by the time we arrived at the site of the Chelsea Flower Show. At the entrance we reassured the security people of our bona fides and they helped us to find Tommy Sloane. Everywhere in the grounds of the Royal Hospital was electric with work and energy. Trucks and wheelbarrows trundled by, carrying materials and plants, as we walked towards the area of Tommy's garden.

Big burly builders in vests and plaster-splattered jeans seemed to make up the majority of the population. They were everywhere. Pushing the wheelbarrows. Driving the trucks. Digging and building and laughing and smoking. Every now and then some other people – tanned women wearing cut-off jeans or long skirts and matching men in white T-shirts and blue jeans – hurried by with the distracted air of creative artists.

Tommy was sitting having tea with his crew when we arrived. He jumped up and shook hands warmly with us. Then he introduced us to the two brickies and three gardeners that he'd brought from Limerick to build the Fairy Fort. He gave us tea in enamel mugs and showed us their progress to date. The garden space was marked out and he'd already planted a small circle of whitethorn bushes, to 'create the nucleus' as he said.

Ian arrived while we were drinking our tea, refusing some himself. A wise move, I decided: I'd burned my lips in at least three places from the rim of the enamel mug. He and I had a quick discussion and decided to begin the collection of interviews we'd need for our documentary by interviewing Tommy's crew.

That was a good idea in theory. In practice, however, it was a disaster. Twenty minutes later, Ian and I took a short walk to try to regroup. Steve was helping to plant some cowslips by then so he paid no attention to our departure.

'How many minutes altogether do you think we got there?' I asked as Ian and I sidled past a man who was somehow carrying a twenty-foot conifer.

'Four – five max.'

'Jesus Christ,' I said, picking pine needles from my hair. 'Did they think we were going to steal their souls if they talked to us?'

Ian smiled.

'I don't know what we're going to tell Sophie if this keeps happening – I mean, I can't actually make a radio documentary out of a series of grunts and "yeah" and "no" and "I don't know".'

'Well, you know the fat guy – what's his name? Kevin?'

I nodded. 'I think so – the stonemason?'

'Yeah – he said that the fans would be arriving tomorrow. Maybe some of those might be better.'

'Jesus, I hope so. What kind of people are fans of a gardener?' I asked.

'I don't know,' Ian said, with a grin. '*They*'re probably wondering what kind of people are fans of a football team who never win anything.'

I narrowed my eyes and looked accusingly at him. 'I never knew you were a United fan – you snake in the grass.'

He laughed. 'Chelsea.'

'It's a wonder that Shane hasn't fired you, so. Anyway, what are we going to do about this bloody documentary?'

Ian looked thoughtful. 'Maybe we could do a bit about the other gardens and a bit about Chelsea in general.'

'OK, that's not a bad idea – we'll need some background . . .'

'I'm glad you said that – as it happens I did Google a little in my brother's house.'

'You're a star, Ian.'

He grinned. 'Did you know that it takes 800 people three and a half weeks to set up the show?'

'I didn't.'

'It's true. Also, did you know that over the five days of the Chelsea Flower Show they consume – on average – 6,500 bottles of champagne, 18,000 glasses of Pimms, 5,000 lobsters, 110,000 cups of tea and coffee, and 28,000 rounds of sandwiches?'

I laughed. 'How in the name of God did you remember that?'

'I'm good with numbers – what else do you want to know?'

'I've no idea – what's in that place over there?' I pointed towards a huge white building with a glass roof.

'That's the Great Pavilion – they launch new species of plants there,' Ian said.

'Cool – I wonder if they have anything good.'

'Like what?'

I shrugged. 'I don't know – maybe a plant that eats United fans?'

'Ha ha – we're getting desperate now.'

Just then we were joined by Steve who was full of

excitement about working with the land. I made a face behind his back at Ian and we all agreed that we'd exhausted the possibilities at the garden and might as well go to LFM to have a look at the studio.

LFM was a very successful local station but it was situated in the most unprepossessing building imaginable. From the outside it looked like an aircraft hangar but inside it was fitted with state-of-the-art broadcasting equipment. Ian was in his element as he was shown around and all he kept saying was, 'Man – Shane'd love this' as he looked at one technological wonder after another.

Sophie had managed to get local dj Ciara Thompson to take my show for two days and I was hoping to be back, broadcasting into Limerick from LFM, the next day. Steve had been harder to replace – Sophie had let John Howard take over the drive-time show the day before while we'd been travelling. Steve was anxious not to miss a second show and good-naturedly hustled until everything was set up for his broadcast at five.

In public Steve and I stayed far away from each other. He sort of initiated it by suddenly changing from the tender attentive lover into a polite but distant work colleague once we'd arrived at the Chelsea Flower Show. I was a bit disconcerted at first but then I told myself that he was probably thinking that we should present as professional a face as possible. Personally, I was finding it hard to stay away from him but I also figured that he was probably right. I talked to Ian about my show for the next day

and then headed off to have a wander around and
see if I could find anything of particular interest that
I might cover during the three days when I'd be
broadcasting from London. Cities are strange places,
full and empty at the same time. For example, I always
find at first when I walk along the streets in London
that it all seems to be a bit of a blur of humanity.
Everybody is completely focused on rushing towards
whatever their destination happens to be. This is
particularly true in areas like Oxford Street and
Kensington.

So to begin with on that day I was overwhelmed
and moved from one Starbucks to another, drinking
coffee and despairing about my show. Gradually,
though, I began to see the individuals around me:
my fascination grew as I could discern the city's diver-
sity beginning to emerge from what at first looked
like an undifferentiated sea of people.

By the time I returned to The Hampshire I had
managed to find three ex-Shaolin monks, a Romanian
fire-eater, and an elderly Irish man who'd slept on
the streets of London since he'd emigrated there from
Roscommon in the nineteen-sixties. I'd also found a
really good band called Fulcrum playing at the
entrance to Sloane Square Tube station. In the lift
there I could have sworn that I saw Jude Law but
when I texted Sophie she said I was having hallucinations.

Back at the guest house as I stepped out of the
shower, my head full of Steve and wondering where
he was, I heard my mobile phone signal the arrival of

a text message. I wrapped a towel around me and tried not to run – it could have been anybody, for God's sake. Sophie was probably still teasing me about seeing Jude Law. It could be my mother wondering if I was still depilating. Or it might be Steve. I picked up the phone with damp hands and read the message.

Hello Sexy.

I dropped the towel and did a little dance, then sat down on the bed and wrote:

You're pretty sexy yourself.

I pressed the send button. Then I slathered on some moisturiser and dressed in the linen suit that Sophie had made me buy. Just as I was emptying the contents of my make-up bag onto the dressing table the text alert sounded again.

Glad you think so. I'll be seeing you.

I read the message and wondered what the second part meant. Had Steve left? It was all a bit odd. I looked at my watch. It was after eight. Surely he should be back from doing his show? My stomach rumbled loudly. I hadn't eaten anything solid since breakfast so, Steve or no Steve, I was going to have to go in search of real food. Just then there was a knock on the door.

'Room service,' a man's voice said.

I opened the door, sure that I hadn't ordered anything but half hoping it might actually be a man with a tray of food. Instead it was Steve. He stepped straight in, grabbed me and kissed me long and hard. My body felt as if it was melting inside my clothes. Steve planted tiny kisses along my throat and I groaned.

'This beats any room service I've ever had before,' I muttered. 'However, good and all as the service is in this hotel, I'm starving and I want my dinner first. Otherwise I'll wilt away and not have the energy to . . . let me see . . . I know . . . to enjoy . . . your . . . ah . . . delivery.'

Steve stepped back and grinned. He looked me up and down.

'You look gorgeous,' he said, sitting down on the bed.

I made myself go back to the dressing table and opened my mascara. 'So now as well as delivering room service you're also bringing me the compliments of the hotel?'

He laughed and threw a discarded T-shirt at me.

'How did your show go?' I said, dabbing at a mascara blob with a piece of tissue.

'Good, really good,' he said, lying back on the bed. 'Unbelievable studio – it's positively space-age.'

'Great,' I said, giving up on the make-up. Hunger was spoiling my concentration. 'Have you eaten?'

'No, of course not.'

'OK, come on, then. I saw a Malaysian place when I was coming back a while ago – it's close by.'

Steve tried to pull me onto the bed with him. But, tempted as I was by the prospect of a roll in the hay, I was also really starving.

The Malaysian restaurant was wonderful. The decor was all soft lights and gentle eerie music while the food was sweet and hot at the same time. I loved it. As soon as I had eaten, my other appetites began to resurface and Steve and I barely managed to keep our hands off each other as we paid our bill and hurried back to my room. After some frenzied love-making we lay wrapped around each other in the dark. Outside the window the London traffic rumbled by and I could hear Steve's heart beating against my cheek. I was just dozing off to sleep when he spoke.

'Put your telephone number in my phone in the morning, will you?' he mumbled in a sleepy voice.

'Mmm. OK.'

I readjusted my position to make myself more comfortable. Then I remembered. I sat up and looked at him.

'You have my number. You sent me texts earlier.'

Steve shook his head but didn't open his eyes. 'It wasn't me, babe – I wanted to call you but I realised I didn't have your number.'

'Shit,' I said as I lay back down and snuggled close.

'What?'

'Nothing,' I said, suppressing a vague sense of unease that was beginning to grow inside me. 'I'm sure it's nothing really.'

17

I didn't think about my stalker the next day – I didn't get a chance, really, because all hell broke loose in the Limerick camp at the Chelsea Flower Show. Steve and I arrived at the gardens at nine a.m. We were nearly run over by an army of delivery trucks.

'Jesus,' I said, jumping out of the way. 'This place is a total building site – I can't see it being transformed into anything decent by tonight when the judges arrive.'

'I believe from speaking with the gardeners that it always looks like this and then – hey presto! It's suddenly the biggest, most influential flower show in the world.'

'Mmm,' I said, stepping around a heap of gravel that had been abandoned on the pathway.

Ian was already at the Fairy Fort when we arrived and he was surrounded by a trio of middle-aged women who were obviously Tommy Sloane's famous fans. Obvious because of the identical T-shirts that all of them wore. The fronts of the T-shirts were emblazoned with the slogan *Tommy Sloane – out on his own* while the backs bore the legend *The Road to Chelsea*.

And it would have all been grand except that the

women were in the middle of a slagging match with
the garden opposite – a space-age job with a Japanese
twist.

Ian shrugged at me as the women hurled insults
at Tommy's rival. Then they began a loud chant of
'Tommy Sloane out on his own' while giving the
bemused onlooking English gardeners the middle
finger. Ian started laughing but good old Steve took
the situation in hand.

'Ladies, ladies, ladies,' he said as he stood in front
of them, his hands up in the air like a referee in the
middle of a brawl.

The women stopped their chanting and looked at
him. Then they began to nudge each other as they
recognised his face.

A small round woman with short streaked blonde
hair spoke first. 'You're him, aren't you?'

Steve smiled charmingly at his now-captive audience. 'Depends on who "he" is,' he said, with a grin.

'Steve Lowe, the RTE fella?' another older woman
with a pierced eyebrow said.

Steve nodded. 'Now, ladies, we have to keep the
Limerick flag flying here at Chelsea so let's not needle
the others . . .'

'Who do they think they are, anyway?' the blonde
woman interjected, winding the other women up as
she did so.

'Diarmuid Gavin my arse with his space garden –
I know the space where that came from,' said Pierced
Eyebrow and they all erupted into raucous laughter.

'They're running scared, all right – trying to tell

us that Tommy Sloane is gone home, cheek of them,'
said Blondie.

My ears pricked up at the mention of this and I
looked at an uncharacteristically worried Ian. 'Looks
like it might be true. The crew said his bed in the
B&B was empty this morning.'

'Did they try his mobile?' I asked.

Ian nodded. 'Yep. And they heard it ringing in his
bedroom.'

'Uh-oh,' said Steve, shaking his head. The women
suddenly looked concerned.

'Where are they now?' I asked.

'Who?' said Ian.

'The workers, of course,' I said, a hint of annoy-
ance in my voice. Tommy Sloane does a bloody runner
just hours before Judgement Day at Chelsea. What
kind of a radio programme would *that* make?

'They're gone across the road to the Horse and
Anchor.'

'Fuck,' I said out loud.

'Fuck's sake, what'll we do if he's really gone?'
said Blondie and then everyone was talking and
swearing at the same time. A Diarmuid Gavin fan
shouted something at us and Steve had to restrain
Blondie as she tried to bolt across the gravelled path.
Jesus, I never realised that the Chelsea Flower
Show could be such a dangerous place and that fans
could be so seriously bonkers – give me football any
day.

'Everybody shut up,' shouted Steve eventually and
it worked.

'I'll go get the crew and we'll look for Tommy,' he said.

'We're coming, too – poor Tommy, no wonder he did a runner, having to look at that space-age crap for the past few days,' said Blondie in a loud voice, her hands on her ample hips.

I looked helplessly at Steve. This was turning into a disaster.

'Do you think maybe . . . naw . . . he wouldn't . . .' said Pierced Eyebrow.

The third woman, a slim, quiet brunette with old eyes, continued the dialogue. 'He might have . . . the pressure gets to him, you know . . .'

Steve nodded sagely. 'Poor Tommy, shoots himself in the foot just as things are working out for him.'

'What do you mean?' I asked.

The women looked at me as if I was stupid and rolled their eyes at each other. Ian shrugged and Steve looked thoughtfully into the distance.

'On the sauce,' said Blondie eventually.

'Off the wagon,' said Pierced Eyebrow.

'Back on the bottle,' said the quiet brunette.

Realisation dawned on me then and, selfish bitch that I was, all I could think about was my show.

'What will we do now?' I asked Steve.

He shook his head slowly, his eyes dark with concern. 'I'm his sponsor, you know. I let him down.'

'No, you didn't,' I said.

'I'm going to look for him. I'll take the lads with me – they might have some idea of the kind of places Tommy might haunt,' said Steve.

'The London Eye,' announced Ian, rooting in his jacket pocket and taking out a bunch of vouchers.

'What?' everyone said.

Ian smiled. 'LFM – the radio station – gave me a bunch of vouchers. Some corporate gig fell through.'

I barely listened as he spoke. My head was already buzzing with the idea of me and these Limerick women on the London Eye. I could get live soundbites as we rotated and I had a feeling that this bunch were a lot more talkative than Tommy's crew.

'Ian, I could kiss you,' I said, punching him on the arm.

'Feel free,' he said, smiling.

Steve checked his watch. 'See you later, ladies.' He bowed low, winked at them and was gone.

A tiny part of me was peeved that he hadn't even made eye contact with me as he left. I didn't expect a big goodbye but some private acknowledgement would have been nice. But then again, maybe this was the way to handle it in public?

'So, can I tempt you all with the ride of your lives?' I said to my three women.

'I wouldn't mind a ride. What about you, Vera? You must be dying for one, with your fella complaining of brewer's droop,' said Blondie, provoking a cacophony of laughter. Ian and I smiled at each other. It was going to be a mad day.

And that's exactly the way it was. We arrived at the ticket office of the London Eye to discover that LFM had booked a private champagne capsule for their no-show guests. The women – who were Eileen

(Blondie), Vera (Pierced Eyebrow) and the quiet Alice – were on high-doh once they heard about our exclusive capsule.

'140 metres high,' said Ian as we climbed inside. My stomach did a little somersault in anticipation and I wondered if I had any of the travel-sickness tablets in my bag.

'It carries over 15,000 passengers each day and you can see twenty-five miles in each direction,' said Ian but nobody was listening. I was too busy rooting in my handbag for drugs and the women were sharing a silver flask of something that definitely wasn't tea.

'But it's not the tallest structure in London,' he continued as the women oohed and aahed and my stomach began a little ceilidh.

'It's the sixth tallest. Know how many tons of steel were used to—Are you all right, Jamie?' Ian asked. 'You look kinda . . . green.'

'Travel sickness,' I said as Vera popped open the first of the two complimentary bottles of champagne.

'But we haven't even moved yet . . . wait . . . hang on . . . we're off at last,' he said and walked to the glass wall of the capsule, where Vera insisted he took a glass of champagne. She came over to me.

'What's wrong, love?' she asked. 'Wait, don't tell me: travel sick?'

I nodded.

'I've the very thing. Miracle drug – don't mind all that shit they give you in the chemist. Try this,' she said as she produced a box from her patent leather handbag and pressed a tiny pill from its foil bubble.

I took the pill and washed it down with champagne – not a good idea but I had a show to do. I realised as I swallowed the pill that I'd just taken an unknown drug from a practically unknown woman. But anything at that point was better than puking all over the London Eye.

And it must have been a miracle drug because it began to work almost immediately. I began to feel better and better and pressed my face against the glass wall, like the rest of the group. The view was stunning and I was delighted to see that Ian had our high-tech tape recorder on as the Limerick women gave a hilarious running commentary on our 'flight' as the attendants had called it when we'd boarded. This will make excellent radio, I thought as we finally reached the summit. The giant wheel stuttered to a full stop then and we all looked at each other.

'Is this a scheduled stop?' I asked.

'Feels like one of those CIE train stops to me – you know, the ones where they stop in the middle of nowhere and don't tell you why or nothing,' said Alice, slugging back her fizzy wine.

The minutes ticked by. My head was floaty from whatever drug I'd taken. I knew that somewhere in my brain that I should be panicking but I didn't have the wherewithal to manage it.

Then the women started a sing-song – 'Long Way to Tipperary' followed by 'Limerick, You're a Lady'.

'Is there any intercom yoke on these things?' I asked Ian in between songs.

He shook his head as someone started singing 'The

Fields of Athenry'. The two bottles of champagne were empty and now all the women had silver flasks in their hands.

'There used to be a commentary piped into all thirty-two capsules but the clients said it interrupted the tranquillity of the flight – you know, the views and stuff – so they disabled it,' said Ian.

'We could be here all night,' I said, taking out my mobile. There was no signal. I couldn't believe that we were so bloody far up and yet we didn't have a signal. 'What if we're stuck here?'

Ian shrugged and the women laughed.

'Might as well enjoy it, love, sure there's nothing we can do from up here,' said Alice, taking out cigarettes and offering them around. I was sorely tempted even though I was a non-smoker.

'I need to pee,' said Alice. 'My bladder is weak since I had the jukebox out.'

'Nothing to do with all that champagne, of course,' said Eileen, laughing.

'Well, fuck me pink,' said Vera, looking south over the river towards Westminster Bridge. 'I don't believe my eyes – is that who I think it is?'

We all followed her gaze. I couldn't see anything or anyone unusual on the bridge.

'Well, knock me down with a feather – it's him, all right. And what's he dragging with him?' said Eileen. 'Jesus Christ – it's a goat. What is Tommy Sloane doing dragging a goat across Westminster Bridge?'

18

We were eventually rescued from the London Eye and I even got a manager to record a piece about the malfunction, with the women interjecting as I interviewed him. He gave us all free vouchers for another 'flight' on the Eye but I knew that the one we'd just had would be my one and only time.

We took the Tube back to Chelsea, all of us hoping that Tommy was heading that way. I phoned Steve en route, a thrill running up my spine as I saw his name for the first time on my screen. It looked like it belonged there. There was no answer so I left a garbled message about Tommy, a goat and Westminster Bridge.

The Royal Hospital was really buzzing now as Judgement Hour approached and I had to admit that Steve had been right: the change in the place was impressive. Though there were still lots of trucks and hordes of harassed-looking gardeners in hi-vis vests running to and fro, by and large everything was taking shape. We passed beautiful model gardens as we made our way to Tommy's Fairy Fort. He'll be hard-pressed to win with this lot, I thought, but I had the foresight not to say it out loud. Tommy's fan base might be small but they were militant in the extreme.

'There he is . . . Tommy . . . yoo-hoo,' shouted Vera as we rounded the corner of a gravel path. Tommy was sitting on some leftover bricks. A black billy goat with ferocious-looking horns stood near him, eating popcorn from a bag. He had a bright orange clothes-line rope tied around his neck and it trailed the ground.

'Where did you go, Tommy? We were worried sick – there's a search party and all gone out to look for you,' said Eileen.

'Nice T-shirts, girls,' said Tommy, smiling up at us from his makeshift seat.

'What's with the goat?' I asked.

Tommy gazed into the sky for a minute. 'I was awake all night trying to put my finger on it . . .'

'On what?' said Vera and the women giggled.

'I just knew in my heart there was something missing – you know, like the final piece of a jigsaw. And then it just came to me. Just as the sky was getting light it came to me.'

'The goat?' I asked.

Tommy looked at the billy goat, who was busy eating the now-empty popcorn bag. 'This is Knacker. Isn't he just perfect?'

We all looked at Knacker and then at Tommy.

'Know how he got his name?' Tommy asked us, smiling.

I was beginning to think that Tommy was seriously losing the plot. We all shook our heads.

'He ran away from the knacker's yard four times. Imagine that! Snatched himself from the jaws of death four times!' said Tommy, glancing lovingly at the goat.

'Wow,' I said.

'Jesus,' said the women in unison.

'I'm starving,' said Ian.

Steve and the lads arrived then. I sneaked a look at Steve as he and Tommy greeted each other like they'd been separated since birth. We heard the whole goat story again. How Tommy was enlightened at dawn, knew the goat was the final pièce de résistance, how he (Tommy, not the goat) walked all the way to Streatham, to a group of travellers living on the edge of the common, and how he bought Knacker for twenty quid.

Steve finally made eye contact with me and smiled briefly before turning his attention back to Tommy.

'I have an idea,' Steve said and beamed at all of us. 'I'm doing my show in an hour but afterwards let's all meet up for a bite to eat. A team night out before the big day tomorrow.'

'Brilliant,' said Vera and Alice. Eileen didn't answer – she was too busy giving Diarmuid Gavin filthy looks as he inspected his completed garden. I smiled and waved at him, in an effort to dissipate any bad feeling, and Eileen turned her evil eye on me.

We agreed to meet up in a small restaurant called Food Et Al. It was directly opposite LFM radio station and we were already seated at a large table near the window when Steve arrived. I'd managed to race back to The Hampshire and shower and change. I wore a trouser suit, a tight blue halter top (chest supplemented by the now-obligatory Wonderbra and chicken fillets) and fitted pants. Sophie had insisted that I wear trouser knickers with this outfit and I was particularly pleased with myself for remembering that fine detail.

But the three women had outdone me by a mile – was everybody just better than me at the Girl Thing? Gone were their T-shirts and tracksuit bottoms in favour of sparkly tops and skirts in the most lurid of colours. Vera wore a loud peach diamond-encrusted job with a plunging neckline and a short skirt. I didn't know what the material was, just that it was synthetic and shiny. The others wore varietals of the same outfit, one in a lime green, the other in blinding pink. All of them wore eyeshadow up to their eyebrows in hues that matched the colours of their outfits exactly. Their clothes and make-up mightn't have been to everybody's taste but for all that they pulled it off with confident panache. Tommy actually surprised me the most – he wore a pinstripe suit and tie and had gelled his long hair into a ponytail. He looked great – bonkers, but great.

But I couldn't take my eyes off Steve as soon as he sat down next to Vera. He regaled the table with stories of RTE and programmes gone wrong and I felt that Tommy's fan base was seriously under threat. The girls didn't give their gardener a second look all night. They were far too busy hanging on Steve's every word. I made an effort at small talk with Ian that lasted all of a minute before he resorted to texting furiously on his phone.

Tommy told me over again all about the goat and

how inspirational animals were in gardens. I smiled and nodded and for the hundredth time that day I thought about the delicious sex I'd had last night and shivered at the prospect of more. Tommy described what a proper snowdrop drift should look like and I nodded knowingly and tuned out. That was a mistake because as soon as I did the stalker popped uninvited into my head. If I was honest with myself I would've had to admit that he was beginning to spook me a little and the fact that I'd accidentally replied to his text last night really bothered me. I'll sort it out when I got home, change my number and that'd be that, I thought as snatches of conversations wafted around me.

Finally the evening was over and we said our good-byes and see-you-tomorrows. I jumped into a taxi, dragging Steve with me. As soon as the taxi joined the long snakelike line of London traffic we started to kiss, our hands exploring, our breath quickening. We reached The Hampshire and Steve hurriedly paid the driver. As he did so I hugged him from behind, my hands under his T-shirt.

We ran into the guest house and up the stairs, laughing and tearing at each other's clothes, just making it through the door of my bedroom. We didn't even bother to undress, we just did it urgently and frantic-ally and with no frills attached. Afterwards, as I lay for the third night in a row in Steve's arms, I felt whole and complete and happy and sated for the first time ever in my life. Well, maybe the second time – but Bill didn't count. As I drifted off to sleep I wished that we could stay in London in this wonderful time-warped first flush of love. It was so special and I didn't want the harsh reality of everyday life in Limerick to destroy it. It wasn't robust enough yet for that.

We arrived next morning to the Chelsea Flower Show press day in glorious spring sunshine. I dressed in a slinky crop-top and matching combats (Karen Millen, Sophie had informed me – it took me a while to work out that she was a designer, and not the girl in the shop that I thought I knew from school). I felt great. Sex first thing every morning beat orange juice hands down and the thought of spending another whole day with Steve near me sent an adrenalin rush through my body. I smiled at him now as we walked together through the foliage and flowers and bustle of the Show.

'The queen is away,' Steve said. 'Only the third time she's missed the Show in its history. She's sending Edward and Sophie.'

'No shit,' I said, thumping him on the arm. 'I wonder – would they give me an interview?'

'You haven't observed the proper protocol – submitted your questions and all that.'

I sighed. Sometimes Steve could be a bit pedantic. 'I know that, Steve but surely if I jumped out from behind a bush with my microphone?'

'You'd be shot by the Special Branch,' he said, laughing.

'Yes, but think of the posthumous prizes the documentary would win.'

We heard the Limerick team before we saw them.

'So what are you going to do about it? Arrest the goat?' a woman's voice screeched. As we rounded the corner at a sprint I could see that the voice belonged to Eileen and that a fracas of some sort was in full swing at the Fairy Fort. It included the Limerick contingent, a couple of policemen, some irate English people and somebody in an Animal Welfare T-shirt. Vera saw us first and came flying down the gravel path, her chest almost hitting her in the face as she ran.

'You'll never guess what happened. The goat went mad in a few of the show gardens,' she said, her breath catching in her throat. 'Jesus, I'll have to give up the fags.'

'Oh my God . . .' Steve said.

'Knacker got loose during the night and . . .'

'Oh no, the Fairy Fort is ruined . . .' Steve said.

Vera smiled and winked. 'That's the funny thing. He didn't touch the Fairy Fort. But he had a real thing for Diarmuid Gavin's space garden.'

'Oh, Oh,' I said as we approached the mêlée. I glanced over at the space garden. The Japanese twist was gone completely, every last leaf eaten as a midnight snack by Knacker. There was a little hill of what looked like brown pebbles at the feet of a fat Buddha statue in the far corner of the plot. Goat shit, I thought as I surveyed the damage and tried to assess the anger levels of the irate crowd. Steve was trying to calm everybody down. Ian was sitting in the sun on a small bench in the garden next door, which Knacker had thoughtfully avoided.

'Where's the goat?' I asked. Everybody stopped talking and looked at me.

'Under the judges' table. He refuses to come out,' said the Animal Welfare guy. Clever of him, I thought as I watched the baying crowd.

'I'll go and see what can be done,' said Steve. 'Maybe the damage isn't that bad. We can all pitch in to help.'

'Poor Diarmuid – he'll be devastated, you know. He's on his way, stuck in traffic in Knightsbridge,' said a Diarmuid fan, a grey-haired woman in a pink kaftan.

'I know I tied that goat up last night – I even double-checked,' said Tommy, shaking his head.

'You should bow out of the competition – it'd be the right thing to do after sabotaging the other gardens,' said another grey-haired woman.

'Rise out of me this minute,' said Vera, chest out, hands on hips. 'The main judging was done yesterday and nobody let the goat out on purpose. That's an awful thing to say, isn't it, Jamie? I hope you're getting all these accusations on tape.'

'Now, now, calm down,' said a young policeman. We all looked at him, which made him turn bright red instantly.

Steve arrived back, smiling broadly. 'It's definitely OK. The judges are aware of what happened but they did their final inspection last night before Knacker went walkies. They decided on a winner when everything was still shipshape.'

'Well?' said Eileen. 'Who is it?'

Steve smiled and shook his head. 'They're announcing the winner at noon. We'll make the evening flight home,' he said, smiling over at me. I smiled back but I didn't mean it. I wasn't ready to go home. Not at all.

Diarmuid Gavin turned out to be dead sound about his half-eaten garden and did a great piece with me and Ian for my show. And at noon we all gathered in front of the judges' table. (Knacker had finally been removed and taken to some animal shelter – he was probably heading back to Streatham already.)

The place was chock-a-block with celebrities – not that any of them would agree to talk to me. The royals were surrounded permanently by minders who were trying to blend in with the crowd but since they looked more like bouncers than flower arrangers they weren't doing a very good job. I followed Ringo Starr for a while but his agent wouldn't let me near him. Finally I managed to get an interview with Ainsley Harriot who showed me how to crush garlic with my hand.

Then it was the moment of reckoning. There was a palpable air of excitement as the judges made their speeches and the magic envelope was produced. Diarmuid Gavin (luckily, as far as I was concerned) won the Show Garden Gold Medal. Vera and the girls had to be restrained by Ian and Steve but they soon changed their tune when Tommy's name as winner of the Silver-Gilt Flora medal was announced. A riot from the Limerick camp ensued which we caught full-blast on tape, Steve doing a great voice-over as the back-slapping and champagne-cork popping crescendoed.

I heard shouts of 'Fix!' and 'Where's the goat?' in the background but they were drowned out by the sheer volume of the celebration. Steve winked at me over the heads of the Tommy fans. I smiled back at him, suddenly sad that it was all over. The Road to Chelsea had turned out to be a very special journey for me. I didn't want it to be over. Ever.

19

The flight home was uneventful and I felt like a completely different person to the one who had flown out of Shannon just a few short days before. OK, I was travel-sick and drugged, that was the same. And my knees were in my mouth on the plane, that too was the same. But in my heart I was different – like I'd made a real connection with someone for the first time in years. As we approached Shannon reality nibbled into my love cocoon like a hungry rat. A parade of faces popped up in front of my drug-addled brain. My mother with a make-up palette, Sophie with her narrowed questioning eyes, Bill with his arrogant disapproving air, Conor in the park, my stalker in the guise of a dark shadow. Jesus, I'll have to give up the drugs I thought as we came to a bumpy stop on Irish soil.

We all shared a taxi from the airport and I was disappointed when Steve sat in the front, chatting away to the driver. Ian and I didn't even attempt to make small talk – we'd used up our quota of that in London. I was dropped off first and I felt lonely as I waved the cab goodbye and opened my front door. He could have sat next to me, I thought as I dumped my small suitcase at the bottom of the stairs and switched on the lights. He could have come in with me, had some coffee, had some sex even. He mustn't feel the same way I do if he can go running home without a second thought.

I went to the fridge and opened it. There was a gourmet hamper inside filled with the most delicious deli treats – stuffed olives, hummus, cheeses, exotic fruit. Jesus, this couldn't belong to Shane, I thought as I examined the hamper. It was open so I got a plate and helped myself. I sat at the kitchen table and tried to eat myself into a better mood. I heard Shane's key in the lock and prayed that Heather wasn't with him. God heard me.

'Jamie!' he said as he came into the kitchen and gave me a quick hug.

'Delicious food,' I said through a mouthful of feta cheese.

'Glad you like it. Came this morning with this card. Stalker, I think,' he said, tossing me a plain white card with the words *Welcome Home* printed neatly across the centre. Shane had his back to me and was leaning into the fridge in his typical pose.

'How was London? The shows were excellent, Soph was dead happy,' continued Shane as I tried to digest the big lump of stalker cheese that had stuck in my oesophagus.

'Stalker food?' I said when I regained my swallow.

Shane turned around and smiled. 'Yeah.'

'Why didn't you throw it out?' I said.

Shane laughed. 'I can't throw out good food – my mother would kill me.'

'Your mother wouldn't know and it's stalker food – tainted.'

Shane broke off a lump of feta and popped it into his mouth, grimacing as he chewed. 'Jesus, give me Calvita any day.'

Tears streamed down my face. Shane pulled up a chair and took my hand in his.

'Fuck the stalker, Jamie. Don't let him get to you – he's only a little fart.' He handed me a tea towel to wipe my eyes.

'It's not him,' I said.

'What is it, so? What's up?'

I began to cry again and I poured out my heart to Shane and swore him to secrecy in the process.

'You're not saying anything,' I said when I finished my long and winding tale.

'What can I say, Jamie? You're a big girl, you know your own mind.'

'And what about Sophie's line, that Steve has more baggage than a Ryanair flight?'

Shane looked at me and smiled. 'Sophie is carrying a lot of baggage herself these days.'

I nodded and began eating stalker food again. My appetite had returned after the chat with Shane.

'There's one thing, though, Jamie. Steve hasn't got a clue about football. Hates it, actually – he told me that last week in the station.'

I laughed. 'So? We have loads in common still . . .'

'Like what?' Shane picked up a mango and began to slice it.

'Well . . .' I struggled to think of exactly what Steve

and I had in common besides lust, 'we both think *Apocalypse Now* is the best movie ever.' I looked at him triumphantly.

Shane laughed. 'Perfect foundation for a lasting relationship – it's in all the self-help books.'

'Smart-arse. And anyway, Mr Ali, what do you and the wonderful Heather have in common?'

Shane didn't answer for a minute. 'OK, let's see – we both like Indian food. And Taytos, we both love Taytos. And, of course, Titbit – who, by the way, has taken a fancy to sleeping in your bed since you went to London . . .'

'Gross! Anyway, Heather hates football too.'

'True. And that's why I'm trying to warn you – if you're going to bother your arse falling in love, then do it with a fellow fan. Makes life simple, that's all.' He smiled at me and winked. 'We should have got it together, Jamie, do you know that?'

I laughed. 'Sounds incestuous.'

'I'm actually not a blood relative. And think of the peace we'd have – Sky Sports all weekend, we could take our holidays around the football calendar, go to matches all the time . . .'

'Too boring. It'd be like having a relationship with myself.'

Shane laughed. 'You have a point. But I see many attractions to the arrangement.'

I got up and stretched my tired body. 'I'm wrecked. I'm off to bed.'

He got up too. 'All that sex is exhausting – now you know why I'm always tired.'

'Shut up, you cheeky thing. You swore you'd keep it to yourself.'

Shane followed me out of the kitchen, up the stairs and into my bedroom.

'Go away,' I said pushing him out of the room.

'I'm just collecting the dog, you eejit,' he said, grinning at me.

I didn't see Steve the next day until after my show and then I only got a wave from him as he entered his office and closed the door. I'd given Sophie a brief account of the events in London, professional and personal, and I was glad when she was called away to a meeting with the directors. I knew by the way she narrowed her eyes during the conversation that she had something to say about all of it.

I sat in my doorless office for the afternoon and worked on ideas for forthcoming shows – I had a lot of preparation to catch up on and I was glad of the opportunity to lose myself in some good hard work. Shane, the little sweetheart, brought me a take-out cappuccino late in the afternoon. My mobile began to bleat. I looked at the name flashing on the screen – Dermot Kilbane. My heart did a cartwheel in my chest.

'Dermot?'

'Hi, Jamie, how are you? I heard you were in London.'

'Any news?'

There was a pause on the end of the line, followed by wheezing.

'Dermot? Can you hear me? Are you all right?'

More wheezing, building up to a crescendo.

'Dermot, are you OK?'

The wheezing began to ease off and I could hear an inhaler being used.

'I'm grand. Just couldn't get my breath there for a second. The old asthma gets bad sometimes. Pollutants in the air, I think.'

'So, what's the news?' I was bursting with curiosity but tried to keep my voice steady.

'Well . . . look . . . could you drop into the office – say, around five? I've something I'd like you to see.'

'What is it? Tell me now.'

'No, not over the phone. Come around at five and we'll talk properly.'

'Is it good or bad? At least tell me that.'

Dermot wheezed and I worried that another asthma attack was under way.

'It depends on the way you look at it. Just come to the office, Jamie, and we can have a chat. I'll see you at five,' he said and hung up. I dropped the mobile and took several deep breaths. My heart was thumping and for some reason I was certain that he'd found Conor and maybe the bad news was that Conor didn't remember us or that he was in jail or . . . I realised that my body was shaking. Before I had time to think properly my phone rang again.

'Hello?'

'Jamie, I know you're probably busy but I can't get hold of Marielouise – do you think Fiona would like the new *Sims* game for her birthday?'

'Bill . . . Bill, I think he found Conor.' It was out before I'd engaged my brain.

'Who did?'

'Dermot Kilbane and I've to meet him at five in his office and what will we do if there's something seriously wrong because there must be something wrong if he disappeared in the first place and—'

'Jamie, where are you and what are you talking about?'

'At work, and I'm talking about Dermot. He's the private investigator I hired to look for Conor.'

'The what?'

'The PI I hired. He's really good, an ex-Garda detective . . .'

'You're not serious.'

I stopped. Why the hell had I told him? Some sort of insane reflex? 'I'm deadly serious – and, actually, goodbye.'

I hung up the phone and swallowed back tears. What kind of timing was that? Of all the people to ring me when I was upset after Dermot's call, it had to be Bill Hehir. Bastard know-all. I picked up my coffee, stood by my doorway and drank it, even though it was cold by now. I had a surreptitious peep around the station to see if there was any sign of Steve but I knew he was psyching himself up in his office for his show. That was his usual routine and he didn't like to be disturbed, which as a fellow presenter I totally understood.

I checked my watch. Four-thirty. I decided to head for Dermot's place and went to gather my belongings. I was bending down to pick up a stray file when I heard Bill's voice behind me.

'Jamie.'

I shot up too quickly and almost put my back out in the process.

'Bill?'

'Jamie, I'd like to go with you.'

I looked at him in his perfect suit, his hair cropped to within an inch of its life, his five o'clock shadow beginning to take over his face, and I had the usual urge to thump the head off him. This was swiftly followed by the sheer comfort of having someone to share the Conor burden with. Someone to share this dark can of worms that I'd recently reopened.

'Why?'

He didn't answer immediately. 'It's about Conor.'

I looked at him and I believed him. This was no time to be grinding axes.

'It's a free country,' I said as I shrugged and dumped files into my briefcase.

'Night, Dee-Dee, night, all,' I said as I walked out the doors of the radio station with Bill in pursuit.

20

'This is it?' Bill said incredulously as we pulled up outside Dermot's neat little semi with the garage extension.

'Yep,' I said and climbed out of Bill's Beemer and marched up to the front door. I knocked and Dermot answered.

'Hi, Dermot, this is Conor's business partner, Bill Hehir. Is it OK if he sits in?' I said.

'No problem, Jamie, come in, come in,' said Dermot as he moved his huge bulk from the door and led us into the 'office' extension. Bill and I sat on two plastic chairs and watched as Dermot lowered himself into his swivel chair. Sweat popped on his brow and he took out a large stripy hanky and wiped his forehead. Then he smiled at us.

'The old asthma acts up now and again,' he said.

'Did you find him?' I asked, unable to wait any longer.

Dermot steepled his fingers and shook his head. 'I'll show you what I *did* find, Jamie.' He leaned across the desk and picked up a videotape, then stood up and slipped the tape into TV/VCR combi that was mounted on the wall behind the desk. We all watched the screen as it flickered to life. My heart was thumping. The jerky black and white images became recognisable as CCTV footage of a department store: Boots – I could make out the logo. The ghostly images paraded – and then I saw him. I knew that Bill did too by his sharp intake of breath.

Conor was in a queue with other shoppers and at one stage looked directly into the camera. My eyes filled with tears as I looked at my brother's familiar face. He reached the cash desk and seemed to chat for a minute with the sales girl. He must have joked with her, because they both laughed as he walked away with his purchases. And then I noticed the date and time at the bottom right-hand corner of the screen. 16.25 p.m. 20/10/04.

'It's the day he disappeared,' I said as Conor walked out of the store and out of our lives. Dermot stopped the tape and sat down on the chair, which protested loudly.

'That was Boots at Heathrow.' He stopped and wiped his brow again. 'Twenty minutes after his flight had left for Shannon.'

'Jesus,' I said.

'How did you get the tape?' Bill asked. I looked at him: his face was ashen and drawn. I was glad that there was somebody with me to share these weird ghostly pictures of Conor. Even if it *was* Bill.

'I was lucky, really. I chanced my arm and asked around and then I discovered that Magma Security were the main security consultants in Terminal One and sure, Jack Maguire runs that company – I know

Jack from Gaelic football since we were knee-high . . .'

'But they never keep the tapes for so long, do they?' asked Bill.

Dermot shrugged. 'Depends on the company. Magma actually keep theirs for five years so we lucked out, really. Would ye like a cup of tea? I baked earlier. Fresh-cream roulade – new recipe . . .'

'No, thanks, we're fine, Dermot. What else did you find?' I asked.

'That's about it. *Nada* on every other front,' said Dermot, shaking his head.

'That's it?' I said.

'I'm sorry, Jamie. I never said this'd be easy. If somebody doesn't want to be found it's a mighty job to track 'em down,' said Dermot.

There was a knock on the door then and a pretty girl in her late teens put her head around the door. 'Sorry, Dad, will I turn down the chicken?'

'Down to 150, Holly, good girl,' said Dermot, smiling at her as she retreated.

'So, where to now?' I asked.

Dermot wheezed a little before answering. 'Conor's wife . . . um . . .'

'Marielouise,' I said.

'That's right. Marielouise. Do you think she'd mind meeting me, having a bit of a chat, a nose around?'

'I'll talk to her. I haven't told her yet that I hired you but I'm sure she'll agree,' I said, glancing at Bill. His face was unreadable.

'Right. You let me know the whens and wheres so,

Jamie,' Dermot said, raising his bulk from the chair and causing another batch of sweat to break out on his face. We shook hands and he escorted us out to the door.

I got into Bill's car and we drove in silence for a while. I checked my phone for messages but then I realised that Steve was on air so I flicked on the radio and tuned it away from Lyric FM and over to Fab City. Steve's delicious voice enveloped me like a silk throw on a rainy day. I was glad of the distraction. Glad to substitute memories of London with Steve for ghostly pictures of missing brothers. I relaxed into listening to the programme. Steve was talking about house prices and first-time buyers but it sounded so sexy.

'Hungry?' Bill asked without taking his eyes from the road.

'Starving, actually,' I said.

'Fancy a steak?'

'Why, have you got one in the car?'

Bill smiled at me. 'No. But I have two in the fridge at home.'

I debated in my head whether to go or not, while Steve's voice filled the silence in the car. In a way it felt right – in spite of everything Bill was the only other person on the planet who fully understood where I was at that moment in time. Not to mention the fact that it'd mean no cooking when I got home. And it'd fill in the time while I waited for Steve to finish his show and ring me. But most of all I didn't want to be alone: those Conor images were too disturbing.

'Sure,' I said, 'as long as you do the cooking.'

I made salad in Bill's operating-theatre kitchen while he fried steak in garlic. He'd put on opera on the super-duper stereo that piped music through to every room.

'So, what did you think of him?' I said as I chopped avocado with a knife so lethal that it could decapitate someone in one swift motion.

Bill had his back to me and was leaning over the stainless-steel six-ring cooker. 'Who?' he said.

'Who do you think? Dermot, of course.' I picked up a perfectly formed red pepper and began to chop that too.

'It's early days,' he said as he opened a bottle of wine and poured two glasses. 'Try that, Jamie. Sancerre – it's your favourite, isn't it?'

I took the glass and sipped the cold wine. 'So you've no comment to make at all?'

Bill leaned against the granite worktop and watched me as I chopped and chopped.

'You really do have a way with knives,' he said.

I grinned and continued my furious slicing and dicing.

'I don't know, Jamie, I don't know what to think – except that it was the weirdest thing, seeing Conor's face on that screen . . .' He paused and ran a hand through his hair.

'I know. I felt the same.'

Bill locked stares with me and I started to blush again. I looked away first. 'Those steaks are done.'

'Yeah, you're right,' he said as he served up the food. We sat at the breakfast bar and began to eat.

'What was he up to, Bill? What was Conor up to that day?' I asked after a few minutes of eating.

'That's the $64,000-dollar question, Jamie.' Bill put down his knife and fork and wiped his mouth with a white linen napkin. 'He gets driven to the airport, books himself on the flight, then goes off and does his shopping in Boots. I thought I knew this guy . . .'

'I thought I knew him too. Inside out. That CCTV footage makes it even stranger, doesn't it?'

He nodded. 'I'm glad I went with you.'

My eyes filled with tears and I tried to fight them back. A lump of steak had lodged in my throat and I picked up my glass of wine and took a large gulp.

'Hey? You OK?' Bill said reaching out a hand that stopped just short of touching mine.

'I'm fine. So, how's work?'

He pulled back his hand and began eating again. 'Same old same old. How are things for you? I heard the London shows – really good.'

'Thanks. London was terrific, actually.'

'Not a favourite city of mine. Give me Barcelona any day.'

'It depends who you're with, though, doesn't it?' I said, smiling at Bill. 'London was magic.'

'Met someone there, did you?' he asked casually.

'Maybe, maybe not.'

'You either did or you didn't, Jamie.'

'None of your business.'

'True, but I'm only making conversation – that's all.'

Just then my mobile rang and I jumped up to answer it.

'Babe, it's me. I just finished my show.'

'Steve, how are you?' I said, walking to the other end of the kitchen.

'Really tired. I'm in a terrible dilemma.'

'What's up?'

'I was going to call over to . . .'

'Please do. I'd love it . . .'

'Well, that's the dilemma. I miss you and I'd love to see you but I'm exhausted.'

'Oh. Right . . .'

'So could we do something tomorrow night?'

'Sure.'

'Brilliant, Jamie. See you tomorrow, so.'

'See you,' I said and hung up. I dumped my phone into my bag and smiled at Bill.

'I'm wrecked. I need my bed.'

'I'll drive you home.'

'There's no need, I'll walk – it's not that far.'

'I'll drive – but are you sure you won't stay? There's football on at nine o'clock.'

I shook my head. 'I'm beat and I have a heavy day tomorrow.'

'No problem – let me just find my keys,' he said.

We walked out to his car. A light mist was falling and again I had that feeling of depression that had enveloped me last night when I came back from London. We drove to my house in silence.

'Thanks,' I said as we pulled up outside. All the lights were off. I looked at Bill in the dusky half-light.

'You're welcome,' he said, his voice low.

'OK – see you,' I said and went to open the door.

I felt him looking at me so I turned to face him. He locked eyes with me, his face inches from mine, and then he leaned towards me as if he was going to kiss me.

'Goodnight, Jamie.'

I could smell his aftershave and something else – something animal and primal.

I turned away, hurriedly opened the car door and stumbled out. 'Night,' I muttered, fumbling for my keys in my handbag.

He waved and drove away and I was glad. Jesus, what in the name of God was *that* about? I asked myself as I opened the front door and almost fell over Titbit. Something kept rising to the surface of my subconscious and as I switched on lights and kicked Titbit out of the way and banged on the kettle I acknowledged it – I'd wanted him to kiss me. I'd wanted Bill Hehir to kiss me.

21

'That was incredible, Jamie,' Steve said as I rolled off him, both of us panting.

'I know,' I said, snuggling into him, our bodies hot and sweaty from sex.

'Such confidence,' he said, kissing my forehead.

I closed my eyes and savoured the post-coital languor. We were in Steve's bedroom in his apartment overlooking the People's Park. Our first time doing it in his bed, I thought as I opened my eyes and looked at his profile. He had his hands behind his head and was staring at the ceiling. I stroked the side of his face with my hand and he kissed my fingers. I'd been really looking forward to spending the night with Steve and had thrown clean underwear and a toothbrush into my handbag before he had collected me.

We'd had dinner in a small Italian place. I'd refused starters and dessert in my rush to have the meal over and the real action begin. It had been worth the indigestion, I thought now. I wound my legs around Steve's and began to kiss him slowly on the neck. He turned his body towards me, kissed me on the mouth and then leaned on one arm and smiled at me.

'I'd better get you home, you little minx, before you get me going again,' he said.

'Oh . . . I . . . OK,' I said, because I didn't know what else to say. My heart sank and I struggled to keep my composure. Steve climbed out of the bed and began to dress. I followed suit, anger and disappointment bubbling inside me.

He chatted away as we drove home and I answered in monosyllables, trying to keep the anger out of my voice. It was early days, I reasoned in my head, and he'd warned me about all his baggage and it was no big deal anyway, was it? Sleeping together all night? Maybe he preferred sleeping on his own – although it hadn't seemed like that in London. We kissed good-night and I let myself in to my dark silent house – the only sound was Titbit's whine of welcome when he heard me come in.

By the following week a pattern had been established between myself and Steve. Roughly every second night we got together, had dinner and then had sex at either his place or mine. We never slept together all night – that seemed to be out of bounds for some reason. Apart from this hiccup everything else seemed to be going brilliantly. I'd changed my phone number and had received no texts, flowers or hampers from my stalker. Work was terrific and the ideas seemed to flow – it was as if the new-found happiness in my personal life spilled over into every-thing else. If only the Conor thing was resolved . . .

Everybody in the station knew by now that Steve and I were an item. Not that we were all over each

other or anything like that at work – that really wasn't
our style and it wasn't very professional either. And
I still hadn't introduced Steve to my family. My
mother was dying to meet him – she had loved him
on RTE and rang me every day, fishing for an invite.

I decided by the end of that week that I might as
well bite the bullet. Steve and I were having coffee
in a small café around the corner from the station.
It was Friday and I'd just finished my show.

'I like the dress – is it new?' Steve asked as I brought
a tray of coffee and chocolate cake to a small table
outside on the pavement. It was a really sunny summer
day. We both wore sunglasses and I had on a new short
pink sundress (Sophie's choice again). Every time I saw
my reflection in a mirror or a window I thought it was
someone else, someone vaguely familiar but much too
feminine to be me.

'Yeah, it's new,' I said, sitting down opposite him.
His gaze travelled appreciatively up and down the
length of my body and as I met his gaze a delicious
secret sexual knowledge passed between us. Lovers'
secrets, I thought as I poured milk into my coffee.

'You look lovely – so summery and gay,' Steve said,
stretching his legs out in front of him.

' "Gay" has many meanings,' I said and smiled at
him.

He laughed. 'Definitely not *that* kind of gay.'

I decided this was a good time to bring up the problem of my mother. 'I've been meaning to ask you . . .'

He picked up his espresso and took a tiny sip.
'What is it, babe?'

'Well, it's . . . it's my mother. She wants to meet you and . . .' My voice trailed off as I saw the look on Steve's face. I was getting to know him now and I recognised that look. It was the same look that said we dared not sleep together for a whole night. I decided to wait it out.

He smiled at me. I didn't return it.

'Your mother?'

'Yep. And my dad, too.'

'Oh, right.'

'It's just a casual meeting, Steve, no big deal.'

'No big deal. When?'

'Tomorrow night? We could call out, have tea with them, an hour max?'

He examined his nails. 'That's a pity.'

'Why?'

Steve took off his sunglasses, leaned over and held my hand. 'Because I had something special planned for tomorrow night. But it doesn't matter – of course I'd love to meet your parents . . .'

'What had you planned? You didn't say anything.'

'Well, it was a surprise, but I might as well tell you. I thought we'd have a – now don't laugh – a love-in.'

I laughed. 'A love-in? Should I let my imagination run riot with that?'

He nodded. 'Absolutely. The whole works. Bubble bath, champagne, DVDs – your choice. I'm cook, host and sex slave for the night.'

'The whole night?'

Steve grinned. 'And the next day. Sunday-morning papers, breakfast in bed – your wish is my command.'

'*Match of the Day*?'

He lifted my hand and kissed each of my fingers. 'If you're very good . . .'

A thrill raced through me. I leaned forward and kissed him hard on the mouth. 'You're on.'

'But if you really want to go and see your parents then we can—'

'Nope. We can do that any time,' I said, leaning over to kiss him again.

'I'd better go to work soon. I've got a dinner thing tonight with some college friends – all ex-alcoholics – I think we should sue the school,' said Steve as he finished his coffee. 'You're welcome to come along . . .'

'Wouldn't dream of it. Work away – I've arranged to have dinner with Sophie,' I said. He leaned over and kissed me this time and I shuddered in anticipation of the weekend to come.

I went shopping with Sophie the next morning. I bought a bikini for the first time ever and I was developing gourmet taste in shoes only weeks after my conversion to Girl Land. The thing I liked about shoes was the absolute simplicity of trying them on. You just had to go into a shop, choose a pair and hey presto! No undressing, no queuing, no matching.

I also bought some really daring and outrageously expensive lingerie in a gorgeous rust colour – knickers (Brazilian, according to Sophie) and a matching bustier. I'd almost purchased a lavender number instead but Sophie and the assistant had insisted, despite my protestations, that rust was my colour. I couldn't afford both but I hid the forbidden lavender job in a rail of pyjamas – there was always next week.

We called in on my mother for a minute on the way home but she was way too busy to nag me about not meeting Steve yet. Every woman in Limerick seemed to be in Poise having something or other beautified. I selected some nail polish with Sophie's help and left the salon with a wave at my mother. Sophie had a date with Rico again that night but she still denied any relationship bar a sexual one. We said our goodbyes and I went home to prepare for my love-in.

This was going to be the best night ever, I thought as I showered and wrapped myself in a terry robe. I'd do my nails first so that I'd have plenty of time to *un*do them if things went wrong. I still found nail-painting very difficult, having missed out on those vital first twenty years of practice. I sat at the kitchen table, my feet up in front of me, and began the arduous task. Titbit sat on the floor next to me, resigned to the fact that his beloved Shane was missing. Even though I was a poor substitute, he'd decided on any port in a storm. When I came home from work now in the evenings Titbit gave me a welcome like no other – hell, I'd called him enough names since he'd moved in and there he was, the poor eejit welcoming me home.

My phone signalled a message just as I tackled my big toe.

'If you were any good, dog, you'd read that text for me,' I said as I put down the polish brush.

Hi Sexy, you looked good today in Secrets.

A cold, icy shiver shook my body as I read the text again. He'd seen me in Secrets – the lingerie shop. I checked the number but I knew that I wouldn't recognise it. The stalker was back – and back with a vengeance. I dropped the phone onto the table and it signalled another text. I picked it up and switched it off. Fuck him if he thought he was going to get to me – I wouldn't read the stupid texts. I resumed doing my nails but my good humour had been dented.

But at least the nails turned out OK: nothing as fancy as Sophie's – hers were like miniature paintings – but serviceable. I went upstairs and put on my make-up – I could actually do it now and not end up looking like Coco the Clown – and slipped into my sexy underwear. It looked fabulous. Then I put on my new clothes – tight jeans and pointy sandals with a slinky beaded satin top. I checked myself in the mirror. Something didn't look right. I took off the top and caught a glimpse of myself in the sexy bustier. Did I dare? Fuck it – this was a love-in, wasn't it? And a bustier wasn't exactly like you were going with nothing on under a mink coat, was it?

I smiled at myself in the mirror. Bustier it was. Titbit was sitting on the bed behind me, watching my every move.

'What do you think? Should I go the whole hog?' I asked him. He wagged his tail and I took that as a yes.

I went downstairs and checked the time. We'd agreed that I would drive over to Steve's at around eight-thirty. I had a whole two hours to kill so I went into the living room and flicked on the TV. Titbit sat on the couch beside me. I found a rerun of *Friends* and settled down to watch it. I hoped that I wouldn't fall asleep after spending so long doing my make-up. Titbit edged closer and put his head on my lap. He looked up at me with big doleful eyes and I rubbed his head.

I was just about to leave my house when I had a brilliant idea. I rushed back upstairs and stripped off everything except my new underwear and my lovely pointy fuck-me shoes. Then I rooted in the wardrobe for a trench coat that I knew I'd owned a couple of years ago. I found it and put it on over my sexy outfit. I scooped up my outer garments and put them in the small overnight bag that I'd packed.

I drove to Steve's feeling daring and sexy and full of anticipation. The small car park next to his building was almost empty and I locked my car and headed for the lift in the foyer, waving at the porter as I did so. I arrived outside Steve's door and buzzed the intercom. The door opened and I began to slip out of my coat. Steve stood in the small hallway and I dropped my bag and coat on the floor and pushed him into the living room, kissing him as I did so. He tried to speak but I locked my mouth to his, forcing him to walk backwards. The living room seemed bathed in candlelight and I pushed him against the wall and pressed my body against his.

'Jamie, Jamie . . .' he mumbled.

'No talking,' I said. 'No small talk whatsoever.' I wrapped a leg around his waist and started kissing him again.

'Daddy,' a child's voice said from behind me. 'Is she a call-girl?'

22

I turned around slowly. Two young girls sat side by side on Steve's bright yellow couch. Aisling and Aoife. All blonde hair and braces and funky clothes. The youngest one, Aoife, had a small teddy bear in her hand. I blushed from my painted toes to the roots of my hair.

'Girls, this is . . . this is my friend . . . Jamie,' said Steve, beaming at his daughters.

'Jamie is a boy's name, isn't it, Aoife?' said the older one.

Aoife looked at me, eyes narrowed, nose cocked in the air. She picked up the remote and turned up the sound on the TV.

Steve had gone into the hall – I presumed to get my clothes – and I stood there half naked in front of the two girls. They continued to ignore me as Steve arrived back and put my coat around my shoulders.

'Why didn't you ring me?' I asked as I followed him into the tiny kitchen.

'I left four messages for you – hours ago,' he said and went to the cooker to stir something steaming in a pot.

I remembered the stalker text and turning off the phone.

'Susan called at around four. Her mother has taken a turn for the worse – she's in a nursing home in Tralee, so she asked if the girls . . . I couldn't refuse . . . sorry, Jamie . . . our weekend will have to wait.'

Steve shrugged and smiled wanly at me. I smiled too. Then he came over and, putting his arms around me, he whispered into my ear. 'You look amazing – so sexy . . .' He began to kiss me and I closed my eyes and kissed him back. He edged me close to the work-top and I opened my eyes for a second. Aoife stood in the doorway watching us, her face expressionless.

'Hi, you're Aoife, aren't you?' I said. Steve whipped around and beamed at his daughter.

'I'm hungry, Dad,' she said and turned on her heel and walked out.

'You'll stay for dinner, won't you?' Steve asked.

I nodded. 'Can I get dressed first?'

He laughed. 'Good idea. Use my bedroom.'

The meal was a disaster. It was as far removed from a love-in as you could get. Aisling and Aoife were extremely polite to me in the presence of their father. They said 'please' and 'thank you' and every time their Dad disappeared to bring in food or remove dirty dishes the younger one turned into the little girl in *The Exorcist*.

'Are you a slapper?' she asked the first time Steve left the table. I blushed and squirmed under the steady gaze of the sisters.

'No, of course not,' I said, playing with my pasta.

'You *look* like a slapper,' she said and smiled sweetly at me.

Steve returned with a steaming bowl of noodles that one of the girls had requested.

'Daddy, the dinner is delicious,' said Aoife in her sugary voice.

Steve went over and hugged his daughter. 'I'm glad you like it, sweetheart,' he said into her hair.

'I love you, Daddy,' she replied and then stuck her tongue out at me. The older girl smiled at me and helped herself to noodles.

'Jamie, how about coming to the cinema with us tomorrow? We're going to see *Pink Fluff – The Movie* and then we're going to Milanos for dinner,' said Steve.

The sisters stared at me and I knew they wanted me to refuse the invitation.

'I think I have something on tomorrow – I promised Fiona and Mark I'd take them bowling,' I said.

The sisters smiled at each other.

Steve smiled at me. 'Isn't that perfect, so? We can all do something together – wouldn't that be fun, girls?'

The girls said nothing.

'Let's wait until tomorrow – I'll ask Mark and Fiona what they think,' I said, trying to kick the Big Day Out into touch.

Dad called to see me the next morning. It was a gorgeous sunny day and had that special stillness that only Sundays have. I suggested a walk so we set off down by the river, Titbit between us on his brand new bright red lead.

'Never thought you'd be a dog person, love,' said Dad as we walked in the sunshine.

I laughed. 'I'm not, but somebody has to walk him. Shane had to go to Dublin this morning and as for Titbit's actual owner . . . she might break a nail.'

'He's a grand dog. How are you, anyway? How's work?'

'Good. Did you hear the London shows?' I yanked Titbit's lead tighter as a huge German Shepherd approached with his owner.

'They were brilliant but I'm a small bit prejudiced. What's this I hear about you and that Steve Lowe fella?'

I laughed. 'What did you hear?'

'Well, your mother thinks he's the greatest thing since sliced bread and she hasn't even met him yet – claims she knows him because she spent five years listening to his show every morning.'

'Great – then there's no need to bring him around to meet her, so.'

We sat down on a bench facing the river, Titbit resting his big head on my sandalled foot.

'Bit old for you, isn't he?' Dad fumbled in his pockets, took out a thin cigar and lit it. I loved the smell of those cigars – they reminded me so much of my childhood.

'He's ten years older than me. That's not a lot, really,' I said, looking at the river. It glistened in the sun and flies danced above its surface.

'It could be a lot – depends on what he was doing.'

I looked at my father, who kept his gaze on the water. What did he mean by that, if anything?

'You'd like him, Dad.' I rubbed Titbit's smooth head.

'I remember this river bank when there was nothing at all here.' He stood up and, taking a drag from his cigar, walked the few steps to the water's edge. The imposing structure of the Clarion Hotel, built in the shape of a ship's funnel, cast a huge shadow on the glasslike river. I got up and joined him, pulling a half-asleep Titbit with me.

'Will we walk back, Dad? I'm collecting Mark and Fiona soon.'

Dad turned around, smiled at me and linked arms with me. 'Lead the way, soldier.'

I laughed. He hadn't called me soldier in years.

The Big Day Out got off to a hairy start from the get-go. Steve had rung me that morning, pleading with me to come. I thought this was a little odd – as if he didn't want to be alone with his own children – but I didn't say anything. I didn't know him well enough in the context of his relationship with his children to comment.

From the minute they met in the bowling alley, Mark and Aoife couldn't stand each other. Fiona didn't feel well and Aisling had a face like a slapped arse – something to do with a new camera phone that she wanted her dad to buy for her. Steve was working himself into a tizzy trying to please everyone and I had the beginnings of a bad headache. The bowling became a blood sport, with Mark determined to beat Aoife and her cheating at every opportunity. Eventually Mark won but the Lowe girls sulked so much that I wanted to strangle both of them. I couldn't wait for the movies. At least when we went to the cinema we wouldn't have to talk.

As we crossed town, me following Steve in his beige Primera, the heavens opened and rain pelted down. The sunny skies were gone, replaced with leaden clouds that promised more rain. It was as if the mood in our Big Day Out group had permeated even the weather.

Another argument ensued outside the Omniplex, this time about which movie we should see. I suggested splitting up but Steve was not giving up on the Big Day Out. Not yet, anyway. The Lowe girls got their way and Steve bought loads of junk in an effort to bribe and placate the troops. And it seemed to work until just before the end of the movie when Fiona vomited on Aoife and Aoife became hysterical. As we ushered the children out of the cinema, one screaming and covered in puke, another as sick as a dog, we walked straight into Bill. He was with Rachel the child-eater.

'Jamie,' Bill said, taking in the scene in front of him.

'Bill,' I said, propping up a very sick Fiona.

'My my,' said Rachel. 'Remind me not to go and see *that* movie.'

'This is Steve. Steve, this is Bill and Rachel,' I said quickly. 'Now if you'll excuse us . . .'

Steve smiled at the couple, throwing his hands in the air. 'The joys of parenthood.'

Aoife had gone to the loo, presumably to clean some of the vomit off her hair.

'I think I'll leave those joys to other people,' said Rachel. 'We just saw the best French movie, didn't we, Bill?'

'Isn't that lovely for you?' I said in my sweetest voice. 'Better get this lot home before they start vomiting again. Steve, will you get the other two out of the cinema? I'll go see if Aoife is OK.'

Steve went off in search of Mark and Aisling. I smiled again and, taking Fiona by the hand, I went looking for Aoife in the loo. 'See you around,' I said over my shoulder. I could feel Bill's stare on me as I walked away. Pity Fiona didn't puke on them, I thought as I pushed open the loo door and heard Aoife's wails as she tried to pick vomit from her hair. After I cleaned up a protesting Aoife I met the others outside the cinema and we all agreed to cancel the trip to Milanos restaurant. Enough was enough.

I dropped Fiona and Mark home, by which time I had a whopping headache. I'd take some paracetemol and cuddle up in front of the telly for the night, I decided as I pulled into my street. The house looked dark and lonely in the twilight. I parked the car, got out and stretched my tension-filled body. As I put the key in the door I heard a noise in the hedge at the side of the front garden. I froze and looked over, fear making my heart pound.

'Who's there?' I asked the hedge. How dumb was that? I swallowed my fear and walked towards the noise. There was nothing there.

I went back to the door, hearing the consoling whines of Titbit in the hallway. He jumped all over me as I entered the dark house and flicked on lights quickly as I made my way into the kitchen. And there on the kitchen table was the lacy lavender baby-doll outfit that I'd admired but hadn't purchased in Secrets yesterday. I picked it up and a note fell onto the table.

Can't wait to see you in this.

I almost puked as I dumped the offending article into the bin. I was seriously beginning to doubt the official take on Pierce Thompson. He was starting to frighten me. As I dialled Sophie's number I knew in my heart that something had changed in my stalker's head.

23

Sophie rang the police about Pierce Thompson first thing the next morning but they said what they always did – *he's harmless, ignore him, don't worry about it.* That was easy for them to say. Luckily, though, I didn't have much time to dwell on stalkers for most of the week because the transmitter at the station broke down. The problem was supposed to be solved by some mythical part that Shane was having shipped in from the States. However, it must have been coming in a currach because on Thursday I was still trying to broadcast with technicians crawling around under my feet.

Then on Friday I woke with a headache, a sore throat and a fever. 'Damn,' I muttered, rolling myself into a ball in the bed as I listened to the rain pelting against my window. Maybe it isn't always such a bad thing to wake up on your own, I thought as I dragged my light-headed self to the shower. I was in no humour to be civil, let alone seductive.

I found my old pink fleecy sweatshirt that I always wore when I was feeling shite and a pair of baggy sweatpants. I forced myself to eat half a slice of toast and then popped a couple of painkillers before

driving the short distance to work. I couldn't face
trudging in the flogging rain when I was already
feeling like hell.

Steve had gone to look at cars that morning so I
knew I wouldn't have to encounter him at all – so it
didn't matter that I looked horrible. And nobody can
see you on radio so that didn't matter either. If I could
just stay upright until lunchtime everything would be
grand. At least the transmitter was fixed.

I slumped in my chair behind my desk, drinking
coffee and feeling sorry for myself until it was time for
my show. Luckily, although I felt as if there was a small
tennis ball lodged in my throat, my voice was actually
unaffected so I didn't have to worry on that score. I
just had to concentrate on staying lucid enough to
function and then everything would be fine.

Courtesy of paracetamol I managed to imperson-
ate a cheery person for the three hours that I was on
air, chatting to callers, reading snippets from the
papers – I even told that joke about the aardvark who
walked into a bar. All the time I was promising myself
an afternoon on the sofa with gallons of hot lemon,
painkillers and back-to-back episodes of *Charmed*. To
hell with the real world, anyway. At two minutes past
one I collected my bits and pieces from around the
desk in the sound booth and decided to go straight
home. The drugs were wearing off. I waved at John
Howard who'd already started reading the news. He
winked at me. I opened the outside door and as I did
so a microphone appeared in front of me.

'Surprise!' I heard a woman say.

I backed against the glass wall in confusion. What the hell was happening? Wasn't that Heather? I blinked and looked again in case the fever was causing hallucinations. No. No. That was her, all right – I'd have known that beautiful cross face anywhere. But why was she in the radio station? Shouldn't she be off 'working' some camera somewhere? She smiled at me. Why did she have a microphone? And who the hell was the old guy with the bald patch and the ponytail? Was that a TV camera he was pointing at me?

'Jesus!' I said, pausing to swallow past the briar in my throat. 'Heather, what the fuck are you doing?'

She laughed that high-pitched annoying laugh of hers and turned her head to smile at Mr Cameraman. 'Jamie – you're a terror – we'll have to edit out that piece. Can we edit it out, Ollie?'

The cameraman nodded.

'OK. Anyway . . .' Heather paused, took a deep breath and shook her head as if she was clearing it. Then she started again. 'Jamie! Surprise!'

She held the microphone in front of me again. I looked at her in terror.

'I'll bet you're a bit surprised to find us here waiting for you when you finish your show,' she said in the same voice that she used to speak to Titbit.

I stared at Heather. She was definitely losing her mind. Or else I was.

'I have a lovely surprise for you, Jamie. You have been chosen as the very first person to receive a make-over for Fab City TV's new fashion programme – *Clothesline*.'

She turned back to Mr Cameraman. I stayed welded to the wall.

'Most of you will know Jamie Ryan by her voice rather than her face . . .' Heather turned her head to look at me and raised her eyebrows. 'Jamie is the voice of Fab City's popular *Morning Show* that's on the air each day from ten till one.'

I started to edge along the wall as Heather spoke – if I could get as far as the door then I might wake up and everything would be OK.

'Jamie!'

I stopped in my tracks. Heather tottered over to me and did that annoying microphone-pushing thing again.

'Well? How do you feel about being our first make-over?'

I looked at her and shrugged. No way on God's green planet was I letting Header More make me over. She hated me and would probably do something drastic like shave off my eyebrows.

'Our stylists will take you shopping for a whole new wardrobe. Then you'll be whisked off to Poise – the best salon in town – where you'll have a complete beauty treatment including hair and make-up, you lucky, lucky girl.'

Now I was positive that I wasn't going to take part in the make-over. Nothing was getting me back into my mother's salon. I couldn't take the feelings of failure evoked by crowds of beauty specialists – including my own mother – standing around me and tutting at how hopeless I was. And I was never going to forget my first – and last – make-over and the way the dye had come so easily out of my hair in the rain and yet managed to stain my skin for a week. I realised that Heather was looking at me as if she was expecting me to do or say something. I shrugged again.

Just then the front door opened. Shane and Ian came in, carrying armfuls of cable. Heather looked at me and winked.

'Back in a sec,' she whispered. Then she started walking towards Shane. Mr Cameraman followed like he was attached to her with an invisible string.

'Here at Fab City Radio,' Heather said in her bright plastic voice as she walked, 'not only do they have a wide variety of entertainment and information for the city of Limerick – they also have something that's very important to me personally.' She paused and looked sincerely straight into the camera. 'I'd like you all to meet my fiancé – Shane Ali.'

Heather finished looking sincere and pointed. Mr Cameraman aimed his device at Shane. Ian stepped aside so that Shane was left at centre stage. Shane's face blanched and his mouth fell open. Then he tried a shaky smile and as much of a wave as was possible with his cable-filled arms.

'Shane,' Heather said and Mr Cameraman swivelled to find her. 'Shane Ali, will you marry me?'

The camera swung back to Shane. 'But Heather, we're already engaged,' he said and moved as though to walk away. She laughed and walked up close to him, barring his exit.

'I know that, silly, but now I have it all arranged

– FCTV are going to show our wedding live on air on 1 July, it's all arranged – so: Shane Ali – will you marry me?'

Mr Cameraman moved in close now and had both of them in his sights. Nobody in the office moved. Outside a truck trundled loudly along the street and the atmosphere was suddenly electric – like just before a gunfight in a saloon. Thinking about it later, I thought maybe that was because everybody knew what was going to happen. Well, everybody except Heather.

'No,' Shane said, lowering his head. 'I'm sorry, Heather, but no.' Then he stepped past her and walked across the open office and out the back door.

Heather didn't move a muscle – even her microphone hand which she'd extended towards Shane was still rigidly held up in the air. Mr Cameraman, though, had moved away and had had the decency to switch off his camera. Slowly everybody crept back to their desks and pretended to be working.

Heather's hand had dropped to her side and the microphone was now dangling, forgotten, from her fingers. But she was still standing in the same place. Her face had gone completely white and, annoying as she was, I felt deeply sorry for her.

Bloody Shane. Why the hell had he done that? But part of me knew. Just like all of me had always known that he and Heather were – other than physically – a match made in hell. I just wished he hadn't arrived at that conclusion in public.

I walked over to her. 'Hey,' I said, softly, touching her arm.

Heather looked at me as though surprised to see me.

'Dean said it'd be great,' she said, fixing me with her beautiful green eyes. 'He said people love reality TV and that Shane and I were the ideal candidates for a TV wedding. Dean said it'd be like Jordan and Peter – everyone would watch it.'

I nodded, wondering how it was possible that she'd spent so much time with Shane and learned so little about him? Shane was nothing if he wasn't private. Plus underneath all the fun and games he was quite a serious individual who was deeply committed to his family and was never going to allow his wedding day to become a media circus.

'Dean was completely sure. He said it'd start off *Clothesline* with a real bang if I proposed to Shane while I was here. It was all perfect . . .'

Heather's voice trailed off and two symmetrical tears flowed down her clear-skinned cheeks. I reached out my hand again and she squeezed it as more tears followed. We stood like that for a full five minutes, in the middle of the office with everybody working around us and Mr Cameraman in the corner drinking coffee with Dee-Dee. I mumbled rubbish that I hoped sounded consoling and wished that Steve would come in early. I didn't care any more if I looked like I'd been dragged through a hedge: Steve was brilliant at all this stuff – much better than me. Heather stopped crying as suddenly as she had started.

'Well,' she said, pausing to blow her nose. 'That's that, I suppose.'

'Look, Heather – you two need to talk – everything will be fine.'

Heather nodded and fixed her hair. Why wasn't her face all blotchy and mascara-streaked from crying?

'I'll be on to you in the next few days about the details of the make-over. So, Jamie – is that OK?'

I looked at her. Shit, *now* what was I going to do? I couldn't possibly put her through a second public humiliation. I took a deep breath. Ah well, it wouldn't kill me.

'Great,' I said, with a false smile.

'You'll be thrilled,' she said squeezing my arm. 'Wait until you see – once they get their hands on you, you won't recognise yourself. I mean, Jamie, in a way you do have some of the raw material to look quite good.'

I bit back a retort. I knew that Heather thought she was being nice to me. Anyway, I couldn't bring myself to hit a woman who had already been floored.

'Ollie?' she called at the top of her voice.

Mr Cameraman stood up and mock-shot Dee-Dee with his index finger. She smiled at him and then rolled her eyes at me as soon as his back was turned. He and Heather gathered up an assortment of leather satchels and aluminium cases and left the office.

After they had gone there was a momentary hush followed immediately by a low gossiping murmur. Now I had to find Shane. I knew he'd be upset by what had happened, but where the hell was he? I had a look in Sophie's office but it was empty. I'd forgotten that she was in Killarney at a day-long seminar on broadcasting. Man – wait until she heard what had happened in her absence! Sophie loved a good public scene so I knew she'd be disappointed to have missed the drama.

I remembered then that Shane had escaped through the back door so I followed his route. The door led out into the radio-station car park and a quick look told me that his car was still there. Which meant he couldn't be too far away. Pretty good deducing, I thought. Maybe Dermot Kilbane had an opening for an assistant?

The rain had stopped but it was still overcast and quite chilly as a strong wind was now blowing up from the river. I stood there for a few minutes, hugging my handbag to me in an attempt to keep out the cold wind and trying to work out where Shane might have gone.

He was upset – that much was for certain. And he'd left his car in the car park though he wasn't at work. Suddenly I knew. I took off at a trot, weaving in and out between the harassed office workers, and then I diced with death as I crossed the busy Dock Road. Once across, I ran the short distance past the bridge and straight into Bob's Bunkhouse – a small wooden-fronted working-men's pub. Sure enough, Shane was sitting at the counter, an untouched pint of Guinness in front of him as he stared unseeingly at the TV behind the bar. He was so preoccupied that he never even noticed me. I pulled up a stool beside him.

'That was dramatic,' I said.

Shane started and turned around.

'She's gone,' I said.

The barman approached and I ordered coffee.

'I can't believe I did it,' he said.

'Makes a few of us.'

He turned towards me on his stool. 'No, really – I've been wondering about Heather and me for a while.'

He paused and I just nodded.

'And then it all sort of came together: she and I want different things – I can't marry her.'

I poured milk into my coffee. 'Pity you didn't tell her that before she proposed to you on camera.'

Shane groaned and lowered his head onto the bar counter. 'I know, I know, but I wasn't clear about it until she said that stuff in the station.'

'You couldn't have lied just for that moment, I suppose?'

He lifted his head and looked at me. 'No point – it wouldn't have been much less humiliating for her, would it?'

I shook my head.

'I think I'll take the rest of today off,' Shane said, picking up his pint and drinking most of it. 'I can't face that crowd at Fab City after what happened – anyway, Ian can cope.'

'They'll be fine,' I said.

'What about you? You look a bit rough.'

'Thanks. I have a sore throat and I feel like shit. I'd just finished work and was on my way home when Heather appeared out of the blue.'

Shane finished off his pint and ordered another. 'Do you want something?' he asked me. I shook my head.

'What exactly was she doing at Fab City with a microphone and a cameraman?'

'I've been selected for the first make-over on her fashion programme. I can't remember what it's called – *Clotheshorse* or something mad like that,' I said, with a loud groan.

'*Clothesline*,' he said, laughing.

'I'm glad you think it's funny, Shane Ali. I was going to refuse to go along with it – shit, they're even going to make me go back to my mother's salon.'

'And? What happened?'

I looked at him long and hard. 'I couldn't refuse, not after what happened with you.'

'Oh,' he said.

'You bloody well owe me,' I said.

'Thanks. I appreciate your sacrifice.'

'Oh no,' I said, pushing my coffee away – it tasted like wool in my mouth. 'Your thanks will not be nearly enough to repay me for this. But don't worry, I'll think of something.'

Shane winked and smiled but his face looked drawn and tired. I felt bad for him. 'I have just one question, Shane.'

He looked at me.

'Who the hell is getting custody of Titbit?'

He laughed then and I was glad to have cheered him up. But I was feeling sicker by the second as the bug that had invaded my tonsils began to have a field day in my body. So it was probably a combination of illness and the shock of what had happened and feeling sorry for Shane that convinced me to have that first hot whiskey. I'm not sure, though, what convinced me that another one would be a good idea. Or the one after that.

I'm even less sure about how Shane and I progressed from sitting at the counter to installing ourselves in a glass-sided snug in a corner of Bob's Bunkhouse. I have a vague recollection of a line of glasses of rum and Coke on the round table in front of us but I'm not sure how many were mine and how many were Shane's. I do remember that the walls of the snug were made out of old smoke-stained wood and coloured dimpled glass and I held forth to Shane about my love of glass-walled places like the snug – and the sound booth at work. Mostly, though, we concentrated on getting pissed and watching rugby on TV and talking rubbish about the world.

It was close to nine when Sophie arrived. She'd called me earlier on her way back from Killarney and Shane and I had provided her with an incoherent version of the events of the day. She and Rico came into Bob's looking like a pair of matching bookends in black suits and white shirts. I put my arms around her as soon as she appeared.

'Sophie,' I slurred, as I dragged her almost onto my lap. 'I love you, Soph – I swear. That Paul fucker is a fool – you're the best.'

Rico started laughing and she shot him a dirty look so he headed off towards the bar. Sophie settled down between Shane and me. She put her hand on Shane's shoulder.

'You OK?'

He nodded slowly but his face looked hurt. 'Why are you and your man dressed in the same clothes?'

Sophie rolled her eyes. 'It was an accident.'

''Scute though, isn't it, Shane?' I said, leaning across Sophie. Shane and I started to laugh as if I'd told a great joke. Sophie put up with it for a few seconds and then she asked, 'Any word from Heather?'

That shut us up but then Shane and I looked at each other and I started to giggle again. I drank half a glass of rum and Coke and gave a loud burp. Shane laughed.

Sophie turned her head to look at me. 'You two need to go home.'

'No way – it's early,' I protested.

Sophie smiled. 'You've been here since lunchtime – you haven't even eaten.'

'No, no, you're wrong there, Soph,' Shane said. 'We had our dinner, didn't we, Jamie?'

I nodded. 'Two of the best toasted sandwiches *I*'ve ever eaten – the onions were divine.'

'I'm telling you, Sophie, there's no sandwiches like Bob's sandwiches,' Shane said, staggering to his feet. 'Look, I'll get you a couple for yourself – Bob! Bob! Throw on a couple of your finest sandwiches for my friend here.'

'No, it's fine, really, I've eaten,' Sophie said, waving wildly at Bob. 'I'll get you again, Bob.'

I suddenly felt exhausted. 'My throat is really sore,' I said to Sophie like a small child telling her mother.

She put her arm around me. 'My car is outside

– I'm going to drive the two of you home.' She stood up and beckoned to Rico who pranced over to our table. What did she really see in him? I nearly asked the question but luckily, though my mind was as free of inhibition as is possible, my throat was so sore that I could hardly speak.

They bundled us into Sophie's car. I remember the short journey and the certainty that I was going to puke all over her upholstery and then the relief when I managed to wait until I was outside my own front door. I remember Sophie convincing me to eat a bowl of soup. I remember being on the couch beside Shane and watching someone shove a tube up a woman's nose on *ER* and that's all I remember until the next day.

When I'd woken up on Friday morning with my sore throat and fever I'd thought it was a shitty start to the day. When I woke up on Saturday, Friday looked like one of my better mornings.

24

As soon as I woke up on Saturday I realised that not only did I have a sore throat but I also had the worst hangover of my life. I leaned out of bed, struggling to open the drawer in my bedside locker without opening my eyes. I knew I had some paracetamol in the drawer. But I couldn't find the locker. Painfully I forced my eyes open. There was no locker beside the bed. I rolled onto my back and groaned with the pain as my head moved position. Why would someone steal my bedside locker? Then I turned my head slightly and looked straight into Shane's big brown eyes.

'Holy shit!' I said sitting upright. The pain inside my head soared. 'Why are you in my bed, Shane?'

He didn't answer.

'And did you take my bedside locker?'

Shane frowned. 'I think we're in my bed, Jamie.'

'Oh.'

'And Jamie – you don't have any top on.'

I looked down at my naked breasts. 'Shit,' I said, folding my arms. 'Why haven't I got a top on?'

He shook his head gingerly. 'Dunno.'

My heart sank. I picked up the duvet and had a quick look. 'Shit, shit, shit,' I said.

'No knickers either?' Shane asked.

'You?'

'Arse-naked,' he said.

I groaned and lay back down in the bed. Wriggling as far away as possible from Shane, I pulled the duvet up to my chin.

'Do you think we—' he began.

'Don't even think it,' I said.

We fell silent for a few seconds. I struggled to work out what had happened. I loved Shane. Loved him like a brother. He was one of my best friends in the world and now it looked like we might have ruined everything between us. And for what? I couldn't even remember the sex.

'Can you remember anything?' I said, turning to look at him.

'No. *ER* and then . . .'

'Exactly the same as me. Maybe nothing happened?'

'We're butt-naked.'

I sighed. 'I know, but maybe we were just too warm.'

Shane raised his eyebrows and a smile started across his face.

'Anyway,' I continued hastily. 'I can't remember anything and you can't remember anything so it can be like nothing happened even if it did, can't it?'

Shane didn't answer for a few seconds. 'OK,' he said, eventually. 'That sounds fine to me.'

'And we don't need to tell anybody about this. Agreed?'

'Agreed.'

I started to calm down. This was manageable – and

anyway, nothing had happened, had it? But, as usual, just as I was sure that things couldn't get worse – they did. The door flew open and Heather stood in front of us. Her mouth fell open and I gasped aloud.

'Heather! Hello! How did you get in?' I heard myself say.

Heather looked at me as if she'd gladly have disembowelled me.

'It's not how it looks, Heather,' Shane said. 'Nothing happened.'

She shrugged and her face suddenly composed itself back into a beautiful mask. Then her engagement ring and a key that looked like it might fit our front door came sailing across the room and landed on the floor beside Shane.

'I want all of my clothes,' she said. 'Put them in my Gucci case – don't miss anything.'

And then she was gone.

Neither of us spoke. We just lay there listening to the sound of her high heels on the stairs and the slamming of the front door. I looked at the ceiling and I could hear Shane's quiet breathing beside me. What the hell had we done?

Suddenly the door opened again and I was seized by a sudden fear that Heather had gone to get a gun and was back to murder us. But it was Sophie who stood in the doorway this time. She pushed at the door with a big wooden tray and Titbit bounded across the room and jumped up on the bed beside Shane. He gave me his darkest look and then snuggled into Shane's side and allowed his belly to be scratched.

'Good morning, you two! Rise and shine!' Sophie chirped as she laid the tray across the bottom of the bed. 'I brought you some coffee and toast and a box of aspirin – thought you might need it. Did I hear the front door close?'

Shane looked at me and then we looked back at Sophie. But neither of us seemed capable of speech.

She shrugged. 'See you later,' she said and was gone with a wave.

'*Now* what'll we do?' Shane said, propping himself up on one elbow as we listened to Sophie's retreating footsteps. This was getting to be a bit of a habit. Titbit burrowed under the duvet.

'I have to follow her and swear her to silence,' I said, jumping out of bed as I suddenly seemed to wake up properly and the seriousness of the French farce that was that Saturday morning really dawned on me.

'Jamie!' Shane shouted, shading his eyes with his hand.

Shit! I'd forgotten I was naked. 'Get over it, Shane – it's not like I'm the first naked woman you've ever seen,' I said as I gathered my clothes from the floor and hastily pulled them on. 'Avert your eyes.'

Shane laughed as he pulled the tray up the bed towards him. 'You must be joking – there's a naked woman in my room and you want me not to look? You've taken leave of your senses.'

'It's just me, Jamie – I'm not a naked woman,' I said, pulling my pink fleece over my head.

'Could have fooled me,' he said to my back as I ran out of the room. Sophie had her hand on the front door just as I reached the bottom of the stairs.

'Well, well, well,' she said, turning around and folding her arms as she looked me up and down. 'You and Shane – who would have thought?'

I covered my face with my hands. 'It isn't like it looks, Sophie, I swear.'

She gave me an old-fashioned look. 'Yeah, right – tell it to the judge.'

'OK, OK, maybe it *is* like it looks, I don't know, I don't remember anything – and neither does he. We're friends, Sophie, that's all – if we had sex it was an accident.'

She laughed. 'That's a new one on me. I mean, I've had a lot of sex – particularly recently – but I don't think I've ever had the accidental variety.'

'Oh shut up, Soph – you know what I mean . . . please don't say anything.'

She looked at me.

'Please,' I begged.

'But there's no Heather any more.'

'That was Heather you heard closing the door.'

Sophie laughed. 'Shit! I was in the kitchen with the radio on – I never even heard her come in.'

'What am I going to do? What if she tells people that Shane and I were in bed together?'

'I thought you said nothing happened.'

'Oh for God's sake, Sophie – I'm *hoping* nothing happened but even I can see it looks pretty bad – especially to Heather.'

'She won't say anything – she'll be too busy trying to save face.'

'Are you sure?'

'Well, I can't guarantee it but I'm pretty sure she won't. What do you care anyway – she and Shane are finished.'

I moved my head and it felt like something important in my brain was irreparably damaged. 'What about Steve?'

Sophie made a face. 'Steve,' she whispered. 'Oh . . . my . . . God!'

'Bitch.'

'Now, now – I have to get going – I promised my mother I'd meet her in the market this morning.'

'Sophie.'

'Ah, get over yourself, girl – who am I going to tell?'

And then she was gone. I went into the kitchen and drank a litre of water and then found some flu medication and took a couple of those. I dearly hoped that Sophie was right about Heather – maybe I should tell Steve just in case? But then again, I didn't want to be courting trouble if there was none around. I groaned. At least I knew that Sophie wouldn't blab so at least *that* problem was solved. Now all I had to do was find a way to carry on being around Shane.

The rest of Saturday wasn't too bad – basically because I was so sick that I didn't care if I lived or died, let alone who thought I'd been doing what with whom. Shortly after Sophie left I staggered upstairs to my own bedroom. My throat was almost closed now and I felt so cold that it could only mean my temperature had soared. I wrapped myself in my duvet and fell asleep almost immediately. I slept pretty much solid until Sunday morning – waking only to pee and drink some of the water that I'd brought upstairs with me.

The next time I woke properly the radio alarm clock said it was 11.43 and was blasting out a Sunday talk show. I leaned over, turned down the volume and tried to swallow. Much better. I curled up in a ball and snuggled back down and then I remembered waking up with Shane. Shit. Now I was wide awake.

I leaned out of the bed and pulled my discarded jeans towards me. My mobile phone was in the back pocket and the small screen told me that I had four new messages. Scrolling through the phone I had a look at my messages. One from my stalker—

Good morning, darling – feeling better?

My skin crawled. I knew it was him because as usual the number was withheld. I wished I could find a way to keep my number from him. I hated that this person knew so much about me even if he was supposed to be entirely harmless. It was spooky.

I kept scrolling. The next two messages were from Steve, both saying the same thing—

Hi sweetie. Where are you? Miss you. Call me.

I hugged myself with delight and opened the last message.

Marielouise and the children are coming for dinner at two. Why don't you come and bring that new boyfriend along with you? Mam.

Was that woman never going to understand that she

didn't need to sign her messages to me? Still, dinner and introduce Steve to the family? Not a bad idea. It'd kill a few birds with one stone. Steve could meet my family – it was about time he was subjected to them. I could eat well without any effort as my mother was almost as good a cook as she was a beautician. And – probably most importantly – it'd keep me away from the house and Shane.

I texted my acceptance to my mother and called Steve.

'Hello,' he said in such a deep, sleepy, sexy voice that I almost hung up and just went round to his place. So I told him that after I'd told him about my mother's invitation.

He laughed. 'Don't let me stop you. There are no kids here – do you still have that raincoat?'

'I'd love to visit you right now but if I did we'd never get to my parents' house for dinner.'

'Aww,' he said and yawned. I had a flash of his body stretching in his bed and it almost broke down my resolve. But I knew I was right – there was no time for hanky-panky if we were to make it to lunch by two.

'Well, we can always call in to water the plants on our way home,' I said.

'I'll hold you to that. What time are we expected at your parents'?'

'Two. I'll pick you up at half-one.'

'See you then.'

I slid out of bed and offered a short prayer of thanks that I'd won the en suite bathroom draw when

Sophie, Shane and I had moved in five years ago. At least I could shower and dress in relative comfort. I was truly dreading meeting Shane after what had happened so I took my time getting ready. Eventually, though, slow as I was, I finished my ablutions and dressing. I looked at myself in the mirror and decided that I was still a bit pasty-looking so I should try putting on some make-up. Which I duly did, though I knew in my heart it was just another way to postpone facing Shane.

I opened my bedroom door and the TV noises that greeted me told me that Shane was already up and in the sitting room. Shit. I'd just have to be grown-up and get on with it. I went to the kitchen and pushed two slices of bread into the toaster. The sound of football lured me towards the sitting room.

'Do you want toast?' I asked as soon as I opened the door.

Shane jumped at the sound of my voice. 'Hi, Jamie! How are you? Is the throat better?' He looked straight at me and my heart sank. Shane never looked away from a match when someone came into the room. Everything was wrong.

I blushed in spite of my resolve. 'Great, great – much better '. . . look, I just realised the time – I promised my mother I'd come over. See you later.'

Shane looked relieved. 'See you, Jamie.'

I grabbed my handbag from a kitchen chair and forced myself not to break into a run. Just as I closed the front door behind me I heard the toaster pop. As I drove to Steve's house my head swirled with thoughts of my own stupidity. How was it possible that Shane and I had ended up having sex? I knew that women often discovered that they were really in love with their male friends but in all the years I'd known him I'd never fancied Shane – not even once. And I was pretty sure the lack of sexual attraction was mutual. And now maybe we were fucked – in every sense of the word. I could only hope that the passage of time might help.

Steve looked surprised to see me at his door.

'You're early,' he said.

I responded by kissing him. He pulled me inside, our mouths locked together as we moved, and then he closed the door behind me. Within minutes we were half clad and almost fully orgasmic, there in Steve's hallway. But you have to work with what you have, I always say and on that basis there's a lot to be said for standing-up sex in a narrow apartment hallway.

After we finished, I noticed that Steve had shaved the stubble off only half of his face.

'What's this?' I asked, touching his smooth cheek.

'You took me by surprise,' he said, bending down to retrieve the razor he'd obviously discarded at some point after my arrival.

'Sorry,' I said, with a grin.

'Don't apologise. Best shaving experience I've ever had, bar none. Any chance you could make coffee while I finish the job?'

'No problem,' I said, making my way to the kitchen while he headed back into the bathroom.

I felt really good – my throat was better and that sex had really energised me. As the aroma of coffee filled Steve's small kitchen I wondered what he'd think if he knew about Shane. How was it was possible that Shane and I had had sex when neither of us remembered anything about it? Either it hadn't happened or else it had been so bad that we'd hardly noticed.

And then something struck me that I hadn't twigged before – what had Sophie been doing in our house first thing in the morning? She didn't still have a key as far as I knew and I was pretty certain that neither of us had let her in. That meant she must have stayed the night. Which also might mean that she knew more about what had happened than I did. As I listened to the sound of Steve's footsteps approaching I poured coffee and decided I'd have to talk to her. She was our best friend – surely she'd think of some way for Shane and I to get past what had happened.

Steve opened the door and I smiled at how handsome he looked in a washed-out denim shirt and cream trousers.

'Coffee?' I said, holding a mug towards him.

That was what I'd do: I'd talk to Sophie – come up with a plan and we'd all live happily ever after. Meanwhile I had to get my head together enough to spend the afternoon with my mother. That in itself was going to take all my resources. My mother loved me dearly and I knew this was true but somehow whenever we were together she made me feel like I was a huge disappointment to her. Still – I kissed Steve and sipped my own coffee. Even Mam couldn't disapprove of Steve so maybe the afternoon was going to go just fine.

25

I was right about Mam and Steve – they hit it off as soon as they met. However, I couldn't say the same for Steve and Dad. Or Steve and Bill, for that matter. I couldn't believe my eyes when I let Steve and myself in the back door of my parents' house and saw Bill Hehir making a pot of tea in their kitchen.

'What are *you* doing here?' I said.

He turned and gave me a slow smile. 'Lovely to see you, too, Jamie.'

Luckily Mam, Dad, Marielouise, Fiona and Mark all arrived in the room en masse just at that point and my rudeness was absorbed in a flurry of introductions and chatter. Steve shook hands with both Bill and Dad and they gave him identical sceptical looks. I ignored them, especially when they started to talk to each other about football. OK – I was a football fanatic myself but even I knew that football talk could be used as a way to alienate the uninterested. I'd done it to Heather often enough myself.

Marielouise and Mam, on the other hand, were mad about Steve. He told them all about Tommy Sloane's Chelsea garden and how the goat had eaten Diarmuid Gavin's plants. Then Mam took both of them outside to see her new Japanese water feature. Fiona and Mark persuaded me to play cards and dragged me into the sitting room.

The three of us were seated on the floor around the shiny mahogany coffee table and I was just about to deal the cards when Bill's tall form plonked down beside me.

'Deal me in,' he said.

I glared at him, the deck of cards poised in mid-air.

Fiona smiled broadly and hugged Bill around the neck. Then she settled herself into the crook of his arm. Mark grinned at him.

'See the match?' he said.

'Pretty good, all right – I'd say things are looking good for Liverpool now. What do you think?' Bill said.

Mark nodded and all three of them looked at me.

'Want me to deal, Jamie?' Bill said, with a wide smile.

I shook my head and dealt the cards. Ten minutes later Mark had cleaned us all out in Snap and was nagging for us to play poker.

'You're eight,' I said. 'Who taught you to play poker?'

Mark gave a long, disgruntled sigh. 'I'm eight and a half and Bill taught me *and* he said I was a really good player.'

I glared at Bill and he gave a sheepish smile.

'Typical,' I muttered.

'He *is* a good player, though,' Bill said. 'Really.'

I narrowed my eyes and increased the scathingness in my look.

'So can we play for money?' Mark said.

'No,' I said automatically. Mark pouted. I turned towards Bill. 'Jesus! Gambling! What next? I suppose you'll be taking him for an initiation in a brothel?'

'What's a broadel?' Fiona said.

'Come on, Jamie, let's play for money,' Mark said.

I glared at Bill and he glared back. Just then my mother shouted at us all to come and have our dinner. I stood up and stormed off to the dining room before I said anything else in front of the children. Bill Hehir was without doubt the single most arrogant and infuriating man I'd ever met.

My father was already sitting at the dining-room table, complaining to Marielouise about the large orchid-and-rose floral display.

'I don't care how much it cost – the smell of those things reminds me of the dead house,' he was saying as Bill and the children and I took our seats. 'Isn't it like a funeral home in here with those flowers, Bill?'

Bill laughed and raised his hands in the air. 'I'm staying out of this.'

My mother sighed and lifted the flowers off the table. 'Now! Are you happy, now?'

My father shrugged. 'At least they're not in my face. Will I carve the lamb?'

'Steve is still in the bathroom,' my mother said, taking her seat between him and Marielouise.

'So? I can surely to God start carving.'

My mother tutted and tossed her beautifully coiffed head. 'Suit yourself. Ah, there you are, Steve – everything all right?'

We all looked as Steve came in. He smiled broadly

and sat down beside me and squeezed my thigh under the table. I smiled at him and then looked up and made eye contact with Bill who seemed to be just staring at me. He looked away as soon as our gazes met. He began to speak with Marielouise and help serve vegetables to the children.

Dad cut the meat and Mam made sure we all had vegetables and gravy. I felt slightly guilty about not inviting Shane who loved my mother's cooking. My stomach tightened as I remembered waking up with him.

As we had our dessert of home-made strawberry cheesecake and coffee, the kids ran off to watch TV, carrying bowls of ice cream. Once they were gone Marielouise told us all about Mark's new business venture. According to his mother he'd taken to hiring himself out to neighbours to run errands and do small jobs. I laughed along with everybody else as she told us about it. But there was something about Mark's new obsession with money that still bothered me, though I couldn't put my finger on what it was.

After the food was all finished, Steve and I volunteered to clean up while everybody else watched the video of Mark's First Communion day. As we filled the dishwasher and scraped plates and cleared off worktops in companionable silence, I fantasised that this would be how it was when we were finally living together. I knew that Steve was right to want to get his old life in order before he embarked on a new life with me. I also knew that it was going to be complicated but I didn't really care. Surely if something was worth having it was worth waiting for?

We were almost finished cleaning when Steve's phone rang. He looked at the screen.

'Aoife? I can't hear you,' he said.

'Go into the garden,' I said, washing out dishcloths at the sink. 'The reception in here is terrible.'

He nodded and greeted his daughter as he made his way out the door. I watched him through the window as I tidied around the sink. He was walking in circles around the horse chestnut tree. That tree had been there for as long as I could remember and I could see the remnants of Conor's old tree house. It was funny that Mam had never had that taken away.

The sound of the kitchen door closing made me jump.

'Where's lover boy?' Bill said, stopping the dishwasher and dropping in a handful of teaspoons. 'I thought he was supposed to be helping you clean up.'

'We're finished,' I said, scrubbing at a tea stain on the draining board. 'He's in the garden, speaking to his daughter on the phone.'

'Oh. Right.'

I searched under the sink for some steel wool and attacked the stain again. Bill stayed in the kitchen. I didn't want to turn around to look at him – and I didn't have to in order to know that he was looking at me. Eventually, when the stain was long gone and I was about to scrub a hole in the stainless steel, I turned around.

Bill had his arms folded and was standing, leaning

against my mother's huge wooden dresser. 'Any word from Columbo?'

I tutted and rolled my eyes.

'Seriously, Jamie – if you are insisting on doing something like hiring a private detective at least hire a good one.'

'Dermot Kilbane *is* a good one,' I said, angrily folding tea towels from the laundry basket.

Bill walked over to the table, took a bunch of folded tea towels and put them in a drawer. 'If it's a question of cash – I'll give you the money,' he said.

'I have money, thank you very much. And what's more, I *like* my detective and I think he's going to find Conor.'

Something unknowable flashed across Bill's face and then disappeared. He reached out a hand for the remaining tea towels and I handed him the final three.

'I know you're mad at me,' he said, not moving.

I shrugged but I couldn't deny it – I was permanently mad at him.

'I just don't want you to get even more hurt,' he said.

I looked into his eyes. They were hazel with dark flecks and for a second I wasn't angry with him – I was just there with him, in the hurt and confusion and loss that we'd all experienced since Conor had disappeared. We didn't move until the sound of the back door clicking closed made us both start and jump apart.

'How's Aoife?' I said, swinging quickly away from Bill.

'Oh, you know teenagers,' Steve said. 'Tell me – do you have any kids, Bill?'

Bill didn't answer for a second and then he said, 'No. I haven't had that good fortune, I'm afraid.'

As Steve told Bill all about his daughters, I was back at the press under the sink pretending to look for scouring power while all the time my head was filled with wondering about the perversity of human beings. How could it be that I could move so seamlessly from wanting to clock Bill Hehir to feeling like he was a part of me?

The kitchen was spotless and I was planning to make good my escape with Steve when Marielouise and my mother came in.

'Jamie! You never told me you'd been selected for the new make-over programme!' Marielouise announced. 'That's brilliant!'

Steve and Bill both looked at me and I was back to square one with Bill who had such a sardonic grin plastered all over his face that I wanted to throw a pot at him.

'How did you know?' I asked.

Marielouise smiled and winked and tapped her nose.

'I told her, of course,' my mother said. 'That beautiful girl – Heather Moore – rang me on Friday morning and we made all the arrangements. We can't wait in the salon! The girls are on high-doh with excitement – I mean, such publicity – you couldn't buy it, could you?'

Bill smiled at me. 'You're being made over, Jamie? How lovely.'

I made a face at him.

'And did they follow you around with cameras for weeks – filming you when you didn't realise you were being filmed?'

I looked at him in alarm. 'Noooo.'

'They did! They did! Won't it be a howl?' my mother said. 'Heather swore me to secrecy.'

My stomach squeezed at the mention of Heather's name but as she didn't appear to have started destroying my reputation yet I calmed myself back down. I tuned back in to my mother talking.

'. . . She said they chose Jamie at their very first meeting weeks ago – isn't that a compliment, dear?'

'Or an insult,' I muttered.

'It'll be good for your career, Jamie,' Steve said.

I raised my eyebrows.

'I swear – people adore that reality stuff, they'll love to see you getting a make-over,' he said. To my surprise I thought I detected a slight note of envy in his voice.

'I think it's great,' Marielouise said. 'I can't wait to tell all my friends to watch it.'

I groaned and covered my face with my hands.

'Surely you don't have to do it if you don't want to?' Bill said.

'It's complicated,' I said from behind my fingers.

'Because of work?'

I looked at him from between my fingers. 'Yes, and other stuff – it's really, really complicated, just take my word for it.'

Marielouise came over and put her arm around me. 'Well, I think you always look fabulous,' she said, squeezing my shoulders. 'Now you'll just be even more gorgeous and we'll all get to watch you on the telly.'

'Thanks,' I said. 'Listen, Mam, Steve and I need to get going – thanks for dinner, it was delicious as usual.' I hurried over and gave her a quick kiss and then Dad and the kids came in as well. We all said our goodbyes and thank-yous and eventually Steve and I were alone in my car.

'You have a nice family,' Steve said as I drove off.

'They're OK,' I said. 'You know yourself – family can be a bit of a pain.'

He didn't say anything for a few seconds. 'You don't appreciate them,' he said eventually.

'Sorry?'

'You heard me, Jamie – you don't appreciate your family.'

'You saw them on a good day, Steve,' I said, indicating to turn left. 'My mother and I could just as easily have had a screaming match at lunch. We don't exactly see eye to eye.'

'In what way?'

I shrugged. 'Nothing that you can easily identify. I guess I'm just never going to be the daughter she wanted – you know, all excited about fake tan and manicures.

'What about your family?' I said, to change the subject. We pulled up outside his house. 'All I know is what you told me – your mother is in a home and you have two younger sisters who live in Los Angeles.'

'And I never see any of them,' he said quietly.

'Never?'

'Not in years – we don't get on all that well.'

'Don't you even see your mother?'

'At Christmas – she's in a home in Dublin – she doesn't really know me any more.'

'Poor Steve,' I said, leaning over and kissing his cheek. He turned and smiled at me but it was a sad, hurt smile.

'No, no, I'm fine about it now, really. Years of therapy.'

We sat in silence for what felt like ages as I tried to figure out the best thing to say.

'When did your dad die?' I said eventually.

He didn't answer for a few seconds. 'I never said he was dead.'

'Oh, I'm sorry, Steve, I suppose I just presumed when you didn't mention him and stuff – jeez, look, I'm really sorry . . .'

Steve put up his hand and shook his head. 'No need. Look, I don't want to talk about it now – it's too much of a downer after our lovely afternoon with your family.' He leaned towards me and kissed me gently on the lips. 'I'll tell you all the gory details some other time. Now let's just go in and have a nice quiet evening in front of the telly.'

'That'd be brilliant,' I said brightly.

Steve smiled and hugged me. 'You really are good for me,' he said into my hair.

I nuzzled his neck, feeling a tiny bit guilty that my enthusiasm wasn't as untainted as Steve imagined.

Sure, I was happy to be spending the evening with him – it was just that now I was also glad to find an excuse to avoid Shane. I was finding that incident increasingly hard to put out of my head.

26

As it turned out that was just as much the case for Shane as it was for me. I dragged my heels at Steve's until well after midnight but even so Shane was still up when I got in. As soon as the front door closed behind me he appeared in the hallway.

'Hi,' I said, carefully trying to gauge the lie of the land. 'How are you?'

'Not too bad now, not too bad, thanks,' Shane said as though he was talking to a stranger.

'Well, I'm wrecked,' I said, forcing a yawn. 'See you in the morning.'

I had just lifted my foot and placed it on the first step of the stairs when Shane did a throat-clearing-cough thing.

'Jamie?'

I turned around reluctantly.

'We need to talk.'

I didn't want to talk. I wanted to go to bed and put the whole incident out of my head but instead I followed him into the kitchen. Shane made tea for us and I sat at the table making little holes in a mound of sugar that someone had spilled.

'About what happened,' he said, plonking a mug

in front of me. I looked up: he was standing by the
table and I knew by his face that he'd probably been
rehearsing his speech all evening. My heart sank.

'. . . So that's why I thought we should talk,' Shane
was saying as I tuned back in to the conversation.

'Oh,' I said, pouring milk into my tea.

'I love you, Jamie . . .' he began.

'Look, Shane—'

'No – let me finish. I love you, Jamie – truly I do
– and I even think you're nice-looking. If I didn't
know you I might even fancy you – but, you see, the
thing is – I *do* know you, so I don't . . .'

'You don't fancy me because you know me?'

Shane shook his head and shrugged. Then he
looked at his feet.

'I should be insulted,' I said, sitting back in my
chair as relief flooded through me.

'I've been thinking about this all day – I didn't
mean to insult you.'

'I said I *should* be insulted, not that I am – to be
truthful, Shane, I'm delighted. I don't fancy you
either.'

He looked up at me as a big grin spread across
his face. 'Really?'

'I swear to God.'

He sat down opposite me at the table. 'That's great
news.'

I nodded. 'Did you talk to Heather since – you
know – the thing at the station?'

Shane sighed. 'Yeah – I met her today for a while
and we had a long chat.'

'And you told her that nothing happened between us?'

He nodded.

'Did she believe you?'

'I don't know – I think so. Anyway, she won't say anything to anyone – she'd be too embarrassed.'

'I hope you're right,' I said.

'Do you know something? I feel lousy about how it happened but I'm not really sorry we've broken up.'

'Was she very upset?'

'A bit – mad at me, mostly, and I don't blame her.'

'It'll all work out eventually,' I said.

Shane nodded and we were silent for a little while as we drank our tea.

'Do you think we had sex, though?' he said then.

I groaned and laid my head on the table. 'I can't imagine it but I suppose anything is possible when you're as drunk as we were.'

'Yeah, I suppose,' Shane said. 'Anyway – we're OK now, though, aren't we?'

'We're grand. Back to normal.'

'Good.' He stood up and stretched. 'I'm going to bed.'

'Well, I'm not coming with you,' I said, feigning shock.

Shane laughed and swatted me across the head. Then we both headed off to our respective rooms and the Land of Nod.

★

I told Sophie all about the conversation next afternoon while we were shooting the breeze in her office, pretending to be working.

'That's so sweet,' she said when I'd finished telling her. 'Are you sure you don't fancy him even a small bit?'

'Not even a tiny, weenchy amount,' I said, sitting back in my chair.

'I have something to tell you,' she said, grimacing.

'What? *You* fancy him?'

Sophie shook her head. 'No – you didn't have sex.'

'What?'

'You and Shane didn't have sex on Friday night.'

'How can you possibly know that?'

'Because you were both so shit-faced you couldn't even get undressed. Rico and I dragged the two of you upstairs and threw you into bed.'

I looked at Sophie and she smiled. 'It was a joke,' she said. 'We thought it was funny – we'd had a few by then ourselves. That's why I stayed in your house. We put you into Shane's bed for the laugh.'

'But we were naked,' I said.

She shrugged. 'It was a warm night.'

'You did that as well?'

'Now calm down, Jamie . . .'

'Bitch!'

'It was a joke – sorry. But look – all's well that ends well.'

'You are a total bitch, Sophie Quinn – how *could* you do something like that?'

She scrunched up her face. 'Look, I'm sorry – I

thought you'd know that nothing happened and then when you were all worried and "*Oh Sophie don't tell anybody*" I couldn't resist stringing you along.'

I laughed then because, much as I wanted to strangle her, I was more relieved to discover that nothing had gone on between Shane and me. Sophie smiled.

'Ah no, no, no,' I said, wagging my finger at her. 'Don't think you're off the hook. I'll get you – just watch your back because you'll never know the day or the hour.'

Sophie sat upright in her chair. 'Bring it on.'

'Did you tell Shane yet?'

She shook her head.

'Put him out of his misery.'

'We'll see.'

Just then my mobile rang and so did Sophie's desk phone. I stood up and pressed the answer button, miming throat-cutting as I backed out her door. It was Dermot.

'Good morning,' he said in his relaxed voice.

'Hi, Dermot, how are you?' I said as I made my way to my own office and sat down behind the desk. 'Any news?'

'A little. Remember I asked if I could talk with your sister-in-law?'

'Sure. I called her and she said it'd be fine.'

'Well, I visited her just this morning – she's a lovely woman.'

'Very nice,' I said, struggling with impatience.

'Anyway, I talked to her – we had tea and stuff

and then she let me have a look around Conor's home office. And do you know what I found?'

'No.'

'Well, it's an amazing thing. Your brother should have been an accountant, he's so neat. But even though he kept every bill and receipt he didn't seem to have kept even one credit-card bill in his own name. There were credit-card bills in Marielouise's name – but not Conor's.'

'So?'

'Well, I thought it was odd. I asked Marielouise about it – thought maybe he was just unusual – didn't believe in credit cards or something like that.'

'And what did she say?'

'Well, she said no, he had one but that the bill went to the company, not to home.'

'There you are, so. Mystery solved.'

Dermot made an *mmm*-ing noise. 'Well, not really. I got onto Bilcon and they said nobody in the company has a company credit card – the employees use their personal credit cards and claim expenses when they pay for work-related stuff.'

'Maybe Conor was the only one – he was one of the owners, after all.'

'I thought of that,' Dermot said, with a low laugh. 'So I spoke to your friend Bill.'

'Really?'

'Yes, and he said neither of them ever had a company credit card – he remembered making a decision about it with Conor. But he still had one of the secretaries search, just in case.'

'And?'

'And she couldn't find anything about a credit card for Conor.'

'So maybe he *didn't* have a credit card,' I said.

'Maybe, but I did a bit of a search and I found a MasterCard and a Visa that could be his.'

'How?'

'My contact did a bit of digging and it turns out that there's a few Conor Ryans with both credit cards. But none of them appear to be your brother, for one reason or another. And then there's this one Conor Ryan – Conor Jarlath Ryan – would that be correct?'

'Yes – Conor Jarlath is his name – after our grandfather.'

'OK, that's what I thought. Anyway, this man opened both accounts around the same time, approximately six years ago.'

'OK.'

'Yes, I know that means nothing. But the interesting thing is that, while the billing address the credit card companies have for this Conor Jarlath Ryan is an apartment in London, most of his purchases up to last year were made in Ireland and in fact most of those were here in the Limerick area.'

My brain struggled with the information. 'So you think this might be my brother?'

'I'm not saying that – just that I think it's worth checking out – if you agree.'

'Definitely,' I said, a sudden surge of excitement whirling in my belly. 'It might be Conor, and if it is it means we'll have found him.'

'Well, maybe so but also possibly not – we'll wait and see.'

'But are the credit cards still active?'

'Yes,' Dermot said. 'Both still being used and paid.'

'So he might be there?'

'Yes, he might.'

'When will you go?'

'Tonight. It shouldn't take too long to find the place the bills go to. I'll get on to you immediately if I find out anything important.'

'Brilliant,' I said. 'Good luck, Dermot.'

'Jamie.'

'What?'

'Don't get your hopes up.'

'Why?'

He took a wheezy breath. 'Well, you'll be upset if it doesn't work out.'

I laughed. 'I'm already upset about it, Dermot. That ship has sailed – it's not going to improve if I just try and cod myself into thinking I don't care whether or not you find Conor.'

Dermot didn't say anything for a few seconds. 'You're absolutely right,' he said eventually. 'Take care – I'll talk to you on Wednesday at the latest.'

I hung up and sat staring into space as I tried to digest all the information that had suddenly come at me. Firstly, Sophie had put me and Shane arse-naked into bed together. That was hard to believe but then again, when I thought about Sophie I could believe it.

Then there was Dermot Kilbane and the fact that he had discovered that my brother seemed to have a secret life with a secret apartment and secret credit cards. That is, if it *was* my brother. Funnily enough, I had a feeling that this was indeed Conor. I really wanted to talk to someone about what Dermot had discovered and was trying to weigh up the benefits of calling Bill against the disadvantages when my mobile rang again.

'Jamie?'

'Hi,' I said, not immediately identifying the voice.

'Hi, Jamie – it's Heather Moore here.'

'Oh hello, Heather! How are you?' Sweat broke out on my upper lip and my hands started to shake.

'I'm great, great, good, terrific – just a quick buzz, Jamie – Poise is booked for nine o'clock Thursday. They'll get started on you then – maybe have to do a bit more later as well but that'll probably be most of the make-up and hair looked after.'

'But I have my show at ten – will an hour be enough?'

Heather sighed a mega-sigh. 'Damn – it'll take hours and hours to make you over. OK, look, I don't suppose you could take the day off?'

'You're right – I couldn't.'

'OK. OK. I'll get it all changed to one-thirty – how about that?'

I gave my own mega-sigh but she ignored it.

'That's settled, so,' she said. 'Hair and make-up and all that jazz Thursday. Then I've booked you in with the stylist tomorrow – he'll take you shopping. We'll finish filming Thursday evening. That way we'll be all set to go for Saturday night's show.'

I listened to Heather and every word out of her

mouth made me regret more and more that I hadn't refused. So what if she'd just been publicly humiliated? Was that any reason why *I* had to be publicly humiliated as well? Heather was still talking as I was thinking and I doubt that she even noticed my lack of response.

'. . . So make a note of the times – one-thirty check in at Poise – Ollie and I'll be there with the camera. Then I need to talk to Colin . . . look, I'll see you then – OK?'

'Fine,' I said, making a decision. 'Heather?'

'Yes?'

'You know that Shane and I are best friends and that's all?'

The other end of the phone was silent.

'We were totally pissed and Sophie threw us into bed together and we slept it off – nothing else.'

Still silence.

'You believe me, don't you?'

Heather coughed. 'Yes. See you.'

I made a face into the phone as she hung up. When I looked up I saw that Shane had appeared in my empty doorway.

'You just missed Heather,' I said.

'She was here?' he said, a look of genuine terror on his face.

'No, fool. On the phone. I talked to her about us being in bed together.'

Shane raised his eyebrows. 'And?'

'Well, it was more of a monologue really – I talked, she transmitted frosty silence.'

'Do you think she believed you?'

'She said she did. I just hope she isn't planning to get revenge on you by going around saying stuff about me sleeping with you. Did Sophie tell you what she did?'

He nodded. 'Bitch. Did you tell Steve?'

I shook my head. 'Nothing to tell – nothing happened.'

'Whatever you say. I'll tell you one thing, though: I was relieved when Sophie told me what they'd done.'

'Me too.'

Shane folded his arms and struck a model-like pose. 'I knew in my heart that if we'd had sex it would be a memorable experience for you, Jamie, not something you couldn't remember.'

'Big-head,' I said, laughing. 'Anyway, that's the least of my worries now – the reason Heather actually rang me was to tell me that my make-over starts tomorrow.'

Shane laughed.

'It's not funny,' I said.

'Yes, it is. Anyway, listen: Ian and I went over those tapes from Chelsea – they're terrific.'

'Good.'

'Yeah – it'll make a great documentary. I especially love the part where you're all stuck up in the London Eye and Tommy appears with the goat.'

'It's beyond sophistication,' I said with a grin. 'Will you put it all together so I can have a listen?'

Shane nodded. 'See you at home later.'

'I'll be late – there's a Celtic League match on in Thomond Park.'

'Kind of a pre-make-over antidote?'

'Exactly,' I said, waving as he disappeared.

Steve cried off when I tried to get him to accompany me to the match, but my dad was happy to oblige. I decided not to tell him about my impending make-over. Not because I thought he'd disapprove but simply because I wanted to put it out of my own head.

Everybody whose arse had ever warmed the Munster rugby reserves bench played in that match but it didn't matter because they won anyway and also managed to distract me. So I counted the evening a huge success. Afterwards Dad and I went for a drink and discussed the finer points of the game and I felt relaxed and happy – a round peg in a round hole. As I fell asleep that night I tried not to think of the beating my self-esteem was letting itself in for as I ventured out of the territory I knew so well and tried to hack it in Girl Land.

27

On my show next morning there was a fight between a man who believed in fairies and a man who didn't. It wasn't a fist fight but that was only because they weren't face to face. I eventually managed to get them off the phone only to be inundated with telephone calls from every part of the city and county on the same subject. Even Tommy Sloane rang in to support the fairy-believers camp – which wasn't a surprise. Tommy was convinced that the Good Folk had had a hand in his success at Chelsea.

All the controversy made for a great show but it was also exhausting. I was seriously contemplating doing a runner after I was finished but the Little People must have tipped Heather off because Ollie the camerman was waiting for me when I came out of the sound booth. He smiled sheepishly.

'Heather sent me,' he said redundantly.

'I figured.'

'Wanted me to film you finishing up today before the make-over.'

I rolled my eyes.

'You just go ahead and do whatever it is you do after your show – don't mind me.'

I grimaced. 'You're hard to ignore.'

'I know but you'll get used to it, I promise.'

I shrugged and went to collect my bag and jacket. All the while being followed by Ollie. I felt like an idiot.

Every other woman I know loves shopping but I think it's different for me. When you're not an average size it can be a little disheartening to trudge through the shops and not manage to find even one thing that fits properly. In my case the sleeves and legs were usually too short, the backs too narrow, the arses too baggy. So it was mostly a bit of an ordeal.

Where was this Colin anyway? I scanned the office for a flamboyant stylist-type person. But there were none to be seen. All of the secretaries were hard at work – even Dee-Dee – and there was a baby-faced man sitting on a chair in my office. He was tall and formal-looking in a navy pinstripe suit and an open-collared blue shirt. His soft blond hair was cut close to his head and though his features made him look as though he was in his thirties his skin looked as smooth as that of any girl. He stood up as soon as I entered the tiny room.

'Colin O'Brien,' he said in a flat Limerick accent as he extended his hand towards me. I saw that each of his fingers wore a silver ring. We shook hands.

'The clothes-stylist person?'

He smiled. 'That's me. You're Jamie?'

'That's me,' I echoed.

He smiled again. 'Will we get goin', so?'

'You're the boss,' I said, following him out of the office.

Colin O'Brien and I became friends almost immediately. It's such a funny thing, isn't it, the way you can meet someone you've never met before and feel like you've known them all your life. At any rate, it's a lot more pleasurable than having some of the people you've known all your life still feeling like strangers.

Colin breezed into Brown Thomas and I soon understood that while I'd never even heard his name before he was a big deal in fashion circles. Firstly, everybody knew him – and like Bill Clinton he also seemed to know everybody's name. All the girls on the make-up counters waved and blew kisses and shouted at him as we passed. It was like being with a movie star.

The reaction to his arrival on the clothes floor was even more dramatic. There the assistants literally flocked to him. They chatted, looked at me, looked at the available clothes and soon Colin was pushing a rail of clothes – and me – towards a dressing room. And all the time I was as passive as a newborn baby.

The amazingly good thing about shopping with a Colin is not the great service but the fact that he's so used to dressing people that he knows just by looking at you both what will suit and what should fit. So as Colin sat outside the dressing room holding court, I tried on one outfit after another and paraded myself for his inspection.

'Too nana-ish.'

'Too slutty.'

'Too horrible.'

'That's nice.'

'That yoke's a joke – throw it in the bin.'

'You look like a man in that, Jamie love – I'd fancy you myself but I think it'd be a mistake.'

'Now *that* works, love. Throw it out to me here and I'll add it to the pile we're keeping.'

I eavesdropped on the conversation outside the dressing room as I struggled in and out of clothes. Through this process I discovered lots of things that Colin had been too modest to tell me as we'd strolled into town. He'd worked with everybody who was anybody in the fashion industry and had spent a long time in Hollywood as consultant stylist to a number of pop stars I'd never heard of – but I got the message that they were big news to the MTV generation.

Ollie tried to get into the dressing room with his camera but I threw a hissy fit and Colin entertained him instead. Somebody brought us coffee after about an hour and Colin allowed me a short break. As soon as I was finished I was dispatched straight back to my cubicle full of clothes. By four o'clock I was exhausted and I'd pulled a muscle in my neck dragging clothes on and off. But I was also happy because we were finished. To be honest, I had no idea whether or not I looked good in the clothes that Colin bought but I was completely relaxed about it as I'd abdicated all responsibility. It was great. Like being a small child again.

Colin and I had a quick drink together and then parted company – me laden down with bags of clothes,

Colin promising to come and help me dress for the *Clothesline* filming. The whole thought of having to get dressed up and go out in public was tipping me back into my disco trauma at the Lismore Community Centre. Lizzie Buckley – I hoped she was stuck in a bad marriage and a dead-end job. I could see where Carrie had been coming from in the movie. I tried to reassure myself that this wouldn't be the same. Colin would never let me go out looking like Big Bird.

By the time I got home Shane was already eating his dinner of nuked pasta and watching a *Baywatch* rerun.

'You look tired,' he said through a mouthful of food.

'Thanks.'

He sat back on the sofa and swallowed his food as he looked me up and down. 'Steve rang me.'

'Oh?'

'He said your mobile must be turned off.'

I fished the offending communication device from my handbag – the battery was dead.

'What did he say?'

'Some sort of a family crisis – he has to go to Dublin straight after his show.'

'Oh really? Anything else?'

Shane – whose mouth was full again – shook his head.

'I might try and call him myself.'

He swallowed. 'He said not to – he'll call you later tonight or tomorrow if he can't manage tonight.'

'All very mysterious,' I said, standing up. 'I don't suppose you'd like some real food?'

Shane shook his head. 'Move, Jamie – I can't see the beach.'

I hit him on the arm and went to the kitchen to find food. There wasn't much there since I'd spent the weekend sleeping instead of doing household chores like grocery shopping. I made myself some scrambled eggs and as I ate hungrily a horrible realisation struck. Maybe Heather was planning to come and film my wardrobe. I'd seen Trinny and Susannah and *Queer Eye* so I had no intention of having anybody pay a surprise visit to my bedroom and make fun of my outdated clothes.

Armed with plastic bags I began the assault on my wardrobe. To begin with I tried to think it all out, then I gave up and dumped almost everything – except for my recent Sophie-inspired acquisitions. How the hell had I managed to buy so many identical plain white shirts?

I threw all my tracksuits and comfort clothes into one of the charity-shop bags and then changed my mind. I couldn't really see myself being parted from that pink fleecy top and my many track pants so I switched them into a separate bag and hid them in the bottom of Shane's wardrobe.

By the time I'd finished that job it was almost nine and I was starting to worry about Steve. What could have happened? Maybe his mother had been taken ill? I changed into my pyjamas and got into bed with a mug of hot chocolate and my book. Next thing I knew it was three a.m. I staggered into the bathroom, brushed my teeth and then fell back into bed with

Titbit who seemed to have taken a liking to me and my bed.

When I woke next morning I found a text message from Steve.

Up to my eyes – will call you and fill you in. Don't worry. Everything all right. Miss you. Steve.

And that was it. At least there were no texts from my stalker, which was a relief. I showered and dressed and made a feeble attempt to do my make-up. Then I set off for work. I had no choice but to drive since I had to bring all my new clothes with me because I was due at Poise at one-thirty.

After my show, where the fairy wars still raged, I greeted Ollie and his camera in reception and left immediately for Poise – arms full of clothes – before I changed my mind and bolted. Heather was waiting in reception when I arrived and she made a great show of hugging and kissing me. She was absolutely perfect-looking. Not a hair out of place, not a dot of make-up imperfectly applied. She smiled and talked loudly about the make-over and Colin and all the time I noticed that her eyes were flat as if they had been drawn on her beautiful face. I felt sorry for her and that was lucky because otherwise I'd have just left while the going was good.

My mother was meeting with a supplier so I was taken off for my salon experience by my friend with the high ponytail. I discovered that her name was Sally, which I thought was a good name for someone so cheerful.

'I hope I don't look fat on the telly,' she said as she began her magic massage on my face and head.

'You're like a rake,' I said, trying not to moan with pleasure. It had been a very toxic and tense weekend one way and another.

'Thanks,' Sally said, as she started with the salad-smelling face mask. 'This is a bit different to the treatment we gave you the last time. This mask is completely new – has the same result as a chemical peel but not as harsh.'

'Great,' I said.

Sally slapped on the goo. 'I wore black, though – do you think it looks all right?'

'You look very nice.'

'Thanks. Me and Karen – she's who'll be doing your hair – anyway, we had a war on Friday about who was wearing black today.'

'And you won?'

Sally tutted. 'Well, not exactly – she wore black too – I hope we don't have to stand beside each other, we look like twins gone wrong – and what harm but she really *is* like a rake – she could wear anything she wanted.'

'Mmmmm,' I mumbled. Whatever ingredients were in this new face mask, I could tell that it definitely contained cement. Maybe Heather was having me encased in concrete and then thrown in the river?

But the facepack was nothing in comparison to the waxing. I never in my life suffered pain like that and as Sally ruthlessly ripped the waxed strips off my right leg I roared like an ass.

'My left leg is almost hairless,' I bargained. Sally smiled indulgently as she ignored me, while placing the hot wax strips along the aforementioned leg. I closed my eyes and breathed through the pain promising myself a wax-free future.

Exhausted, I resigned myself to the rest of the process, allowing myself to be taken over by the experts. I moved when, where and how I was told, flicked through magazines when I was alone, nodded and chatted when appropriate and wasn't even fazed when my mother arrived to check on my progress. As for Ollie – he'd been telling the truth. Every now and again I'd notice him in the room pointing his camera at me and I just learned to pretend he wasn't there.

I doubt that I could have maintained my relaxed state if Heather had appeared. But luckily she'd had to rush off to do something or other so I was reasonably safe. Because this was for TV, *Clothesline* had ordered that I should not be allowed to see myself until the very end of the day. I didn't care. I was resigned to my fate by then.

By five o'clock I'd been processed to within an inch of my life by almost everybody at Poise and the unveiling was nigh. Karen – the hairdresser who'd come in to put the finishing touches to my hair after Gretta the make-up lady had finished with my face – ran through the salon and announced the great event. Everybody who'd as much as shaken hands with me that day packed into the small room. My mother smiled and waved at me and generally acted like I was a six-year-old in a school concert. Ollie

stood himself on a table so that he could get a better
shot of the proceedings and Gretta swivelled my chair
until I was facing the wall of brightly lit mirror. I
steeled myself and . . .

'Shit!' I said as I focused on my reflection. 'I look
great!'

Everybody in the room cheered and clapped and I
tried to take in what I was looking at. My hair was still
short but somehow it was softer with sort of feathery
layers and copper-coloured highlights. My make-up –
which had taken over an hour to do – was so subtle
as to be almost invisible. I just looked clear-skinned
and bright-eyed and – I was happy to see – quite pretty.
For the first time in my post-pubescent life I looked
like a girl.

To my horror my eyes filled with tears that I
hurriedly blinked back and then everybody was kissing me and hugging me and Ollie was doing a little
dance on the table. Just as the excitement died down,
Heather appeared. The crowd parted to let her
through. She stood behind my chair and assessed me.

'Not bad,' she said, making eye contact with Gretta
and my mother instead of with me. They grinned
and looked relieved and I supposed Heather was the
equivalent to the woman from Del Monte. Heather's
approval was obviously heady stuff for the staff of
Poise.

'Now this is the way it works, Jamie. The show goes
out on Saturday week – did I tell you that? The directors have moved us to a prime-time slot.' She looked
at me expectantly so I smiled. What in the name of

God had they filmed that they thought would make Saturday-night viewing? This had to be bad.

'Anyway, we've been running promos – have you seen them?'

'Not unless they're showing on Sky Sports,' I said.

Heather continued unabashed. 'Anyway, from tomorrow we'll be revealing you in the ads – just to get the viewers behind you . . .'

'Jesus,' I said. Heather smiled and I wondered again if she was going to humiliate me on national television.

'We'll need to cover the mirrors once Colin arrives to dress her – she can't see herself until the reveal,' Heather said to Sally.

I tried to smile agreement but inside I was cringing. What had I let myself in for? Just then Colin arrived. He winked at me and I relaxed immediately – maybe he could protect me from Heather? We were whisked off to a small makeshift changing room.

'This is crap,' I said.

'Jamie, Jamie, Jamie – you're an awful woman. Other people would die for this opportunity,' Colin said from behind the curtain.

'Yeah, right. An opportunity to make a complete fool of myself on telly,' I said, eyeing the clothes that he'd selected for me. An aqua silky skirt thing with a big diamond-encrusted belt and a shimmery top with a plunge neckline. I climbed out of my jeans and T-shirt and into the clothes, glad at this point that mirrors had been banned. Colin whistled a Britney Spears tune as I dressed. I couldn't decide which of the three pairs of shoes was meant for the skirt. They never taught me that at journalism school.

'The blue Nine West shoes with the tiny heel go with that skirt, love,' said Colin as if he could see through the curtain. At least he wasn't fazed or disapproving about my complete ineptitude with all things girl. I slipped on the shoes and tried to see what I looked like. I felt all gangly and awkward as I emerged. Colin wolf-whistled when he saw me.

'You're one gorgeous babe and if I ever change my sexual persuasion I'll be knocking on your door,' he said as he held my hand and twirled me around.

'Shut up, Colin, I feel like someone who's pretending to be a girl,' I said as I walked self consciously to the makeshift studio, Colin leading the way.

We walked in to a Trinny and Susannah-type set. A small crowd of people had gathered, including my mother and Heather. Cameras rolled as I made my entrance and everybody applauded. Heather whisked me in front of the covered mirror and spoke to camera. I didn't understand a word that she said and could feel colour rising in my face. Great. I'd have a big beetroot head on top of the transvestite body.

And then she whisked the cloth away and I stood there looking at myself – no – looking at somebody who vaguely resembled me. Somebody who looked like she'd stepped straight off the catwalk. I was absolutely speechless at the transformation. I could hear Heather asking me what I thought and I could feel my eyes filling up. Jesus, I was crying on telly. I tried to compose myself and I think I managed to gabble a few coherent sentences as I twirled in my fabulous outfit. I'd never in a million years have thought to put these clothes together and at that moment I wanted to marry Colin and have him dress me every day. Girl Land was great if you had a Colin.

They made me try on all the outfits and I had to admit that one was nicer than the others and I was actually beginning to enjoy myself just as Heather called it a day. My mother was shiny-eyed with delight and kissed me as the camera crew wrapped up. I reluctantly changed back into my own clothes but cheered up instantly when I discovered that I could actually keep the wardrobe that Colin had chosen for me. It was almost worth the trouble.

The staff at Poise badgered me to go for a drink but I'd had enough of Girl Land. Even though it seemed to be going my way for once I was tired and wanted to be by myself. So I hugged and kissed them all – including my mother – and made my excuses and ducked out to my car. I piled my new clothes into the back and fished my phone out of my handbag. That was good – three missed calls from Steve. I switched on the radio and Steve's voice filled the car which meant he was on air so there was no point in calling him. I'd call him later.

I drove off towards home in the light early-evening traffic. Steve played a Robert Palmer track and I grinned to myself at his lounge-lizard taste in music. When things between us were more settled I really was going to have to try to educate his musical taste.

I stopped at a red light and my phone rang. I

glanced at it, intending to ring back, but then I saw the caller's name. It was Dermot. My heart did a backflip. 'Did you find him?' I said before I could think about the words coming out of my mouth.

Dermot laughed wheezily. 'Maybe.'

'Where are you? Are you still in London?'

'No, I'm back at home – I just got in the door.'

'What happened?'

'Well, I found the apartment building – Gladioli Villas in west London. I had a good look around but there doesn't appear to be anybody actually living in number fifteen.'

'How do you know that?'

'I asked the neighbours. Some of them knew nothing but there are a couple of nosy old women in the building. I showed them a photograph of Conor and they both said that he was the man from number fifteen. One of them said he was always there on the first of the month . . .'

'How does she know that? Does she know him?'

'No, but that's the day her pension comes and she always goes to the post office and says she usually meets him – I don't know how reliable that is but it'd make sense if he was just using the place as a holding address.'

'So what now?'

'I'll go back over next Wednesday – which is the first – and stake the place out, as they say.'

'Thanks a million, Dermot,' I said.

'Jamie . . .'

'I know, don't get my hopes up.'

'No, actually – I take your point about that. No, I was going to say good luck with that TV show.'

'How did you know about that?'

'Well, I am a detective, you know.'

'Very funny, Dermot.'

'All right – my wife was in the salon today when you were getting all the stuff done. She said you were lovely.'

'Tell her thanks.'

'Talk to you later, Jamie.'

I hung up and pure unadulterated excitement flooded my system. Conor was alive. I knew it was complicated and I knew it was weird and still part of me didn't care as long as he was alive. I resolved to call Bill as soon as I got in and had made a huge mug of coffee. He'd have to eat his words about Dermot now. It really was an added bonus.

My head was full of Conor and at first when I pulled into the driveway I didn't notice that there were two people sitting on my doorstep. Jesus! I squinted: Aisling and Aoife.

Aisling stood up as soon I got out of the car but Aoife stayed sitting on the concrete step, a look on her face not entirely unlike Titbit's malevolent stare.

'Hi, girls!' I said, hoping I sounded more enthusiastic than I felt.

'Hi, Jamie,' Aisling said. Aoife sort of grunted.

'What brings you two here?'

'Dad – he told us to come and say hi while he was on air. We were bored.'

'Well, it's lovely to see you both,' I said, sidling past

Aoife and opening the front door. 'Come on in. Are you hungry?'

Neither girl answered me but they both followed me to the kitchen. Titbit scraped wildly at the back door as soon as he heard my voice and I let him in. He ran towards the two girls who suddenly lit up. The girls petted the dog and talked to him like he was a long-lost friend.

'Mum says we can get a dog,' Aoife said, forgetting to ignore me.

'That'll be lovely,' I said.

'Can we come and get Titbit and bring him for walks while we're here?' Aisling said.

'Of course.'

Aisling looked at her sister. 'That'd be good, Aoife, wouldn't it? We'd have something fun to do every day.'

Aoife shrugged and stroked Titbit but I could see that she agreed.

'Are you on holiday from school already?' I said as I poured boiling water into the teapot.

'Yeah,' Aisling said.

'And will you be staying with your dad for a couple of days?'

They groaned in chorus. 'We have to stay here for the whole summer,' Aoife said, bitterly.

'The whole summer?' I echoed.

They nodded glumly and I tried for a big happy smile.

'That'll be great,' I lied as I looked into their sullen faces. 'Really, really great.'

28

I made a lasagne while the girls fussed over Titbit. All attempts at conversation had just about run dry when Steve arrived, a large bunch of flowers in his arms.

He kissed us all and sat at the kitchen table and put his head in his hands. Aoife stood behind him and began to massage his neck.

'Poor Daddy,' she said in her sweetest voice, 'you're so tired. Let's go home.' She grinned at me.

'In a little while, sweetie,' said Steve as I handed him a plate with the last piece of lasagne and some salad. 'Thanks for this, Jamie. At least I don't have to cook dinner now. My show was hectic – some breaking-news story – prisoners on the roof of the jail – and just . . . oh . . . loads of stuff . . .' He stopped talking and sighed. I looked at his face and noticed dark circles under his eyes. He looked exhausted but seemed very agitated at the same time.

'You're coming down with something, Steve,' I said, feeling his forehead. His temperature seemed normal.

'My sinuses act up this time of the year,' he said and blew his nose.

Aisling and Aoife had brought Titbit out into the small back garden. Steve pushed the food around his plate. I stood at the window and watched the children throw a ball that Titbit refused to fetch.

'Did the girls tell you about their mother?' he said.

I looked at him and he smiled wanly. 'All they said was that they were staying with you for the summer.'

He blew his nose again. 'Susan is doing this humanitarian aid mission in Africa . . .'

'And she gave you no notice? That's kind of hard, isn't it? I mean, the girls will need something to keep them occupied while you're working and stuff . . .' I hoped that I didn't sound as though I didn't want them around. I did, for Steve's sake, but I wasn't stupid: I knew that it wasn't going to be easy – most of all for me.

'She was called out suddenly – she's an engineer, did I tell you that already? Anyway, they wanted her sooner than was planned so . . . so I stepped in.' He came over to the window and stood behind me, twining his arms around my waist. We could see the girls chasing Titbit, squealing and giggling as they did so. Steve nuzzled my neck.

'It's going to be a wonderful summer, Jamie. I can feel it – you, the girls, we'll have a great time. And they'll be going to Irish college on Inisheer in a couple of weeks – maybe we could holiday there at the same time.'

He kissed the back of my neck. I watched the seemingly idyllic dog-chase in the garden and I fought off the thing in my head that was saying *nightmare summer* as I turned around and kissed Steve hard on the mouth.

'We'll go to dinner tomorrow night, Jamie – I feel like we haven't had any time together in ages. I miss you.'

I snuggled close.

'I'll book that new restaurant that everyone is talking about.'

'Super Macs?' I said, with a grin. 'I heard the ads on my show.'

Steve laughed. 'I was thinking more along the lines of La Boucherie.'

'I know. That'll be great.'

I slept badly that night. My dreams were vivid technicolour snapshots of make-overs and Conor and Steve's girls, all mixed together in what seemed like some new insane sitcom. This was interspersed with sounds from Shane's bedroom that should have been X-rated. I was glad that Shane was getting some action but did he have to keep me awake at the same time? Who the hell was he in bed with? Hopefully not Heather. And that train of thought made me think of when I might see a little action again myself – considering the presence of our newly acquired beady-eyed chaperones.

I got up early and showered and dressed. Shane came into the kitchen as I buttered toast.

'You owe me,' I said as he filled the kettle. His hair was dishevelled and he wore jeans and nothing else.

'For what? I won all the football bets again this season,' he said, grinning at me.

'A night's sleep, fool. What were you doing that was so noisy? Wait – don't answer that.' I laughed and bit into my toast and noticed for the first time ever, that I could remember, Shane's face turning an exquisite shade of puce.

'Shane Ali, what's going on? Who's the mystery girl?'

He turned away and began to fill the already full kettle again. 'Nobody. Did you watch any of the game last night? Heard it wasn't great . . .'

'It's someone I know, isn't it? That's why you're so mortified. Is it Heather?'

'No – don't be stupid.'

'Bet it's someone from work – Dee-Dee?'

Shane smiled at me. 'No, it isn't Dee-Dee.'

Just then I heard footsteps on the stairs, followed by the sound of the front door opening.

'I'll just wave her off, thank her for the sound night's sleep,' I said, running towards the kitchen door. Shane tried to grab me but I managed to wrong-foot him – years of playing football had its advantages. I ran down the hallway and opened the front door. And I couldn't believe my eyes as Sophie's shiny Peugeot pulled away from the kerb.

I ran back into the kitchen but Shane was gone.

'Shane,' I called up the stairs. 'Confession time. Come down – it won't take long.'

No answer.

I took the stairs two at a time and barged into his bedroom. Shane was sitting on the bed, pulling on socks.

'Confess all,' I said, sitting down beside him on the unmade bed.

'You should have knocked – I could have been balls-naked,' he said without looking at me.

'Don't mind that, I've seen it all before. Now tell me everything.'

Shane grinned at me and shrugged. 'Nothing to tell.'

'Liar. You just slept with our best friend and there's nothing to tell?'

'I'm taking the fifth.' He went back to dressing himself.

I stood up and smiled slyly at him. 'That's fine, because I'll get Sophie to tell me. You know how it is with us girls – we tell each other everything. Especially about guys. Oh, and by the way it is true – we do rate them on a scale of one to ten.'

I waved and walked out of the room and could hear Shane muttering as I left.

I arrived at work and went in search of Sophie, who was conveniently tied up in a meeting. I sent her an *I saw you so you better confess* text and began preparing for my show. I hoped to God that the fairy wars were over – they were beginning to bore me now.

And then there was the bloody make-over show. What kind of footage did they have of me? Jesus, that was really worrying. I cleared my head as I entered the sound booth and my show went smoothly despite my inner turmoil.

The minute the show ended I went in search of

Sophie. She was in her office, filing her nails and reading a report at the same time.

'Well?' I said, plonking myself down on the chair opposite her. 'You look exhausted.'

She smiled. Putting down the report, she concentrated more intently on her nails.

'I'm pretty tired myself. It was kind of noisy in our house last night,' I went on.

'Is that right?'

'Yeah, it is. And you know I saw you leaving this morning so don't try to pull that one on me.'

Sophie's eyes were round with feigned innocence. 'I don't know what you're talking about, Jamie. All set for fame?'

'Bitch. Don't try to change the subject, I'm not a fool. I know what happened.'

'*How* do you know?'

'Feminine intuition – it's a *Girl Thing*,' I said in a bad impersonation of her voice.

'Ha ha,' Sophie said. 'Really, how do you know?'

'Shane spilled the beans.' I smiled at her and noticed that finally I had her undivided attention.

'What did he say?' she asked, abandoning the nail-filing.

'Oh, this and that. The usual. What do you say when your two best friends – who are themselves best friends – end up shagging each other?' I gave an exaggerated shrug.

'Nothing happened.'

'Right. So it was the soundtrack from a porn movie that kept me awake.'

'Jamie, sometimes you're so vulgar . . .'

I examined Sophie's face and she looked away. 'You like him, don't you?'

She didn't answer.

'Sophie, you like him – I never realised that you fancied him . . .'

She didn't answer.

'*Do* you fancy him?'

She ran a hand over her perfectly smooth hair. 'It was just one of those things.'

'How did it happen, anyway?'

Sophie smiled and looked away. 'We went for a drink after work and then we went for food and then . . . well, we kissed outside Friar Tuck's and I have to admit, Jamie, it bowled me over. We got a taxi . . . and, well, you know the rest.' It was her turn to shrug.

'And then you ran away this morning before I could meet and greet you.'

'Exactly. You'd have done the same thing.'

'Absolutely.'

The phone rang and we heard Dee-Dee's voice crackle on speaker. 'Hi, Sophie. There's someone looking for Jamie . . .'

'No problem, Dee-Dee. Tell them she's on her way, all bright-eyed and bushy-tailed.'

'Be careful, Soph,' I said, grabbing her arm.

She looked at me. 'Don't blow it up out of proportion – it happened, it's over, we're both on the rebound. A bit of fun.'

I didn't say anything, though I thought it was a bit more complicated than that. But I didn't have time to think about it too much as we walked together out of Sophie's office. The minute we went into the open-plan area I could see Ollie coming towards me, pointing a camera in my face.

'Extra footage for the show,' he said and I rolled my eyes in exasperation. Steve was standing at the door of his office, smiling and waving at me. Sophie was smiling too but I was too distracted to gauge her reaction when Shane appeared from behind a dividing screen, a roll of cable in his hand.

Ollie filmed me as I left work and headed to the car park. I didn't speak at all: I was like Tommy Sloane's crew when I'd tried to interview them in Chelsea – I didn't have anything to say. I drove away as fast as was legally possible.

When I got home I took Titbit for a walk, glad to be out in the bright sunshine. As we walked by the side of the Shannon my phone rang.

'Hi, Jamie.'

'Hi, Steve. What's up?'

'Nothing. It's just that I know we'd arranged to go to dinner tonight and . . . well . . . Aoife isn't feeling well and she wants me to stay at home.'

Of course she does, I thought.

'That's fine, Steve – don't worry about it.'

'Are you sure? I'm really sorry. I was so looking forward to hearing all about the make-over. I bet you'll look terrific on TV.'

'Mmm,' I said, thinking that he hadn't said anything yesterday even though he'd seen me immediately after I left Poise.

'Are you mad with me?'

'No, of course not. Aoife's sick, she needs you.'

'We'll take a rain check. Maybe tomorrow night?'

'No problem. Talk to you later.'

I made my way home, feeling suddenly deflated. I tried to work out what had upset me about my conversation with Steve. If the child was sick then she was sick – it wasn't really that. Maybe it was something about Steve's tone – but what? As I let myself into my house the strangest thought struck me: Steve had sounded relieved.

29

I couldn't face cooking so at about eight o'clock I made my way to the Thai takeaway on Hyde Road. As I got back into my car, arms full of cartons of food, my attention was taken by the sound of a laugh that I recognised. I looked across the road and saw two men standing smoking outside a run-down pub. I couldn't believe my eyes. One of them was Steve – no doubt about it. I watched as he walked into the seedy-looking pub, laughing and talking with his companion. The fragrant aroma of the Thai takeaway that I'd just purchased filled the car. I debated whether to follow him into the bar but I decided not to. Tears stung my eyes as I started up the engine. Why had he lied to me? And worse still, why had he used his child in the lie?

I drove home and by the time I reached my front door I'd calmed down considerably. There could be a reasonable explanation for all this – I shouldn't jump to conclusions. I'd talk to him tomorrow, I decided as I opened the front door.

'Shane, I'm back,' I called out as I plonked the food on the worktop and went in search of clean plates. Shane came into the kitchen, his hair wet.

'Nothing like a shower after a long day,' he said, rooting in the bags.

'And a long night,' I said. I began opening cartons and ladling food onto plates.

'Want a beer?' he asked as he stuck his head into the fridge.

'Any wine?'

'Yep. I'll be posh and have a glass with you,' he said.

We brought our food and drinks into the living room and Shane flicked through the channels until he found a rerun of *World Cup Classics*. We ate in silence for a while.

'So, are you seeing Sophie again?' I asked through a mouthful of green curry.

'Tomorrow. At work.'

'Smart-arse. You know what I mean.'

He laughed and shrugged. 'Yeah, and the answer is that I don't know.'

'Bad answer. It's a yes-or-no question.' I looked at Shane as he polished off his glass of wine in exactly the same way as if it was a glass of beer. He shrugged again. 'I think I want to but I don't know if she does and it might make everything weird . . .'

'I know what you mean: look what happened to us – and we didn't even do anything.'

He grinned.

'How did it happen, anyway?'

'I undressed her slowly, then she—'

I threw a paper napkin at him. 'Stop! Too much information. You know what I mean.'

'It just happened. But it was bad timing. I wish it was next year, so the Heather thing would be well out of the way. I mean, Sophie has had a shit time and . . . it could be all wrong . . .'

'It could be all *right*, too.'

'I don't know – I think it was a mistake.'

'She does have one flaw all right, Shane: she's not great on football.'

He laughed and switched channels. *Punk'd* – which we both loved – came on. There's nothing like a TV programme where some poor unfortunate is set up in a horrible situation and filmed secretly to give you a laugh. And then I had the best idea ever.

'Shane, let's do it,' I said, standing up in my excitement and pointing at the TV.

'What? Let's do what?'

'Let's punk Sophie.'

An evil grin spread across Shane's face. 'How?'

I did a little war dance. 'You'll love it – *Pimp My Ride* meets *Punk'd*.' *Pimp My Ride* was another one of our favourite American shows, where they take your car and jazz it up – fur, leather, alloys, the works.

'The new Peugeot?'

I nodded, grinning from ear to ear.

'We couldn't – she'd go mad.'

'She put us in bed together, let us think the worst, let us stew . . .'

'She'd go ballistic.'

'Coward. You fancy her now so you're letting her off the hook, you coward, Ali.'

'How would it work?'

I rubbed my hands in glee. 'We take her car, pimp it up good – paint it, decorate it, tacky and cheap is what we're looking for. We pretend we're filming it for a new programme – watch her reaction as she sees her beautiful car seemingly destroyed . . .'

'Seemingly?'

'Yeah, of course. All the stuff will be removable, even the paint job. That's the *Punk'd* part of it.'

Shane smiled. 'It could work – I could get some of the lads from the TV station to help. How would we get the car from her?'

I picked up my wineglass and took a sip.

'You'll ask her for a loan of it – urgent business in Nenagh.'

Shane shook his head. 'Good idea – except for one thing. I can't drive.'

I laughed. 'I keep forgetting that. OK – we could hot-wire it – no – she'd have the cavalry out. You couldn't steal her keys, could you?'

'How?'

'Jesus, Shane, am I the local criminal? Have you any ideas at all?'

'Let's do it the simple way. Take her keys, let her think she's lost them. All we need is a morning. Actually, isn't there a directors' meeting next Wednesday?'

I nodded. 'Excellent idea. She'll be locked in a meeting all morning, she probably won't even miss her keys. Now, who do we know who could help us?'

'Fucking hell – look at that, Jamie!' said Shane. I turned around to face the telly and looked myself straight in the eye. The *Clothesline* promo was in full swing. I could hear a voice-over saying: '*Are you a hopeless case? An ugly duckling? A trackie tramp? Jamie Ryan was until* Clothesline *called . . . tune in on Saturday 12 June to see how Jamie changed from a fashion disaster to a catwalk queen . . .*'

And the pictures that they ran with were of me at the bloody TV bash – standing in the foyer with the red dye running down my chest (which I could see now was lopsided – one of the chicken fillets must have moved when I ran in the rain).

Shane was bent over double from laughing and I picked up a cushion and beat him over the head with it. He sat up and wiped tears from his eyes.

'I can't wait for that show, Jamie,' he said and started to laugh again.

'Some friend *you* are – and it's your fault I had to do it.' I beat him again with the cushion.

'Oh Jamie, you made my night. This'll be the talk of the town tomorrow. I can't wait to go to work.'

And Shane was right. Everybody was talking about the forthcoming show. Dee-Dee and Raina Burke giggled when I came into reception but I silenced them with the darkest glare that I could muster. I made my way to my office and wished that the door was fixed. Jesus, how hard *was* it to fix a door?

Sophie came in then and I glared at her too. She put her hands up in the air in mock surrender.

'I didn't say anything. Not one thing, Jamie.'

'Keep it like that, so.'

'They could have shown the shrunken-dress bit – although they might be saving the really good bits for Saturday week.'

I smiled at her and pictures of her precious car – all pimped-up and tacky – popped into my mind. 'What goes around comes around,' I said.

My phone rang. Sophie waved a silent goodbye as I answered.

'Hi, Mam.'

'Everybody's talking about it. You're famous, do you know that?'

I said nothing.

'Jamie, are you still there?'

'Yes.'

'Anyway, I can't wait for the show – you'll have to make a big effort now.'

'What do you mean?'

'Well, people will recognise you and they'll be watching what you wear and, well, you'll have to keep up appearances . . .' My mother laughed as if she'd just cracked a joke but I knew there was a sting in that particular tail. I felt like I was eight years old and she was telling me not to play ball in my new patent shoes. Or climb walls. Or have any fun at all.

'There's two chances of that, Mam: none and zero. Actually, I'm sitting here in my grey trackies and a lovely dri-fit vest I found in the bottom of my wardrobe.'

'I'm only trying to help you. There's no need for that tone, Jamie.'

Conversation died and I let the ensuing silence stretch out between us, nice and long and awkward.

'I'll do your make-up for you – just call in to the salon any time and I'll get one of the girls to look after you,' she said eventually.

'Thanks,' I said, both of us knowing that it'd never happen. 'I'd better go, I'm up to my eyes here. See you.' I hung up without waiting for the goodbyes, her words still ringing in my ears: *people will be watching you – you have to keep up appearances*. If that was true then it was a sad world we lived in. And my mother was at the helm in that sad world. I hated it all in that moment – the make-over, my stupidity in agreeing to it, the invasion of privacy to come. The sad reality is that women have to constantly decorate and preen or they face condemnation and the worst part is that it's mostly by their own sex.

'How's the Trackie Tramp?' Shane said from the doorway. He was gone the second he saw me lift a stapler off my desk.

I did my show. And struggled through it for the first time in ages and as if that wasn't bad enough I cut my shin on the bloody transmitter sculpture in the studio on the way out. Then I went in search of Steve. His mystery visit to the pub the night before was gnawing away at me. I limped into his office without knocking. He had his back to the door and shot around the minute he heard me.

'Jamie!' he said, smiling at me. His nose was red and he sniffed loudly.

'Steve. How's Aoife?'

'Aoife? Oh, she's fine. A twenty-four-hour bug – much better today.' He grinned at me and stood up and came around the desk.

He hugged me to him and nuzzled my ear. 'I miss you, babe.' Then he kissed me gently on the mouth. I didn't respond. He pulled away and held my face in his hands.

'What's up, Jamie? It can't be that *Clothesline* programme because we saw the promo last night and it's going to be terrific for your career. The girls are dying to see it . . .'

I looked into his lovely sexy eyes. 'It's not that.'

Steve kissed me lightly again. 'So what's up? Tell me.'

I stepped back a little so that I could see his whole face. 'I saw you last night.'

Confusion clouded his eyes and I could see him wrestling with this new information.

'Where?'

'You were going into a pub on Edward Street with someone.'

'You must have been mistaken.'

'Steve, please don't make this worse. You lied to me. I'd like to know why.'

He looked into my eyes and reached out and traced my mouth with his finger. I pulled back slightly.

'Why?' I asked again.

'OK. I'll tell you the truth, Jamie, even though I shouldn't.'

'Why not? Is it all right to lie to me?'

He shook his head. 'In the fellowship . . .'

'Fellowship?'

'Alcoholics Anonymous. We're sworn to secrecy, especially sponsors and, well – Tommy Sloane's brother rang and said he was in a bad way and I met the brother and we went and got Tommy . . .'

'And Aoife?'

'Do you think I'd lie about that?'

I shrugged.

'Aoife was sick – I left her with Aisling while I sorted Tommy out.' Steve looked at me, his face full of hurt. I moved towards him and then we kissed hungrily and he whispered in my ear as our kisses became more urgent. The situation was just getting out of control when there was a knock on the door. Then the phone rang.

'The gods say go back to work,' said Steve, winking at me. 'Come in.'

Dee-Dee came in with a sheaf of files for Steve. She looked at me and smiled knowingly as she retreated.

'I'd better prepare for my stint. Listen, Jamie, let's have a really nice night tomorrow evening – dinner at La Boucherie – coffee at your place.'

'Love to,' I said. 'What about the girls?'

'Well, Aisling is old enough to babysit for a couple of hours.'

'Brilliant – can't wait,' I said and backed out the door, smiling at Steve.

30

'This is really good,' I said, cutting a piece of tender steak. Steve was sitting across from me and hadn't looked away since we'd begun our meal. It was an incredible turn-on and it was all I could do to concentrate on the food. Plenty of time for dessert later, I thought as I smiled at him. The thing about Steve was that he had this air about him like royalty or movie stars. He looked like a special person and people were drawn to him because of it. I felt so lucky, especially now that Aoife had stopped phoning every five minutes to complain about her sister. I had a feeling that it was going to be a good night.

'Would you like another glass of wine?'

'Steve Lowe, are you trying to get me drunk so you can take advantage of me?' I said, holding out my glass as he poured.

'I was hoping *you*'d take advantage of *me*,' he said, smiling.

I rubbed my leg against his under the table. 'That'd be my pleasure entirely.'

'Not quite,' he said and leaned over and kissed me on the mouth. I was oblivious to the other diners as

I responded to the kiss. It felt like years since we'd had sex.

'Dad, Aisling hit me and I told her I'd tell on her and she's a mean bitch and you shouldn't leave me alone with her . . .'

Steve and I jumped apart. Aoife stood at the table, tears streaming down her face.

'Aoife, what happened, for God's sake? And where is your sister?' said Steve just as Aisling made her way through the packed restaurant.

'Dad! I'm not minding her any more – I hate her and I wish she was dead.'

The woman at the table beside us tutted loudly and I could see the maître d's concerned face looking over at the rumpus.

'You started it, Witch Face – I'm telling Mum too. And Dad, she rang her boyfriend in Dublin and stayed on the phone for hours and she let me watch an over-eighteens' movie and she said fuck off to me . . .'

Aisling pushed her younger sister. 'No, I didn't – *you* said fuck off first and you said Jamie was gay . . .'

'You said she was disgusting in the ads and that she was a slapper and . . .'

'Girls! Give it over at once,' said Steve and nodded at a hovering waiter for the bill. The girls bickered on as we got our coats and paid for our meal. They were still fighting on the pavement outside and fought the whole way back to my house. Steve walked me to the door and we could hear them arguing as he kissed me goodnight.

'Sorry, babe – I was so looking forward to tonight.'

I shrugged. A wail sounded from Steve's car and he waved and left.

I let myself into the dark house and sat on the couch with Titbit and a bottle of Shane's beer. I flicked through the channels, knowing already that there was no football on – the season was over. The *Clothesline* promo ad came on so I flicked over to another channel and cursed Steve's girls for ruining the night. My phone signalled a text and I picked it up, thinking it was Steve apologising again.

You shouldn't have done the programme. You hurt me.

That was all I needed. A message from my stalker on my phone with the new sim card. Great. Without thinking I hit 'reply'.

Why don't you fuck off and leave me alone you wanker?

Then, realising what I'd done, I switched off my phone and checked that all the doors were locked. I brought Titbit up to my bedroom and let him sleep at the bottom of my bed.

The slagging about the *Clothesline* show escalated and by the middle of the following week I felt like the whole city knew me – and that was just from the promos alone. What would it be like next Saturday when the show itself was aired?

I spoke to Dermot Kilbane on Wednesday morning and he seemed more interested in the show than in the information that he wanted to relay to me. It wasn't much, anyway – stuff I knew already, like the date he was flying to London and what he planned to do there. As I hung up after speaking with him I realised that the make-over thing had one good advantage – it stopped me, albeit temporarily, from dwelling on my missing brother.

But the biggest distraction of the moment was Jamie's Revenge on Sophie. Shane, fair play to him, had everything organised and had managed to secure a spare set of car keys that he'd discovered she kept in a drawer in her office. She was safely ensconced with the directors right now and Shane had given the keys to his friend Paul at the TV station.

We'd lined Ollie up to mock-film the whole thing and I couldn't wait to see Sophie's face and her dilemma in trying to be gracious in front of the camera. Sophie was a trouper and wouldn't let the imaginary programme down, no matter how hard it was to hide her shock. We planned to do the reveal after my radio programme that morning – a special on the growth of the cosmetic surgery industry in Limerick. It was an excellent show and I was elated when I'd finished. I always knew when it had been a good show by the reaction of my colleagues and when I came out of the sound booth and Johnny G and John Howard began clapping my heart felt like it would burst. I loved my job at moments like these – absolutely loved it – and I knew how lucky I was because how many people could honestly say that?

We brought Sophie out to the front of the building at around four o'clock. She was all excited and curious at the same time. Johnny G pretended he was fronting the pilot for the new show. He was brilliant and a small crowd had gathered on the front steps with Johnny and Sophie.

'So, Sophie Quinn, we are thrilled to inform you that your car is the very first to be featured in this new show *Changing Rides*.'

Johnny paused and Sophie looked puzzled. He continued. 'We took your Peugeot 307 – yes, your Peugeot – and glammed it up. Your boring silver car is gone – to be replaced with *this* . . .' He waved as a car – if you could call it that – pulled up near the steps. It was driven by Paul from the props department of Fab City TV.

There was silence as everybody looked aghast first at the car, then at Sophie and then back at the car again.

It was canary yellow in colour with turquoise speed stripes down each side. As we all made our way down the steps we could see bright pink fur seats. The dashboard had pink, yellow and turquoise jewels embedded in it. The mirror was a mini-dressing-room job with tiny bulbs surrounding it. The sunroof looked like the glass had been tinted pink and it made Paul's face appear eerie as he smiled out at us from the driver's seat.

The inside roof was yellow satin and a state-of-the-art car stereo with surround sound belted out hip tunes. Paul got out of the car and we could see the interior in all its shiny glory. Some of the crowd were tittering now and Shane was desperately trying to keep a straight face. But it was Sophie's face that was the most comical. Emotions ran across it at speed: first absolute horror, followed by dismay, and then the horror again.

'So, Sophie, why don't you take a seat in your gorgeous glammed-up ride?' said Johnny G, who was surpassing himself in the role of show host. Ollie looked as if he was earnestly filming every detail.

Sophie looked like she was going to cry but climbed into the car and looked out the driver's open window as Johnny spoke to her. 'So, Sophie, what do you really think? Don't you just love it?'

'I . . . I kind of liked it silver . . . I don't know what to say,' she said, horror written all over her face.

'I like that – so overcome that she's speechless. Anyway, Sophie, do you know who was behind the restyling?' said Johnny.

'Laurence Llewellyn Bowen?' asked Sophie sarcastically.

'Your good friends Shane Ali and Jamie Ryan. You can thank them for this wonderful job.'

Sophie glared at us and we smiled at her. Johnny held the mike out towards us.

'So folks, are you pleased with the results?'

'Absolutely delighted,' I said. 'It's turned out way better than we imagined – I mean, it's so Sophie!'

There were titters from the crowd.

'Enjoy it, Sophie, we love you,' said Shane, winking at her.

She looked bewildered sitting there, her face pink from the tinted glass, the music making the pink furry dice shake even though she'd turned it down.

'Anything to add?' said Johnny, holding the mike out towards Sophie.

'Um . . . I liked it silver . . . I don't mean that I don't like this . . .'

'Do you like the new look or not?' asked Johnny.

'I . . . yes . . . I know that people worked hard . . .'

'Yes or no?'

'Um . . . yes . . .'

'Well, that's a miracle, Sophie Quinn, because *we* all think it's crap,' said Johnny and everyone started laughing. Sophie looked puzzled.

'Sophie, you've just been Punk'd, you big eejit,' he said.

Realisation dawned on her then and she got out of the car as everybody cheered and clapped. She made a beeline for us. 'I'm going to kill the two of ye.'

'What goes around comes around, Sophie – I tried to warn you. Karma – if you'll pardon the pun,' I said, and grinned. She glared at me and then fixed on Shane.

'Her idea,' said the cowardly Shane, pointing at me.

'Liar. His idea, Sophie, believe me,' I said.

'Feel like a pint?' asked Shane.

'I feel like a whole bevy of them,' said Sophie. 'Give me five minutes. And by the way, we're walking – unless you can get the car cleaned up right now.'

'Coming?' asked Shane as Sophie left.

I shook my head. 'I've got plans,' I lied. I didn't want to be a gooseberry. Even there in the street I could feel a new energy between Sophie and Shane and no matter what either of them said I had a feeling in my water that there was more to this than they thought. I knew I was destined to spend the evening alone. Steve was taking the girls to the cinema later and although he'd asked me to come I really couldn't bear to spend the evening with the two sulkers. Titbit was a better option.

But Sophie had the last laugh. *Clothesline*, unfortunately, was a real programme and I was its reluctant star. At first I wasn't meaning to watch it at all, just do the ostrich thing and bury my head in the sand and pretend it wasn't happening. But my family and friends made that impossible. Steve was taking the girls to a concert in Dublin where James Blunt and Daniel Beddingfield were the star attractions on the Saturday night and I was glad that they'd miss the make-over show. But Aisling and Aoife had assured me that they'd set the video recorder and couldn't wait to watch it when they came back on Sunday evening.

My mother had wanted to throw a party on the night and hire a projector screen for the show. But she'd dropped the idea immediately once she'd heard me swearing at the other end of the line. Sophie was coming to our house to watch it – supposedly with me but really with Shane. They were pretending that they weren't seeing each other – Sophie was even still going out with Rico occasionally – but any fool could see that there was something going on between them even if they couldn't.

I woke on the morning of the show in great form

initially. Steve had come back to my place the night before and we'd had terrific sex. It was so good that it was almost worth the wait. But then reality dawned and I buried my head under the duvet and wished the day would just go away. No such luck.

My mother rang about forty times, hardly able to contain her excitement. A huge bunch of flowers arrived at my door and I was just about to dump them when Shane read the card – they were from Steve. Bill sent me a text message saying he couldn't wait to see the show. Bastard. Marielouise rang and said the kids were on high-doh and that Mark hoped I'd be wearing the new Liverpool strip when they revealed the made-over Jamie. The only person who hadn't contacted me was my stalker. I hadn't even bothered to change my sim card this time – I mean, he seemed to know my new number sooner than me so what was the point?

We settled down in front of the TV that evening, a bottle of wine on the table in front of us. Shane sat next to Sophie, his arm draped casually behind her on the sofa. Titbit sat next to me, his fat body curled into my side.

The ads finished and *Clothesline* started. I peeped out over a cushion. The show opened with secretly filmed shots of me walking to work in my grey trackies, another of me in my favourite pink fleece which looked hideous on screen. There was me in jeans and a T-shirt that actually had a hole on the sleeve, which the camera zoomed in on. Me in my Liverpool jersey, running out of the station. Jesus, what did I look like at all? Me and Mark playing football in the park, a huge streak of mud festooning my red sweaty face. Shane and Sophie were guffawing and I was slugging back the wine like there was no tomorrow.

But the worst bit was to come. The bastards had filmed my wardrobe before I'd done the big clean-out. There was Heather standing in my bedroom as she and Colin rummaged through my clothes. Colin held up the pink fleece like it was something the dog slept on and Heather held my favourite jeans up against her perfectly attired body saying they were *so Nineties*. Tears of laughter were streaming down Sophie's face and I'd run out of cushions to throw at her.

My wardrobe looked pitiful, even to me. T-shirts, jeans and one skirt. And the worst part was when they got to the shoes. Doc Martins, sneakers, even a pair of ancient football boots. I closed my eyes and groaned, wishing the programme over.

Then it moved on to the make-over. My mother in her element, beaming at the camera, not a hair out of place. Heather all smiles and giggles, Colin talking clothes and make-up and shoes. And then the big reveal. I peeped out through my fingers as the sheets were stripped off the mirror and the camera focused on me and my reaction. And I must say I was stunned once again at how good I looked.

Shane wolf-whistled and Sophie screamed. And then the credits rolled and the agony was over.

'You looked fantastic, unbelievable,' said Sophie. 'I won't be a bit surprised if they'll offer you TV work. Amazing.'

'Jamie, you were fantastic – the whole show was brilliant,' said Shane.

I shook my head but I was secretly pleased at the way it had unfolded. I knew it was just the fact that so many people had worked on me – polished me up until I gleamed like a revamped car. *Pimp My Person.* I knew that it was temporary but the results were pretty amazing. Even I could see that.

'More wine,' said Sophie. 'Let's celebrate!'

As I headed to work early on Monday morning I got some inkling of exactly what my new-found fame entailed. People waved at me from their cars. A bus pulled up beside me in O'Connell Street and all the passengers waved at me and gave me the thumbs-up. Everybody in the station was buzzing about it and Dee-Dee had four journalists ringing her for interviews with me. My show was inundated with callers and well-wishers and by lunchtime I was fit to tear my hair out.

I sought refuge in Sophie's office, bringing two coffees with me.

'Sophie, can you believe all the bullshit? Spare me, there's no way I'm doing interviews . . . Sophie what's wrong?'

She was sitting in her chair, her face the palest I'd ever seen it. Her eyes were red-rimmed and when she saw me a single tear rolled down her cheek.

'I think I'm pregnant. No – correction – I *know* I am,' she said. And then the tears came in earnest.

31

Sophie's news took over my entire consciousness for the next few days. On the one hand I couldn't believe that she was pregnant – as in she was about to produce a small human being from her body. On the other hand every time I looked at her pale and worried face I knew it was true. But possibly the worst part of it all for me was that she refused point-blank to discuss it.

'It's my problem,' Sophie said as she lifted a huge bunch of files from her filing cabinet the day after she broke the news. She dumped them on the desk and began to painstakingly read through each piece of paper. 'I'll deal with it.'

'Will you tell Shane?' I asked.

She shook her head and bent over a sheaf of paper.

'But you're going to have the baby?' I asked.

'Yes – that's the only thing I'm definite about.'

'Then don't you think he might guess as time passes?'

Sophie looked up and I could see the dark bruises of sleeplessness around her eyes. 'I don't know if it's his baby.'

'Oh,' I said, grimacing. 'Rico?'

She shrugged.

'Have you told him?'

'No.'

She laughed wryly. 'Jesus, Jamie – would you like to be going to parent-teacher meetings with Rico?'

'Well, no, but if it is his baby . . .'

'Look,' Sophie said, slamming the open drawer of the filing cabinet. 'Rico, Shane – what does it matter? Neither of them was in the business of procreating when we were having sex so in a way it's nothing to do with them. Do you know something? I don't even want to know which of them is the father. It's definitely *my* baby – I know that much and at the moment all I can deal with are things I'm definite about.'

She turned away and emptied another load of papers out onto the desk and began to super-concentrate on them. I watched the top of her head: I felt very, very sorry for her and I didn't really mean to ask the question but it sort of popped out.

'What about the baby?'

She looked up at me, puzzled.

'Doesn't he or she deserve to know who his or her father is?'

Sophie's face clouded over and two huge glistening tears rolled down to her chin. She sank onto her chair behind her file-strewn desk and, putting her face in her hands, she began to sob. I ran over and put my arms around her and held her tightly as she cried. Jesus – mothers, fathers, children, parents – why was it all so complicated? I stroked her hair and she cried and cried and cried. Eventually she stopped and sat back and looked at me.

'I'm fine,' she said, with a watery smile. She blew her nose noisily. 'I'm scared but do you know something, I'm kind of glad I'm pregnant as well in a mad way – does that make any sense?'

I nodded. 'Mother Nature – ruthless bitch will do anything to populate the world.'

Sophie laughed. 'But I don't know what to do about the father issue now. I was thinking about it in terms of me and Shane and Rico all along – I never thought of it from the baby's point of view.'

'You have a long, long time to sort those things out,' I said.

'Do you think so?'

'Of course.'

She sat staring into space for a few seconds and I was really sorry to have raised the subject in the first place. Eventually she looked at me.

'You're right – I don't have to make every decision this minute, do I?'

I shook my head and smiled. Sophie bent down and pulled her make-up out of her handbag. Then she leaned to the side and produced a mirror from a drawer. She emptied the miscellaneous make-up onto a space among the still unsorted files and without saying another word set about repairing the tear damage. I watched in absolute fascination. Within minutes you'd never have guessed that she'd been crying at all – except perhaps for the slightly haunted look in her eyes.

'You're a genius, Michelangelo,' I said.

Sophie looked up from the mirror and smiled.

'Why, thank you – I've a meeting with the directors in half an hour and I've no intention of going in there with a blotchy face. I want them to give me more money for the station, not start worrying that their manager is losing her marbles.'

'They'll never think that,' I said.

She piled all the make-up back into its bag and then stood up and straightened her skirt. 'Do I look OK?'

'You look great,' I said.

She walked around the desk and stood in front of me. 'Thanks, Jamie.'

'For nothing,' I said, standing up and hugging her hard. Her body felt small and frail and I was suddenly swamped with worry for her.

'You sure you're OK?'

Sophie walked towards the door. 'I'm fine.' Then she waved and was gone.

I left the station a few minutes later, my head still full of Sophie and her problems. Who was entitled to know and if and why and all the other imponderables. On the way out I met Dermot.

'Jamie!' he said, stepping back into the blinding lunchtime sunshine.

'Dermot,' I replied, amazed at how hot the day had become since I'd gone into work. 'How are you?'

We faced each other on the footpath. The sun beat down on my head.

'Great! Great! Lovely day, thank God, isn't it? If we had weather like this all the time wouldn't we have the grandest country in the world?'

I nodded as Dermot fished a large cotton handkerchief from his trouser pocket and wiped his face. There was something odd about him – and not just the usual oddness of being a wheezing, obese detective. Something else.

'I'm glad I ran into you,' he said, replacing the handkerchief. 'Have you time for a quick drink?'

I was supposed to be going to the supermarket to pick up some food before collecting Mark and Fiona at half-two but I figured I could abandon the food shopping until later.

'OK,' I said. 'Dillons'? It's the closest.'

He agreed and we walked the short distance to Dillons' Sports' Bar – the Fab City local. Dermot insisted on buying the drinks and sent me to find a seat. I sat down at a table in a quiet corner near the back door. The pub was almost empty – it really wasn't the weather for hiding yourself indoors. Raucous laughter from the small courtyard on the other side of the door told me that most of the customers were either out there smoking or had joined the smokers in order to take the sun.

Dermot arrived at our table with a cup of coffee for himself and a misting glass of sparkling water for me.

'When did you get back from London?' I said as soon as he'd seated himself.

'Last night.'

'And?'

He smiled and stirred two spoons of sugar into his coffee. 'The curate's egg.'

I frowned and shook my head.

'Good in parts.'

My chest tightened. 'What does that mean, exactly?'

Dermot gave a long sigh and unpocketed his sail-like hanky. He looked at me with his intelligent eyes.

'I found Conor,' he said, quietly. He dropped the handkerchief onto the table and pulled a small attaché case onto his knee. After a few seconds of fumbling he handed me a bundle of photographs. My hands began to shake as I sifted through them. Each one had a picture of the same man: walking along a city street, eating in a restaurant, holding the hands of two small children I'd never seen before. A tall, angular man with dark hair – The Man in The Park – Conor. The last photo confirmed it beyond a shadow of a doubt. It was a close-up of Conor's face. It filled almost the whole frame and hot tears sprang into my eyes as soon as I looked at it.

'He's laughing?' I said incredulously to Dermot.

He nodded sympathetically.

'How can he possibly be laughing when we've all suffered so much since he left?'

Dermot pressed his lips tightly together, reached over and held my hand.

'Oftentimes people don't realise the effects of their actions,' he said. Dermot squeezed my hand. 'I'm sure it wasn't his intention to cause any of you any pain . . .' His voice trailed off.

'Did you talk to him?' I said.

'Yes. Yes, I did.'

He put more sugar in his coffee and began to stir the frothy liquid.

'And?'

'He wouldn't talk to me – said he didn't know what I was talking about and if I didn't leave him alone he'd have no choice but to call the police.' Dermot sighed again. 'Look, Jamie – I don't know Conor but I know a man on a mission when I see one. Whatever is going on in his life, it's no accident that he left.'

'What does that mean?'

Dermot shrugged. 'What I'm saying is that it looks to me like he made a decision to walk out of his life in Limerick and – I'm sorry, Jamie – I don't think he has any intention of coming back.'

I looked down at the photo of a laughing Conor that I'd dropped onto the sticky table. Surely Conor would never do something like that – hurt me and Mam and Dad, Bill, Marielouise – his *children*? He wasn't exactly Mother Teresa but I'd never known him to be gratuitously cruel – it wasn't his form. In a way it was easier to believe that something bad had happened to him. At least if he'd been murdered or abducted we would all have suffered at someone else's hands – not at Conor's.

'I need to talk to him,' I said.

Dermot grimaced. 'Might be difficult.'

'But you know where he is now.'

'Weeeellllll,' Dermot drawled, 'we *did* know where he was – I made a few phone calls this morning and it seems that Conor has cancelled his credit cards and the lease on that apartment.'

'What?'

'I suspected he might, which was why I checked it out this morning.'

'So now we're back to square one,' I said.

'Not exactly square one – at least we know he's alive.'

I drank my tepid fizzy water in one long gulp. 'There has to be a reason for this,' I said, slamming the empty glass back onto the table. 'I want to see him – talk to him myself. Can you find him again, do you think?'

Dermot played with the hem of his handkerchief. 'I can have a go. We can follow the money.'

'What does that mean?'

'Well, he has to be financing his new life somehow. Maybe siphoning money from Bilcon.'

'But that'd be embezzlement, wouldn't it?'

Dermot shrugged. 'I can look, Jamie – get permission to go over Bilcon's books. The thing is, you might not like what I find.'

'I don't care. I want to know the truth no matter what it is.'

I exhaled a shuddering breath. Suddenly I felt cold and longed for the feeling of the hot sun on my skin.

'The thing is, Jamie love, that I can't guarantee I'll be able to find him again. Especially as he now knows we're onto him.'

I shrugged, a new determination forming inside me. 'I want you to try.'

Dermot didn't answer immediately. He just drained the dregs from his cup and placed it noiselessly back on its saucer.

'Will you try, Dermot?'

He nodded and I patted the back of his hand. 'Thanks.' I picked up the photographs and looked through them once again. Pausing at the image of my brother with two children I scrutinised the picture. The children were both girls and also quite young – maybe three and five – younger than his own children, anyway. Both had thick mops of black hair and were holding Conor's hands as if it was the most natural thing in the world.

Who could they be, these tiny girls? Was he a bodyguard or a minder of some sort now? But there was something domestic-looking about the photograph – I couldn't have said what exactly but it was undeniably so.

'Do you think he could be involved with some other woman?' I asked Dermot.

He shrugged and nodded simultaneously. 'Possibly.'

'And do you think these might be her kids?'

He nodded again. I traced Conor's photographed face with my fingertip. 'Where did you take this picture?'

'I followed him from the apartment. He went to a nearby day nursery and came out with the children.'

I nodded but didn't say anything. Dermot took a deep breath that made his wheeze ring out so loudly that the barman looked at us. 'I spoke to him shortly after this picture was taken. He put the children in his car and I was worried I'd lose him if he drove away. Nice car, too – silver BMW 5 Series.'

'Was that when he refused to talk to you?'

'Yes. He kept looking into the car at the children and to tell you the truth he was a bit agitated.'

'Agitated?'

He nodded.

'Like maybe he was afraid of something?' I asked.

Dermot nodded again. 'The only thing is, Jamie, there could be a number of explanations for agitated behaviour like that.'

'Such as?'

'Well, I don't know.'

'Maybe he's ill,' I said, as possibilities flooded in.

'Maybe.'

'Or afraid.' I realised I was just repeating myself.

'Maybe,' Dermot said again. 'Or maybe he just doesn't want to be found.'

'I want you to contact him. What about that car? Is it registered in his name?'

Dermot pulled a single A4 sheet from his folder and pushed it towards me. *Kelly Smith 138 Gladstone Road London NW2 5EH – possible address for Conor Ryan?* was written in neat script across the top of the page.

'Who is Kelly Smith?' I asked.

'The BMW is registered in her name so she must at least know him if he had her car.'

I looked at Dermot.

'I could contact her – see if she knows Conor's whereabouts if that's what you want me to do.'

'Please – please do that.'

Dermot smiled kindly and nodded. 'There's one small problem. The wife's niece is getting married in

Belfast on Saturday – big affair – and the whole lot of us have to go up on Friday and we won't be back until Sunday night. I was thinking that if you wanted me to go I could go Monday. How would that be with you?'

'That's grand with me. Dermot, I must owe you a fortune by now – you've been back and forth to London a couple of times.'

'Look, don't worry about it, Jamie – I got the cheap flights and I always stay with my sister in Shepherd's Bush. We'll sort it out when I'm finished.'

I opened my bag and fished out my chequebook. 'How about if I give you five hundred now so at least it won't be piling up on me?'

Before he could answer I wrote the cheque – it was worth it, who needed a deposit for a house anyway? I handed him the cheque. 'You'll never put those children through college if you don't charge the clients, Dermot.'

He laughed and nodded.

'Can I have a copy of those photographs?' I asked.

'No problem. Take the whole folder – I have copies of everything at home.'

He handed me a green paper folder. I didn't say anything, just took it from him. He looked at his watch. 'Is that the time? I promised the wife I'd drop in to her mother this afternoon – cut the grass, tidy up around for her.'

I tried to hide my surprise as we stood up. Had his wife and mother-in-law heard him pant and wheeze recently?

'You OK?' he asked as we made our way back into the brilliant sunshine. I blinked like a vampire and shaded my eyes with my hand.

'Fine.' I smiled at the now perspiring smooth-skinned detective standing in front of me on the busy footpath. 'Look, Dermot, when you find him, this time I'll talk to him.'

'I'll do my best for you,' he said, grasping my hand in a sweaty but hearty handshake and then hurrying off. I hoped to God he wasn't going to keel over and die cutting the old lady's grass. I was growing quite fond of Dermot. He was a thorough and methodical detective and I could see how he'd have made a great cop. But he was also an insightful and kind man. I looked at my watch: two-fifteen – time to head towards the school. As I began to walk up Henry Street my phone rang.

'Steve,' I said, my heart jumping as I saw his name on the small screen. 'Oh Steve, I'm so glad you called, you won't believe what's happened – I just met Dermot Kilbane and he found Conor but Conor ran away from him and it looks like he doesn't want to be found but I just can't believe he'd do something like that without a good reason . . .' A huge avalanche of tears erupted and I bawled.

A thin middle-aged woman wearing a skintight halter top and sprayed-on pedal pushers stared straight into my face as she passed. Steve murmured softly into my ear and as I reached the corner near the school I stopped walking and crying and stood there in the middle of the footpath, my head full of confusion.

'Jamie?' Steve's voice called after a few seconds.

'Yes,' I said sniffing loudly.

'You OK?'

'I'm fine, Steve, thanks, love.' I blew my nose and tried to drag myself up out of the emotional hole I'd fallen into. 'Why did you call? Did you want me for something? I never even asked you.'

'Just to tell you that I have to go to Doolin after the show.'

'Why?'

'The girls are going to Irish college in Inisheer today.'

'Oh, I forgot.'

'I could do without this drive ahead of me after a day's work.'

'I know,' I said, beginning to walk again.

'It's unbelievably hard for me at the moment. You don't know what it's like for me trying to keep all the balls up in the air. It's incredibly stressful . . .'

I tuned out as Steve launched into a rant about how difficult his life was and how nobody understood. A disloyal part of me wanted to say that I'd be happy to swap with him right at that moment but I knew that was just a reaction to the news I'd received from Dermot. It wasn't Steve's fault that my life was so full of shit.

'. . . So it'll be late when I get back – how about lunch tomorrow, maybe?'

'That'd be nice – call me in the morning,' I said.

We said our goodbyes and then hung up. As I walked slowly towards the school in the sweltering heat that tiny disloyal part of me began to bitch about Steve. Sure, he made the right listening noises – but did he ever really engage with what was happening to anybody else? I beat back the question.

He was preoccupied. His life was difficult – having those two wagons as daughters was more than enough suffering for any one lifetime. He probably meant to be more interested in me and in what was happening to me but was just a bit caught up in his own stuff. It didn't mean that he didn't care about me.

The children were already milling out into the sunshine by the time I reached the schoolyard. Mark was earnestly discussing some kind of collector cards with a group of serious boys his own age while Fiona – as unbuttoned as always – was playing tag with a group of squealing little girls.

They saw me immediately and my heart actually ached in my chest as I hugged and kissed them. How could Conor abandon these two willingly? It just couldn't be true.

The three of us struggled along the hot, dusty city street – me carrying both their school bags and the kids arguing and scuffling and petitioning for drinks and ice pops. I had promised them that they could come and hang out at my house for the afternoon. Marielouise was to pick them up on her way home from work and meanwhile the three of us were going to eat junk and just be together. Needless to say, when we'd been planning this afternoon I hadn't antici-pated hearing that my brother had wilfully walked away from all of us. Maybe it was just as well that I

had the children to distract me under the circumstances.

The air in my house was stuffy and dead so I opened
all the windows and doors as soon as we got in. It didn't
make much difference. I made us some sandwiches
and searched the freezer until I found ice cubes to add
to our drinks. That was always the trouble with extreme
weather in Ireland – we were so used to our in-between
nondescript climate that we were never really prepared
for either heat or cold.

Fiona and Mark settled down in front of the Disney
Channel and demolished the plate of sandwiches. I
could hardly eat a bite so I just sat there between
them on the sofa, sipping cold 7-Up and trying not
to think about their father. After they'd eaten I tried
to persuade them to go outdoors but they protested,
saying it was too hot and they were too tired and I
was too mean if I expected them to go outside in
that heat.

'We'll get skin cancer,' Mark said, throwing himself
onto a cushion on the floor in front of the TV.

I looked at him.

He shrugged. 'We might, you know.'

Fiona was stretched along the sofa, half asleep, and
a tiny breeze was moving the air in the sitting room.
Thank God for a house across the road from the
river.

'All right, so,' I said, relenting. 'But we have to go
for a walk down in the bird sanctuary after the movie.'

They agreed and we all settled down to watch a
movie about a boy and a bear. Fiona nodded off and

Mark became engrossed in the story but I couldn't concentrate. All I could see were those photographs of Conor.

What had happened to my brother? And what the hell was I going to do about it? I sat, melting onto the sofa, internally debating my next step. Finally common sense prevailed and I went and got my phone. Locking myself into the kitchen so that the children couldn't hear me, I made the call I'd been longing to make ever since Dermot had delivered his news in Dillons' pub.

32

'Is that right?' was all Bill said when I finished telling him what Dermot had discovered.

I closed my eyes and counted to ten – had this man no emotions? 'I just told you that your best friend may have embezzled from your company and that's all you have to say?'

'What do you want me to say?'

'Sweet fuck all, Bill. See you round.' I jabbed the hang-up button and threw the phone across the kitchen, cursing myself for once again mistaking Bill Hehir for a human being – the man was definitely a robot. No wonder Conor ran away – I'd run away too if I had to work with that fool.

I took Dermot's green folder from my bag and looked again at the photographs of Conor. How could this be happening? What did it mean? I picked up the A4 sheet with the London address – who the hell was this Kelly Smith? His girlfriend? A friend? His employer? I was suddenly overwhelmed – none of it made any sense at all. I shoved everything back into the folder and made myself a cup of coffee before going back in to the kids and the Disney Channel. I forced myself to concentrate on the movie and was just starting to succeed when the door-bell rang. When I opened the door Bill Hehir was standing on my doorstep. I was too annoyed even to speak so I just turned on my heel and walked away.

He followed me straight through the kitchen and out into the back garden. By then I was shaking with fury and began to pull madly at the weeds growing between the paving slabs. Nobody said anything for a full five minutes. For once, though, Bill's face wasn't a mask: he looked hurt but I didn't care. If I was to be honest I wasn't really angry with Bill but I was so confused and upset myself and he was such an arse-hole anyway that it seemed like a good idea to focus all my anger on him.

'I think I found a dummy company,' Bill said.

'Pity you didn't find it eighteen months ago.'

Bill gave a wry laugh. 'Eighteen months ago I was worried that my best friend had topped himself, not looking to see if he'd robbed me.'

'And has he robbed you?'

'I think so – I found a non-existent subcontractor who's been in receipt of monthly payments for the past five years.'

I stood up and made my way slowly over to my rusting garden bench.

'Five years? But he only left eighteen months ago,' I said, plonking myself down on the wooden seat.

'I know it's weird but it looks like it was planned.' Bill sat down beside me. And as we sat there in silence I felt as if I'd been emptied of everything – words, feelings, everything – and Bill looked like a man trying to digest a concrete block.

'And you want Columbo to find Conor again?'

I nodded. 'There has to be an explanation.'

'Sure – how about your brother is a bollocks?' Bill said, standing up. 'That's a good explanation.' He took off his suit jacket and threw it down beside me on the bench. Then he pulled at his tie until it came free, opening his collar button as he paced back and forth in front of me. I squinted into the sun as I watched him and somewhere a car backfired.

'Maybe something is wrong with him,' I said quietly.

He stopped pacing. 'Like what?'

I shook my head. 'I don't know. That's why I want to talk to him. Come on, Bill – don't try to tell me you don't want to know why.'

Bill didn't answer. I was glad because I wasn't sure I wanted to hear what he was thinking anyway. I was too vulnerable. A small noise caught my attention and made me look towards the patio doors that led from the kitchen to the garden. Though I wasn't positive I thought I saw Mark's back disappearing from view. I jumped up and grabbed Bill's shirt-sleeved arm.

'Mark,' I hissed.

We stood together, looking towards the empty kitchen.

'Did he hear us?' Bill asked.

I shrugged. 'I don't know.' I walked into the house and straight into the sitting room. Fiona was still asleep and Mark was sprawled on his tummy, chin in his hands, watching TV. He looked up when he heard me come into the room.

'OK, love?' I asked.

He nodded and smiled and turned his attention back to the television. I thought that maybe I saw something in his eyes but I couldn't be sure and I couldn't really ask him. All I could hope was that he hadn't overheard anything: *I* was hardly able to bear the weight of what had happened – I was positive that it would crush an eight-year-old. I went back to the kitchen where Bill was now standing, staring out the window, a full glass of water tilting and forgotten in his right hand.

'Well?'

I shrugged. 'I don't think he heard – I hope he didn't.'

'Good.' Bill remembered his water and took a sip. 'You shouldn't keep looking for him, Jamie.' He turned around to face me. 'Really, if he doesn't want to be found we have to respect his wishes.'

I raised my eyebrows. 'You don't mean that.'

Bill smiled for the first time since he'd arrived. 'You're right, I don't. But I still think you should forget about him.'

'He's my brother.'

'And my best friend and if he doesn't want us I think he can go fuck himself.'

'But what about the children?' I asked.

Bill sighed. 'I don't understand how he could do it to them – bastard – but they're better off without him if that's all he thinks of them.'

'He might need our help.'

Bill laughed a long, low, mean laugh. 'You're deluding yourself. It's high time you faced up to the truth and stopped acting like a child.'

I felt the rage rising inside me. 'Fuck off, Bill Hehir. You think everybody is like you – cold and calculating and always in control.'

He stared at me, his face expressionless, and the anger inside me exploded until all I could feel was the heat and the pain of it. Bastard. Why had I called him in the first place? I might have guessed how he'd react.

Bill took a deep breath. 'Really?' he asked. 'That's what you think of me? Cold, calculating and always in control?'

I nodded. 'The truth always hurts.'

He shook his head. 'No, not always – sometimes, though, people can decide that something is the truth. Now *that* can hurt OK.'

I picked at the skin around my cuticles. 'I don't know what you mean, Bill. It's always the same with you – disappear off into your own head as soon as the going gets tough. You didn't want me to look for Conor in the first place and now it turns out that I was right to do it.'

He laughed again. 'Are you sure? Do you feel better now than you did before?'

I shrugged. 'It makes no difference what I feel – we now know that Conor is alive and well and living in London.'

'And doesn't knowing that make it worse?' he said, moving slightly towards me.

I backed away. I knew he was right but I didn't care. 'No,' I lied. 'Now I can talk to him and if he's in trouble I can help him and we can sort everything out.'

Bill exhaled an exasperated breath. 'Best of luck to you, Jamie – Boutros Boutros-Ghali himself couldn't sort out this heap of shit.'

'I don't agree and I think if you weren't such an embittered cynical bastard you'd see that what I'm saying is true.'

'If being a realist and living in the world makes me a cynical embittered bastard then I'm guilty as accused. You, on the other hand, Jamie Ryan, are an ostrich – you believe what you want to believe, mould the world to suit your view. Well, off you go, I won't try to stop you. But I won't help you to cause more pain.'

'I have no intention of causing more pain.'

'Then I'm warning you – don't tell your parents and don't tell Marielouise.'

I started. How had he known that I was thinking of telling them that very night? He stared at me and neither of us spoke for a few seconds. 'Don't tell them,' he repeated. 'It wouldn't be fair.'

I shrugged, walked towards the sink and turned on the tap.

'Promise me,' he said.

I turned around, my heart thumping with fury. 'I'm not a child, Bill – don't give me orders.'

'Use your brain, Jamie.'

'Why don't you have a look and see if you have a heart, Bill?'

He gasped slightly and threw his jacket over his shoulder. 'This is like a bad scene from *The Wizard of Oz*. See you around.'

And then he was gone. I turned back to the sink and began to scrub the draining board. I heard Bill say goodbye to the children and then I heard the front door slam.

I finished cleaning the sink and went immediately into the garden where I repotted all my house plants. Why the hell had I called him, anyway? I was really never going to learn my lesson about that man.

Mark and Fiona joined me in the garden and as the afternoon cooled we had a late picnic and played some Snap. Inside I was bruised and sore but I decided to box up the whirling confusion until I could have an opportunity to think it all out later, when the kids had gone home.

Marielouise arrived at around five and joined us in more cool drinks. As I looked at her happy face and saw that she was finally beginning to recover from the trauma of Conor's disappearance I suspected that maybe Bill was right. Maybe I should keep what I knew to myself for a little while longer – at least until I had some good explanations to ease the pain of the blow.

I waved the children and their mother off and made myself a salad for dinner. But I still couldn't eat so I lay on the sofa and tried to watch some old Serie A football and wished that Shane was coming home instead of going to his parents for dinner. I couldn't focus properly on the handsome Italians and between the heat and the trauma and the general weight of life I must have fallen asleep because the next thing I knew someone was banging on the sitting-room window.

Groggily I stood up and staggered towards the front door.

'Steve?' I said, peering into the balmy night.

'Took you long enough,' he said, walking past me into the house.

I stepped back and looked at him in surprise. 'I was asleep on the couch.'

He didn't answer, just continued on into the kitchen. I followed. By the time I'd arrived he was looking into the open fridge.

'Any food?' Steve turned his head to look at me.

'Not a lot – I didn't get a chance to shop. There's some salad and cold chicken if you'd like that.'

He slammed the fridge closed, giving an exasperated moan. 'I should have known there wouldn't be anything to eat.'

I looked at him. His eyes were wide and darker-looking than usual and his face was slightly flushed as though he had a fever. 'Are you feeling OK?' I asked as I filled the kettle.

'Fine. Good. Never better. Did I tell you I've had an approach from LFM? The powers that be there heard my broadcasts when we were over covering Chelsea and they're looking for someone like me. Want to interview me.'

'That's brilliant, love,' I said, yawning loudly.

'Oh – sorry to bore you,' Steve said.

I looked at him. 'I've had a long, hard day – I'm tired.' The kettle boiled. 'Would you like some tea?'

He shook his head and made a face. Then, without warning, he walked over towards me and pulled me close. My body stiffened as he began to kiss my neck and I tried to pull away.

'Oh Jamie,' he murmured into my hair. My head swirled. Only seconds before he'd been looking at me with an expression close to contempt on his face – now this sudden rush of amorous attention? I couldn't figure it out but I knew that something was seriously wrong.

'Look, Steve – no . . .'

He ignored me and pushed his hands under my T-shirt. I pulled away.

'Steve!'

He looked at me as if he was seeing me for the first time, which made me wonder who he thought he'd been kissing. And then, like tumblers in a lock, everything came together – Steve was a fuck-up. It wasn't even his fault that he couldn't love anyone because he was the centre of his own universe. Steve's needs, Steve's wants, Steve's worries – nobody else had a reality for him. A massive wave of exhaustion swept over me.

'I'm going to bed.'

'Anything you say,' Steve said, sidling up, a leer on his face.

I pushed him away. 'Alone. Let yourself out, Steve – I'll talk to you tomorrow.'

I pulled free of him, walked out of the kitchen and

went upstairs. My body felt like lead as I slowly climbed the steps and went into my bathroom. I turned on the taps in the bath and went out to the hot press on the landing to get a towel. Steve was at the top of the stairs. His face was pale now and drawn and his eyes were haunted-looking and I didn't care – I just wanted him gone.

'See you, Steve,' I said, opening the door of the hot press.

'Don't ignore me, Jamie – I won't be ignored.'

I grabbed a fat red towel and turned around. 'Won't you? Too bad,' I said. 'Goodnight.'

Steve stepped forward and caught me by the arm. 'I'm not finished speaking to you yet.'

I stumbled towards him. 'Let go!' I shouted, freeing my arm. 'Look, Steve, I don't know what you should do – call your sponsor, I suppose – do whatever it is you need to do, but get out of my house. I'm going to bed.'

'How dare you speak to me like that,' he said, coming close up into my face, white spittle collecting at the corner of his mouth that had turned from being Steve's mouth into a hissing, cruel orifice. 'I am not doing anything – clean and sober – I told you.'

'Not any more,' I said, anger battling with a sudden burst of fear inside me.

'Fucking know-it-all bitch,' he said, jerking his hand forward. I looked at him in surprise as his fist made contact with the centre of my chest. Then I reeled back and fell down the first three steps of the stairs, landing with a loud shout as I banged my head against the wall. I lay there crumpled for a few seconds, trying to work out what was happening. Steve ran past me and I heard his feet on the stairs and saw his back disappear through the front door. My head thumped and rang and I puked where I sat. I tried to get up but my legs weren't working. Then maybe I passed out or something because the next thing I knew Shane was crouched beside me, calling my name over and over.

33

'What happened, Jamie? Did he hit you?'

I was sitting on the couch in the living room. My whole body was shaking, despite the blanket that Shane had wrapped around my shoulders.

'Ouch!' I said, pulling away from the bag of frozen peas that he was holding to the side of my very sore head. A lump the size of a grapefruit had formed almost instantly and I had a really bad headache.

'I rang Sophie, by the way – she's coming over,' he said. 'Did you take the Nurofen? Maybe we should take you to the hospital and we should definitely report it . . .'

'No, Shane. I'm fine and I can deal with this. It was an accident, really it was . . .'

'I don't believe you, Jamie. I saw him flying past me on the stairs – only a guilty coward would do something like that. I've a good mind to—'

'You'll do no such thing, Shane Ali. It was an accident, it's nothing.'

Just then the doorbell rang. Shane ran out and returned with a concerned-looking Sophie. The minute I saw her I burst into tears. She sat down and put her arms around me and I cried like a baby.

'That's it, Jamie, let it out,' she said into my hair.

After what seemed like an age Sophie spoke, her voice quiet and calm. 'Tell me what happened.'

I looked at my friend, her pale face worried and drawn. 'I'm sorry for dragging you out of bed, Soph, I'm fine, I . . .'

'Tell me,' she said, looking into my eyes, her hands gripping mine.

I lowered my head and looked at our entwined hands as I spoke in a monotone. 'He was really weird when he came in, Sophie, not like himself at all, not like Steve . . . No, that's not true – he *was* like Steve.' I stopped and took a deep breath as she tightened her grip on my hands. 'We had a fight on the landing and he pushed me . . .'

'The dirty cowardly bastard, I'd love to . . .'

I shook my head. 'I don't think he meant it, not really . . .'

'Yeah, right. Jamie, there is absolutely no excuse on God's Earth for him to raise a finger to you. It doesn't matter whether he meant it or not – the fact is he did it.'

'I know, but it was more a reaction than an action. Anyway, I stumbled and fell down the stairs . . .'

'He pushed you down the stairs? Fucking hell, this gets worse, we should report the bastard . . .'

'No, Sophie, I stumbled – only about three steps and I walloped my head off the wall, that's how I got the bump. And I kind of passed out because then the next thing I knew Shane was calling my name. Where is Shane?'

'I've no idea. Listen, Jamie, you should report him – make him pay.'

I shook my head. 'I just want to forget about it. I want it to be over. And anyway, what good would it do? It's my word against his – I did a programme on domestic violence.'

Sophie loosened her hands from mine and placed them on my shoulders.

'Look at me,' she ordered.

I did as I was told.

'You can't go back with Steve, you know that.'

Tears welled in my eyes and spilled down my cheeks. 'Did I deserve it? Did I do something to deserve it? Is there something wrong with me?'

'No way. Remember when Paul did the dirt on me? You stayed up one whole night telling me that I didn't deserve to be treated like that. Well, it's the same really, Jamie. I got slapped too – not physically but it hurt the same. Nobody deserves to be treated like that – that's the bottom line.'

I knew in my heart that she was right but in that moment I wanted Steve to undo it all, I wanted it not to have happened. I wanted Steve to treat me with love and respect and he'd done the opposite and it made me feel like a shit person.

'I'm starving,' I said and we both looked at each other and burst out laughing.

'I'll get Shane to go get takeaway, how's that?' said Sophie as she went in search of him.

My headache was finally lifting and the leaden concrete feeling had moved and had now taken up residence in my heart. I felt hollow and drained and really hungry.

Sophie returned with a dejected Titbit at her heels. 'I found him sitting looking at the front door with his big sad eyes – Shane is on the missing list. Maybe he read our minds and has gone for the takeaway.'

'Or else he's gone to give Steve Lowe a hiding,' I said.

A mean twinkle flickered in Sophie's eyes. 'Mmm – Shane beating seven kinds of crap out of Lowe-life.'

'Seriously, Sophie, Shane has a terrible temper. He'll kill him.'

'Good. Now let's have a look in the cupboards for food, I can't wait any longer.'

Sophie made us scrambled eggs and toast and lovely hot tea and we sat in the living room, eating. I was glad of her company.

'No more Steve,' she said, munching on her toast.

I smiled wanly at her. Now that I had food in front of me my appetite had deserted me.

'I listened to you when I got caught up with a rat fink – so you have to listen to me now. Drop him – you're too good for a fuck-up like him. I'll make it easy for you: I'll fire him.'

'You can't do that. There are laws about sacking people.'

'Yeah, but if he's shoving cocaine up his nose again then it's only a matter of time.'

'And do you think he is?' I asked.

Sophie shrugged. 'If I was a betting woman . . .

not that it matters, anyway. There's no excuse for what he did.'

I tried to eat some scrambled egg but it tasted like sand.

'I took your advice, by the way,' she said after a few minutes of eating.

'About what?'

'The daddy issue. You were spot on, Jamie, when you asked about the baby's rights. So I told them, both of them, Rico and Shane.'

'What? Are you serious?'

She nodded and smiled.

'And? How did they react?'

Sophie laughed. 'Rico was planning an autumn Portuguese wedding – he's a devout Catholic, apparently, but he can't be *that* devout if he's having sex before the magic sacrament . . .'

'Portuguese wedding?' I echoed.

'That was shelved the minute he heard that Shane was . . . well . . . in the running too.'

Sophie looked at me and shrugged as if she didn't understand Rico's concerns. We both laughed. It was a deadly serious subject but sometimes all you can do is laugh.

'And Shane?'

Her body language changed, like she was going back into herself or closing down or something. She shrugged and smiled at me and picked at a crust of toast on the plate in front of her.

'Come on, tell me.'

'He was great. Brilliant, in fact. Maybe too brilliant.'

'What's that supposed to mean?'

'Well, we've been friends for years and suddenly both of us are single and bonking each other and within a couple of weeks I'm pregnant. He feels sorry for me so he's brilliant about it . . .'

'That's not true. Shane really likes you. I know he does, I can tell.'

Sophie smiled. 'Maybe – maybe not. But this baby clouds everything now. How will I ever know if he's just sorry for me?'

'What exactly did he say?'

'Well, I told him the score, told him about Rico and how I'd made the decision to keep the baby and that I didn't expect either of them to stick around . . .' Sophie stopped and examined my lump. 'It's gone down a little. Anyway, he was really quiet for ages and then he looked straight at me and said he loved me, I was a friend and more and that he'd be there for me and that it was great really about the baby.'

'He said that? And what about the Rico situation?'

'You mean who is the daddy?' Sophie shrugged. 'Shane doesn't seem to think that matters.'

'That's my Shane,' I said.

She smiled. 'I think he just feels sorry for me – he knows I've been dumped on. It doesn't matter, anyway. I told them I'd have a paternity test done after the baby is born.'

'It's a pity about the wedding,' I said, and smiled at Sophie.

'What wedding?'

'The Portuguese job that'd make you a good Catholic wife . . .'

She threw a cushion at me and we both laughed.

'So is Rico out of the picture?'

'Pretty much. He wants to support the baby if it's his.'

'And Shane?'

'He wants to help whether it's his or not.'

'By the way, I never asked you – what's he like in the sack?'

Sophie shook her head. 'Not saying. Classified information – and sure don't you know already?'

'I hope he's a bit more energetic than *that*! I love Shane, he's like a brother to me.'

'Speaking of brothers – how did Dermot get on in London?'

'You won't believe what happened.'

'He found him?'

I nodded.

'Why didn't you tell me before this, Jamie?'

'I didn't get a chance.'

'Jesus, that's some news to be keeping to yourself. Your mother must be delighted.'

'She doesn't know. Nobody knows except Dermot, Bill and now you.'

'Wow, this is unbelievable. So, what's the story?'

I gave Sophie a quick recap of Dermot's findings, and also of Bill's opinions on same.

'I see his point,' said Sophie when I finished.

'Who? Bill's? Easy for him to lay down the law – he's as cold as Siberia, that man.'

'Don't you think he's hurt by what Conor did at all, Jamie?'

I shrugged and played with a piece of toast.

'Dermot said the same thing as Bill – Conor doesn't want to be found.'

Tears welled up in my eyes and I sniffed loudly. Sophie caught my hand in hers. 'Maybe they're both right, Jamie. Leave it be. It seems that Conor wants to stay hidden so . . .'

'What would you do if it was *your* brother or sister? What would you do if it was *me*? And maybe I was in trouble and you didn't bother to find me, to ask me to my face?'

Sophie ran a hand through her hair. 'So what are you going to do?'

I sniffed again. 'I'm going to find him.'

'Look, Jamie, I don't have a great feeling about this Conor thing and I don't want you and everybody else involved to get hurt all over again, that's all. Be careful.'

I wiped my eyes with a disintegrating tissue, stood up and looked out the window. 'Where in the name of God has Shane gone? I hope he didn't follow Steve.'

'I hope he did,' said Sophie, smiling at me. 'I hope he gives him one good kick in the balls, that'd do for starters.'

'I'm such an eejit. I thought I loved him.'

Sophie laughed. 'Welcome to the human race. We all make mistakes – look at me.'

I yawned. 'Jesus, what a night.'

'Let's go to bed. I hope Shane hasn't murdered Steve – I couldn't be arsed going down to bail him out now,' said Sophie, laughing.

'Not funny,' I said.

'Can I stay here, Jamie?'

'Of course,' I said, standing up and stretching. 'I could do with the company.'

Sophie came over and hugged me. 'It'll all be fine, wait and see.'

I closed my eyes tight and the pain in my heart took my breath away. At that moment I hated Steve.

34

I didn't want to go to work next morning. Sophie insisted that I not only go but also wear one of my new killer outfits and hold my head high. Shane, thankfully, appeared at the breakfast table in one piece but only shrugged when asked where he'd disappeared to the night before.

So I marched into work, flanked by my two closest friends in the world. I did my show without a blip – breezed through it, in fact – and was just getting ready to leave when Steve appeared in my doorless office.

'Jamie.'

I didn't look at him. I just kept fiddling with a bunch of files on the desk.

'Jamie . . . babe . . . look, I'm so sorry. I was under pressure yesterday and I couldn't get hold of my sponsor and—'

I raised my hand in front of me like a traffic cop. 'Please go. Leave,' I said and looked directly at him. When I did I almost laughed out loud. Steve had two black eyes, and the most self-pitying look on his face. He looked like a panda, a weak petulant panda.

'Jamie, I love you, I'd never hurt you . . .'

'Get out, Steve.'

'Please listen to me. I'm sorry – can't you forgive me? Didn't you ever make a mistake, Jamie?' He took a step closer and I shut my eyes tightly. He must have read that as a signal that I was softening because suddenly he was crying and hugging me. I stayed sitting in my chair like a statue. Tears were beginning to come but I squeezed them back in. I wouldn't cry. No way. I stood up, Steve still clinging to my neck.

'Oh Jamie, I need you now, more than ever and I knew you wouldn't let me down, I need someone like you in my life – someone who understands me . . .'

I grabbed his arms and pushed him away from me. 'It's over, Steve.' My voice was calm and I meant what I said. It was over. There was no going back from last night. I could see Shane and Sophie and Johnny G watching the proceedings from a distance and I knew that if Steve put a foot wrong he'd be getting another hiding.

'Jamie, don't be like that.'

'Like what? Like somebody who just got punched by her boyfriend? I'm really sorry that my behaviour is upsetting you, Steve. Gee, hang on a minute and I'll start a little sing-song,' I said, slamming files into the cabinet.

'Is it really over? Is that what you want?'

'Yes.'

He nodded, turned slowly and walked out. I looked at his dejected figure as he went into his office and for a moment I felt sorry for him and thought that maybe I was overreacting. Maybe I was being too hard? But that thought only lasted a second. There

was no going back, whether I wanted to or not. I
packed up my bag and marched out of the office,
my head held high.

'How's it going, Rocky?' I said to Shane.

He shrugged. 'I didn't do it, Jamie, I swear on my
mother's life.'

'He says he didn't do it,' said Sophie.

'I didn't do it either, but I wish I had,' said Johnny
G, squeezing my arm. 'Fuck him, Jamie. He's only a
coke-head. You know what they say: once a coke-
head, always a coke-head.'

'You just made that up,' I said, laughing.

'Yeah, but it sounds good, doesn't it?' said Johnny
G and walked away, with a wave of his hand.

'You all right, Jamie?' Sophie said.

I nodded reassuringly. 'Great. I told him it was
over.'

'Good girl. Way to go.'

'See you later,' I said, conscious now that the whole
station had been observing the proceedings. I wanted
to get out of there fast.

'Look, I'll call later. Shane is cooking for me.'

'At our house?' I asked.

'No – at my place.'

'Hope you like Koka noodles, he does a really good
curry version,' I said. And, mock-punching Shane on
the arm, I left.

The tears came as soon as I hit the pavement. Why
did I feel humiliated when I'd done nothing wrong?
It was bad enough that I'd fallen for a self-centred
bollocks. Now it seemed unbelievable that I couldn't

see him for what he was and even more unbelievable that he'd hit me. Nobody had ever hit me before and for the first time I understood how victims can feel complicit when their partners belt them. It made no logical sense but part of me was afraid that I'd some-how attracted that violence to myself.

I called to see my dad later that evening. I knew I wouldn't tell him any of the stuff and that included the new information about Conor. But I craved his reassuring presence and as we sat and watched some golf tournament on Sky Sports I felt safe and secure and childlike. Mam was doing a fashion show at Castletroy Park Hotel so it was just the two of us. I was glad about that.

We talked a little and watched the golf and I felt a whole lot better by the time I was due to head home. Dad walked me to the door.

'Are you OK, love?' he said as he opened the front door for me.

'I'm fine.'

Dad looked at me and then he did something unusual. He hugged me to him and I'm almost sure he said something like 'I love you' into my hair. But I didn't ask him to repeat himself. I just went home.

There was a huge bunch of flowers in reception when I finished my show the next day.

'Stalker?' I said to Dee-Dee when I came out of the sound booth. The florists must love him, I thought as I admired the fragrant bouquet that was destined for the bin or else some colleague's sick relative.

'Nope, not stalker,' said Dee-Dee in a whisper. That grabbed everybody's attention. 'From Steve,' she mouthed.

'Anybody need flowers?'

'My sister just had a baby,' said Raina Burke from behind a filing cabinet.

'Help yourself,' I said and walked into my office. Ger, the janitor, was already there with a new door propped up against the wall. He was looking at the door and shaking his head.

'Wrong door?' I asked.

He smiled at me. 'Wrong hinges. I told them what to get, I even wrote it down.'

'Biggest job in the world – hanging a bloody door,' I muttered as I sat down and opened a bottle of warm mineral water.

'You're right there, love. There's an art to hanging a door. It's not as easy as it looks,' said Ger.

'Obviously,' I said, worried that my sarcasm was losing its cutting edge. I wanted my door back, now more than ever. I checked my post as Ger left, still shaking his head. There was more fan mail: I'd begun to get it after the TV programme and now I kind of looked forward to it in a perverse way. Guys had even sent me their pictures and phone numbers and Sophie agreed that some of them didn't look half bad. But one stalker was enough to be getting on with.

There wasn't much today: a woman in Rathkeale who wanted to know the name of my hairdresser – I'd forgotten that already – and a vertically challenged guy who was looking for a wife. Weird. And then I saw it on my desk – a plain white envelope with my name written on it in beautiful script. I eyed the envelope like it was a letter bomb and then I opened it. Inside was a white invitation card with flowers embossed on the front. Like a wedding invitation.

And that's exactly what it was – a wedding invitation to my own wedding. The room seemed to become suddenly chilly as I read the gold print.

You are cordially invited to the wedding of Jamie Ryan and Pierce Thompson on 21 June 2006, 3.00 p.m. at Cratloe Church and to a reception afterwards at Knappogue Castle.

Then he'd handwritten underneath:

Is the date ok with you? That was the only available date for next summer. Everybody's copying us! If you don't like the card design I can change it but I know you like flowers.
Regards
P

I tore and tore the card until it was a mound of tiny pieces like snowflakes and then I threw them in the bin. I knew immediately that I should have kept it as evidence – that I should have shown it to somebody. But there was something so sinister and eerie about it that I just couldn't bear the thought of it existing in the world with me.

'Jamie.' I looked up into Steve's black-rimmed eyes.

'Go away,' I said, thinking that every day was going to be Groundhog Day with Steve. I grabbed my bag and walked out of the office. I could feel everybody's stares on me as I walked through the open-plan room towards the doors. Steve followed me out.

'Please, Jamie, I made one tiny mistake . . .'

I whipped around and faced him. 'It's over: finito, understand? Now please have the courtesy to leave me alone. I have a stalker already, thank you very much. I don't need another one.'

I marched off down the road, suddenly angry with the whole world.

35

The next morning started off badly. The night before I'd loaded some of my new wardrobe into the washer-dryer and went to bed thinking that I'd have lovely clean clothes for the rest of the week. Which was exactly what I got – except they were miniature versions of everything. As I pulled out item after item I cursed and swore and even kicked the machine.

'A bad workman always blames his tools,' said Shane as he came into the kitchen.

I held up what had once been the fabulous skirt I'd worn on *Clothesline*. Now it looked like a hanky. 'Shut up, Shane, if you value your life.'

He padded over to the fridge, opened it and buried his head inside. 'Read the labels.'

'What?' I asked, rooting around to see if anything had escaped.

'The labels on the clothes. A lot of them have to be dry cleaned,' he said, smiling, a chicken wing in his hand. 'Heather drummed that into me.'

I couldn't believe that even Shane knew the rules of Girl Land. 'And did she tell you that our washing machine was actually really a shrinking machine?'

He laughed and bit into the chicken.

So I went to work in my old jeans and an ancient black T-shirt that had somehow escaped the Big Clean-Out.

Ger was in my office when I arrived at work, a measuring tape in his hand.

'What's wrong today?' I asked as I plonked myself down in my chair and began sorting stuff for my show.

He scratched his head. 'The door. It fitted perfectly yesterday. It just needs a shave, that's all,' he said and left.

As I worked I eyed the door, which was still propped up against the wall, and wondered if I should buy a beaded curtain from Argos while I waited for the door to be fixed. Although then my office would look like Madame Lena's parlour. I smiled at this thought and then wondered if I could make a programme about fortune-tellers – that was a good idea.

I tried not to look up as people came and went in the station – I didn't want to see Steve. My upcoming programme was about the Iron Man competition being held in Austria in July: we had four solicitors, all from Limerick, vying for the title. I'd invited all four on the show and I knew it was going to be a cracker since they were already bitching about each other to me.

Just as my Iron Men arrived in reception Marielouise rang. 'Hi, Jamie, you're collecting the kids, aren't you? I said I'd give you a quick ring just to remind you.'

'Hi, Mar. I'll be there, don't worry about it.' I

prayed she wouldn't ask if I'd heard anything from Dermot Kilbane. I didn't know if I'd be able to lie to her.

'They're really looking forward to it. Keep an eye on Mark – he didn't look himself this morning. I'll see you lot later, so – around seven, is that OK?'

'Take your time, Marielouise. See you later.'

I hung up and walked out to meet my Iron Men. They looked like they'd had their first row already. The programme lived up to my expectations – that was until two of the four Iron Men fell over the transmitter sculpture on their way out of the studio. I suppressed a laugh as they examined themselves minutely for serious injury. Luckily they were fine and in spite of that – or maybe because of it – for the first time in days I felt normal. Sophie called me into her office after the show.

'That was hilarious, Jamie. Those Iron Men turned into right bitches,' she said, laughing.

'I know. The leg-shaving thing was a scream, wasn't it?' I sat down on a swivel chair opposite her.

'What was that about? I missed some of it.'

'They shave their legs – they say it makes them faster.' I looked at Sophie and we laughed.

'Steve was here while you were on air. He had some news.'

'Is that right?' I picked up a pen from Sophie's desk and played with it.

'You know that LFM have offered him a position?'

'He said something, all right.'

'Looks like he's going to take it.'

I didn't answer, just digested the news. Part of me was glad but another part of me was sad – sad that a relationship that initially had seemed so full of potential had so quickly become something distasteful.

'He'll be here for another while: I've got to find a replacement. So, what do you think?' asked Sophie.

I shrugged. 'Whatever makes him happy.'

'It's classic behaviour with guys like him, Jamie. I knew it in the back of my mind when I was hiring him it was too good to be true – getting such a big name to come to Fab City.'

'I feel so stupid.'

Sophie shook her head. 'Don't. You did nothing wrong. Guys like him make a mess wherever they go and then run away from it all.'

'I suppose.'

'I'm proud of you, Jamie.'

'*I*'m not so proud of me. I'll never trust myself again.'

'Yes, you will. You got out straight away – no second chances, no bullshit excuses – that was brave. And Jamie, I've been there too and for much longer than you.'

I looked at my friend. What she said was true – she'd been with Paul for years: they'd bought the house, booked the wedding, even bought the dress, for God's sake. And he'd done the dirt on her. Suddenly I realised that although I had been dealt a shit hand I'd got off lightly in the end.

'Thanks.'

'For what?'

'For being there. Shane, too. And for laughing at me through the whole *Clothesline* programme.'

Sophie grinned. 'What are friends for? Anyway, I thought the Iron Man with the shaved head was very good-looking. Did you get his phone number?'

'They all had shaved heads, Soph. I better get going: I'm picking up Mark and Fiona from school, and I have to go home first to collect my car.'

'You should have driven to work.'

'It takes too long and I don't have the patience to sit through the traffic any more. There are advantages to living so near town.'

'See you later, Jamie. I've a meeting with the directors at four – I have to break the Steve news and make myself look good at the same time!'

'Best of luck. See you later, Soph.'

I left the station, went home and got my car without going into the house. Titbit was sitting on the sitting-room windowsill, looking out beseechingly at me as I backed out of the drive. I checked my watch as I headed into the traffic-congested city. Two o'clock – plenty of time, I thought, glad that I'd allowed a full half-hour for traffic jams. At ten minutes to three I was still in town, the traffic reduced to crawling pace. A knot of tension was building inside me and I had an urge to abandon the car and sprint up the road.

I finally arrived at the school, twenty-five minutes late. Parking crookedly on a double yellow line I dashed across the road and through the school gates. There was still a gaggle of children waiting with a teacher. I watched Fiona's little face light up when she saw me and she came bounding down the steps and into my arms, pigtails flying.

'Jamie, can we go to McDonald's? You promised last week. Look, I got a prize for best picture.' Fiona dropped to her knees and began rooting in her Barbie school bag.

'There,' she said triumphantly, pulling out a picture of a beach with orange sand. 'I couldn't find my yellow marker. Do you like it? You can have it, I was going to give it to Mom but I'll make her one with yellow sand at home . . .'

'Where's your brother, sweetie?'

'Don't know. Do you have Blu-Tack in your house?'

I scanned the schoolyard. 'Did Mark come to school with you this morning?'

Fiona gave me a puzzled look and then nodded.

'Let's go and find him. Which way is his classroom?' I took Fiona by the hand and we walked back into the school. We passed the bright empty classrooms until we came to Mark's. I could see a teacher inside.

'Mr Roast,' whispered Fiona, pointing through the glass door. I smiled. A sign on the door said *Class 7 – Mr Roche.*

I knocked on the door. A couple of seconds later a man opened it, smiling as he did so, and invited us into the room.

'Hi, I'm Jim Roche. Can I help you?'

'I'm Jamie Ryan, Mark Ryan's aunt. I'm collecting him but he seems to have gone walkabout . . .'

'Mark wasn't at school today.'

'Are you sure?'

Mr Roche smiled at me. 'Of course. I missed him first thing this morning because our class computer went on the blink and Mark is the only guy who can fix it when that happens – kinda sad when an eight-year-old can run I.T. rings around you!'

I barely heard what he was saying. Panic was rising in me, and my thoughts were unfocused. What should I do?

'Are you OK?' asked Mr Roche, looking earnestly at my face.

I shook my head, my eyes filling up with tears.

'Are you Fiona?' said Jim Roche, turning to her. 'Mark told me all about you. Can you do something for me? Can you go and play with our hamster, Bertie Ahern? See him over there in the corner?'

Fiona looked up at me for affirmation, her eyes shining. She loved animals. I nodded at her and she ran off to the far corner of the room.

'Look, don't panic. This is probably just a mix-up. Maybe he was unwell and his mother kept him at home and Fiona's forgotten.'

'No. Fiona says he came to school with her and I spoke to his mother this morning. He should have been here.'

I could see the panic that had engulfed me begin its work on Mr Roche.

'We'll go to the Principal's office, it's just across the hallway. Fiona, could you mind Bertie for a few minutes while we go and see Mrs Harris? Good girl,' he said as he led the way.

The Principal – a kind-faced middle-aged woman – rang the Guards immediately once she heard that Mark should have been at school. Then she rang Marielouise and I tried to hold on to some semblance of reason as horrible scenarios invaded my brain. I didn't realise I was crying until Mr Roche handed me a tissue. The Guards arrived at the same time as Marielouise. Her face was ashen as both of us answered their questions.

A female police officer – with model good looks – asked most of the questions.

'I wonder if Mark could have sneaked back home after you went to work,' she said kindly to Marielouise.

Fiona came into the office and I could see that she'd sensed that something was very wrong. Marielouise knelt down in front of her and hugged her as though she was afraid that she'd disappear as well.

'What did Mark say this morning, Fiona?' I said.

'Nothing,' said Fiona.

'Are you sure, honey?'

Fiona nodded. 'Where is Mark?'

'We'll find him – don't you worry about a thing,' said Marielouise. The Guards began asking more questions and Marielouise and I answered as best we could. Lists of friends, relatives, places he liked to go. Marielouise rang my mother on the off chance that he'd called in at the salon. No luck.

'Bill – he might have gone to Bill's,' she said

excitedly, jumping up and dialling his number. The Guards had gone with Mr Roche to check out the CCTV camera at the street corner near the school. It was all like a surreal dream – how could it be happening that *another* member of our family had gone missing? I felt like I was in some sort of TV drama and that suddenly the ads would come on and real life would resume. My brain churned so I sat down. Then my mother and father arrived. Dad's face looked crushed.

'We'll find him, love,' said Mam to Marielouise, patting her on the arm. I looked into my mother's face and I could see the terror in her eyes. 'It's probably just a prank,' she continued in her mock-cheerful voice. 'He's looking for a bit of notice. I remember Conor went missing when he was about Mark's age. We were in town and one minute he was there and the next he was gone.'

He made a bit of a habit of that, I thought as Mam continued. 'Anyway, we found him in the police station, sitting on the desk with a big ice cream in his hand. Don't worry, love, he'll be fine.'

I listened and I knew that my mother was trying desperately to believe her own words. Fiona had started to cry so I pulled her close.

'I can't get Bill,' said Marielouise. 'His phone is switched off. What'll we do now? I can't get him and he doesn't know and what'll we do . . .'

I looked at my sister-in-law. Her face was drawn and pale, her eyes were huge with fear and she stood in the middle of the Principal's office and frantically picked at the skin around a thumbnail.

'I wonder, did he remember his lunch? Mark is a terror for leaving his lunch on the kitchen table.'

My heart ached for her. How much of this could somebody bear? Where the hell could Mark be? And then something rose to the surface in my confused brain. I needed a chance to tease it out.

The door opened and a very tall heavy-set policeman with red hair smiled at us.

'The best thing to do now is probably to go home and wait – you'd be surprised how many children go missing and turn up hours later, wondering what all the fuss is about.'

So Mam and Dad went with Marielouise and Fiona and I told them that I'd follow them in a little while. I jumped into my illegally parked car and rang Bill. This time he answered immediately.

'Mark is missing,' I blurted out.

'Missing?'

I started to cry. When I heard myself saying the words out loud it made it more real and scary.

'He went to school as normal this morning and . . . I went to collect the kids and there was no sign of him. His teacher says he never came into class.'

'Did you call the police?'

'Yeah. Mam and Dad have taken Marielouise home now. She's distraught.'

'Where are you, Jamie?'

'I thought of something while I was in the Principal's office. I think I might know where he's gone. Can you meet me at my house?'

'I'm on my way.'

I threw the phone into my open handbag and drove at breakneck speed. Bill was there before me. I ran into the house, went to the fridge-freezer and took down the green folder that Dermot had given me with the details of the search for Conor in it. I leafed through the various papers.

'It's gone, Bill. The sheet of paper with the address is gone.'

'Whose address?'

'Some woman called Kelly Smith – Conor was driving a BMW registered in her name.'

'But what's that got to do with Mark?'

'The thing is that on that piece of paper Dermot had also written something like *possible address for Conor.*'

'Are you saying that you think Mark has gone to London?'

'I don't know for sure but I've been thinking – do you remember the day you were here and I thought Mark might have overheard?'

Bill nodded.

'I was very freaked-out and I think I left the folder Dermot gave me on the kitchen table.'

I rooted in my bag for my phone.

'Clever kid,' Bill said.

'Yeah, but I wish he wasn't,' I said. The phone burred in my ear.

'Hello?'

'Dermot, it's me, Jamie.'

'Jamie. How are you?' wheezed Dermot into the phone.

'Not great. My nephew Mark is missing and I think he's gone to London to find his dad. He seems to have taken the sheet with Kelly Smith's address.'

'Actually, Jamie, I was just going to ring you about that. I did a bit of work and it turns out that the rates for that address are billed to Conor Ryan.'

'Do you think it's *our* Conor?'

'Well, it's a huge coincidence if it's not. Jesus, what age is the young fella again? He'd never manage to get to London.'

'You don't know him. He's eight going on thirty.'

'Well, if there's anything I can do to help, Jamie, just ask.'

'Thanks. Can you give me that address again?'

'No problem. Just give me a sec.'

I motioned at Bill for a pen and paper and I wrote the address down quickly.

'Good luck, Jamie. And remember, if you need anything just ring me.'

'Thanks, Dermot. Goodbye.'

I hung up and looked at Bill. 'London?'

Bill nodded. 'We'll have to go to Marielouise's first. You know that.'

'Yeah. Let's go.'

We drove in Bill's car and he spoke to his secretary on his state-of-the-art car phone, asking her to book flights to London for us.

'God, this is such a mess. How did I let him overhear me that day?'

'Don't go blaming yourself.'

I looked at Bill's profile as he drove, his face

serious. 'I thought you'd be blaming me, telling me I should never have meddled, that I should have—'

'There's only one person to blame for all this, Jamie. And that's Conor. He's responsible for the whole sorry mess.'

'I brought it all up again.'

'No, you didn't. Mark is hurting – if he hadn't done this he might have done something much worse down the road. And do you know something, Jamie?'

We were pulling into Marielouise's long gravelled drive.

'What?'

'I'll never forgive Conor. I'm finished with him.' Bill looked at me, his hazel eyes hard and steely. I knew he meant it.

'It's not what he did to us. I could almost forgive that. It's what he's done to his children. Abandoning them like that. You wouldn't do that to a dog.' He climbed out of the car and I followed, dreading the job that lay ahead of me.

36

Marielouise looked as though somebody had punched her in the stomach.

'Are you sure?' she asked, her voice quiet and ultra-calm.

I nodded. 'The PI, Dermot Kilbane, had pictures and all.'

'And he walked away?' she said, her arms wrapped tightly around her middle. My mother was crying softly in the background. I could hear Fiona's shrill voice in the garden, playing some childish game. It was as if time had stood still.

I didn't answer Marielouise. There was nothing to say. I couldn't look at her, she was in too much pain.

'So Mark took the address? How did he know what was in the file?'

Bill looked at me. 'Jamie and I were talking in the garden and he must have overheard us . . .'

'How could you, Jamie?' she said.

'I'm sorry, Marielouise. I should have checked, I should have been more careful when—'

'No, that's not what I meant. How could you not tell me?'

'It's . . . I thought it was for the best . . .'

'I told her not to. I made her swear she wouldn't tell,' Bill said, edging closer to me. I could feel the heat from his body, he was that close. My mother was still crying and Dad put his arm around her shoulder.

'I want my son back. I'm going over there,' Marielouise said then.

'Look, let Jamie and I go. We might be wrong, Mark might turn up here. We'll go, Marielouise. It's better like that,' said Bill.

She looked at him without seeing him. 'Excuse me,' she said and ran from the room. I followed her and found her kneeling over the downstairs loo, throwing up her lunch. I held her hair as she retched and then I wiped snot and tears from her face with a damp sponge.

'Jamie, what's happening? I keep thinking it's a bad dream or a sick movie and I'll wake up soon and Mark will be here and Conor . . .'

I held her in my arms in the tiny room and she cried and cried.

'Maybe Bill is right – I'll wait for him here,' she said eventually and splashed water on her pale worried face.

'It's the right thing to do, Mar. The Guards said you should stay here and if he's gone to London we'll bring him straight home, I promise you.'

We walked back to the living room. Bill was on the phone to the police, filling them in on the new information. Mam was playing hostess and was presiding over a tray of tea things. Fiona had come in from the garden and sat quietly on the sofa, eating a biscuit, her solemn eyes watching everything.

'They're sending a Guard around. They strongly advise that you stay here, Marielouise . . .' Bill said as he joined us.

'She's decided to stay,' I said.

He nodded. 'Good. Listen, could I have a look in Mark's bedroom? I want to see if there's anything there that might help us.'

Marielouise sighed. 'Come on, I'll show you.' She went out to the hallway and up the stairs, all of us following. Mark's room was a shrine to Liverpool FC. The curtains bore the logo, as did the duvet cover. The walls were covered in posters of the team and a giant flag was suspended from the ceiling. Bill searched the room like a pro, looking in the strangest places for clues.

Fiona stood by the door, watching us search, her eyes round and innocent – a bit too innocent. I'd been a kid once, with an older brother, and I recognised the look.

I knelt down in front of her and pushed some stray blonde hair behind her ears. 'Do you want to tell us anything, Fiona?' I asked, holding her two little hands in mine.

'I never took money,' she said.

I smiled at her. 'Of course you didn't.'

Her eyes filled with tears. 'I only took the torn one 'cos he wouldn't let me watch the Disney Channel.'

'That's OK, honey. Where does he keep his money?'

Fiona wiped her tears with the back of her sleeve and walked out onto the spacious landing. Then she opened the hot press and pointed. 'Under the red towels,' she said.

Marielouise pushed aside the towels and unearthed a silver money box. It was empty. 'He'd have had quite a bit of money – his Communion was only . . .' Tears welled in her eyes and Mam hugged her.

Bill's phone rang and as we went downstairs I knew from what he was saying that it was his secretary, Annie, confirming our flights.

'We need to leave straight away,' he said and I nodded. Just as we were climbing into the car a squad car pulled up in the drive. Bill went and spoke to the young Guard and then finally we drove away towards Shannon and our waiting flight.

We checked in as soon as we arrived and went straight upstairs to the departure area. As we emerged from the metal-detector queue there was a half-audible announcement about the Heathrow flight. Bill went off to find out more and I sat on a chair, watching as the departure lounge filled up. He returned with two coffees. 'I got you a coffee – you might need it.'

'Why?' I asked, pouring milk into the steaming cup.

'Flight delay.'

'Shit. How long?'

Bill shook his head. 'They don't know. Something technical, I think.'

'Brilliant. We could be here all night.'

'I know. I offered to go up and fix it for them but

they wouldn't let me.' He smiled and sipped his coffee. 'Nothing we can do but wait here.'

'Shit,' I said again and checked my watch. 'What time were we due to fly out at? Nine-thirty, wasn't it?'

Bill nodded. I drank my coffee and picked up a discarded *Irish Times* and turned to the sports section. Bill closed his eyes and I knew he'd fallen asleep when his head dropped onto my shoulder. I could smell his hair – coconut – and his dark lashes were long. Sophie'd kill for those, I thought as I shifted slightly so that I could turn the pages of the newspaper. His arm was now on my lap. An elderly couple sat opposite, watching us.

'Your husband is having a grand sleep,' said the man. 'I wish I could do that.'

'What, love? Fall asleep in a chair, or next to a beautiful young one like her?' said his small grey-haired wife. I blushed to the roots and smiled and pretended to read the business section of the paper, deciding not to explain the husband bit. There was another announcement over the PA which startled Bill awake.

'Jesus, I'm knackered – no sleep last night,' he said, looking up at a monitor to check our flight status. Still delayed. He yawned and rubbed his eyes.

'Out on the town?' I asked.

He laughed. 'God, if only you knew the truth. I'll tell you sometime.' He paused and looked as if he might be considering telling me whatever it was right then but the PA interrupted him, finally calling our flight. We headed to the departure gates and the knot in my stomach began its gnawing again, this time in earnest. I didn't know what I was going to find in London – on any front.

37

I looked at Bill as the big black taxi pulled up outside 138 Gladstone Road. The address that had repeated itself over and over in my head since Dermot had read it to me on the phone. Echoing like a mantra as we drove to Shannon and flew to Heathrow. And now we'd arrived at the mythical place.

'Is this it?' I asked as we peered out the window at the quiet, sleeping street. Bill nodded and leaned forward to pay the driver. I opened the door and stepped out, beginning to shiver as soon as my feet hit the pavement. The house looked too ordinary to contain that truth.

'Cold?' Bill asked as he slammed the cab door.

I looked at him and actually smiled. Bill looked like he'd slept in a hedge – his hair was standing up on one side of his head. Black stubble covered his chin and neck and he had dark circles around his eyes. Funnily enough, it suited him. He smiled back at me.

'Freezing,' I said as I hugged myself to stop the tremors that were running from my head to my toes.

He put an arm around me and squeezed me tightly, letting me go almost as soon as he touched me. It made me feel so much better that I wanted to ask him if he wouldn't mind repeating it and slowing down but it wasn't exactly the time or place.

'Nearly there,' he said as we both turned and surveyed number 138. It was a small red-brick terraced house with a bay window and a standard rose tree in a pot by the green front door. I looked at my watch. Three twenty-five a.m. Bill opened the gate and I walked ahead of him up the short path and rang the doorbell before I could change my mind.

We stood together by the rose tree and listened to the sound of the bell in the dark hallway. There was no response. I was gripped with a sudden terror. Maybe it was just a coincidence and it wasn't our Conor and we'd never find Mark. Or if it was him maybe he'd gone already? He knew we were on to him so maybe he'd upped sticks and run away again? If that was the case then we really were in trouble.

Bill reached out and rang the doorbell a second time. Through the glass panels in the door I could see a light going on at the top of the stairs. A dark shape began to descend. My heart thumped wildly as the shape got closer. I reached out and grabbed Bill's hand. His fingers tightened around mine and my heart slowed marginally. My breath caught in my throat at the sound of chains and latches being undone. The door opened a fraction.

Conor stood in the hallway in his bare feet, wearing a tattered grey tracksuit bottom and a green T-shirt. I reeled slightly at the sight of him.

'Jamie. Bill. What's wrong? What are you doing here?'

'Did the police contact you?' Bill said.

Conor shook his head. 'I was away. Just got back late last night.'

'Mark is missing,' Bill said, stepping slightly in front of me. 'Since yesterday – we think he might know you're here and . . . have you heard from him?'

'No.' Conor ran a hand through his sleep-dishevelled hair. 'Nothing. Why would he look for me? How the hell could he find me in London?'

Bill's hand, which was still gripping mine, tensed and relaxed and then tensed again until he was holding my hand so tightly that I thought he might break one of the bones.

'We think he found your address in my house,' I said.

Conor looked at me and I looked back at him and it was like falling. Nobody said anything for a few seconds until I heard Bill clear his throat and say. 'Can we come in?'

Conor stepped back and waved us into his house ushering us into a small, untidy, over-coordinated sitting room. Everything matched: it struck me that somebody had obviously put a lot of thought into the decor despite its present state of disorder. Bill and I perched uncomfortably side by side on a red sofa. My brother – suddenly risen from the dead – sat opposite in a matching armchair and produced a packet of cigarettes. He offered us one and when we refused lit his own with shaking hands.

'So?' Conor asked after a long nicotine exhalation. 'Tell me what happened?'

My first instinct was to tell him what to do with himself. But instead I began to relate the nightmare of the day before, my stomach churning as I relived the events. Nobody else spoke and I felt strangely detached as I described how and why we'd ended up in London in the middle of the night.

When I had finished, Conor lit another cigarette and we sat in more silence. I looked around the room: wooden floor, soft red sofa, subtle cream walls hung with dark-framed family photographs. The two dark-haired little girls whom I remembered from Dermot's pictures were there smiling at us as chubby-cheeked babies. A big glossy photograph by a weeping cherry tree of Conor and a woman – laughing and dressed up as if for a wedding. And all four of them together. The happy family.

'I presume the police checked the airports?' Conor said, suddenly breaking the silence.

'Obviously,' Bill answered.

'And no luck?'

I shook my head. 'He's only a kid – you have to be at least fourteen to fly by yourself. I know he's tall but . . .'

Conor sat forward in his seat. 'What about the seaports?'

'They were checked as well – absolutely no evidence of an unaccompanied child on board any of the ships,' Bill said.

'I can't believe that nobody missed Mark until school was over yesterday,' Conor said, suddenly angry. He jumped up from his seat and began to pace. 'I mean, for God's sake, you'd think they'd notice an eight-year-old wasn't at school, wouldn't you?'

'I already told you,' I said. 'Marielouise thought he'd gone into school but he doubled back and probably went home and the school thought he was at home and then . . .'

'I find it hard to credit,' Conor said. 'You'd think they'd be more responsible.'

Bill let out a long, angry breath and I put my hand on his arm. He turned his head to look at me and then sank back into the sofa.

'Oh my God!' Conor said loudly.

We looked at him.

'What?' I said.

'Did you check the computer, Bill?'

'Which computer?'

Conor put his cup down on the coffee table and stood in front of Bill. 'Our computer – the home computer. The history.'

'Christ!' Bill said jumping up from the sofa.

'What?' I said, jumping up as well, though I had no idea what was going on.

Bill looked at me. 'The history – see what websites Mark might have visited recently – I can't believe I didn't think of it.'

Conor was shaking his head as he dialled a number on the phone. He paused as he listened to the phone by his ear. 'Marielouise?'

I gasped.

'I'm sorry to wake you – OK, OK, I know you weren't asleep, I see that. Look, I'm sorry but would you go and check the Internet history on the computer and see if you can find out if Mark was on any sites recently that might give us a clue about where he is.'

Marielouise obviously didn't answer and just hung up immediately. I didn't blame her.

'Will she do it, do you think?' Conor said to Bill who gave an exasperated laugh.

'For fuck's sake, Conor – of course she will.'

Conor's face reddened as though Bill had slapped him and he walked over to the window.

'What now?' I said.

'We wait,' Bill answered.

'Anybody want a drink?' Conor said. 'Shall I make tea? Are you hungry?'

'No, thanks,' I said. Bill didn't answer. Conor lit another cigarette and opened the curtains.

I felt sick as everything swirled around inside my head. What if somebody had abducted Mark? He was only eight, after all, no matter how clever he was, or how grown-up or adept with computers. Eight years old and all alone in an airport or on a boat or some such dangerous place. My thoughts were interrupted by the shrill sound of a mobile phone. Bill fumbled in his jacket pocket.

'Yes?' he said. I held my breath as I watched his frown deepen while he listened. 'OK, thanks – I will. You OK?' A pause as he listened some more. 'I know. Don't worry, he'll be fine – you'll see.'

He punched a button and looked at us. 'CIE – or whatever the hell it's called now – Bus Eireann, is it?

Mark was on their site on Monday night, on this Eurolink part which is all about buses to London.'

'I knew it!' Conor said triumphantly.

'And did he book himself onto a bus or something?' I said.

'She doesn't know yet – she's getting onto the police right now so that they can see if Mark booked anything. I presume they'll have to wake up some-body at Eurolink to go check if there's any trace of him there.'

'How long will that take?' I asked.

Bill shrugged. 'A little while, anyway.'

My eyes filled with tears and I sniffed hard. 'I hope he's on one of those buses – at least he might be safe.' Bill put his arms around me and pulled me close. I leaned in against him and allowed the tears to come. I was so exhausted that my skin hurt but if only Mark was OK then I wouldn't care about anything. Behind me I heard the sound of Conor lighting up and pacing. Finally, when I'd stopped crying, I pulled away from Bill. Though I'd have preferred to stay put. I blew my nose and sat down on the sofa. Conor and Bill stayed standing.

'How could they not notice an eight-year-old by himself?' Conor said.

I shrugged, exhaustion tugging me downwards.

'No, really. What kind of incompetent carry-on—'

'Oh for fuck's sake, Conor!' Bill said turning to face him.

Conor frowned and then looked surprised. 'I'm just saying—'

'Just saying what? That the school should have minded him? That Marielouise should have? Even that CIE should have minded him? What about taking some responsibility for it yourself? I mean, let's face it, Conor, if you hadn't fucked off and deserted your family, your eight-year-old would right now be tucked up asleep in his bed. Instead of God only knows where, with God only knows who.'

I couldn't take my stare from Conor's face as he listened to Bill.

'Nothing changes, does it – you know everything, Bill,' Conor said, his face set, jaw clenched. He walked right up to Bill.

'I know one thing, Conor: if you're looking for someone to blame then blame yourself.' Bill leaned forward until they were almost close enough to kiss. One lanky and blond, one blocky and dark. Both wound up and ready to explode. As I watched them I figured that someone was about to throw a punch – the only question was who?

'Everything is so black and white in your world, isn't it, Bill? The biggest irony of all is that if you actually knew why I had to leave my family you more than anybody would understand.'

'I wouldn't understand – there can be no excuse for what you've done. Don't think you can talk your way out of this: nobody is falling for your shit any more. Have you any *idea* of the suffering you've caused?'

Bill took a sharp breath as if he'd been running. Then he walked over, pulled back the curtain and looked out on the still dark street. Conor looked hurt but funnily enough all my sympathy was with Bill. The truth was just the truth. I looked at my brother who seemed shorter and thinner than I remembered and, though I didn't know why, he reminded me of Steve. He tossed his cigarette end into the empty fireplace but continued to stand in the centre of the room.

'Do you think I don't know that?' he said to Bill's back. Bill didn't turn around.

'*I* think you don't know it,' I said. Conor turned towards me. 'Not really. I think you couldn't know it and still do what you did. Not unless you're a psychopath or something.'

Conor didn't say anything for what felt like ages. He just looked at me and I remembered the day in the park and a knot of anger began to form inside me.

'I'm sorry, Jamie.'

I shook my head. 'Not good enough, Conor. Not nearly good enough.'

'You don't understand – it wasn't straightforward – I love my family.' He paused. 'And my friends. It's just . . . things got complicated and I had to go. To be honest, you start to wonder if anybody would even want you back after . . . after all that happened.'

Bill turned around. 'And what about your children?'

'I saw them every few weeks.'

'Like the day in the park?' Bill said.

Conor nodded. 'And other times. It's very hard

not to see your kids – I couldn't bear it. I went over every six weeks or so and just watched them. I'd hide out in the park or near the school – wherever I thought I'd catch a glimpse of them.'

'What kind of a bastard are you?' I shouted, jumping up and punching my brother in the chest with all my strength. He staggered back and looked amazed. 'If it was hard for *you* not to see them – what the hell do you think it was like for your *children*?' I hit him again. He grabbed my wrist but I wrenched it free and thumped him harder. 'I mean, really, Conor – your own kids just thrown aside – how could you do something like that?' The more I hit him the better I felt. Conor raised an arm to protect his face and I thumped and thumped until Bill's arms encircled me from behind and he gently pulled me away. I started to cry temper tears but I didn't resist Bill. Conor stood in the middle of the floor, arms hanging loosely by his sides and a look of utter defeat on his face. 'You're a selfish bastard,' I said as the adrenalin that had pumped through me abated. 'Just discarding your children like unwanted baggage – especially as you seem to have plenty of time for other people's children.'

Conor didn't say a word. Just looked at me, puzzled. I pointed to the photographs of the smiling little girls on the walls. He took a deep breath. 'They're not other people's children. They're mine.'

38

'What?' I said, though even as I spoke it was all beginning to make some kind of sense. The domestic look in the photographs. Why hadn't I copped it before?

'But how can they be your children?' Bill said as if he was inside my head. 'Surely they're at least four and five?'

Conor nodded. 'Polly is six, in fact – since May – and Jilly is almost five – end of October.'

'But you haven't been gone for that long,' I said. 'Not even two years . . . how . . .'

Conor looked at the floor and didn't answer. He didn't need to.

'You bastard,' I said, moving up so close to him that I could see the stubble on his chin and the pores in his cheeks.

'All the time you were playing the good father in Limerick you were screwing some woman in London and having babies with her?'

'It wasn't like that,' he said.

'Ah, for God's sake – what *was* it like, so, Conor?' I said.

'We were married.'

'What?' Bill and I said together.

'How?' Bill continued. 'Before or after you married Marielouise?'

'After.'

'But how can that be?' I asked.

Conor sighed. 'They don't check very closely.'

'For God's sake, Conor,' Bill said. 'I can see having a fling—'

'Lovely,' I interrupted.

'No, really,' he said. 'I'm not defending it, Jamie, it happens – but did you have to get married?'

Conor slowly looked up at Bill. 'Yes, I did. You see, it wasn't a fling, Bill. I loved Kelly.'

'And what about Marielouise?' Bill said.

Conor shrugged. 'I loved Marielouise as well. I wasn't able to choose between them – and especially not between the children.'

'So you had two families?' I said, incredulously.

Conor turned to face me as he nodded.

'For how long?' I asked.

'About seven years.'

'Christ,' Bill said.

'I had to honour all of them,' Conor said. 'I owed it to them.'

'That's elephant shit,' Bill said. 'You just wanted everything. And do you know something, Conor? When I think about it, I'm not surprised. You were always greedy. Always thought that the rules didn't apply to you.'

'Fiona is almost the same age as that other little girl . . .' I said as the reality of it gradually dawned.

'Jilly is a month older than her.'

I shook my head. 'I can't believe it.'

Conor sighed, 'It's true.'

'So why did you disappear?' Bill said, a hard edge to his voice.

'Kelly has problems . . .'

'Don't all your families,' I said, sitting back onto the sofa, my whole body beginning to fill with disgust as I listened to my brother.

'What kind of problems?' Bill pursued.

'Depression. Attempted suicide – the works.'

'So you fucked off out of your life?' I interrupted.

'It wasn't as simple as that. Kelly was . . . is . . . look it's too complicated but the short version is that I did fuck up, even I admit that. But things weren't going all that well with me and Kelly and I told her everything—'

'You told her that you had a wife and children in Ireland?' I interrupted.

'Not exactly – she knew about the kids but she didn't know I was married. I told her I was leaving.'

He paused and lit a cigarette. He took a deep breath. 'And then I left and it's lousy to say it but the truth is that I was relieved and then . . . I was at Heathrow . . .' He stopped again.

'There was a phone call just before I was due to board the plane: Kelly had cut her wrists – in front of the girls. A neighbour found her – rang me . . . I came back.'

Conor ran his hand through his hair. The silence in the room was truly deafening. I was struggling to make sense of his words.

'And stayed, obviously,' Bill said quietly.

'It wasn't the plan but the children were distressed and Kelly – well, let me put it like this: Kelly is still in a psychiatric hospital.'

Conor looked at us and obviously didn't see as much sympathy as he was expecting so he continued. 'Somebody had to look after the children and then . . . well, then the longer you're away the harder it gets to go back.'

'And what about Fiona and Mark?' I said.

He shrugged and raised his hands. 'At least their mother wasn't slitting her wrists with a vegetable knife in the kitchen.'

'And you couldn't tell us any of this?' I said.

'How could I?'

'Weren't the phones working?' Bill said.

'That's not what I mean,' Conor said, his face suddenly peevish. 'I had to look after my little girls. Neither of you have children so you can't really understand.'

'For fuck's sake,' Bill said and stood up. 'Why couldn't you tell your family? I'll tell you why – you couldn't tell them – or me – because if you did you'd have to face up to your lies and then what would everybody think of the wonderful Conor Ryan? The fair-haired boy turns out to be an embezzling bigamist.'

'That's not fair,' said Conor.

'Well, fair or not, it's true – you allowed everybody else to suffer so that you wouldn't have to do the hard work. I don't understand any of it,' Bill said, turning back to look out the window. The first pink streaks of dawn were beginning to appear in the sky. I looked at the exhausted hunching of Bill's shoulders and then at Conor's face and I didn't understand any of it either.

Conor and I had always been close. My big brother. Always there for me, always willing to give me money when I was broke and haul my arse out of trouble. My mother and I hardly ever saw eye to eye except concerning Conor. We both thought he was better than sliced pan.

And then there was Bill. Always seeming to be standing on the sidelines of life, watching everybody else. My mother had a real soft spot for him – always had had. As I sat there and looked at both of them in that North London sitting room it struck me that I might have misjudged Bill. What with Steve, Conor and Bill to make sense of, it was looking like I definitely needed to adjust my meter for judging people.

When the chips were down Bill was the one who turned up – tie fastened to choke-hold and sarcastic attitude at the ready. But, notwithstanding all that, he was there, doing what needed to be done when the shit hit the fan. Conor was better than Bill at talking the talk, but right then I couldn't see much evidence of him walking the walk.

In the middle of my philosophical musings Bill's phone rang. He turned around and looked at me as he answered. Conor and I both stared at him. 'Marielouise,' he said. My heart jumped.

Then Bill was silent as he listened. He fumbled in

his jacket for a pen and I ran towards him and handed him a magazine I had found by the sofa. He smiled as he took it from me and made *mmm*-ing noises as he wrote. Conor didn't move. Didn't even light a cigarette.

'OK, thanks. I'll get back to you as soon as I know anything,' Bill said. 'Talk to you later – try and get some rest.'

He hung up.

'So?' I said, unable to contain myself for another second.

'That was Marielouise.'

I raised an eyebrow.

'OK, OK – the police woke up a few techies and they've found a booking – made with Marielouise's credit card. It's for a Eurolink bus that left Limerick yesterday afternoon at four and arrives at Victoria Coach Station at eight this morning.'

'And is Mark on that bus?' Conor asked.

Bill shrugged. 'They called the driver and he says there is a boy who fits Mark's description all right but that he appears to be with a woman.'

'Can't they just ask everybody?' I said.

'Well, the bus had already arrived in England by the time they got in touch with the driver. The police in London have been contacted and the consensus seems to be that there's no point in panicking Mark – especially as we're here. Marielouise wants us to go and meet the bus.'

'That's fine with me,' I said. I looked at my watch – it was after five. 'How long will it take us to get to

Victoria Coach Station from here?' I asked Conor.

He started like I'd woken him. 'Um, I don't know – an hour? I think it's somewhere near Buckingham Palace so, yeah, an hour should do it.'

'We need to leave about six, so,' Bill said. 'Just in case there's any traffic. Better to be early than late, under the circumstances.'

'Definitely,' I said. 'I couldn't bear not to be there when the bus gets in.'

'I'll drive,' Conor said, all of a sudden. 'Give me ten minutes to get a babysitter – I can't leave the girls by themselves. I'll ask Brenda across the road.'

Conor lit the inevitable cigarette.

'OK, how about this, so: I'll get dressed and we'll head off immediately – avoid all the early morning traffic. Once we get to the general area of Victoria Coach Station, I can park the car and we can grab a bite to eat in a café or something,' he said, like someone planning a military manoeuvre.

He looked at us as if he was waiting for something – I wasn't sure what. Agreement? Approval? I didn't care. I just wanted to get to the bus station in plenty of time so that we could find Mark.

'That sounds like a plan,' Bill said eventually, in a flat voice.

'Great,' Conor said, making a flapping motion with his hands before disappearing out the door. We stood in his sitting room and listened to the sound of the front door close. I walked over to where Bill was standing by the window. We watched as Conor disappeared into a house across the road. I looked out on the early-morning street. Neat red-brick houses full of sleeping and waking families. A couple of cars passed as we stood there in silence, just watching the day wake up on Gladstone Road.

'Who would think that a man who led a double life lived in this perfectly ordinary house?' I said.

Bill didn't answer. I turned my head to look at him and his face was contorted as if he was trying to control himself.

'Bill?'

He nodded but kept his eyes focused on the street. I stood in front of him. 'Bill?' I repeated. His face continued to move for some seconds and I gradually realised that he was trying not to cry.

'Mark is on that bus,' I said.

He took a deep breath and nodded. This time he looked at me. 'I hope so.'

'He's on it,' I said, moving close. 'I know he is. I know that little bugger and it all makes loads of sense now. Jesus! Credit-card fraud at eight!'

Bill smiled a wobbly smile and continued to look at me. I reached out a hand and touched his face. Then I moved close and kissed him on the lips. Immediately his arms were around me and the gentle gesture of gratitude and tenderness that I'd made jumped about ten notches and became a hungry, searching, passionate kiss. My skin felt as if it was on fire. He backed me against the wall and I felt his hands under my T-shirt just as I was trying to free his shirt from his waistband. I knew it was insane but I didn't care: the comfort and distraction outweighed my misgivings – and anyway, desperation is a powerful aphrodisiac. Our mouths separated and I groaned with pleasure, throwing back my head until it made sudden contact with the wall.

'Ow!' I squealed.

Bill pulled away. 'Sorry – Jesus, Jamie, I'm sorry. What did I do?'

I smiled at him as I rubbed my sore head. 'Nothing – it's not you – I have a bump on my head and I hit it against the wall.'

Bill reached out and laid his hand over mine, gently making contact with my scalp. Sore as my head was even that contact felt good.

'Poor Jamie,' he said. 'Is it very sore?'

'A bit.'

He rubbed my head tenderly. 'Bastard.'

'Absolutely,' I said, not wanting even to think about Steve, let alone talk about him. As the pain in my sore head subsided all I wanted was to get back to what we'd been doing before I'd knocked my bump on the wall. And then it struck me. 'How do you know what happened?'

Bill moved his hand from my head and rested it gently on my waist. 'Shane told me – I met him when he was out looking for Steve that night.'

I sighed. 'Shane Ali – that fella has a mouth the size of the Shannon estuary.'

'He's a good friend, though. He was just upset for you.'

'I know. He spent hours looking for him.'

Bill pulled me in close to him so that our whole

bodies were touching. 'He really did – it wasn't his fault that he couldn't find him. He looked everywhere for him – pub-to-pub search – that's how he met me. I was in Hayes' Bar having a drink after a meeting.'

I pulled away and looked at him. 'But he did – find him, I mean.'

Bill shook his head. 'I don't think so. I mean, it was a fluke that *I* found him – pure coincidence that I just happened to be driving up Edward Street as he came out of that pub. Who would think of look-ing in that place for him?'

'Was it this real seedy place?'

Bill nodded. 'An awful dive. Anyway, forget that fool – where were we?'

Bill leaned forward and kissed my neck and the fire started all over again in my body. But meanwhile my mind kept working until I had it all figured out.

'Bill!'

'What? Your head again?'

I pulled away altogether and looked at him. 'No – you beat the crap out of Steve, didn't you?'

Bill rubbed his face with a cupped palm. 'I'm sorry, Jamie, but when Shane told me what Steve had done to you . . . and then I just saw that fucking weasel coming out of a pub. It was like Fate: there he was, all puffed out, cock of the walk holding court with some lowlifes – I couldn't stop myself. I was out of my car, had thumped him in the face and was back in my car and driving away before I could think about it.'

I covered my face with my hands.

'Sorry,' Bill said after a few seconds. 'I know it's all macho shit but I couldn't bear what he'd done to you – but I am sorry.'

I parted my fingers to have a look at him. Where was his tie? I saw it poking out of his jacket pocket. I dropped my hands.

'Don't be sorry,' I said, taking one of his hands in both of mine. 'He deserved it. I'll do as much for you some day, if you ever need me to thump somebody for you. Just say the word.'

'OK, all ready,' Conor's voice said as the door opened. 'Has something happened to you, Jamie?'

Bill stepped aside.

'No, no, just a bit of a bump on the head, that's all – Bill was having a look.'

'You're all right, though?'

'Absolutely fine.'

'Great – let's get going, so.' An elderly plump Afro-Caribbean woman appeared from behind Conor.

'Brenda, this is my sister Jamie and my friend Bill.'

Brenda smiled and shook our hands. 'Best of luck – I'm sure the boy will be on the bus,' she said kindly.

We murmured assent and said our goodbyes. Then we followed Conor through the hallway. We were just about to step out the front door when we heard a voice.

'Daddy?'

We all turned. A small, fine-boned little girl with long dark hair was standing in a pink flowery nightdress at the foot of the stairs.

'Polly,' Conor said, moving back towards the child.

He crouched down in front of her and kissed her cheek. 'Go back to bed, sweetie. Daddy has to go out for a little while. Brenda's here.'

Polly rubbed her big brown eyes with the back of a chubby hand. 'Can I watch TV?'

'It's too early – go back to bed for a while.' Conor stood up and turned Polly by the shoulders, then he gently propelled her towards the stairs. We stood and watched as she padded up, pausing on the top step to have one last look at us. Once she'd gone, Conor led the way down the quiet street to a silver BMW. I recognised the car from Dermot's photographs. In silence we all got in, Bill and Conor in the front, me in the back. Conor drove carefully out onto a main road and we began our journey.

Probably to drown the silence in the car, Conor switched on the radio and as chart music rolled over me I offered a silent prayer to God to make my authoritative statement about Mark being on the bus true. If he wasn't on that bus we were all out of options and I couldn't even bring myself to think about what might have happened to him.

39

After two minutes in the back of the BMW I thought I was going to throw up all over Conor's beige leather upholstery. I really should have sat in the front but I couldn't bear the thought of trying to make conversation with Conor. Not that Bill was trying all that hard. In an effort to fight off the feelings of overwhelming pukiness I lay back and closed my eyes. It had been a very long twenty-four hours in a very long week, one way and another. I was not only pukey and frightened and confused by everything that had happened, I was also exhausted.

After driving for what felt like hours we were finally in the centre of London and Conor was pulling into an underground car park. My mouth felt like a sewer. I found a stick of Spearmint in my handbag and folded it into my mouth.

'We made good time,' Conor said, swinging into an empty space and switching off the engine. He looked at his watch. 'Not bad at all. Not quite seven.'

Bill looked over his shoulder at me and smiled. I smiled back at him, my body giving a shiver as I remembered the wave of desire that had overtaken me in Conor's sitting room.

Nobody spoke as we made our way out of the car park and onto the early-morning London street. Cars and pedestrians were already beginning to fill up the streets and footpaths as another day in the city got under way. Conor began to speak as we walked, about London and Buckingham Palace and tourists and commuters and statistics. I didn't really listen – couldn't – all I could think about was that bus that was wending its way towards us.

We went into a small French-style café and the men ordered coffee and croissants while I went back onto the streets and found a newsagent's. I bought three newspapers and distributed them between us. We all set to reading to take our minds off the bus and to relieve us of the burden of trying to find something to talk about. We spent a solid half-hour like that, shifting in our uncomfortable plastic chairs and rustling paper as we turned pages.

I read a full-page article about global warming, all the world news reports, the TV pages, the sports section, an interview with David Mellor and the letters page. And it worked. I didn't have to speak and I didn't have to think. Perfect. I didn't know what Bill and Conor were reading but they must have had similar success as neither of them looked up from their newspapers the whole time. Eventually it was Bill who broke the silence. He noisily folded his broadsheet and coughed. I lowered the page I was reading.

'Seven forty-five,' he said.

Conor and I nodded and folded our papers while

Bill found the waitress and paid. In unspoken accord we headed for the doors of the restaurant. It had started to rain. A thick grey drizzly rain that soaked through my T-shirt as soon as I stepped outdoors. I didn't care. In the distance I could see the London Eye towering over everything. I remembered the day I had been trapped there with the fans, looking at Tommy Sloane and his goat crossing Westminster Bridge. It seemed more than a lifetime ago.

After about five minutes' walking we saw the coach station and went inside. Bill asked about buses from Ireland and was informed that one had just arrived. We hurried to where the Bus Eireann coach in its familiar colours was parked. The doors hissed open just as we reached it and before the first tired-looking travellers could descend Conor climbed the steps.

'Is this bus from Limerick?' I heard him ask the cranky-faced driver before forcing his way in against the flow of disembarking passengers.

Bill and I stayed by the steps as the driver came out and opened the baggage hold. Two police officers – a man and a woman – approached him and had a word and I was just about to ask them if they were on the same mission as us when suddenly I saw Mark. He was wearing a red jacket and carrying a bag that looked very much like his school bag and he looked exactly what he was – a runaway eight-year-old. But his face, though white as paper, was shining like a torch with the huge smile plastered across it.

'Mark!' I called out as he and Conor descended

hand in hand from the bus. He looked around in surprise and waved wildly as soon as he saw me.

'Jamie! I found him! I found Dad!'

I ran towards them and hugged both of them at the same time. Both lost. Both back. Like father, like son? I didn't care about anything at that moment. Not about why or what or anything else – even about Conor – I was just so relieved and happy to see them alive and well. If only life could remain as uncomplicated as that.

As we disentangled ourselves from our embrace, Mark shouted Bill's name and ran to give him a hug, announcing the same news about his Dad as he reached him. I looked at Bill and my eyes filled with tears as he bent low and swung Mark up into his arms. Mark hugged his neck and as soon as his feet touched the ground he ran back over to Conor. Bill was almost as pale as Mark – notwithstanding the black stubble that was already threatening to become a full beard. I went to him and squeezed his arm.

'He's safe,' I said.

Bill nodded.

I fumbled in my handbag, looking for my phone. 'I need to call Marielouise.'

'Already did it,' he said.

I smiled. 'You're a star.'

'What can I say – it's true.'

Bill put his arm around my shoulders and I leaned into him and we just watched as the police officers spoke to Conor and Mark. After they had finished they all walked towards us. Conor introduced us to

PC Foley (the woman) and PC Harrison and they invited us to come back to the police station with them.

It was within walking distance and after a short conversation with a corpulent middle-aged sergeant who reminded me of Dermot, Bill and I were dismissed as Conor dealt with the legalities in an office. Mark was inseparable from his father so we went out to the tatty reception area to wait. I bought us two cups of shitty coffee from a vending machine and we drank it – too tired to talk. Eventually, Conor and Mark emerged and joined us.

'So?' I asked my brother as they sat down beside us on the plastic bucket chairs provided.

'All's well that ends well,' he said, with a smile.

I couldn't smile back as a wave of anger rose up my throat. But I didn't want to say anything in front of Mark so I looked down into my plastic cup.

'Will we try to get Mark onto a flight home with us?' I said, without making eye contact with Conor.

'I'm going with Dad,' Mark said.

I looked up.

Conor shrugged. 'I was speaking to Marielouise and Aer Lingus and the flights are pretty full. Mark and I can get on a flight early this afternoon – they gave us the last two seats. I took the liberty of asking about seats for you two as well – you did fly Aer Lingus, didn't you?'

He paused and both Bill and I nodded.

'That's what I thought,' Conor continued. 'Anyway, this evening at seven is the best they can do for you. I said we'd call and confirm – what do you think?'

Suddenly I felt so exhausted and wrung out by the whole thing that I didn't give a shit what happened.

'That's fine,' Bill said when I didn't answer. 'I'll call and confirm.'

Conor shifted in his seat and ran a hand through his hair. Mark yawned loudly and leaned against his dad. 'We'll need to get going, Mark and I, if we're to make it to the airport in time.'

I listened to my brother giving orders and organising everyone as if he was the great saviour when really he'd caused the whole sorry mess in the first place. I watched Mark's trusting face as he gazed up at his father and wondered how he was going to handle the discovery of his half-sisters. All's well that ends well, my arse. I jumped up.

'Conor – a quick word. Markie, sit there with Bill a minute. I need to talk to your dad.'

I walked out the front of the station and Conor followed. With every step I took the anger inside me increased tenfold. 'What the fuck are you up to?' I shouted, whirling around to face my brother. He was, of course, lighting a cigarette.

'I beg your pardon?'

'Did you tell Mark that he has two new sisters?'

'Well, no . . .'

'So what's the plan? Will you drop him off like a DHL package and then come back to London? Or maybe now you're planning to abandon your English children?'

'Jamie, listen . . .'

'Oh, I've got a great idea – how about Paris? You could start a French connection – you could have children all over Europe.'

I stopped, suddenly breathless. For once Conor didn't speak. He just stood looking at me as he smoked his cigarette.

'Well?' I said eventually.

Conor flicked his cigarette onto the pavement and sighed. 'I know I fucked up. I know all of this is my fault.'

'So? What are you going to do?'

'I'm going to bring Mark home – it's the least I can do. Brenda will hold onto the girls.'

'And what about Fiona? Are you just going to deposit Mark and leave immediately? Surely he thinks you're coming home for good?'

'Look, Jamie, I don't how I'm going to manage it but this time I'm going to sort out the mess and do the right thing. I just spoke to Brenda on the phone and she is flying over with the girls tomorrow – I've booked us into Jury's and I don't know what'll happen but I suppose I'll just stay put and take my medicine . . .'

'Dad?'

Conor and I spun around. Mark's eager face was peeping at us around the front door of the police station.

'Hi, soldier,' Conor said. Mark ran over to us and caught Conor's hand. 'We'll talk more at home, I promise.'

I shrugged. There was nothing he could say to me that was going to make everything all right.

'We'd better be off. Will you two be OK?' Conor said.

'We'll be fine,' Bill said, appearing in the doorway.

'See you, so,' I said, bending to kiss Mark on the head. Conor looked as if he was considering giving me a hug but he got the stay-away signal that I was putting out and just smiled weakly.

'See you, Bill,' he said instead.

Bill didn't answer him. 'Bye, Mark – see you at home,' he said. Then Conor and Mark waved and set off. Bill and I stood in silence and watched them disappear into the crowd.

'So?' I said eventually.

Bill looked at me with bloodshot eyes. 'Do you feel like shopping?'

I moaned.

'Well, Harrods isn't a million miles away.'

'If they were giving the stuff away for nothing I couldn't be arsed.'

Bill stretched his hands high in the air behind his head as he yawned loudly.

'Exactly,' I said.

'I confirmed that booking – we fly out at seven.'

'That's grand. But what'll we do until then?'

Bill grinned. 'I took the liberty of booking us into the Heathrow Hilton for a few hours.'

I squinted and rubbed my eyes. 'Probably a bit expensive for me.'

'You can owe me.'

I leaned towards him and kissed him gently on the lips. 'I already owe you. Thanks for everything, Bill.'

He smiled. 'You're more than welcome. Come on, let's get a cab.' I followed him down the bustling street and within seconds he'd managed to flag down a black cab. We got in. The traffic was appalling, forcing the cab to move along in this slow jerking motion that for me was like being tortured. I leaned my head against Bill's shoulder and moaned softly.

'I take it that's motion-sickness moaning as opposed to the pleasure-related sort,' he said into my hair.

'Comedian,' I mumbled against the fabric of his jacket.

'Go to sleep,' he said.

'I'll try,' I said, moaning again and squeezing my eyes shut. I didn't sleep but for the hour or more that it took to get to Heathrow I stayed put with my eyes closed, fighting nausea, exhaustion and the rising consciousness that being there with Bill – even in those circumstances – was the right place for me to be.

I think he must have slept on the journey to Heathrow because he hardly moved and never spoke. As soon as the cab stopped I jumped up and paid the driver over Bill's protests. He laughed at my insistence and led the way into the hotel. The lobby was reasonably empty – a couple of men in suits reading newspapers at low glass tables. Bill smiled at me as we waited for the uniformed man behind the desk to give us his attention.

'This looks bad,' I said, leaning on the blond-wood counter.

Bill raised an eyebrow. 'What?'

'Checking into an hotel for a couple of hours in the middle of the day – no suitcases – what'll they think of us?'

Bill grinned and looked as though he was about to say something when the man behind the desk approached.

'May I help you?' he asked in a refined accent, obviously doing his best not to react to the cut of the two of us. I smiled broadly at him.

'Hehir,' Bill said. 'I rang and made reservations.'

The man dropped his gaze to a flat computer screen. 'Certainly, sir. Here we are: Rooms 287 and 285 – just across the corridor from each other.' He tapped the keyboard and handed us a swipe card each. I took mine from his manicured fingers as a blush crept slowly from my toes the whole way up my body and onto my face. I couldn't believe it. Two separate rooms? Why? Well, I suppose the question was why not? And I'd said all that stuff about what would the hotel think so Bill knew I'd been presuming that we'd be sharing a room.

My stomach knotted with mortification. Thing was, I hadn't thought it out. I'd just presumed . . . and remembering the carry-on in my brother's house . . . But that was it, wasn't it? I'd been mistaken again – well, that wasn't much of a surprise, considering everything. 'Jamie?'

I started.

'You OK?'

'Sure . . . yeah . . . fine . . . can't wait to throw myself into that shower and then lie down in a real bed and get some sleep.'

Bill narrowed his eyes and looked at me. I squirmed under his gaze and tried for a big, broad, happy smile.

'Will that be everything, sir?' the reception man said and we both looked at him. Oh great, I'd forgotten him and now there was another person who thought I was insane.

'Better get going, so,' I said in my happy voice. 'Is that the lift? Look! Quick. Run before the doors close.'

I legged it across the lobby and into the open lift, almost falling onto a woman in a mauve twinset. Bill followed, stepping inside just as the doors closed.

'Second floor,' I said, leaning towards the panel of buttons. 'Anybody else need me to press another floor?'

The other occupants of the lift – the mauve twinset woman and a short man in a grey suit who looked like Fred Astaire's thirty-year-old grandson – shook their heads and then looked away quickly. I clasped my hands in front of me and looked at the floor. As the lift swooshed swiftly upwards I glanced once – quickly – at Bill and found that he was looking at me, his face a picture of puzzlement. But I looked away – I was running out of happy smiles.

Within seconds we were on the second floor and I was charging down the carpeted corridor, looking for Room 287.

'Great!' I announced as I found it. Why was this

mortification making my voice rise by ten decibels? I pointed a finger at Bill in a way that reminded me of Ollie the cameraman, swiped my card, shouted, 'See you later' and escaped into Room 287.

Once inside I leaned against the door with my heart pounding, my face still burning and a beginning sense of loss growing in my chest. The room was dark, the curtains were drawn and though I eventually worked out that that was because I was required to insert my swipe card in a slot by the door, I decided I liked the dark better. I pulled off my T-shirt and jeans, turned down the white sheets on the neatly made bed and climbed under the covers. My body ached with lack of sleep as well as with tension and travel-sickness and as soon as my head hit the soft cool pillow I began to cry.

My heart was sore. Conor had betrayed me – us. Mark might have been killed, or worse. My boyfriend who I'd thought was the love of my life had punched me down the stairs. And now I'd jumped the gun with Bill and made myself look like a complete slapper. Jesus, how many curve balls can life fling at a girl in any one week?

40

As soon as I'd finished my bawl I fell asleep, not waking until four-thirty. I still felt raw but at least I also felt a bit better and that was something. I undressed and stood under the shower until I woke up properly and then put my smelly clothes back on. I had to dry my hair with my fingers because I didn't have a comb in my handbag – though I did have a small make-up bag. Sophie would be proud of me, I thought as I put on a smear of make-up and a quick flick of mascara. I looked in the mirror and apart from the fact that my hair did definitely look like I'd forgotten to bring a comb I thought I didn't look too bad. If only I'd had clean underwear I'd have been nearly happy. Well, maybe 'happy' was an exaggeration.

I sat down in a squashy armchair and flicked on the TV. But even though I religiously surfed through every channel I couldn't seem to concentrate. Inside myself I was still full of confusion. So much had happened that it was all like a dense ball of string and I couldn't find the start of it in order to begin the unravelling. Still, I told myself as I started to feel sorry for myself again, Mark was fine – home by now – and that was all that mattered.

At five-fifteen there was a knock on the door. Before I opened it I knew it was Bill coming to collect me so that we could go and check in for our flight. I composed myself as best I could and stepped into the hallway. He looked and smelled as though he'd showered as well, though he still had that devastatingly attractive stubble going on.

'Now I feel human,' I said as I closed the door behind me. 'Did you sleep?'

He nodded and smiled but I could see he was appraising me as though he wasn't quite sure if I was going to turn into a maniac again at any minute. I didn't blame him.

'Like a baby,' he said.

We stood in reasonably companionable silence in the descending lift.

'We've plenty of time,' I said, struggling for topics of conversation. 'All we have to do is settle up with the hotel.' I looked at him as I finished speaking.

'I already paid,' he said.

I shook my head as the lift stopped and we walked out into the lobby. 'Then I need to repay you.'

He smiled. 'Forget about it.'

'No.'

'OK then, owe me – I like it when you owe me.' He stopped walking as he said that and a slow grin spread across his face. But I wasn't about to go down that road again.

'Go away with that, Bill Hehir!' I said, once again adding decibels. What the hell was this shouting about? 'The cheque will be in the post as soon as we

get home. Come on, we'd better hurry. We don't want
to miss our flight.'

Bill's face closed up and he gave a tight smile.
'Definitely not,' he said.

The next half-hour or so was spent finding our
way to Terminal One and then locating our check-in
desk. I was relieved to discover that we had to sit
apart during the flight.

The journey home was uneventful. I found myself
sitting between two middle-aged country women who
talked across me for the entire journey. Even though
they didn't know each other when they embarked at
Heathrow, by the time we disembarked at Shannon
they had discovered that they had at least a dozen
acquaintances and one in-law in common.

Bill and I met up again at the door of the plane. We
walked in silence straight past the luggage-collection
point – since we didn't have any – and I wished that
I'd driven myself to Shannon. But it was too late.

Neither of us said much on the drive into Limerick.
It was dark and raining and I was tired again. I was
also wondering what would happen when the relief
at Mark's return wore off and the Conor-shit really
hit the fan.

'Hungry?' Bill asked all of a sudden just as we
were approaching the final roundabout before
Limerick.

'Starving,' I answered because it was true. I was
absolutely ravenous.

'My house is closest – want to come back and get
something to eat?'

I thought of my empty fridge and also of a night by myself thinking about Conor and Marielouise and all the shit that was going down in my family. Complicated as my feelings for Bill were becoming, it still seemed like an easier option.

'Great,' I said.

Bill nodded and turned off the Ennis Road towards his house. Twenty minutes later we were in his kitchen and he was straining the water from a pot of fresh pasta. He mixed in some pesto while I sat on a high stool and watched him work. I leaned over and grabbed some Parmesan and the grater – I felt that I should be doing some work. The atmosphere between us became considerably more relaxed as we assembled our meal.

We ate at the breakfast counter. Bill found a bottle of Riesling which we took along with us on our coffee tray when we'd finished eating and retired to the sitting room.

I sank into his gigantic sofa and sighed a long deep sigh. He sat down beside me, a glass of wine still in his hand.

'Full?'

I nodded.

'Tired?'

I nodded again. 'You?'

He sat back and turned so that he could see me. Then he didn't say anything for a very long time – just looked at me. Eventually I couldn't stand it.

'What?' I said, sitting forward in my seat. 'I know I look like I've been pulled backwards through a hedge but give a girl a break – I've been wearing these clothes for two days now.'

Bill smiled. 'That wasn't what I was thinking.'

'So? What *were* you thinking?'

He closed his eyes and slowly opened them again. 'Probably the short answer is that I was thinking the opposite to that.'

He paused and I shrugged. 'Like what?'

'That you look lovely. That I love your eyes and how they look like they change colour depending on the mood that you're in. One minute they're so dark that they look almost black, the next they're bright green.'

Bill moved closer to me on the sofa and reached a hand towards my face, lightly brushing my cheek. 'I remember the first time I saw you. You were only a kid – thirteen, fourteen . . .'

'Fifteen.'

He smiled again. 'Fifteen. Even so, you were probably the most alive person I had ever seen.'

'What does that mean?'

'I don't know. It's just the way you were . . . are.'

'Alive?'

'And now, as well as that, I think you're probably also the most beautiful person I ever saw.'

'The make-over,' I mumbled as he got even closer. I could smell and nearly taste him in the air in front of my face.

'Nothing to do with it,' Bill said and I could feel his breath as he spoke. I was mesmerised by the moment and could feel myself falling deeper and deeper into an abyss that was a lot more than an uncomplicated roll in the hay. Going against every signal that my body was giving me, I forced myself to stand up. I covered my mouth with my hands and looked at him. He looked up at me from under his eyebrows.

'Bill,' I said as soon as I could speak. 'We've had a difficult and emotional few days and I don't think we should – you know – complicate matters even further. I'll call a cab. Go home. Let you rest.'

He stood up and I wrapped my arms around my body to stop myself reaching out and pulling him towards me.

'I don't want to rest,' he said.

I didn't say anything for a few seconds. 'But maybe you need to,' I said.

Bill reached out and pulled me towards him. My resolve shattered like glass. To hell with it. Maybe I couldn't have what I really wanted from Bill – but shit, at least I could have this. I kissed him hungrily and he kissed me back and our hands found each other. Then he pulled away.

I almost screamed with frustration.

He looked into my eyes and I looked back at him. My heart was pounding like a horse's hooves and the air around us felt thick with electricity.

'I want to ask you something,' he said.

I looked at him with his stubble and hazel eyes and funny hair that stuck up at one side when he was tired and I wanted to say '*Be fast about it and let's get down to business*.' Instead I said. 'OK. Ask me.'

'Is this another one-night stand?'

I guffawed. 'What?'

Bill's face clouded over and he looked as if I'd hit him.

'Why are you asking me that?' I said softly.

At first he didn't answer. He just stepped back from me and caught hold of both my hands in his. We stood there in silence for what felt like ages, face to face, holding hands like a couple having a real conversation. I tried to read his expression but it had suddenly changed to being its old inscrutable self. I had no clue what he was thinking, let alone feeling.

'Why?' I repeated.

He took a deep breath. 'Because I don't want it to be.'

'Me neither,' I said before I launched myself at him and began to kiss his mouth. He tasted like balsamic vinegar. He pulled my T-shirt over my head and I unbuttoned his shirt and then everything slowed down as Bill led me to his bedroom. We undressed each other in turn, savouring the sight and smell and touch of each other as we tenderly made love. Afterwards I fell asleep almost immediately.

Next morning I awoke to the quiet sound of Bill's breathing. I glanced at the clock – six-fifteen – and snuggled against his back. He turned around and kissed me lightly on the lips.

'Good morning,' he whispered.

I kissed him back and ran my hands along his chest.

He groaned. 'I have an early meeting.' He kissed

my neck and moved down. 'How about a shower?' he mumbled.

'Too comfy,' I said. 'You go ahead.'

'You must be joking,' he said and then we were off again. The night before had been tender and loving – but morning sex with Bill was another story entirely.

41

After our morning wake-up call, we took turns in the shower – we'd have been there all day if we'd gone in together. Bill dropped me off at my house: I was in dire need of clean clothes and much as he tried to tell me that his underwear suited mc men's boxer shorts aren't exactly my idea of comfort.

I changed quickly and had a short cuddle with Titbit before walking off into work. It was a beautiful summer morning – in keeping with my mood and the stupid smile that wouldn't stay off my face. Every time Bill's face popped into my head a shiver ran through me and I could barely stop myself ringing him just to hear his voice. I hugged the secret of us to myself because I knew how fragile this new relationship was, especially after the Steve debacle. I had no intention of telling anybody what had happened between Bill and me. Unfortunately, however, the first person I met was Sophie.

'And Mark booked himself onto a bus to London?' she said, grabbing me by the arm as I tried to open my new office door.

I turned around. 'How do you know?'

'Well, not from you, obviously – do you ever answer your phone?'

'It was dead. How do you know?'

'Your mother. Isn't it brilliant that Mark is OK?'

I nodded.

'And Conor – what the hell was going on there? It's unbelievable.'

I shrugged. 'Long story.'

'Give me the potted version, I'm dying of curiosity.'

'OK. Turns out my lovely brother – the White-Haired Boy – had got not one but two wives . . .'

'Holy shit!'

'But wait: he also has two more children.'

'Fuck off!'

'I'm dead serious and though you might think this is the story from an episode of *Footballers' Wives* apparently one of his harem is bonkers and is locked up because she tried to kill herself.'

'Jesus, that's a mess,' Sophie said, following me into my office.

'Who are you telling?'

I sat down behind my desk.

'How did you and Bill get on in London? Any fist fights to add to the drama?'

In spite of myself a huge grin spread across my face.

Sophie's eyes widened. 'You didn't!'

I pretended to look for something in my desk drawer.

'Oh – my – God! You can't be serious!'

'He was brilliant the whole time,' I said.

'I always knew he had staying power in the sack – he just has that look about him.'

'Oh, shut up – that's not what I mean! Bill was incredible through the whole Mark thing – mind you, he's incredible in the sack as well!'

Sophie squealed. 'At long last! I'd go and get pissed to celebrate your new romance, except I'm off the booze. We could go and eat five tins of Ambrosia creamed rice if you like – that's my latest craving.'

'Yeuch!'

'I've got great news, by the way – Balloon Balls has left.'

'Steve?'

Sophie nodded. 'Well, you know he's going to London anyway and I'd say that the atmosphere in the office for the last few days has been a bit frosty. Let me put it like this: even Dee-Dee and Raina had stopped saluting him.'

The mention of Steve's name diminished my good humour. Sophie must have noticed something in my expression.

'What?' she said. 'Are you upset that he's gone?'

'No, I'm glad he's gone.'

'So?'

'What if I'm walking into another big mess with Bill? I mean, fuck it, Sophie, I was absolutely mad about Steve and it was only a few weeks ago and now I think I'm in love with Bill and . . . how are you supposed to *know*?'

Sophie smiled and her pale morning-sickness face warmed. 'You're asking the wrong person. Tell me one thing: did you ask him about Dublin? Who was that woman asleep in his bed?'

My mood took another nosedive. 'No.'

'You should probably do that just to clear the air.'

I nodded. She was right but I wasn't sure I wanted to hear the answer. My phone rang.

'I'll leave you to it – I want more details later,' Sophie said, waving as she left the office.

I looked at the screen of my phone. Mam. Oh God, I hadn't talked to her at all since before I'd left for London. I really should have called her.

'Hello, Mam.'

'Hi, Jamie. I'm glad I caught you before you went on air. Isn't it great?'

'About Mark? It's brilliant.'

'And Conor – oh Jamie, I'm over the moon!'

'About what, Mam – the second marriage? The surprise grandchildren? The lies? The deceit?'

I stopped, my heart thumping with anger. Was there nothing that Conor could do that would blot his copybook as far as our mother was concerned?

'I'm not saying it's an ideal situation . . .'

I laughed.

'The thing is, though, he's my son and he's alive. I know you're mad at him, Jamie, but we're family and we have to try to get past this whether we like it or not.'

'Well, I *don't* like and I don't have to get past anything.'

My mother sighed. 'I'm actually calling to invite you to come home to dinner tonight.'

'Will Conor be there?'

'Of course – I thought if we all sat down around the table and . . .'

'I'm not coming.'

'Please, Jamie, I'd like you to be there.'

'I don't want to be in the same room as Conor unless I have absolutely no option.'

'Do it for me.'

'Aw, Mam.'

'Please.'

That was low – using the 'for me' card. I sighed. 'What time?'

'Good girl – seven o'clock. I'll cook your favourite chicken casserole and we'll have flan for dessert.'

'You're evil, Mam – you know I can't resist chicken casserole.'

'See you later, love.'

I hung up and began to prepare for my show, rooting in the filing cabinet for my fall-back programme plan. Paddy Shine had subbed for me while I was away – I didn't think *Shine On* twice a day was fair on the people of Limerick. I pushed away all thoughts of brothers and dinner and even Bill. I didn't want to have to think about any of it and now I didn't need to because I was off into my haven of a studio for a couple of hours. Suited me grand.

After my show – which went well, all things considered – Dee-Dee handed me a message.

In meeting all day – will pick you up at six for dinner at your parents' house. Bill was scrawled across a pink Post-It. I blushed under Dee-Dee's knowing gaze.

'Thanks,' I said, grabbing the slip of paper and hurrying into my office. My mother was totally irrepressible – who the hell else had she invited to that bloody dinner? Nelson Mandela? There was a knock on the door and Shane came in.

'Just had a call from Heather,' he said perching on my desk.

'Shit – has my mother invited her to dinner too?'

He looked puzzled.

'Forget about it,' I said. 'It's a long story. What did Heather have to say for herself?'

'Just that she wants me to keep Titbit – she's going to Milan for six months.'

'I thought we already had him.'

Shane shrugged. 'I know.'

'Still – I love that ugly mutt now, I couldn't bear Heather to take him. Good job he isn't a child, though, with that kind of careless attitude to custody. Speaking of children . . .'

Shane looked at me with a perfect poker-player's expression – completely unreadable.

'Well? Sophie told me about the baby – how do you feel about it?'

'I suppose it's not the way you'd plan it but these things happen and sometimes they work out, don't they?'

'They do. What about you and Sophie?'

'She thinks I feel sorry for her.'

'And do you?'

Shane shook his head. 'No – and worse than that, I really like her.'

'What does "really like" mean, Shane? Are you saying that you love her?'

'She's one of my best friends, I always loved her.'

'And now?'

'Everything is different.'

'Good different or bad different?'

'It might be good if I could convince Sophie that she isn't a charity case. Heard Conor is back – was he The Man in The Park?'

I nodded. 'Little fucker.'

There was a knock on the door and we both started.

'Come in,' I called. The door opened and Marielouise stood in front of us. She wore a crumpled biscuit-coloured linen suit and her face was so pale that she looked luminous. Her blonde hair was lank and she wasn't wearing make-up – most unusual for her.

Shane coughed. 'Hi, Marielouise – better get to work. How are you?'

'I've been better,' she said with a wry smile. Shane waved and disappeared.

I got up, went over and put my arms around her. 'How are you love?'

Marielouise began to cry. Her thin shoulders shook with the exertion of emotion. I held her tightly but didn't speak – there was nothing to say. When she finished she blew her nose.

'Jamie, the reason I'm here is that your mother rang and I promised her I'd go to dinner tonight but I just can't.'

'I don't blame you.'

'Will you apologise for me?'

'Don't worry about it. Of course I will.'

Marielouise's eyes filled with tears. She swallowed hard and blew her nose again.

'Dillon's?' I said. 'A couple of stiff drinks wouldn't go astray.'

She gave me a wan smile. 'I'd murder a gin and tonic.'

'And possibly my brother?'

Marielouise laughed and I grabbed my handbag.

42

'It's my round! It's my round!' I said, winding my arms around Marielouise's neck.

'No! No! It's my turn. Anyway, Jamie, it isn't every week that your husband comes back from the dead.'

We looked at each other and roared with laughter. Marielouise stood up carefully, wobbling slightly as she walked to the bar. There was no denying that we were pissed. It was five o'clock and we were still in Dillon's. Even though we'd started off talking about Conor and abandonment and children, somehow we'd segued into a drinking session. At about four I texted Bill to ask him to pick me up in Dillon's and Marielouise texted her sister to make sure that the kids were OK. Once we'd dealt with that bit of house-keeping we warmed to the task of downing as many gin and tonics as we could manage without falling over.

I knew that Marielouise's heart was broken and she knew that Conor's carry-on had devastated me and my parents as well. But after a couple of good bawls and three gin and tonics we were ready to change the subject. We needed some light relief and it was great to see my sister-in-law laugh and joke. There'd be plenty of time to face up to the shit.

When Marielouise returned from the bar this time she'd thoughtfully bought a double round. A sing-song had broken out at the back of the pub where a group of young fellas were getting a stag under way. They were singing 'Blue is the Colour' at the top of their lungs.

'Bloody Chelsea fans!' I hissed venomously.

Marielouise rolled her eyes and gulped gin.

'Watch this,' I said as the young fellas cheered and clapped when they finished singing.

I jumped up from my seat and began to sing 'You'll Never Walk Alone'. Two builders at the next table joined in and soon half the pub – including the Chelsea fans – were singing. As soon as I stopped Marielouise launched into that *Dirty Dancing* classic whinge, 'Time of My Life'. Probably to stop her singing 'Hungry Eyes' one of the plaster-encrusted builders sang 'The Fields of Athenry' and the whole of Dillon's joined in the chorus. I drank back my gin and before anybody else could get in I jumped to my feet again and belted into 'Hey Jude'. It went down a bomb and just as we crescendoed to the final chorus Bill appeared in front of me. Much to his amusement I serenaded him and then kissed him long and hard on the mouth. The bar erupted in catcalls and applause and I took a bow.

'We'd need to be going to your mother's,' Bill said,

sitting down on a stool and smiling at Marielouise. She beamed at him and leaned over and kissed him on the cheek.

'The man who found my son,' she slurred. 'I love you and Jamie does too.'

I thumped her on the arm and we screamed with laughter. Bill rolled his eyes.

'How are you, Marielouise?'

'Never better and I have the very song to prove it to you.'

Marielouise climbed up on her stool and stepped onto the round bar table. Bill grabbed the glasses just as Marielouise launched into 'I Will Survive'. Bill and I laughed and I draped myself around him and nuzzled into his neck.

'I know you don't want to hear this, Jamie, but we need to leave.'

'How about we go home first . . .' I said, pausing for a nudge and a wink. 'And we can just go to my folks for dessert? I can't stick having to look at Conor's ugly head all night.'

'We have to go – is Marielouise coming?'

I shook my head and the room spun. 'No, she can't face it. Maybe we could bring the builders, though? They're great singers.'

Bill stood up and, smiling at me, gently pulled me to my feet. Marielouise's audience clapped and roared and she got down from the table.

'We have to go,' Bill said to her. 'Come on – I'll bring you home.'

She looked at him and a flash of her hurt and pain

flitted across her face. Bill must have seen it too because he hugged her.

'I wish he was dead,' she said, two tears running down her cheeks. 'Am I terrible?'

'No,' Bill said.

Marielouise sniffed loudly. 'But then I look at the children and they are so delighted to have their daddy back and that makes me glad that he's alive. But it'd be easier for me if he was dead . . .'

I hugged her.

'Ah, fuck him!' Marielouise said, straightening up.

'My sentiments exactly,' said Bill, gathering up our belongings and steering us towards the door.

Luckily he'd parked his BMW just outside because the minute the air hit us Marielouise and I developed jelly legs. Which, of course, we thought was hilarious. I fell asleep as soon as the car began to move and vaguely heard Marielouise being dropped off. I didn't wake up properly, though, until Bill shoved a cup of garage coffee under my nose.

'Drink this or your mother'll kill you.'

I moaned. 'Nooooo.'

'Do what you're told.'

I took the cup from him and sipped the scalding liquid. It made me feel sick but I knew he was right: my mother *would* kill me if I turned up at her house in such a state. By the time I'd finished three cups of coffee and done four laps of the forecourt I managed to convince Bill that I was sober.

'How can you be so composed about spending an

evening with Conor?' I said as we drove towards my parents' house.

'This evening is about your parents – not Conor,' he said, his jaw set in a determined line. I noticed that the sexy stubble thing was going on again and stroked his cheek. He turned his head briefly and smiled at me.

'But he robbed you,' I said.

Bill sighed deeply. 'I know. But that's half resolved – Conor came to see me today . . .'

'What! You never told me!'

'Well, Jamie, you were busy singing when I met you and it isn't often I get serenaded so I didn't want to ruin the mood.'

'What did he have to say for himself, anyway?'

'He's resigned from the company. Technically he didn't really rob us – just channelled his own money into that account . . .'

'Even so, how could you trust him?'

'I couldn't and he knows it, which is why he's resigning. I'm buying him out but, to be fair to him, the price is very low.'

Bill stopped the car in front of my parents' house. 'Let's do this,' he said, leaning over and kissing me on the lips.

I burped and laughed and so did Bill, which at least took my mind off what I was facing.

My mother was like somebody on a mixture of cocaine, speed and ecstasy. She was coiffed and made-up to within an inch of her life. I imagined that every beautician in Poise had been engaged that day in preparing her for this dinner.

'Sorry we're late,' Bill said, kissing my mother's cheek.

'Not at all, not at all – I'm delighted ye came, I was afraid . . . well, you're here now.'

'Marielouise sends her apologies,' I said without too much slurring.

My mother's eyes filled with tears and her bottom lip quivered. I put my hand on her arm. 'Look, Mam, it's just too hard for Marielouise . . . too soon.'

My mother bit her lip and nodded. 'I didn't want to leave her out but I didn't really expect her.'

I shrugged. 'Why are we doing this dinner thing, anyway? I don't see the point. A nice dinner isn't going to make everything all right.'

'Don't you think I know that, Jamie?'

'So?'

'We're still family and we have to find a way past what has happened.'

'Happened?' I said though I couldn't believe my ears. My mother's face had reset into its Poise mask. Surely she couldn't mean that. My head filled up with all the stuff that Conor had done to us and now my mother was talking about it as if we were victims of a natural disaster. I could feel my temper rising and obviously so could Bill.

'Something certainly smells delicious,' he said, taking my arm and propelling me towards the dining room. 'What's cooking, Anna?'

'Chicken casserole. Jamie's favourite.'

My mother looked at me and though I felt the whole dinner thing was pointless and painful under the circumstances I could see the mixture of sadness, desperation and hope in my mother's eyes. I figured that one evening of discomfort wouldn't kill me.

Bill and my mother had started up a conversation about Mark as we walked into the dining room. Conor and Dad were installed at either end of the table, both of them looking extremely uncomfortable.

'You're just in time, really – I was only saying to your father that maybe I'd told you half-seven by accident but I had to take the casserole out because it gets ruined if it's in too long. Sit down, sit down – let me just dish it up for you.'

Bill and I sat down and my mother discreetly cleared away Marielouise's place setting before handing us all steaming plates of food. We all tucked in. Anything to avoid conversation.

'Miss Limerick was in with me again today – lovely girl! And do you know who else is one of mine?' my mother said, pausing to look around the table. Needless to say, none of us answered.

'Dolores McNamara,' she said.

We all looked blank.

'The woman who won the European lottery. Salt of the earth, a lovely woman. Sally did a great job with her hair yesterday – she's off to Marbella for the weekend again. Well for some.'

Silence fell on the table as soon as Mam stopped motor-mouthing. The only sound in the dining room was that of cutlery and plates clinking. The atmosphere was leaden and as the food began to sober me up I decided that I couldn't bear reality.

'Is there any wine?' I asked.

Dad nodded. 'Half a case in the garage. I'll get it, love.'

He jumped out of his chair and shot out of the room before anybody else could offer to go. More eating. More clinking. I looked surreptitiously at my brother as I filled my mouth with food. He looked old and I was glad. He'd caused so much suffering. Bastard. I looked back down at my dinner.

Dad came in with two open bottles of wine and filled everybody's glass. He sat back down. I gulped the entire glass and helped myself to a refill.

'Great wine, Jimmy,' Bill said.

'You should know – you bought it,' Dad said.

'Did I?' Bill answered, leaning back in his chair. He looked as if he was about to speak again and then he stopped himself and concentrated on his dinner plate. The atmosphere in the room took a nosedive – if that was possible – and my parents and Bill all looked embarrassed. I scrutinised them, trying to work out what had just happened. Why were they suddenly mortified? It was only wine, after all – and then I remembered.

'For Mark's communion,' I said, leaning towards Bill. 'Remember, it was Cup Final Day and we had a big party and everybody was there . . .' I paused and drank more wine. The alcohol was metabolising nicely and I felt as clear as a bell and as brave as a lion. 'Oh, hang on a minute . . . I'm mistaken – *you* weren't here, Conor, were you? You were on that long, long flight home from Heathrow. Eighteen months of a flight – did ye go over the Bermuda Triangle, by any chance?'

Conor didn't answer. He just looked at me.

'So tell me, Conor – any more weddings on the horizon? Should I buy a hat? Bill can get you a discount on the wine. He has great contacts.'

I held Conor's gaze with mine and was glad to see the hurt in his eyes.

'Cut me some slack here, Jamie,' Conor said defensively.

'Go fuck yourself!' I retorted.

'Jamie!' my father's voice called and I looked in his direction. My mother stood up, almost knocking her chair to the floor.

'I need to just go check the . . . check the . . .' she said as she fled towards the kitchen.

Nobody spoke for a few seconds. I finished my glass of wine in one go.

My father cleared his throat and we all looked at him. 'Your mother went to a lot of trouble to cook this meal and we won't have this carry on at the table.'

'But Dad . . .' I began.

He shook his head. 'No buts from either of you. I won't have your mother upset.'

I considered just standing up and leaving – I wanted to be anywhere else but sitting there with my bastard of a brother, pretending to be a real family. But my father hardly ever laid down the law and so if it was that important I supposed I had to stay. I swallowed my anger and nodded. Just then Mam came back and we all continued as though nothing had happened. Our old friend awkward silence returned as we finished off our casserole and began work on dessert.

'Absolutely delicious food, Anna,' Bill said.

My mother smiled a wobbly smile at him.

And then more silence. I could almost hear the cogs in my mother's brain turning in a frantic effort to find a neutral topic of conversation.

'Linda – Miss Limerick – is off to Milan for a week. I believe Shane's girlfriend Heather got a fabulous contract with an Italian fashion house.'

'Ex-girlfriend,' I said.

'Oh, I didn't know,' my mother said. 'That's a shame.'

'Ah, it's not too bad. Shane got custody of the dog,' I said. Bill and my parents laughed and even Conor cracked a smile.

'Linda's lovely – from a lovely family, too. Wasn't she great on your show, Jamie?'

'Fabulous,' I lied, remembering how hard it had been to beat conversation out of her and the argument I'd had with my mother before the show. Linda, the only woman who ever needed a bikini wax before a radio interview.

'She's the favourite to win Miss Ireland, you know,' my mother said, obviously relieved that the conversation seemed to be flowing at last. 'You know her brother,' my mother said, turning to Conor.

He shook his head.

'You do – Johnny Doyle – don't you remember you and Jamie gave him that laxative chocolate? What was it called again?'

'Ex-Lax,' Conor and I said at the same time. We looked at each and roared with laughter as the memory of Johnny Doyle's pained expression resurfaced.

'He had the scutters for three days,' Conor said.

'Conor!' my mother said.

'Trots Doyle,' I said, recalling the nickname we'd given him after that. For a few seconds Conor and I were joined in the memory and the laughter. Magically, as if none of the bad stuff had happened. And then I remembered and it was like being doused with cold water. I stood up from the table and blindly made my way out into the back garden.

43

It was misting slightly in the garden and I could smell freshly cut grass. I thought of the scene that I knew was unfolding at the dinner table and I knew it wouldn't be long before my mother sent somebody to find me. I needed to escape but as driving was out of the question in my state of inebriation the tree house seemed like my only option.

I found that somebody – probably Mark – had made a new rope ladder. I gingerly climbed up its wobbly length and hoisted myself into the tree house. Or Conor's tree house as we'd always known it. It looked much smaller than I remembered but smelled the same – woody and earthy and slightly damp. Mark had put up new Liverpool posters and there was a stack of *Shoot!* magazines in the corner. I pulled out a tatty beanbag and plonked myself into it. I wiped my eyes and wished that I had something to blow my nose on – Mark was a bit short on tissues. What a fiasco. I should have listened to my gut and not to my mother. I understood why she wanted us all together but sometimes you just can't fix things.

I started as I heard a noise. Conor's face appeared.

'Go away,' I said.

'I knew I'd find you here,' he said, ignoring me and pulling himself into the tiny house. He looked around. 'The old place looks just the same as the last time I was here.'

I didn't answer.

'Jamie – talk to me.'

'There's nothing to say.'

'Please.'

I shook my head.

Conor didn't say anything for a few seconds, just sat down beside me on the floor, pulling his legs close to his chest and resting his head on his knees. He looked up. 'If you won't talk to me then will you listen?'

I looked away.

'There's no excuse for what I've done – none whatsoever. I fooled myself the whole way down the line. Firstly, I fooled myself into thinking that I was entitled to have everything I wanted – so even though I had Marielouise and I loved her I married Kelly as well because I loved her too. Then, when I wanted out of that relationship, I fooled myself into thinking that I could just walk away . . .'

Conor lit a cigarette and took a few deep drags before continuing.

'I stopped fooling myself when Kelly had the breakdown – that was my wake-up call, I suppose. I knew then that not only could I not have it all, I'd actually thrown away loads. I'm not making excuses for myself but it was the worst time of my life. Six weeks of hell – the girls were traumatised after finding their mother in a pool of blood, I was completely in over my head. Kelly was bonkers, tried suicide a few times more even in the hospital. She insisted that I visit every day.

'It was a complete nightmare and by the time I woke up I'd been missing from here for nearly two months and I just didn't know how to get out of the hole I was in. The top of my game was putting food on the table and minding the girls.'

In spite of my anger I was getting a picture of the misery that Conor was describing. But then I remembered Dad crying as we watched a Liverpool match and the anger surged again.

'You caused so much pain, Conor – Mam, Dad, Marielouise, Mark, Fiona, me, Bill. We thought you were dead or worse.'

'I know, and in some ways I was dead. But, as I said already, there's no excuse.'

'Why didn't you just come home or phone and tell us everything?' I jumped up off the beanbag and hit my head on the low timber-plank roof. 'Ouch!' I sat back down. 'Apart from anything else, Conor, we would have helped you if you were having such a hard time.'

He looked at me. 'Are you sure, Jamie?'

'What do you mean? Of course.'

'Even considering that I'd be ringing you up to tell you that I had a second wife and a couple of kids by her and that I'd been siphoning money from Bilcon to finance my double life?'

I didn't answer.

'Are you really sure you wouldn't have just told me to fuck off?'

'Maybe I would have but Mam and Dad wouldn't.'

'That's probably true. I can't undo what I did but I can try to make it up to them and my kids.'

'What about Marielouise?'

Conor laughed. 'She wouldn't spit on me if I was on fire and I wouldn't blame her. She told me to expect the divorce papers and I'll just sign everything. No contest.'

Conor lit another cigarette.

'Give me one of those,' I said.

He looked at me in surprise but he obeyed. I lit the cigarette, coughing and spluttering as soon as I tried to inhale. Conor laughed. 'You were never any good at smoking, Jamie.'

'Shut up.' I inhaled again and my head spun. 'Christ – is there alcohol in these?'

We sat and smoked in the darkening tree house.

'Are you and Bill an item?'

'None of your business.'

Conor laughed. 'It's true, so. I'm glad for both of you. Bill is a great person – you don't know the half of it, Jamie,' he sighed. 'I'll miss him.'

'Why? Is he going somewhere?'

He smiled. 'Very funny. He's not going anywhere. But I'm afraid that, like in all the best mafia movies, as far as Bill is concerned I'm dead to him.'

I didn't comment and we sat in silence. I could hear the birds' chorus and a distant mower and the theme music from the nine o'clock news. I didn't know where Conor and I were going. I didn't know if I could ever forgive him or trust him but I had to try – not for him but for our parents.

We finished our cigarettes. Then, without talking about Conor's behaviour any more, we climbed down from the tree house and went back indoors. Bill and my parents were in the sitting room surrounded by photographs from Mark's communion. Bill looked exhausted. I smiled warmly at him. He really was turning out to be a truly good and reliable person: if only I could get up the guts to discuss what had happened all those years ago in Dublin then everything would be perfect.

Mam made us drink coffee which she served from some new ornate silver coffee pot she'd just bought. What with the food and the coffee and the trauma I was stone-cold sober by the time we said our goodbyes and left.

'Your parents are taking the whole thing remarkably well,' Bill said as we drove away.

'Mmm,' I said, admiring his profile.

'How are you, Jamie? You've had a hard night.'

I stretched and turned on the radio. Paddy Shine's voice filled the car and I laughed as he introduced the Eagles' song 'Take It Easy'.

'I'm fine, Bill, don't worry about me. But I don't want to even think about the Conor situation, let alone talk about it.'

I put my hand on his thigh. 'Actually, what I *really* want is a bit of distraction – your place or mine?'

He laughed. 'You choose.'

'OK – your place, so. It's quieter.'

As soon as Bill closed the front door behind us I was all over him like a rash. He ran his hands down my back and unfastened my bra. 'Jesus,' he said breathlessly as we backed up the stairs.

'What?'

'I must ask your mother for the recipe for that casserole – it's obviously an aphrodisiac.'

We staggered into the bedroom, both completely naked by then. I pushed him down onto the bed. 'Try this for a recipe,' I said and even though it was a stupid joke we both laughed. Then we got down to business. Afterwards I fell asleep almost immediately.

When I woke, Bill was gone and his bedside clock said seven-fifty-five. Sunshine was streaming into the room, pooling on the floor by the bed. I curled up in a ball and looked at the puddle of light, thinking about the night before. The sex – the wonderful, exquisite, screamingly good Bill-sex – was a great antidote to the current family crisis. My mind started up into its usual whirl of why and if and maybe. I shut it down. I didn't care if I should feel the way I felt about Bill. So what if it was foolish? All that mattered at that moment was that he seemed to feel the same way too. What more could I ask?

I stretched languorously in the big comfortable bed and then had a shower in Bill's neat en suite bathroom. Searching through his chest of drawers I found a white T-shirt and a pair of hilariously small Y-fronts.

Not much but better than wearing my smelly old underwear again. I needed to go home and get clean clothes. I made my way through the silent house and into the sunny kitchen. On the fridge was a huge note scrawled in red marker. It was fixed in place with a magnet of a Gaugin painting.

Jamie,

Had to go to work. Will you call me later?

Love, Bill

I smiled as I read the note while sipping a glass of orange juice. The word *love* floated towards me. I knew it was just a word. A possibly meaningless social convention. A way of signing off that didn't necessarily mean anything. But still.

A sudden noise behind me made me turn. I was expecting to see Bill. Instead, a tall, magnificently beautiful woman with a mane of wild black hair and chocolate eyes was standing in the kitchen doorway.

'Is Bill here?' she said. She gathered her hair in one hand and held onto it. I shook my head.

'Who are you?' she asked, taking a step towards me. She stopped again, her eyes darting around as if she was searching the room for something.

'Jamie Ryan – and you?'

She didn't answer, just went to a cupboard and took out a crystal wineglass, then searched in another cupboard until she found a bottle of wine. She opened it and poured herself a glass. I watched as if I was at a play. There was something about the way she totally ignored me that was compelling. Without ever looking at me she sipped at the wine.

'I'm back,' she said, looking into the dark liquid. 'I've come back to Bill at last. I go away from him but he knows I'll always come back. He's the only one . . .'

She looked at me suddenly and it felt as if she had grabbed me. 'Bill loves me like nobody else loves me and I get angry with him sometimes and forget how much I love him too. But I do, you know . . . I do love him. Do you believe me?'

She took another dainty sip from her glass and my stomach contracted as I recognised her. The woman in the hotel in Dublin. The same woman in the photograph behind me in Bill's kitchen. I hadn't known he'd ever been seriously involved with anyone – but then, when I thought about it, I knew very little about Bill.

Conor and he had become friends when they were at college. I knew from Conor that Bill's family were from somewhere in County Tipperary. Apart from that I knew that they were wealthy and fucked up and that was about it. The woman walked over to me and repeated her question.

'Do you believe me?'

I looked into her dark eyes and noticed a smear of red wine by her mouth.

'Yes,' I said. 'Yes. I believe you.'

The woman smiled, bent her head and sipped more wine. Then she looked at me.

'Good, because it's true. And now I'm back with Bill and I won't leave ever again.'

I nodded and swallowed hard to manage the

tears that had sprung into my eyes. I should have known that Bill was exactly the type of person to have his very own mad lover. Well, fuck that for a game of soldiers – I was no Jane Eyre.

'Excuse me, I have to get to work,' I said, walking past the woman who still hadn't told me her name. I didn't care. Mrs Rochester. The bunny-boiler. It didn't matter what she was called. It was nothing to do with her, really, and everything to do with him. Fuck him. After all the things he'd said to me. But then . . . what *had* he said? Nothing. No wonder he was such a successful businessman: he was a master at clinching deals without promising shit.

44

I slammed the front door of Bill's house behind me. It was a mild sunny day, breezy and blue-skied with those fast-moving fluffy clouds. I looked at my watch and saw that it was twenty to nine. If I ran I'd have enough time to call in at home and find something to wear before going into work. Because that was where I was going. Into my glass booth where I was in control of the world and nothing bad could happen to me.

Tears pricked my eyes but I fought them off. I'd cried enough. I had no idea how I'd fucked up so badly. To have your heart broken once in a fortnight was bad luck. But twice? That was beyond belief. It wasn't like I had a history of hooking up with bad boys – sure, I hadn't found the love of my life but I also hadn't been so irresistibly drawn to shits like Steve and Bill.

Maybe it was my age? I didn't think I was desperate to find someone but maybe I was and I just hadn't realised it yet. It was like I'd said to Sophie – Mother Nature is a ruthless bitch. Whatever the reason, I was going to call a halt: better to spend my life alone than locked into a relationship with a bollocks. Anyway, I'd never really be alone – I always had football.

I took a series of deep breaths as I walked. I'd let my guard down and trusted Bill and then . . . I couldn't even begin to think about it. I was going to freeze it in a ball in my head and maybe later, when my show was over or when I felt it wouldn't destroy me, I'd tell Sophie and she might have some answers. But not right then.

I started off along the leafy North Circular Road at a slow jog. It made me feel a bit better to be pounding the pavement with my feet. The rhythm calmed me. I speeded up and ran and ran and ran until I reached my house. It was silent, of course, since Shane was at work. Titbit greeted me with licks and excited barks. I sat on the floor and stroked him as he slobbered all over me. The affection threatened my resolve to keep away from emotion, so I disentangled myself and forced myself back into my robotic state and went to find something clean to wear.

Bill floated back into my head as I walked around the hushed house. But I forced all thoughts of him away and concentrated on finding clean clothes. I rooted through the pile of shrunken clothes still in the laundry basket: not one stitch was actually wearable – unless you were a really, really skinny pygmy. And that was another thing: what was this whole girl kick I'd been on? What was that about? Maybe that was more of the same insecure, desperate rubbish that'd been going on in my relationships.

I picked up the shrunken clothes and carried them out into the back garden where I unceremoniously dumped them into the wheelie bin. Shit, I was finished with that as well. *I yam what I yam*, I thought going back indoors. Like Popeye.

I'd been through the girl school and I'd learned good stuff – useful stuff – and I didn't feel doomed to look like a failed transvestite for the rest of my life. But it suddenly struck me that the reason I wasn't any good at girly things wasn't entirely because I couldn't do it. Part of me had always known something true: make-up and dressing up and all that palaver was only good if it was an option. If it became something that you *had* to do – something that defined you – then it was just another tyranny. And I was like a recently freed slave – determined to avoid all tyranny. OK, now I was finally getting a bit of clarity. Rule One – be yourself. Rule Two – if the *yourself* in question happens to be Jamie Ryan, then don't buy clothes that have to be dry-cleaned.

Along with developing my philosophical stance, I searched for ordinary clothes. However, the few pairs of jeans and trackies that I'd been left with after the recent cull were all in the laundry basket. I flicked through the pathetic few items still hanging in my wardrobe and then flicked through them again. The only viable option seemed to be a formal black tuxedo-style suit that I'd bought in a sale one Christmas. It was a little over the top for a stint in Fab City morning radio but as it was the only normal-sized item of clean clothing I could find, I figured it'd have to do. I found a strappy white vest to wear underneath so that I wouldn't melt while I was doing my show. Then, grabbing an apple from the kitchen, I got into my car and drove to work.

As I pulled into the car park behind the radio station I looked at my watch. Nine-thirty: that was good going – less than an hour since I'd been faced with Bill's other woman.

I arrived at the station and headed straight to my office, closing my beautiful new door behind me. No more private conversations with the entire workforce earwigging. No more being constantly on display.

Before I even sat down there was a knock on the door.

'Hi, Jamie. Sophie left these files for you.'

'Thanks, Dee-Dee.'

I took the files from her outstretched hand. She stayed standing in front of my desk. I looked at her enquiringly.

'How was your dinner?' she asked coyly.

I rolled my eyes. 'You don't want to know.'

'Well, it couldn't have been too bad if you were with Bill Hehir – he's a total ride.'

'Do you think? You can have him, so – I'm sticking to dogs and football from now on.'

Dee-Dee laughed. 'You're a holy terror, Jamie. I'd better go out and do some work. See you later.'

'See you, Dee-Dee.'

As soon as she closed the door I felt another rush of humiliation. To stop it invading my head I planned my show. I had no guests that morning so I was relying on my trusty clippings folder and the newspapers that were waiting for me in the studio. It was my

favourite kind of show – harder work but more chal-
lenging. And that suited me.

At exactly ten o'clock as the news headlines
were being read I headed towards the sound booth.
I waved across the open-plan office at Johnny G
and he gave me a thumbs-up. As the ads played
out over the speakers I took a deep breath and
cleared my head of all the shit. I was back in the
world I loved. The world where I was completely
in control.

I didn't get to start on any current news stories.
As soon as the show began, Harry O'Fee, our local
TD and Minister for Agriculture, rang in with a rant
about the negative profile of Limerick in the national
press. I pretended to be listening but in fact I was
scanning the newspapers while he was talking.

As Harry droned on I found a great piece about a
man in Dublin who had bought what he thought was
a laptop computer, only to discover that it was a briefcase containing four cartons of milk wrapped in corru-
gated cardboard. I was laughing silently at the advice
of the Gardai not to buy computers on the street when
the door of my studio flew open and then slammed
closed.

It was all so fast that I almost didn't see Pierce
Thompson come into the room. He was in and had
bolted the door closed before I fully realised what
was happening.

'Hi, Jamie,' he said, reaching into a pocket of his
navy suit and producing a gun.

I laughed nervously. 'I'm very sorry but you're not

allowed in here,' I said as though he was an ordinary passer-by who'd wandered in accidentally.

He smiled and sat on a chair next to me. 'You're wrong, Jamie. This is exactly where I should be.'

Harry O'Fee was still ranting in the background and I saw Shane run past the glass window of the booth. There was a loud thumping on the door and I could hear shouts from the other side. Pierce sat back in his chair and pointed with the gun towards the second mike.

'Would you mind switching that on, please?'

I stared at him and didn't move. Was this really happening? Was I really locked into my sound booth with an armed stalker? I'd never seen a gun before but as I scrutinised it I was sure that it was a fake. It looked exactly like a novelty cigarette lighter. I just decided to sit still and let Shane and the lads break down the door like the last time. Pierce straightened his plain red tie and smiled.

'Oh, I see the problem – you don't think the gun is real? Hang on a minute.' With that he leaned to the side and aimed at the wicker waste-paper basket in the corner. In one fluid movement he pulled the trigger and the bin jumped into the air, landed on its side and scattered its contents on the floor. I couldn't believe my eyes as I stared at the dead bin. Holy fuck! A real gun! My ears rang with the proof.

'Jamie – my mike?'

I reached out to the control panel with a shaking hand and flicked it on. Pierce tapped the microphone and cleared his throat. I noticed that whoever had been pounding on the door had stopped.

He leaned forward. 'Excuse me, could the people shouldering the door of Jamie's studio please pay attention to what I have to say? I don't intend any harm to Jamie. However, I do have a gun and I won't hesitate to use it on you. Please refrain from attempting to gain entry.'

He smiled at me as if he'd announced the news headlines. My heart was thumping as the full reality of my situation hit me. I'd always known that Pierce Thompson was more dangerous than the police imagined. But even I hadn't realised that he was a full-blown psychopath. Without taking his stare from my face he produced a small CD pouch.

'I brought my own music.'

I must have looked puzzled because he continued. 'These are songs that have great significance for me. Each one marks a milestone in my relationship with you.' He flipped open the pouch and handed me a CD.

'Track three – play it, please.'

I read the tracklist and realised that he wanted me to play my least favourite song – 'Love Cats' by The Cure. Under normal circumstances I'd have told him to shove it. However, a gun is a compelling argument. As Robert Smith began whining I wondered if I could overpower Pierce. I mean, I was twice his size – but then, there was the gun.

'This song was playing the first time I saw you,' Pierce said, settling into his seat and his role as captor-cum-dj. 'It was in HMV and you were asking the girl behind the counter about *Eternal Sunshine of the Spotless Mind*. I was waiting behind you in the queue. It was a Saturday and I was calling in to pick up the Blodwyn Pig album I'd ordered . . .'

His eyes glazed over and I caught a glimpse of Dee-Dee's head darting in front of the glass for a quick look. I sincerely hoped that they were out there hatching a plot to free me.

'. . . The moment I heard you speak I knew. It's strange, that, isn't it? How one minute you're this disembodied voice and the next thing you're right there in front of me. Do you believe in kismet?'

Kismet? Was he the frog in the Muppets? I had no idea what this lunatic was talking about but it made no difference. I shrugged.

'It's simple, really – you just don't understand yet but you will. I see the men you've been with and I know what women think they want – what they think will make them happy.'

A loud banging on the glass window of the booth interrupted Pierce. I didn't know whether to laugh or cry when I saw my mother's angry face. She thumped again on the glass and mouthed something that we couldn't hear. But you didn't have to be a lip-reader to know that she was ordering him to let me go.

'You look more like your father than your mother.'

Pierce pointed the gun at me and gave a dismissive wave to my mother. She went berserk, thumping and shouting like an irate ape in Dublin Zoo. Pierce's mouth tightened and he waved her away again but she was undaunted. I could see that he was beginning to lose his temper and I was hoping that my mother could see it too. Somebody must have been picking up on the vibe because suddenly Shane yanked Mam from view. Pierce took a series of deep breaths as if to calm himself. He shook his head philosophically.

'People don't get it. You never answered my question, Jamie.'

I shrugged and nodded. Then I shook my head.

'Do you? Do you believe in kismet?'

'Well . . .' I said, stalling for time. 'I'm not sure – do you?'

'Of course. Otherwise I wouldn't be here, would I? It's our destiny that motivates me.'

I looked at a blob of spittle that was forming at the corner of Pierce's mouth. I couldn't just sit passively at my microphone and let this happen. I made my living talking – surely I could have a stab at talking this lunatic out the door.

'Pierce,' I said, tilting my head to one side and smiling my most charming smile. 'I'm flattered, I really am – that a man like you would be interested in me . . . and maybe at another time it might work between us. But right now I'm just coming out of some very bad relationships and I need some space to get my head together. Maybe if you call me in a couple of months? We could have coffee – see a movie – whatever you like.'

My heart thumped and I clasped my hands together so that Pierce wouldn't notice they were shaking. He seemed to be considering my proposition and I began to get my hopes up. He reached for his CD holder and handed me another disc.

'Fred – you play this band a lot – I like that track "Four Chords and the Truth". Can you play it now, please?'

I tried to hide my disappointment as I slid the CD into the player. Now what was I going to do? What the hell was going on outside – surely the whole of Limerick knew by now that I was being held captive by a stalker with a gun? Where was Harry O'Fee now that I needed him? Where were the police?

I tried to think of another plan of escape but my thoughts were being confused by fear. As the music played I struggled to calm myself down. I had to be focused or I was fucked. Suddenly I had an idea.

'Pierce?'

'Yes?'

'Would you mind if I ran out to the loo? I'll be right back.'

Pierce shook his head and smiled. 'It won't be long now, my love. It won't be long.'

My eyes widened but I was afraid to ask him what he meant by that.

'Our flight to Aruba is in a couple of hours. Lovely place, Aruba – you'll love it there, Jamie.'

'Oh,' I said. 'I'm sure I will but I really, really, really need to use the loo now – I'll be straight back.'

'I'm not a fool. I know that if you go out now you won't come back. It's too soon and you don't understand yet. But you will, my love, you will.'

Now I was terrified.

'If we could be alone together for one week then I just know that you'd understand how our destinies are intertwined. One week, that's all I ask.'

I bit my lip, afraid to answer in any way.

Out of the corner of my eye I could have sworn that I saw Dermot. His face popped up and then disappeared so fast that I couldn't be sure. I almost jumped out of my skin as the telephone light lit up. Pierce leaned forward and punched the button and the music automatically dipped.

'Hello?' he said.

'Is Jamie there?'

Pierce nodded at me.

'Hello?' I said.

'Riveting show, Jamie – the girls and me are here in the factory and we're glued to it. It's Vera – remember us from the London Eye?'

'I remember.' My voice sounded shaky – did this mean that the whole town thought that what was happening wasn't for real? I sincerely hoped not. At least my mother and the others outside my booth in the station knew that wasn't so.

'Is it a play? Is it one of those EV+A arty yokes?'

'Not really.'

'Anyway, love, 'tis brilliant, whatever it is. Keep up the good work – 'tis making the time fly here on the line. See you, Jamie.'

'See you, Vera,' I said forlornly.

A loud rapping noise made me look up. My mother was standing at the window a huge false smile on her face, holding a big cardboard sign towards us.

Let her go, please. She's my only daughter, it said in big red letters. I started laughing. This couldn't be really happening. She threw that first placard over her shoulder and revealed a second message.

I love her and I know you love her too but if you really did love Jamie you'd . . .

Pierce and I were transfixed by the messages. Just as I was beginning to wonder what she was saying, Mam flung card two away and produced the rest of the sentence.

. . . *let her go. If you love someone you have to set them free. I know it's hard but it's for the best.*

Shane appeared behind her and tapped her gently on the shoulder. He said something to her and she shook her head and pointed to the sign. He spoke again and to my horror my mother's eyes filled with tears. Shane put his arm around her shoulders and led her away from view. I felt anger bubble up inside me. Fuck this bloody man, anyway: it was one thing to upset me but it was another thing entirely to upset my mother like that. Especially after all she'd just been through.

'Pierce – enough is enough – we need to stop this nonsense right now.'

He smiled and a shiver ran down my spine. This was really out of hand. Oh, where the fuck were the cavalry when you needed them? Pierce handed me yet another CD.

'Track two – that Limerick classic "There is an Isle".'

I sighed and cued the song.

'That was the next time I saw you – well, saw you properly. It was in Thomond Park, you were with your

dad and that Ali bloke. I was beside you – I couldn't
believe my luck. And then you hugged me, remember?'

'I'm sorry, I don't remember.'

'It doesn't matter. Munster scored a try and you
turned to me and hugged me and that was when I
really knew beyond the shadow of a doubt.'

Pierce pulled his satchel onto his lap and produced
two red Munster jerseys.

'One each – you put yours on first.'

I shook my head. I was sick of taking orders from
this squirt.

'Jamie,' he said in a warning voice. He quickly
pulled his jersey over his head. 'Now, see – you next.'

I shook my head again. I didn't care, he could
shoot me if he liked. The telephone light lit up again.
This time I switched the phone on.

'Hello?' said a man's deep husky voice that I didn't
recognise. There was a tap at the glass. A tall, angular man with a drooping Mexican moustache waved
at us. He was speaking into a mobile phone.

'Joe Laffan,' the voice said. 'Detective Joe Laffan.'

'Look, I've nothing to say to you – I've already made
my position clear. Goodbye,' Pierce said authoritatively.

'Hang on, hang on – I've someone here on the
other line who wants to talk to you.'

A woman's voice broke in on the conversation.
'Pierce! I want you to come home this very minute
and give over that cod-acting. This is Mammy.'

45

Pierce's face blanched and his fingers tightened around the gun.

'I don't want to talk to you,' he said in a low voice. The air in the room became electric with his obvious suppressed anger. I felt like rapping on the glass and berating the detective for involving the psycho's mother. How the hell did they think he got to be so mad in the first place?

'This is not your business,' Pierce said.

'If you're going to drag the family name through the mud I'm afraid it *is* my business. Get out of there this minute and stop disgracing yourself – you never lost it.'

Pierce began to become agitated. As I listened to his mother's clipped and ostensibly civilised voice and watched the effect it was having on her son I almost felt sorry for him. The undertone of cruelty was unmistakable: I couldn't imagine growing up with that. He jumped up and began to pace and mutter to himself.

'Your father is turning in his grave, Pierce Thompson,' his mother continued. 'God between us and all harm . . .'

Pierce leaned across the desk and flipped the off switch, letting out a triumphant shout as he did so. 'For once in my life I don't have to listen to you.'

He stood in the middle of the tiny room and took deep breaths. 'Stick to the plan, stick to the plan, stick to the plan,' he said over and over.

I briefly considered making a run for the door but I was afraid that he was now so rattled that he might actually shoot me. I looked at Detective Laffan and hoped he could see the damage he'd done. He put his mobile phone to his ear and the light on my control panel began to flash again.

'Don't answer that,' Pierce shouted. I sat back in my seat and threw my hands up. He handed me a CD and I put it on.

'This speaks for itself,' he said. 'Bell XI – "Eve, The Apple of My Eye".'

He seemed to be calming down and I smiled at him in the hope that that might help.

'Put on your Munster jersey,' he said.

After what I'd just seen I figured it was time I started to cooperate. If I did what he wanted we'd soon be leaving the sound booth and the sooner the better. Once we were outside then the troops that I was hoping were massing might be able to save me. I pulled the jersey over my head and smiled a big fake smile at Pierce.

He smiled back delightedly. 'It suits you.'

As we listened to the song I watched the policeman outside the window give up trying to contact us by phone. He knew as well as I did that it was useless.

He looked at me and I saw that his eyes were brown and kind. He smiled reassuringly. I tried to smile back but I couldn't. He gave me a small wave and disappeared from view. I was alone again and really scared now. My eyes filled with tears and I blinked them back. Pierce leaned forward and pulled the microphone towards him.

'OK, folks, here we go. I want a car outside the front door in five minutes. Nobody is to talk to us. Nobody is to try and stop us. We can be civilised about this or we can do it the hard way – it's your choice.'

He sat back in his chair and smiled at me. 'How did that sound?'

'Good. Great,' I said.

'That's good because I really don't want any unpleasantness – there's no need for it.'

'I totally agree,' I said. 'No need at all.'

'This is so great, Jamie, I can see that you're starting to see things my way – aren't you?'

'Oh, I am, Pierce, definitely.'

There was a rap on the window. My mother stood there, teary mascara marks on her face. Pierce handed me yet another CD and as he did so my mother quickly flashed up a sign.

How's your asthma?

I was confused: I didn't have asthma. This time the song was Bill Withers' 'Lovely Day'. As it began, Pierce started to tell me how Bill Withers held the record for the longest note ever in a pop song.

I made appropriate noises as I tried to decipher my mother's message. Asthma? Suddenly I understood. There was some plan hatching. Thank God. I tried making a wheezy breath. What did Dermot sound like? I tried again. This time it was more convincing – I was getting the hang of it. I took another few ragged breaths and held my chest.

'Jamie? Are you all right?' Pierce asked.

'I'm fine, it's just my asthma.'

'Poor thing, I never knew you had breathing difficulties.'

'Only when I'm stressed out.'

'Do you have an inhaler or something?'

'Not here.' I leaned forward and began to cough. It was so convincing that I started to wonder if I really did have asthma. Pierce poured me a glass of water from a bottle on the desk.

'The climate in Aruba will do wonders for your chest.'

I nodded and continued to wheeze. Fair play to my mother. Edgy and all as our relationship was, when the chips were down she was still the mammy and I was still her little girl. I pitied Pierce. I wheezed loudly just as my mother reappeared. She held another sign up to the window.

Let me in – she needs her inhaler.

I noticed then that she was holding an inhaler in her hand. She rapped loudly on the window and pointed to the inhaler, mouthing *Let me in*. Pierce shook his head. *Please*, my mother mouthed. He leaned over and switched on the microphone.

'Give me Jamie's inhaler,' he said.

My mother shook her head. *Let me in*, she repeated. Pierce shrugged and sat back in his seat. I wheezed and held my chest. He looked at me and quickly looked away. Bastard. I wheezed again and this time I moaned and coughed as well. My mother banged on the window again. Pierce folded his arms across his chest and I could tell that he was starting to get rattled. Mam began a slow thumping on the glass. He held his hand up.

'Stop!' he shouted. 'Stop that right now.'

But my mother had moved into a new groove and the low thumping noise continued. I slumped a little in my chair as I wheezed.

'Give me the inhaler,' Pierce shouted into the microphone.

Mam shook her head and shrugged. It was a stand-off. I knew by my mother's face that she had no intention of budging.

'Please let her in. I need my inhaler,' I croaked and took off on another coughing jag.

Pierce stood up and handed me a glass of water. I pushed it away and it crashed to the floor. Mam was still thumping away and his breathing became faster as he paced up and down behind me. He ran up to the glass and banged hard.

'Give me her inhaler,' he screamed.

'Let my mother in,' I gasped. 'I need her.'

'No,' he said. 'She can give it to me.'

'Please,' I begged, slumping to the side and pretending to pass out.

Pierce came over and rubbed my face with his papery-dry hand. 'Jamie! Jamie! Wake up.'

I wheezed and continued to play possum. 'Please, Jamie. Oh God! Oh God, what'll I do, what'll I do?' He shook me by the shoulder. I moaned and let my head slump further forward. Pierce covered his face with his hands and muttered to himself. Then he walked up to the window.

'Just you,' he shouted.

I watched through slitted eyes as Mam nodded eagerly.

'I'm warning you,' Pierce said, turning to point the gun at me. Mam nodded again and disappeared. Two seconds later there was a soft knocking at the door of the studio. Pierce – whose breathing was now faster than mine – slid the bolt and opened the door just enough to let my mother in. He slammed the door behind her and shot the bolt back into place.

'Give it to her and get out,' he said.

My mother looked at him like he was a piece of shit stuck to her shoe and came over to me. She put her arms around me and whispered, 'Work with me.'

Then she took a deep breath. 'Poor Jamie. Here, take this,' she said in a loud voice. I took the inhaler and pretended to use it, all the time keeping up the appearance of a severe asthma attack. Mam chattered on and on as she bent over me. Pierce moved to stand beside her.

Through my half-open eyes I could see that though he was still holding the gun he'd let his hand drop to his side. Suddenly, Mam swivelled around. In one swift movement she slid a small can of hairspray from the sleeve of her cardigan and sprayed it directly into Pierce's eyes. He screamed with pain. I jumped up, grabbed the ugly transmitter sculpture from under the desk and, swinging it with both hands, walloped Pierce in the side of the head. With a loud groan he folded to the floor.

Mam grabbed the gun and the door burst open. Suddenly the room was full. Two uniformed policemen were the first in. They immediately handcuffed Pierce who was already starting to come round. Detective Laffan appeared in front of me.

'Are you two OK?' he asked and I almost laughed aloud because he looked so like an extra from *Three Amigos*.

My mother put her arm around my shoulders and squeezed me tightly. I began to cry and shake.

'We're fine, aren't we, love – you're not hurt, are you?'

I shook my head but I couldn't speak.

'Well done, Mrs Ryan,' the tall Guard said. 'We could do with a couple of women like you on the force. If you ever think of changing your job . . .'

Mam laughed. 'Mothers are the fiercest in every species, aren't they?'

Detective Laffan smiled.

'Anyway,' she continued. 'I've been telling Jamie for years that those handbag-size Elnett hairsprays are very handy and you should never leave the house without one.'

'It's a Girl Thing,' I said. Then I laughed and hugged my mother because that was surely the ultimate girl lesson.

But I'd learned a more important lesson than that. I suddenly saw my mother in a new light: you don't mess with her cosmetics, you don't mess with her house but most of all you don't mess with her kids.

46

My mother led me to the outer office but I was so overcome I found that I could hardly walk. It seemed to be crammed with people both familiar and strange. Dermot, Dee-Dee, Shane – Sophie's white face appeared in front of me and she said something to my mother. Then the two of them brought me into Sophie's office and closed the door.

It was eerily silent and I realised the reason was that for the first time ever nobody was broadcasting on Fab City Radio. I seemed to be in a cocoon, separated from the world around me. I couldn't believe that the events of that last hour had really happened. Had a stalker really held me hostage at gunpoint in my own sound booth?

Sophie handed me a cup of coffee and I sipped as she and Mam chatted. Every so often they tried to include me and though I nodded and smiled I really felt that I was on a different planet.

There was a gentle knock on the door and my Mexican detective appeared.

'Sorry to disturb you – how are you feeling, Jamie?'

I tried to smile. 'Not too bad.'

He looked kindly at me. 'It'll take a little while but you'll be grand.'

'I know.'

'Anyway, Sophie – any chance of a few words with you?'

'No problem, Joe.'

She moved towards the door.

'And there are other loose ends that need to be tidied up – I know you're not feeling the best, Jamie, but I was wondering if your mother would oblige us? What do you think, Anna? Can you join us for a chat?'

My mother looked at me and I smiled reassuringly. 'I'm grand – really.'

'I won't be long,' she said, kissing me on the top of my head.

And then they were all gone and I was alone and glad to be so. The speaker on the wall crackled and Johnny G's chirpy voice filled the room. Ridiculous as it was I felt relieved that the show was going on. I leaned back in Sophie's chair and covered my face with my hands as the events of the morning reran over and over inside my head.

The sound of the door made me jump and I opened my eyes. Bill was standing in front of the desk. My heart flipped in my chest at the sight of him and my instinct was to go to him. But then I remembered the beautiful woman with the wild eyes. The memory pinned me down in the chair.

'I just got here. Are you all right?' he said.

'What's it to you?' I said.

He looked baffled. 'What do you mean?'

Suddenly I was filled with a rush of anger. I jumped up off my chair. 'You swan in here full of concern, asking about my welfare as if you actually give a flying shit about me or what happens to me.'

I paused for breath.

'I understand that you're traumatised – Jesus, that man could have hurt you . . .'

'At least all he'd have done was shoot me.'

Bill laughed. 'Jamie, what the hell are you talking about?'

'Stop the innocent act – you know exactly what I'm talking about. You bull-shitted me into bed and I know that I should have seen through it. After all, I've had plenty of experience lately with arseholes who want to fuck me – and not in a good way.'

'What *are* you talking about?'

'I met your other woman – no, hang on, maybe I'm the other woman. Are you doing the same to her as you're doing to me? I bet you are. Maybe there's more than two of us? Have you one for every day of the week? We could all wear knickers with the days of the week printed on the front so you won't get confused. Now there's a plan. A pack each for every gullible woman who thinks you're something special . . .'

Bill's face was serious. 'I still don't know what you're talking about – *what* woman?'

'The woman who let herself into your house this morning and told me she was staying for ever – told me about how much she *loved* you and how much you *love* her. If only she knew . . .'

'I do love her, as it happens – thing is, she's my sister.'

My righteous indignation evaporated like mist. 'Your *sister*? I never knew you had a sister.'

'You never asked.'

I stood there looking at him, my mouth hanging open, feeling like the biggest idiot in the world. 'Siblings,' I said eventually. 'More trouble than they're worth.'

Bill looked at me for a few seconds and then a huge grin spread across his face. 'At least yours hasn't been in a secure facility since he was fifteen.'

I widened my eyes. 'Maybe he should have been.'

Bill laughed. 'I know it must have been a shock to you but I'm quite glad to hear that Amanda is in my house. I had a call from the hospital as I was driving here, in fact. At least that means one of my problems is solved.'

'What's your other problem?' I asked.

He walked around the desk and stood in front of me. 'I can't believe you thought that I'd use you or anybody else.'

I looked into his face and for the first time ever I saw past the façade of arrogance and seeming detachment.

'I'm sorry,' I said.

Bill held my gaze and then, still serious, said, 'I must say, though, I was a bit chuffed to hear that you think I'm something special.'

'I didn't say that exactly . . .'

'Noooo – you said a big load of confusing stuff

about knickers and days of the week but I seemed to hear a compliment buried somewhere in all that. Was I wrong?'

I moved closer to him. 'No,' I said, kissing him lightly on the mouth. 'You were right.'

He pulled me tightly to him and we kissed again. Properly this time. As we drew apart he looked into my eyes.

'Good,' he said. 'Because I think you're special too – I told you that the other night. I've always thought you were special.'

Bill smoothed my hair with his hand. 'What a week,' he said, with a loud sigh. 'But I suppose the important thing is that that mad bastard didn't hurt you.'

'You should have seen my mother with her Elnett – I can't believe what she did.'

'I can – Anna is a tough cookie. Why are you surprised?'

'It's not that. It's stupid, I suppose, but I always felt as if I wasn't the daughter she'd have liked. You know, no good at the girl stuff – and, worse than that, no real interest. A bit of a disappointment.'

Bill laughed. 'You're a terror for jumping to conclusions, do you know that? As long as I've known her your mother has thought you were the bee's knees.'

He kissed me, cupping my face with his hands. 'Jamie Ryan, could you do something for me?'

'What exactly do you have in mind?' I said, putting my hands on his arse.

He groaned. 'Hold that thought – I have one other thing I want to say to you.'

'Mmmm,' I said, my thoughts elsewhere.

'In future, before you do judge and jury on me will you promise to ask questions first?'

I pulled away and looked at Bill. I was going to ask him what he meant but suddenly I knew. When I looked at people I only saw what I wanted to see – or what I was afraid of. Maybe he was right, maybe if I asked more questions and looked a little harder and longer then I could stop doing that.

I had been right about one thing, though: I'd always known that Pierce Thompson wasn't harmless. As if on cue my mobile phone beeped, announcing the arrival of a message. I started and momentarily panicked as all the stalker messages came flooding back into my mind. But I knew that it couldn't be Pierce so I made myself pick up my phone and read the message.

Hurry up and ride him – I can't keep your mother out of my office for much longer.

If there was one rule of Girl Land that I was happy to obey it was this: always do what your best friend tells you. I started to laugh as I moved back towards Bill.

'Now, exactly where were we?'